Because it turns out,
we are far more magical
than we imagined.

WOVEN IN TIME

BOOK ONE

JESSICA ANN

Publisher: Jess Ann Creates www.jessanncreates.com

ISBN (Paperback): 979-8-9938164-1-8

ISBN (eBook): 979-8-9938164-0-1

Cover design by: Juan José Padrón at www.jcovers.com

Interior design by: Jessica Ann with Atticus at atticus.io

Library of Congress Control Number: 2025923670

Printed in the United States of America

NOTE:
This book contains sexual content.
It also contains subject matter that may be difficult for some readers,
including violence, sexual assault, and emotional abuse.

However, it is through love, through stories, through connection,
that we heal.

For the dreamers, the sensitive souls, and anyone who has ever felt we were made for so much more.

P.S. You are.
You're magical.

PART ONE

"We must be willing to get rid of the life we've planned, so as to have the life that is waiting for us."
— Joseph Campbell

Chapter 1

MIRYAM

Oakeshire, England, In the year of our Lord 1307

I f getting that apple meant changing her fate, she would go out on that limb, despite the risk. Gazing up at the ancient tree, Miryam clenched her fists as she plotted her ascent. Its gnarled roots spread like a web across the orchard grass. The curved trunk twisted and turned, its age revealed in layers of fungus and rot. The few apples it bore were speckled with mildew, most of them infested with worms.

Miryam cared about her safety and somewhat about what others would think.

Those things were just *less* important.

Shifting her attention to her sister, Isabella, with a pained look, Miryam said, "Father is marrying me off, and I've no say in the matter."

"He meant not what he said," Isabella said, frowning. "Come. Let us walk home and talk it through."

"He meant exactly what he said," Miryam retorted, heat rising in her cheeks. She seized the lowest branch as bark crumbled beneath her fingertips.

"You know this is dangerous," Isabella pleaded, her voice dropping to a whisper. "Village folk say the tree is ... cursed."

That was precisely *why* Miryam meant to climb it.

The tree was rumored to have been placed under a witch's spell centuries ago, and whoever ate from its largest apple would be granted their heart's greatest desire. But such gifts came with a price, as magic

2

often does. Even so, it never stopped the bravest of villagers, most often foolhardy boys, from scaling the tree each year.

This year, it was Miryam's turn to try.

Anything to keep from marrying a man she did not know and living the boring existence of a weaver's wife. She had already been a weaver's daughter for seventeen years. Must she go through the rest of her life never knowing the fullness it could offer? She dreamed of true love, heartbreak, and adventure. Until now, she had only heard of such things in fables and books, when she was lucky to get her hands on one. But when she did, she absolutely consumed those tales, and, well ... her father rather regretted teaching her to read.

Miryam gathered the folds of her wool dress in one hand. "Why must we wear these cursed gowns at all times?"

"Speaking like that is why you cannot find a nice boy to wed you," Isabella said, pursing her lips.

Miryam knew her sister loved her, but Isabella cared far more about others' opinions of her climbing that tree. Though they were only a year apart in age, with Miryam being the elder, Isabella always played the more mature role.

For as long as Miryam could remember, Isabella had judged her for her ways. At the market, for instance, when they were meant to be selling woven blankets and goods beside their father, Isabella would remain the dutiful daughter—tending the stall, charming the buyers, and somehow always looking radiant. Miryam, meanwhile, would be drifting into daydreams or striking up conversations with the most curious of passersby, often with no thought at all for their weaving trade. Worst was when Miryam would have some wild notion to do something 'un-lady-like,' such as playing games with the street children or racing teenage boys to the water wheel. Her sister would give her more than enough advice on account of those larks.

With a huff of frustration, Miryam hauled herself onto the first branch with her free hand, though it would have been far easier had she been wearing trousers. A glob of oozing black sap clung to her leather boot. She scraped her heel against the trunk, trying to rub it off to no avail.

"What if someone were to see you?" Isabella hissed.

There it was. *The truth.*

Miryam reached for the next branch.

"Or worse, God forbid, a knight," — Isabella's voice rose an octave — "or the earl."

Miryam climbed on. With each pull upward, her anger fueled her, turning into sheer determination. If there was any escape from her fate, she prayed this apple would be the key. Wincing as her arm scraped against a branch, she climbed higher still. Sweat stung her eyes as the midday Sun beat down on her upturned face.

"Come down, I beg you," Isabella called from below. Her voice, once cautious, was now more frustrated. "Father only seeks the best for you."

It was not proper for a lady to climb any sort of tree, let alone this one. But Miryam no longer cared. She'd grown weary of waiting for someone else to dictate her future. Tired of simply being a weaver's daughter—or future wife.

The fungus-speckled skin of the largest apple gleamed red and yellow before Miryam. She was so close. Single-minded, she stretched her arm to its full length, a stitch in her sleeve tearing with the strain. Her fingertips brushed the waxy fruit.

Just a little farther.

She edged out from the trunk, the branch beneath her groaning and swaying. At last, her hand closed firm around the apple. Plucking it triumphantly from the tree, she held it out high. "Look, Bella, I have it!"

Snap. The teetering branch gave way, and gravity wrenched her downward. Miryam cried out, clawing at empty air, but the old tree offered no mercy. *Was this the price to pay for getting this apple?* She struck the ground hard, the breath torn from her chest.

The apple slipped free and rolled from her hand.

"Miryam!" Isabella cried, dropping to her knees beside her.

The world blurred and shrank around Miryam. A sharp ache throbbed in her skull. She opened her mouth to speak, but no words came. Tiredness washed over her like a wave in the sea, too strong to fight. Her eyes closed as she strained to stay conscious, lying on the hard, damp Earth.

Isabella whispered a brief prayer over her body. "Hold fast. I will fetch help, dear sister."

As the footsteps faded in the distance, Miryam's world went dark.

~~~

"Do you feel it?" A woman's voice drifted above Miryam's still body.

"I know not," came a man's reply—his voice young, almost boyish. "It is not my gift to sense such things. What is it you feel?"

"'Tis strong ... bright ... yet *thick*." The woman enunciated each word with care, the last tinged with unease.

"What does it mean?"

"We must take heed. There is a great polarity in her—light bound with darkness. She might go either way. Best we leave her be."

"Leave her?" he protested. "She clearly needs our aid."

Miryam's eyes fluttered open. The bright Sun shone high in the sky, bombarding her vision. Squinting, she made out two vague shapes standing above her, an aged woman and a young man, both cloaked in long black robes. Her head throbbed as she tried to remember what had happened. She strained to understand what they were saying about her, but the words blurred in her mind. *What was strong, bright, and thick?* They weren't making any sense.

The woman bent down, resting her hand on Miryam's shoulder. At her touch, a gentle warmth coursed down Miryam's arm and into her core. The pain lessened.

"I am Sophia," the woman said softly. "This is Ved. Are you able to sit?"

Miryam struggled, pulling herself into a half-sitting posture. "I know not if I—" She broke off, leaning forward with her head in her hands. Hot saliva collected in her mouth.

Quickly, she turned aside, retching on the grass.

Wiping the bile from her lips, she longed only to sink down again into sleep. Instead, she forced herself upright as Sophia held her back to keep her steady. Once more, a warm wave flowed into Miryam, easing her sickness.

"Ved, would you fetch the mead from my satchel?" Sophia asked her companion.

He drew a small leather pouch from a nearby bag and pressed it gently toward Miryam's mouth. "Here, drink."

Ved held the flask steady for her, and the lukewarm sweetness of honeyed wine washed away the bile. Relief spread over Miryam almost at once.

"Thank you," she murmured, letting her gaze linger on this new stranger.

A loose strand of his dark hair had fallen across his brow, with the rest pulled back neatly. His skin had a warmer hue than most villagers she knew, yet his eyes were the clearest blue—just like her own. When their matching eyes met, Miryam felt suddenly exposed, as if Ved could see right through to her heart.

The ache from her fall seemed to fade faster with each passing moment, replaced by a flutter stirring in her belly. Her thoughts strayed to what it might be like to press her lips against his. "I am Miryam." She bowed her head with a soft smile.

Ved held her gaze.

Flustered, Miryam turned her eyes to Sophia. "I thank you both for your aid. I was but trying to pluck an apple when I fell."

"You seem mended well enough now," Sophia replied. "Come. Can you stand?"

"I believe so," Miryam said, pushing herself from the ground, surprised again to find her aches magically gone as though they had never been there. "That is odd ... I feel much improved."

Sophia's lips curved into a knowing smile.

Miryam cocked her head.

Without a word, Sophia grabbed her satchel, motioned to Ved to follow, and started toward the forest path. Ved obeyed, but not before glancing back once more at Miryam.

"Wait!" Miryam yelled after them, questions tumbling out in a rush. "Whence came you? How is it I've never seen you in the village? What were you saying of me? Shall we meet again?"

"Time will tell," Sophia said, not breaking her stride.

In a moment, both had vanished between the trees.

"But ... I do not know where to find you." Miryam's shoulders slumped. She turned back toward the village just as Isabella came running, their father panting hard a few paces behind.

"I am so glad to see you up and well. I feared the worst." Isabella pulled Miryam into a fierce embrace. "Who were you speaking to?"

Miryam cast a glance toward the forest opening where her two mysterious visitors had disappeared. "I know not ... They wore black robes and spoke of the oddest things." Her eyes lit suddenly, wide with wonder. "Oh, but, Bella, you should have seen *him*. A boy, so handsome! His eyes, the very color of bluebells in springtime."

"I *know* you must be mended if you are already thinking of boys once again," Isabella replied dryly.

"No," Miryam whispered, still staring at the trees. "I think I might die."

Their father, Simon, broke in. "Shall we fetch the apothecary? Quick, Isabella—take her arm. I shall take this side."

"Faaather, I am well." Miryam chuckled, wriggling out of his grasp. "I only think I might *die* because I have met possibly the most handsome, most mysterious boy, and I know not if I shall ever see him again." She plucked a dandelion from the ground, twirling it as she spun once around. Then, she stilled. "Not that it matters. Since you are marrying me off to someone else," she said with sass.

Simon's face hardened, unamused.

Miryam knew she would get a scolding—and probably extra chores—for speaking to her father like that, but she didn't care.

"Oh, Miryam, every week at market you find the 'fairest boy you ever saw,'" Isabella said, rolling her eyes. "All that matters now is that you are unhurt, and that no one saw you climbing that dreadful tree." She cast a wary look at the behemoth.

"Come now," Simon said, drawing both daughters into his arms. "Isabella speaks true. This is no hour for worry. We shall speak of your future another day. For now, let us go home before the light fades."

"You should have heard the strange things they spoke of," Miryam pressed. "They spoke of forces, of light and darkness, and—" Her lips parted, then closed again. "Never you mind. Let us go."

Her father and sister would not understand.

They never did.

As they turned back toward the village and home, Miryam remembered the apple. Scanning the orchard floor, there it was—bruised, yet intact. She scooped it up, brushed the dirt away, and lifted it to her mouth.

With a single defiant motion, she took one huge bite.

CHAPTER 2

LEAH

Anaheim, California, USA 2017 C.E.

"I can sense there's something important about to happen. Something *big*. It will shift your life path," Leah said, observing the young woman sitting across from her.

The woman wore a light blue cardigan buttoned to the throat. Hair pulled into a messy bun. Holes for three earrings in each ear, but only one filled with short, metallic heart earrings. Her book bag hung open, exposing a half-eaten banana in a Ziploc next to a copy of *God, Is He the One?*

Leah leaned in. "It has to do with your past, something you've repressed from childhood. It's going to affect your current relationship. You've been unsure about it."

The woman's eyes widened. She bent closer, intrigued. "Can you tell me what's going to happen?"

"The future isn't fixed. I can only see ... possibilities." Leah closed her eyes and tilted her ear up, as if receiving hidden messages from above. She waited for a dramatic pause, counting in her head.

One ... two ... three.

Snapping her eyes open, Leah planted her palms on the table, her gaze locked on the woman. "Only you'll know when it comes. Wait for the pull in your gut that says, *this is it*. The answer is already within you."

Confusion spread across the woman's face. The gears turned as the woman searched her mind. And then it came—that *aha* moment when someone makes a connection where there hadn't been one before.

Once it happened, Leah had them hooked. The rest was easy.

"Ohhh, I see," the woman said, a smile slowly spreading across her face. "You're right. I've been wondering whether my boyfriend is about to propose."

Leah listened, but mostly, she watched. She studied the woman's facial expressions and movement, making mental notes. People were so unaware, always giving away so much information. However, she noticed things. Knowing how to use her observations was why she was so good at her job as a psychic.

Finally, Leah held up a finger. The woman stopped talking.

"That right there," Leah said, spinning to face the classroom full of community college students, and her anxiety spiked. She swallowed hard, remembering she wasn't in the comfort of her small office giving a private reading. "Did you see what happened?"

"But I really think—"

Leah gave the woman a smile and nodded toward the audience. The woman looked a little disappointed and returned to her seat.

"Why do we want to know the future? Is it all predetermined, or do we have free will?"

A few students raised their hands.

Leah went on. "I'd suggest you pay more attention to the now. It may sound very Zen, but it's actually biological. We have nothing outside *this moment*. The past is gone; the future has yet to come. The present is all we can truly know. And *that* is our best guide for predicting what will happen."

A girl in the front row wiggled her hand high in the air.

Leah called on her.

"So, what do you believe? Free will or destiny?"

"What do I ... believe?" Leah dragged the words aloud, immediately hearing her mother asking her a similar question when she'd told her she was going to work as a medium so many years ago.

What sort of person becomes a psychic, throwing away their career in psychology? You could have been something. Could have been someone.

But instead ... Leah cringed and shook her mother's voice out of her head.

She glanced at the clock. Two more minutes until the end of class. She could distract. It was what she was good at.

"The debate of fate or free will is tricky. Some of the world's top scientists don't even believe free will exists. And over eighty percent of the world follows some religion. But the better question is, what will your future clients believe? As young psychologists, it's important to consider your clients' spirituality and take their worldview into account."

The bell rang. Students shoved books into bags and shuffled out.

Leah raised her voice. "That's the end of class. Thank you for having me as your guest lecturer today. And if you ever want a future reading, come visit us at the store."

She waved, but no one was looking.

What the fuck am I doing here? Teaching a room of psychology students had once been her dream. So why did it feel so hollow? And why were these headaches getting worse?

Shrugging the questions off, like most things in her life, Leah gathered her things and headed back to her full-time job.

~∿~

The front door of the metaphysical shop chimed as Leah entered. She did a quick scan. No customers. *Good.* She plopped down on a patchouli-scented couch. "Ugghh. This headache won't go away. Not even ibuprofen or coffee did the trick. Is it too early for wine?"

Behind the counter, Kat fussed with a display of crystals. "And hello to you too, my favorite business partner and best friend in the world."

"Hi, Kat. Sorry. It's just ... this headache is about to turn into a raging migraine." Leah rubbed the spot between her eyes, willing the pain away.

Kat came around and plopped onto the couch beside her. "No wine here. But how did your first college lecture go? That's so exciting!" Her tone dropped. "Why aren't you excited?"

"It was fine. Just community college. Honestly, this woman droned on for at least ten minutes—never mind." Leah waved it off. "It still amazes me what the human mind can connect. But hey, first college lecture. Yaaayyy." She raised her hands in mock celebration.

Kat squinted, unimpressed. "You know I don't like it when you make fun of clients. They come to us looking for answers. Even if you don't believe in it, you shouldn't be so judgy ... Wait, that was judgy of me to say." She closed her eyes, taking a deep breath. "I'm letting go of my negative thoughts, and I ask that you join me. Also, I have some herbal tea you can take for that headache."

She popped up to snatch her purse and began rifling through it for the tea. Kat exuded so much positivity it simultaneously drove Leah insane and made her jealous. If Leah was a glass half-empty of red wine, Kat was a glass half-full of kombucha.

They balanced each other.

"You're right. My negative thoughts are going in the trash can of my mind—sorry, *the compost bin*—where they will turn into happy thoughts." Leah smirked. "But can I at least keep the sarcastic ones?"

"Of course, you wouldn't be *you* without them."

"I still don't know why you put up with me."

"I'm not sure either." Kat laughed. "Maybe so you can help unload these boxes. Would you, before we head out for the day?"

"For you, of course."

They had to put away five boxes of crystals, incense, and Wiccan and esoteric books. Kat had always dreamed of opening her own metaphysical shop, and ten years ago, she finally did—with Leah's help.

And while Leah was an atheist, she was one of the city's best damn psychics.

It had started when they were seventeen. Bonded by the shared burden of overbearing mothers, Leah and Kat had been inseparable ever since. Kat—full name Ekaterina Mikhailova Fedorov—had come to America as a baby with her mom. She never knew her father, but somewhere along her search for her Romani roots, she found a deck of Tarot cards instead.

Leah pulled a stack of books from a box and began shelving them on the freshly dusted display. One cover read: *Easy Guide to Understanding Tarot.*

As it turned out, *she*, not Kat, was better at giving readings.

Kat couldn't give a Tarot reading that didn't end with, "... and then you'll live happily ever after." It was sweet, but not always what people needed to hear. What began as a fun teenage game quickly turned into a side hustle for them, and then somehow a full brick and mortar business.

Leah flipped through *Are We All Really Psychic?* before sliding it onto the shelf. She didn't hate giving fortunes or doing readings. She just didn't believe in them.

Twenty years later, she still felt like a fraud. But people loved her sessions, and she loved Kat, like the sister she never had. So, here they were. Leah kept telling herself that someday she would have plans to finish her PhD in psychology, but for now, this was what life had handed her.

Once they finished restocking the shop, Leah settled behind the front counter and flipped open a new magazine Kat had subscribed to. The cover headline read: "Guided Meditations. Do They Lead to Intense Visions?" She wouldn't mind reading that one, mostly to see how they defined *intense*. Plus, it'd make Kat happy.

"Hey, would you grab the mail? I realized I never brought it in today," Kat called from the back of the store.

"Sure," Leah said, setting the magazine down with a sigh.

Outside, the California Sun hit her face, and the warm breeze loosened her shoulders. She hadn't realized how tense she was. She scooped the mail from the box and flipped through it on the way back in.

Junk. Junk. Bills. More junk.

Then—a scribbly, handwritten letter.

With Leah's name on it.

Just her first name. Not even an address or stamp.

Frowning, she opened it and pulled out a black-and-white coupon that looked like it had been cut by a five-year-old. *Buy one book, get one free*, it said, *only at Baba Yaga's Books and More.*

"What the hell?" she muttered.

"What is it?" Kat asked.

"A coupon for a bookstore, hand-addressed to me. About as bizarre as me accepting that guest lecturer invite." She tossed the coupon onto the counter. "None of those students are going to wander in here, either."

Kat furrowed her brow for half a second, then lit up. "Oooooh! Maybe it's a sign from the Universe!"

Leah rolled her eyes. "Not everything is a sign. It's probably—"

Her phone vibrated in her pocket.

"Oh shit, that's Hana. I have to get this." Leah stepped away to answer her daughter's phone call. "Hey, sweetie."

"No sweetie here," said the cold voice on the other end.

Her jaw tightened.

"Seth." Her ex.

"Leah."

His voice was flat. She could practically hear his raised eyebrows.

"I just wanted to let you know I picked up our daughter—Hana, remember her?—from school. *Again*," Seth said, each word cutting. "It was your turn."

Leah checked the time. *Shit!*

"That's the third time this month. What the hell is going on with you?" Seth's voice sharpened.

Leah's stomach twisted. She hated it when he talked to her like this. The last few weeks had been a blur of mind-splitting migraines, scrambling her brain like eggs. They were coming more often, harder to ignore. Even so, not an excuse. Not to Seth. Especially not to Seth.

"Never mind," he snapped. "I don't care *why*. Just pick her up at my place on your way home."

"I'm sorry. I got caught up at work—"

"I don't need excuses. I need you to be a responsible parent. Actually, no. You'll find out soon enough when you get the letter. I'm filing for full custody. My lawyer will be in touch."

The line went dead.

Leah stared at her phone. *Filing for full custody?*

Suddenly, the room seemed to collapse around her, air being sucked out like a vacuum. She gasped, but her lungs didn't cooperate. Her vision blurred as tears welled, uninvited. She blinked them back. No. Not here. Not now.

"Leah?" Kat's voice broke through. "Was Seth giving you shit again? That guy walks around with a cloud of negative energy."

Leah's lips parted, but nothing came out.

Hana.

Her daughter. Her anchor. The only thing that made sense in her life. And now, Seth was trying to take that away. It was enough that she had to split custody with him, but *this*. It was too much. She could feel herself folding inward, walling off the ache. A migraine bloomed, hot and sharp, behind her eyes.

"I need to go get Hana," Leah muttered, pressing a thumb hard against her temple.

"Talk to me," Kat pleaded. "What did he say?"

"He's filing for full custody." Leah spun to leave.

Kat reached out, grabbing her arm and drawing her into a tight hug. "Oh, honey, we'll get through this. He won't take her away."

Leah's body tensed—but she didn't pull away.

"I'm here for you," Kat said, rubbing her back. "We'll find a good lawyer. Plus, you know, moms almost always win these things. There's nothing to worry about."

There's always something to worry about.

Leah stepped back, wiping a lone tear off her cheek. "I have to go."

CHAPTER 3

KARAIA

SECTOR ONE, NEW SOTERIA, 2307 C.E.

Karaia stepped out onto the main transit tube. The clink of sanitized metal beneath each footfall reverberated around her. She was alone except for the ever-present hum of the news echoing through the corridor. Seamless windows curved up to meet the long ceiling's artificial lights, occasionally interrupted by maintenance hatches or elevators leading to one of fifty other tube levels. Every ten minutes on the dot, a silent railcar floated effortlessly on its magnetic strip.

That evening, she chose to walk home.

Not necessarily because she wanted to, but because her stomach felt uneasy, and walking always made her feel better—calmer, more in control. This was on top of the five NeuroCredits she'd purchased and taken earlier in the day. But they never seemed to help with her gut. Only with her mind's anxiety.

Seromela Corporation had just promoted her to Head Marketing Analyst. At twenty-seven, she was the youngest person ever to hold the position—in the company, in the country, maybe even in history. At least that she knew of. While Karaia would never admit it out loud, because she told herself she was a badass at everything she did, this new assignment unnerved her.

As the country's elected corporation, Seromela shared its building complex with the New Soterian government. Nearly every day since her Official Assignment there ten years ago, she'd gotten off work at

5:30 p.m., boarded Rail 87, and called her grandma on the way home. New Soteria encouraged all citizens to stick to a daily routine, taking the rails whenever possible.

Yet another thing she wouldn't admit out loud—changing up her nightly route was her little way of rebelling.

No one needed to know.

And it wasn't technically illegal.

Thirty feet below her, the lifeless Earth stretched out in dusty brown, riddled with disease. No one lived down there anymore, not since the Great Fall. *Too dangerous*, they said. But the moment she thought about the ground beneath her, Karaia wondered what the dirt would feel like between her toes.

NIVA. She spoke silently to the Neuro-linked Intelligent Voice Assistant that every New Soterian citizen had access to with their mind. *Open NeuroCredits. Buy one credit.*

NIVA responded in Karaia's head. *Would you like to transfer now?*

Yes, transfer.

One NeuroCredit transfer complete. Enjoy.

A sweet blend of serotonin, dopamine, and other feel-good chemicals flooded her brain, calming her instantly. She let out a soft sigh.

With each step, the tension in her shoulders loosened, and her worries about work melted further away. She peeked through the tube windows and imagined a faraway Sun setting, painting the sky and clouds in shades of pink and orange. At least, that's what she thought a sunset might look like, based on holo-images. She'd never actually seen one, not past the endless grid of skyscrapers and transit tubes that connected one building to another. Still, she smiled as she walked on.

What Karaia could see was the faint steam curling from her lips. It was winter, and the transit tubes weren't fully heated. Since most people took the rail system everywhere, they never noticed the slight temperature in the tubes. But she did.

She noticed a lot of things, more than most.

Her 'sixth sense,' her dad used to call it. *A strange, old saying.* Karaia figured it probably came from a time when people still believed in religion and gods. Those days were long gone. Humanity had evolved past believing there was an ancient deity in the sky judging them.

Nevertheless, she wondered where her sense of *knowing* came from. Outwardly, she remained modest, telling people she was just especially observant. But deep down, that wasn't quite it.

Sometimes ... she just *knew* things.

Today was one of those days. Karaia's conscious mind told her she was walking home because she was nervous about her new work assignment and walking calmed her, but something else—something from deep within her gut—told her she was supposed to walk home.

Call Grandma, Karaia thought as she pressed the communication device implanted near her left temple as she walked.

A hoarse voice answered quickly. "Karaia, is that you?"

"Yes, Gram," she said, chuckling softly. "Do you have another granddaughter who calls you every day on her way home from work?"

Her grandmother, Cecelia, ignored the question and proceeded to tell Karaia about her day as usual. "I was just finishing up a game of Alutrien Train with Delores from down the tube. You know, the lady with the cute little dogs, Dags and Wags?"

Karaia knew all about Delores, Dags, and Wags. Her grandmother talked about them almost every day. That, or the latest pandemic outside New Soteria's walls, or some war breaking out across the ocean.

"Yes, I remember."

Cecilia continued, "Well, it was down to one point. She was about to beat me, but then I came back with a double jynx flush. Can you believe it?!"

"Nice job, Grams." Karaia turned onto the next tube. "I wanted to tell you—"

"That Delores, she's such a sweet lady. I do hope she paid for a NeuroCredit or two to make up for losing to me. You know, she's always going on about—"

Karaia never found out what Delores was always going on about.

Someone crashed into her right shoulder, jolting her off balance. At the moment of impact, she felt a sharp prick in her arm, followed by a dull ache radiating down her side. She stumbled, catching herself before hitting the hard metal floor. Blinking up through the tube's fluorescent lights, she caught a glimpse of a dark-hooded figure darting away.

She reacted on instinct. "Hey! Watch where you're going!"

"What's that?" her grandma asked, her voice crackling through the comm.

Karaia had forgotten she was still on the line. "Sorry, Gram, I've gotta go." She pressed her temple again, ending the call.

"Put your hands up!" someone shouted from behind.

Karaia froze mid-step.

Two armed New Soteria officers marched up to her. Their uniforms matched New Soteria's colors: ash gray and cobalt blue. One moved quickly around to block her path. Their faces were hidden behind dark, reflective visors built into standard-issue helmets. She couldn't see their eyes.

Both had their laser guns aimed directly at her.

"We said *hands up*," the one in front barked. He jabbed her chest lightly with the tip of his laser gun.

Karaia slowly raised her shaking hands. Her heartbeat pounded fast and uneven, chopping her breath into short, ragged bursts. All the feel-good chemicals released from her last credits had disappeared.

Of course, New Soteria had armed officers.

She saw them every day—at work, in the tubes, on the rails. They were there to protect people from terrorists. But it still didn't change the fact that having a gun pointed at her made her feel like she'd done something wrong. Yet she hadn't.

Or had she?

"I had nothing to do with it, whatever it is you're after," she blurted. "I saw someone run by just a few seconds ago. I couldn't see their face, though."

She hoped that was enough.

Adrenaline surged in her bloodstream. Her pulse thundered in her ears. *Just get through this. You can buy another NeuroCredit after.*

"Ma'am, we're looking for someone. A woman." The officer lowered his weapon and flicked his wrist, projecting a holographic image into the air.

A blurred figure running. The holo-image was grainy, probably pulled from a transit tube camera. The face was obscured, but the dark hood was unmistakable.

"They just came by here," Karaia said, hand trembling as she gestured up and to the left. "They went that way."

Before she could say another word, the officers rushed past her.

Karaia rubbed her arm and shivered. *NIVA, open NeuroCredits. Buy five credits.*

NIVA responded, *would you like to transfer them now?*

Yes, please. Now.

NeuroCredit transfer complete. Enjoy.

Karaia waited for the familiar rush of chemicals to flood her brain. She closed her eyes, took a deep breath, and willed herself to feel good again.

Nothing happened.

No calming wave. No shift in mood. No credit transfer.

Her logical mind kicked in. Maybe the government had temporarily restricted the NeuroCredit system in her area because of the woman they were chasing. Sometimes, in cases of suspected terrorist activity, they'd limit access to key systems. But that was always outside New Soteria's walls, not within.

Either way, Karaia needed to get home. There, she could connect directly to her household NIVA hub and take as many credits as she needed.

Thirty-two agonizing minutes later, Karaia deeply regretted her decision to walk. She nearly cried with relief when her apartment came into view. *Almost there.*

Just before she reached her door, shouting echoed from the alley tube to her right. It stopped her in her tracks. Half-hidden behind an incinerator chute, the two officers cornered the hooded woman they had been after. They were arguing but too far away for Karaia to hear the words.

But she could see.

One officer slapped the woman hard across the face. Blood trickled from her lips. She spat in his face and yelled something back.

The woman tried to run away, pressing and kicking off the hard tube floor. One officer grabbed her roughly, locking her in place. She screamed, but he clamped a hand over her mouth, stifling the sound.

She was trying to break free.

Like a caterpillar emerging from a chrysalis.
Like a butterfly.

There it was—Karaia knowing something she couldn't possibly know. She had never seen a butterfly. Had never even *heard* of one. And yet, suddenly, an image bloomed in her mind. A delicate insect with majestic wings, wriggling its way out of dormancy before fluttering into a brilliant blue sky, surrounded by endless miles of greenery.

She didn't know how she knew. But she *knew*.

The woman writhed, still locked in the officers' grip.

Karaia curled her lip at the sight, trying to make sense of what she was seeing. Everything felt surreal, like she was watching a show on the holo-screen. Distant. Disconnected.

The woman bit down on one officer's hand. He yelped and let go for a moment.

She broke free. *Was the butterfly free?*

Then, the second officer pulled something from his side.

Zap! And slump. Life evaporated from the woman.

There would be no more butterfly.

Blood sprayed the wall behind her, then dripped down the building's hard plastic-alloy exterior. The officers caught her limp body before it hit the ground.

Karaia almost screamed, pressing her hand hard over her mouth. Adrenaline surged throughout her body, dominating her being. Her stomach churned inside, refusing to quell.

This wasn't a simulation. This wasn't a news flash.

This was *real*.

And it was a genuine possibility that she could end up the same way as that woman if she were caught watching this bloodied scene. Yet she stood frozen, gaping, her feet unwilling to move.

The officers began dragging the woman's body toward the main transit tube. They still hadn't seen Karaia.

But her feet were locked in place.

Move, she commanded herself.

Move. Now!

Snapping herself out of it, she forced her legs to push off the ground and flee the rest of the distance to her apartment. At the door, she

21

raised her palm to the sensor. But her hands were shaking so badly she couldn't keep them steady enough. The scanner blinked red—unable to recognize her print. A lump formed in her throat as tears streamed down her cheeks, salt coating her lips.

She tapped her foot frantically, begging the door to open.

Finally, it unlocked.

Karaia rushed inside, slamming it shut behind her. Leaning her back against the door, she slid to the ground. Her head dropped into her hands, eyes squeezed tight.

NIVA, open credits.

Nothing.

Her thoughts were too scattered, too erratic.

She gasped out loud, "NIVA ... open ... credits." Short, uneven breaths punctuated each word. Tears blurred her eyes. It was so unnatural, crying like this. The last time she remembered sobbing was when her parents left. She'd been four years old.

NIVA waited silently for her next command.

"Buy ten credits," she choked out. "Transfer all now."

Ten NeuroCredits transfer complete. Enjoy.

Karaia waited for the flood of bliss to enter her system.

She held her breath and waited.

Waited.

But nothing happened.

The gentle deluge of serotonin didn't come to wash away her feelings. It wasn't there to erase the scene replaying in her head. And nothing arrived to ease the ache that tossed and turned in her gut.

Why had she walked home?

CHAPTER 4

MIRYAM

Setting aside her loom, Miryam crossed their small cottage to the window. A thin layer of dew still clung to the fields from the night before. The Sun barely crested the trees, pressing the morning fog back toward the sea, yet the village was already astir. Townsfolk bustled about doing their daily chores—feeding animals, tending crops, preparing for market. A rooster wailed in the distance. The sharp air carried the promise of autumn.

"Work, work, work. That is all we do," Miryam groaned to her sister. She drew in a deep breath, her gaze fixed outside. "Do you not long to see the world beyond our village? Or feel the salty breeze across the sea? To walk the streets of unknown lands?"

Isabella arched her brows as she folded a stack of woolen blankets into a wooden crate. "You would do better to mind how we sell this wool before winter instead of prattling with merchants—or chasing after fair-faced boys at market."

"But do you not wonder at such things?" Miryam sighed, already knowing her sister's answer.

"I do wonder sometimes," Isabella replied. "Only ... 'tis not our life. The sooner you accept that, the happier you shall be. Come. Help me finish these blankets so we may get them to market."

Feeling dejected, Miryam drifted back to her loom. Isabella had always felt more comfortable in the circles that made Miryam balk. As wool merchants, they were just under the ranking of clergy. Their father, Simon, was a sought-after and skilled tradesman, and even landowner, descended from generations of weavers—father to son.

Then came Miryam and Isabella.

With their mother gone, there would be no son in their lineage. Thus, tying themselves to the right families was essential to continuing the family trade and securing their futures.

At least that's what Isabella and their father repeated incessantly.

Miryam could not fathom why it was so vital to bow to these invisible rules and pretend that she cared about these wealthy nobles that bought from them. It all seemed absurd to her.

Yet she cared about Isabella and her father—more, perhaps, than she let them see. And for their sake, she would play her part for as long as was necessary. Until the day arrived when she'd marry for love and be whisked off to some faraway land where she could explore the great mysteries of life and romance.

Assuming her husband agreed to such fancies.

On second thought, maybe she didn't need a husband at all. Better to live as an old maid, or a temptress, or take her pleasure when she chose—just as men did. *Why shouldn't women do that?* The thought made her laugh softly to herself.

"Miryam?" Isabella's voice broke her reverie.

"Hmm?" Miryam blinked, setting her hand on her finished blanket. The black and white wool interlaced in an intricate pattern. It was one of her best. There were only a few slight mistakes that no one would notice, except Isabella, of course.

"That's simply it, Bella. I will not accept this life. I cannot!" Miryam flung her arms wide and began pacing the room.

"Here we go again ..." Isabella rolled her eyes, hauling bundles of wool toward the door and out to the cart.

"Because I cannot accept it, I shall never be happy. And since I shall never be happy, then I may as well live as I choose. What I want is ... well, I know not exactly." Miryam stamped her foot, glaring up at the ceiling as though the spider in its web might offer her the answers she sought. "I only want the chance to find out. Men have that right. Why not women? I want the freedom to choose *my* life." She collapsed onto a pile of woven fabrics, her head hanging low.

Isabella strode back in. "You are overreacting. *Again.* And get off those blankets." She pursed her lips until Miryam rose.

Miryam resumed her pacing. "What was Father thinking? I have not even met this man—this man he expects me to spend my life with! What if he were to be covered in warts, or bent with a hunchback? What if he has six toes on one foot? Or worse—what if he is dull?"

"You are being selfish," Isabella snapped. "If you refuse to marry, we are left with naught. Do you know how hard Father worked to be noticed by Dempsey, the Earl of Norfolk's personal tailor?"

"You know I want to marry," Miryam huffed. "I simply do not want to marry *Dempsey.* Or anyone I do not love."

Isabella seized Miryam's hands, her face alight. "But you would live in the castle! How wondrous that would be."

Miryam's heart sank at the thought of stone walls. "I care naught for such things. Not as you do."

"But this is not all about you," Isabella retorted, gathering the last of the blankets and motioning for Miryam to follow her outside.

Miryam scoffed, noticing her sister's fingers lingering on the mistake she had made in the blanket. Isabella's words stung, yet she was right. Their father was not cruel; he only sought what he believed best for the family, as he always had.

Their mother had died giving birth to Isabella, when Miryam was but a year old. Since then, their father had raised his two daughters to be strong and clever, even teaching them to read when many grown folks never learned. They knew everything about the weaving trade and ran their small business most days while their father tended to the sheep and farm chores. However, they would never own it, or the land it sat on, because they were women. The only way to keep it alive was through marriage. And Miryam, as the elder daughter, was expected to wed and secure their family's livelihood.

"You are right. Forgive me, sister." A heaviness pressed against Miryam's chest as she helped tie the stack of wool blankets onto their cart.

"Marriage can be one of the most thrilling moments in a woman's life." Isabella smiled, trying to cheer Miryam up. "Gawain and I cannot wait to be wed. You know he is training to be a knight like his father?

With your betrothal near, I expect he will soon ask Father for my hand."

With Miryam set to marry soon, Isabella's dreams might at last be within reach. Dreams she had cherished since she and Gawain were barely twelve. While they couldn't openly court, Gawain met them at the market every week, often buying more fabric than his family required. A grunt escaped Miryam's mouth. *Why is it that Bella has her dreams come true?*

"I am happy for you, truly, sister. I wish only that we might both find happiness. Who knows? Perhaps this year I shall gain what my heart most desires as well." Miryam grinned, thinking of the apple as they waited for their father to join them.

"For believing such a dangerous tale, you ought to seek holy confession," Isabella said sharply. "'Tis witchcraft you are inviting in."

Perhaps Isabella was right.

Perhaps Miryam could be content with a simple life.

Perhaps ... Yet, she doubted it.

Even her name set her apart. *Miryam*—a Jewish name in a Christian land—was near blasphemy. Simon had wished to call her Marian, the Anglicized form, but the name Miryam had come from her mother's bloodline, and that blood ran deep. In the end, he agreed with his wife's desires.

A year later, she was gone.

From birth, Miryam knew she was cursed. If all was already set against her, then why not strive for something more? That was why biting into the apple had not scared her. Why not make this life worth living, especially if she was doomed from the start?

She wondered what her mother would say.

"You know, Bella, you're not right about everything." Miryam's eyes searched her sister's, hoping for agreement. But she knew better.

Isabella just sighed. "I hear Father coming now."

"Hold a moment." Miryam darted back into the house. At her cot, she pulled it slightly from the wall, revealing a tiny hollow in the Earth hidden beneath a scatter of straw. Here were her treasures—*her secrets*—safe from the world. Bits of pretty flowers she had found in fields. A seashell she had bought at the market. Her cherished books.

Her fingers closed around an old scrap of fabric. It had once been part of a blanket her mother had woven when Miryam was a baby, the last physical bit of when she was still alive. Sometimes, she just enjoyed carrying it around with her. Miryam tucked it into her dress bodice, covered the hole with straw again, fixed the bed, and scurried out the cottage door once more.

Their father, Simon, checked the bundles in the cart, making sure all was tied fast, then fixed the horse to the traces. Selling in the larger city of Norwich always brought more coin than in their own village of Oakeshire, and it wasn't far away. Even with the crown's taxes on wool rising, the family fared well enough for their modest farm and trade.

Pulling into the town square, Miryam tried to forget her current woes and willed herself to simply enjoy seeing all the different folk at the market. A small dirt-smeared boy chased a chicken. An older woman pulled a cart full of cabbage and leeks. A barefoot beggar wandered the street asking for bread. Merchants abounded, selling food and goods of all kinds and bringing tales of far-off lands.

Amidst the crowd, a well-dressed young man approached their booth as they unpacked their goods. "M'lady, Isabella." He bowed low. "'Tis an honor to be graced by your presence."

Isabella's cheeks flushed a bright red, and she dropped a curtsy. "Gawain."

"Miryam, Master Simon—I am at your service as well." He bowed again.

"It is good to see you," Miryam said cheekily, "but we all know whom you came for." She tilted her chin toward her sister.

"I cannot deceive you." Gawain's smile widened, his shoulders easing as his eyes lingered on Isabella. "Have you heard? The new Earl of Norfolk speaks in the square today."

"Oh, Father, may Miryam and I go hear him once the market is done?" Isabella pleaded as she clapped her hands together.

King Edward II had recently appointed the new earl to succeed Sir Roger Bigod, 5th Earl of Norfolk, who had died the year before without an heir. All the nearby villages murmured with talk of this mysterious nobleman and his first public address.

"So long as you are home before the evening chores," Simon said.

"What is his name again?" Miryam feigned interest.

"Lord Amalric de Dunne. He arrived this very morn with his lady, Adeline, and his heir, Edwin. They are to dwell at Yorkington Castle in Oakeshire, not Framlingham ..." Gawain watched Isabella fit the pieces together. "Which means I shall live closer. And we may spend more time together," — he turned to Simon with a hopeful look — "only if it pleases you, sir."

Simon nodded. "I think we may arrange that." He smiled at Isabella, who gazed dreamily at Gawain. "And we have good tidings to share with you as well. My eldest daughter, Miryam, is soon to be betrothed." His laugh rumbled from his belly, which jiggled with pride.

All the color drained from Miryam's cheeks at his words.

"'Tis wonderful news. To whom?" Gawain asked.

"She is to wed the earl's own tailor and weaver, Dempsey Slye. We have corresponded these past months, and after some persuasion, he has agreed." Simon clutched Miryam's icy hand. "In return, he will inherit my farm, my sheep—and my daughter."

Miryam felt as if she might retch.

"He comes from London, said to be among the finest weavers in all England. Once wed, Miryam shall dwell within the castle walls. Imagine it, child—you, among the nobles!" Simon's voice swelled with pride. "We are to meet him at the village dance this Friday eve."

"That is joyous news," Gawain agreed.

Miryam could bear no more. Heat flushed her face, like the day in the orchard, the day she had heard her fate. She pressed her lips tight, choking back the fury she wanted to release. She longed for freedom, for expansion, not to be bound behind castle walls. It was as though her life had been taken, shrunk to the size of a silver penny, and pressed back into her hand.

"Pray excuse me, Father. I must get some air." Not waiting for an actual answer, Miryam curtsied and fled the stall. Walking as fast as she could, she wove through the market. When she made it out of the square, she tried to remain lady-like as she hit a jog. But seeing the forest's edge, she abandoned all pretense and took off sprinting full speed, not caring who saw her.

It felt good to run. To be unbound. Her heart thundered, and her lungs burned. Bursting through the tree line, she halted, panting. Holding the bottom of her dress to her mouth, she bellowed, "Hrrrr-mmmmm!" The sound tore from deep within her throat.

Miryam collapsed beside a fallen log. The tears came next. Flowing out of her like the cresting tide, unable to stop, wrung from her by some unseen force. She wept until her sleeves were sodden. *Why must I do this to myself? Why cannot I accept the life set for me?*

Lowering her gaze to the forest floor, she tried to ground herself. A small caterpillar inched past her foot. She scooped it up and sat on the log. Its tiny body crawled along her hand, up her arm, and back again. Its steady movement calmed her sobs.

"Tell me, little one," Miryam whispered, "what is freedom like? You may go where you please. No one commands you. No one tells you what you must become. But at any moment, a bird might snatch you up." She held the caterpillar up to her face, looking closely at its little head nosing around. "Perhaps the safer path is right. But what if there is more to life than safety? I feel it *here*," — she pressed a hand to her chest — "in my bones, in my very essence. Yet I know not what it is. What say you, little caterpillar?"

She waited in silence, eyes following its slow crawl.

"Well then, what did it say?" A voice called from behind, startling her.

Miryam shrieked, flinging her hands—and the caterpillar—into the air as she toppled backward over the log, landing squarely in a bed of stinging nettles.

CHAPTER 5

LEAH

T he alarm clock blared beside Leah's bed. "Fuuuccckkk ..." she grumbled, smacking snooze for the second time, eyes still closed. Ten minutes passed.

It screamed again.

Leah blinked her eyes open and squinted at the ceiling. *How is it morning already?*

After picking up Hana from Seth's the day before, she had flopped promptly into bed, not wanting to think any more about the impending custody case.

Well, not exactly promptly. A pizza box graced the kitchen table outside her room, while a half-drank wine box, plus an empty ice cream pint, had found a new home on her nightstand.

Leah could see the day peeking over the top of the concrete wall that surrounded her tiny apartment patio, where a sun-bleached plastic chair sat alone, two dirty beach towels draped across it. *Laundry. That was the other thing I needed to do ... yesterday.*

She pulled the blanket over her face.

Willing herself to disappear, or at least sleep for another hour, Leah grabbed her phone from under her pillow. The lock screen glowed with a photo of her and Hana. Life had a way of sneaking up on her, kind of like a carnival funhouse's last clown or those pesky wrinkles around her eyes. *Where the hell did those come from?* She didn't even smile much. Definitely not enough to *earn* crow's feet. But one day, there they were. A permanent reminder that time didn't care whether or not you were paying attention.

Leah exhaled. She was thirty-seven years old, and some days, it felt like she'd never really lived at all. *Here I go again. Existential crisis before my feet even touch the floor.* She rolled her eyes at herself.

Stop overthinking. Get up. Face the damn day.

Or ... she could lie there just a little longer and doom scroll social media. The latter thought won. Even her internal monologue was too exhausting to argue with.

Right on cue, her daughter, Hana, bounded into the room and jumped on the bed, dressed, wide awake, and ready for school. "Morning, Mom!"

A thirteen-year-old going on thirty. Scratch that—forty. Hana was more responsible than Leah on most days. Honestly, her bright, unshakable optimism might've been the only reason Leah got out of bed most mornings.

That ... and coffee.

Hana nuzzled up to her and gently peeled the blanket down. "Time to get up. The Sun is shining, and it's a beautiful day." She kissed Leah's cheek.

"It's always beautiful and sunny in California," Leah retorted.

"That doesn't make it any less true."

"How did you get so wise?" Leah smiled and pulled her into a big, sleepy bear hug. "And so ... awake?"

"I've got things to do, Mom. *Duh.* Robotics club is after school today, so I won't be home until five. Savannah's mom said she can drive me, so you don't have to pick me up."

Her *conversation* with Seth from the night before came flooding back to her, complicating her thoughts, so she closed her eyes and lowered her head, not letting Hana see the sneer that crossed her tightening lips. She looked up at Hana and smiled. "Thank you, sweetie. I'm so sorry about yesterday. These headaches have been awful, and I'm losing track of time."

"Mom, don't worry. Dad is just being *Dad*. He'll find any reason to get one over on you," Hana said. "I wish he wouldn't put me between you two. I love you both."

Leah could see the ache in her daughter's eyes. "Then that means you don't want to live with him full time?" she asked, bracing herself for the answer.

"Of course not," Hana replied.

A sigh of relief washed over Leah. "Oh good, I started to worry this was something you and your dad had talked about."

"I can't believe you would even think that. I want to live with both of you. Yes, your lives are different, *very different*, but I like them both equally." Hana traced the patterns on her mother's blanket with her finger. "I mean, well, he does have a huge mansion, a pool, and he lets me do whatever I want," — she smiled coyly — "but look at this cute apartment! It's way cozier than his cold marble floors any day."

"Don't rub it in. I know your dad can give you way more than I can." Leah's eyes shifted down.

Hana lifted her chin and looked directly at her. "Kidding, Mom. But really, this is my home, no matter the size, and I will always want to be with you, wherever that is." With that, Hana tugged at Leah's arm to no avail. "Now, time to get up."

Leah helped drag her tired, middle-aged body out of bed. "It makes me so happy to hear you say that. And you're right, you shouldn't be in the middle of our shit ... I mean, junk. But now, he's filing for custody, and I just ..." — she pulled Hana into another tight embrace — "I just can't lose you."

Hana was the only person in the world Leah felt she could be completely vulnerable with and comfortable around at the same time. And thirteen years ago, she became Leah's reason for living.

Because thirteen years and nine months ago, Leah had tried to end it all at the bottom of a pill bottle. Luckily, she failed, and one week later, she found out she was pregnant. That changed everything for her. She vowed to be a better parent than her mother or father had ever been to her. And when her relationship didn't work out with Seth, it didn't matter because Leah had Hana, and Hana was her world.

Now, Seth was threatening to take it all away. Leah's chest tightened.

"I'm going to be late for school!" Hana exclaimed, unwinding herself from her mom's arms.

"Don't forget that your dad is—"

"Picking me up at seven o'clock for dinner, I know." Hana nodded as she spoke. "He texted me a reminder this morning. We're going out to some special dinner with *Delilah*."

Leah cringed at the idea of her daughter hanging out with Seth's girlfriend already, but they had been dating for six months now, and Delilah was moving into his house. However, she couldn't help thinking that this was just another way Seth was rubbing his perfect life in her face. She couldn't keep hiding from it either. But she could try.

Pushing that thought to the back of her brain, she felt another migraine coming on. She rubbed her temples. *Not today, please.*

"I need to get to the school bus," Hana said, "but promise me you'll make an appointment with a doctor about those migraines. I can tell just looking at you, another one is coming on, isn't it?" She pointed a finger at Leah.

"That obvious?"

"Yeah, I know you."

"Okay, I promise." Leah kissed Hana on the nose. "What would I do without you?"

Hana skipped toward the door and was nearly out of the room when she peeked her head back in. "Oh, and I started your coffee. It should be ready now. Love you!"

She left in a flash, leaving Leah alone, fingernails digging into her palms, resenting the amount of grief her ex blindsided her with constantly. Seth had sabotaged her life umpteen times since their relationship had ended. Why Leah had ever thought dating him in the first place had been a good idea, she didn't know. Or maybe she did? Something about the feeling of punishing herself for something unknown. It made her loathe her own self-betrayal.

Now, she would have to figure out how to salvage her life and beat him in court. Her world depended on it.

CHAPTER 6

KARAIA

Time was a strange thing. When Karaia was enjoying life, it passed by effortlessly, never once making its presence known. But now, sitting on the floor of her apartment, pleading with the minutes to go by faster, beckoning sleep to take her, and wishing she could take a credit to calm herself, time seemed to last an eternity.

Her mind wouldn't stop replaying the scene. The zap of the laser gun. The woman's blood splattering against the wall. Her final breath. The officers dragging the lifeless body down the alley.

Over and over.

Karaia couldn't comprehend why she couldn't erase the feelings that flooded her body. No credit transfers. No serotonin release. Nothing.

Except blood.

And *murder*.

Murder was supposed to have been eradicated from New Soteria.

Karaia's eyes were swollen from crying, and her throat raw from sobbing. A small mass of vomit emitted a vile stench from the floor to her right. She didn't even remember throwing up.

She whispered, voice raspy, "NIVA ... access credits. Buy and transfer one credit."

I'm sorry, Karaia, you have reached your 24-hour limit. If you think this is in error, please contact Seromela Tech Support. Would you like me to connect you now?

"No, thank you, NIVA." She peeled her achy body off the floor. Her stomach grumbled, and her mouth felt dry.

Karaia stepped into her kitchen. Everything looked so normal and neat.

"Holo-screen on," she croaked.

A holographic projection blinked to life, displaying two newscasters—Brian Holster and Vee Maddox—floating midair. Their show, *On the Verge*, was one of the most popular news programs in the nation, often streaming through the transit tube airwaves to keep citizens updated on the latest climate crises or the country's most recent threats.

"What is our world coming to?" Vee said, enunciating each word with exaggerated weight.

Karaia wrinkled her nose at the woman's theatrics. She disliked the way Vee pulled her head back, bulged her eyes, and sipped her cinnamon latte with extra foam, nonchalantly commenting on the state of the world.

Karaia grabbed a towel, wetted it, and fixed her eyes on the other broadcaster.

"Honestly, I don't know, Vee." Brian shook his head in practiced frustration.

Karaia rolled her eyes. Everything she watched felt so ... hollow. So performative and meaningless. Compared to what she had experienced last night—

She trembled.

"Just last night," Vee continued on-screen, "we received a report of yet another attempted attack on New Soteria. Two torpedo drones were launched at our outer walls. Luckily, they were destroyed before impact by our security-bots. Brian, what are you thinking about all this?"

Karaia cleaned up her mess on the entryway floor.

"I'm thinking, this is the fifth time this month!" Brian slammed his palm down on the arm of his chair. "We are lucky that none have breached our walls yet. But when are we ever going to be safe from those who want to destroy everything we've built? I say we take the fight to them. End it for good."

Vee nodded solemnly. "It's frankly disgusting. However, the report states that the drone couldn't be identified from the wreckage. The perpetrators are officially unknown. But isn't it clear who continues to target us?"

"Of course it is." Brian looked directly into the camera. "This is the work of the Defiers."

Vee sipped her latte and agreed. "But where are they? There's no confirmed base of operations for these vicious terrorists. Some say they're in New Liberty, the Settlement, or even the California Keys. Others point all the way to United Europe or the Krussian Empire." She raised her eyebrows. "Some even say they could be right here in New Soteria itself. They could be *anyone*."

"But we haven't had an internal attack in years," Brian replied. "Not since Stellan and Kai Marshall's kidnapping. Aren't we safe inside our walls, at least?"

"I hope so," Vee said, taking a deep breath. "I sure hope so."

"The best way we can stay calm," Brian continued, "is by taking a credit as needed and always reporting any suspicious activity. Which reminds me ..." He straightened his coat and puffed his chest a little. "This broadcast is brought to you by Seromela, New Soteria's Official Corporation, founder of NeuroCredits, keeping you safe, happy, and healthy for the last fifty years."

"And with that, I'm taking one now." Vee laughed, leaning back in her chair. Her shoulders relaxed visibly as the serotonin washed through her body.

Karaia let out a quiet snivel of jealousy as she watched.

She tossed the vomit-soaked towel into the kitchen incinerator and pressed the button. Seconds later, she placed her hands under the sanitizer.

"What about this weekend's festivities?" Brian asked on-screen, shifting gears. "Want to give us a preview of what citizens can expect for the 50th anniversary of Seromela as New Soteria's Official Corporation?"

Karaia turned down the volume. She already knew everything about the anniversary celebrations—she was on the planning committee, after all.

Crossing the room, she waved her hand above the food preparer's sensor. "Americano, hot. And scrambled eggs with bacon."

"Good morning, Karaia," the machine replied in a rugged male voice. "Your order has been received. Would you like to add a dessert this morning?"

"No," Karaia said out of habit.

But then she thought about the previous night.

The image of the lifeless woman flashed again behind her eyes. She shivered. Her stomach twisted. Squeezing her eyes shut, she tried to block out the memory—the fear and sadness that gripped her heart. A tear slipped down her cheek. She wiped it away quickly. She yearned for a credit to make it all better. She seriously *needed* to figure out why her credits failed to disperse, having never experienced this maddening technical difficulty.

Yes, after what she'd gone through ... she deserved a little extra.

"Actually, give me a chocolate dessert. Like, *a lot* of chocolate. And make it a double shot on the Americano." She'd need the extra caffeine too.

"Order amendment received. That will be $1,307.00. Transfer funds?"

"Yes," Karaia replied.

She grabbed a mug. Her hand trembled as she slid it into the machine's slot.

Fuck. She didn't know how much more of this she could take. Living without credits was hell. *How did people do this before?*

Two shots of espresso poured into the mug, followed by steaming water.

As she waited for her food, she pulled up her social media feed on the kitchen holo-screen. She tapped the 'Latest News' tab. Nothing about the shooting from last night.

The sinking feeling in her gut said there never would be.

Murder. Suicide. Depression. Assault. Even anger and sadness—they had all officially been eradicated from New Soteria.

There hadn't been a reported murder in over seven years. A new record. Crime was at an all-time low. All thanks to the development of Seromela's NeuroCredits technology. All people had to do was purchase a credit—or more—and transfer it the moment a negative emotion came on.

Then, *instant bliss.*

It had revolutionized the world.

Seromela Corporation had won every New Soterian election since NeuroCredits launched. They'd even sold their proprietary tech to the highest global bidders. And now, Karaia lived in the richest, safest, happiest country on Earth.

Or so they said.

Karaia realized her jaw had been clenched this whole time. She opened her mouth wide, stretching her neck back and forth. Checking the time, she counted down the minutes until she could get to work and ask Arjun for help with her credits. He was her best shot at fixing all this. And the only person she trusted to tell.

Since 2299, New Soteria had made it illegal to opt out of having NeuroCredits linked to your internal NIVA system. Some dissenters had fought against the law, choosing to live without the brain-linked technology.

They were known as the Defiers.

And then there were others, people who were inexplicably immune to the NeuroCredits' effects. Despite multiple studies, no one could explain why or how. But regardless of science—or consent—the New Soterian government had decided it was too dangerous to allow anyone to live in an unregulated society. Both groups were forced to leave the country. Many sought refuge in the Settlement, a mysterious, primitive country, north of New Soteria. If you could even call it a country. There were gruesome rumors of in-fighting, disease, and lawlessness. Some thought it didn't even exist and that those who left for the Settlement were ... dead. No one knew for sure though, because no one ever came back.

Karaia knew that best of all. Her parents had left for the Settlement when she was just four years old. Her grandmother said they had promised to come back for her and her brother, Cass. But they never did. Like everyone else.

So now, if someone found out her NeuroCredits weren't working ... well, Karaia couldn't let that possibility into her mind. Not yet.

Arjun will run the tests. He'll find out what's wrong, fix it, and my life will return to normal.

That's what she told herself, anyway.

After scarfing her breakfast, a slice of double chocolate cake, and a second Americano, Karaia dressed and headed toward the door for work. But not before taking a glance at herself in her hallway mirror.

Leaning forward, Karaia turned her face to one side, then the next, gazing at her smooth brown skin. She was beautiful. Well, that was being modest. She was drop-dead gorgeous and knew it. And thanks to access to the latest in biotechnology, her face was nearly perfect too. Flawless, except *now* tiny red squiggles edged out from her dark pupils due to the night of crying and lack of sleep. Nothing could cure that. And her hair—normally straightened—frizzed out in a heap of tight black curls around her head. *What will they think at work?* She couldn't remember the last time she'd gone out in public without taming her wild hair. But this morning, she didn't have the energy or the time.

None of that mattered anyway—not if her credits never worked again.

Staying focused on one problem at a time, she stepped out the door and into the transit tube. But when her foot clinked against the metal floor, memory yanked her back to the night before. Feeling as if someone had punched her in the gut, she shuddered. As she made slow, deliberate steps toward the rail, her breaths came in fast and short.

She swallowed hard.

Time slowed with each footfall.

Desperately, she wanted to run back inside, curl up in bed, cry her eyes out, and fall fast, fast asleep, hoping this was all a bad dream or a VR trip. She kept walking forward, eyes fixed ahead. *Avoid the alley. Just get to the rail. Just get to work.*

She passed by the alley tube.

Don't look. Don't look.

She looked.

Down the alley, there was no limp, lifeless body. It was as if nothing had ever happened there. Only *she* knew it had.

About to turn and continue on, something caught Karaia's eye—a small white object wedged beneath the incinerator chute. It stuck out against the tube's pristine cleanliness. She hesitated. Part of her wanted to move forward, to get to work, to pretend everything was normal. But her feet took her down the alley instead, curiosity over caution. She scanned the ground where the cleanup crew—whoever they were—had done their job well. There was no trace of blood, no sign of a struggle, no evidence there had ever been a murder here. The place had been scrubbed spotless.

Almost spotless.

She reached down and picked up the small piece of ... *what was it?* It was slightly smooth, rigid, and rectangular in shape. Her brain searched for the word. *Paper.* It was a piece of paper, an old form of communication. No one used paper anymore. The writing—hand-written—was imperfect and messy.

It read, *240052 East 85th Tube.*

Karaia frowned, pondering if this address had anything to do with the woman from the night before. And where it led. And what she was doing. And why they killed her. She flipped the paper over in her hands, staring at its words, hoping for answers.

She shook her head.

None came.

Shoving the paper into her pocket, Karaia also shoved all the questions to the back of her mind too as she walked toward the rail stop. Along with the feelings. The confusion. The emotions she didn't know what to do with.

Focus on one thing at a time. Just get to work.

Stepping onto the next rail, she tried to remember the actual work she had to do that day—but came up blank.

Chapter 7

MIRYAM

M iryam cried out as sharp needles dug into and pricked her bare skin. Flailing in the brush, she dragged herself out of the nettles and rubbed vigorously over her skin, breaking their grip on her.

Once she settled, she shot glances all around. "Who is there?!"

"I beg your pardon. Let me aid you," the voice called again, nearer now.

"Why doest you spy on me? Show yourself!" Miryam shouted. Spinning in every direction, her eyes fixed at last upon her intruder.

Her shoulders went slack.

The young man from the orchard. *Ved.*

Still clad in the same black robe—and still as striking as ever—he approached Miryam with caution.

Her anger quelled, her heart leaping in its place.

"I mean no intrusion. But I saw you running ... and then, crying. I wished only to see you safe. Yet now ... I see I have trespassed upon your solitude. Pray forgive me." Ved lowered his gaze, awaiting her reply.

Miryam inched forward. Steadying her demeanor, she fixed all her attention on him. He stole a glance upward. She narrowed her eyes. "I suppose I may forgive you. But I am beginning to think you are trailing me." A mischievous grin spread across her face. "How is it we met twice in one week?"

Ved's lips twitched, the edges teasing a curl. "We are but delivering our monthly alms to the poor. Any other cause for our meeting lies in God's mind alone."

"What are you?" Miryam stepped closer, her heart quickening. "I mean, what order are you with?"

"I am a novice at the Benedictine Abbey at Woodbridge." Ved spoke in a soft but hurried voice. "I have not yet taken my vows. That will come when I turn eighteen, two months hence."

Miryam tilted her head, her curiosity peaking. "What kind of name is Ved, anyway? It does not sound Catholic. Why do you not wear your hair as the other monks do? Is it because you are a novice? And why have I never seen you before?" She began her usual pacing as she spoke, her excitement growing with each step. Not waiting for answers, more questions tumbled out. "What is it like living in a monastery? Do you pray all day long? Are you even permitted to speak with women? I suppose I saw you with a woman at the orchard. Why were you with that woman, Sophia, the other day? Do you have nuns at the abbey as well?"

Ved drew a long breath. "You ask many questions." His voice grew solemn. "I should return. The almoner will be waiting for me."

Miryam froze and crossed her arms. A swirl of leaves danced about her boots. "You cannot do that."

Ved lifted his eyes, piercing her with his stare. He was hard to read, and Miryam loved that.

"Do what?"

"Leave."

"Why not? You are correct. I ought not linger with a young woman in the woods alone." He turned to go.

Without thinking, Miryam grabbed his arm.

Ved turned back sharply, their faces but inches apart.

The scent of hard labor and lavender fields filled Miryam's nostrils. She had never been this close to a man before, especially not one who stirred her heart. Dizziness swirled in her mind, yet she held her ground, drinking him in. A bit of sweat beaded his tan brow. A dirt smudge adorned his cheek. The firm muscles through his robes teased her imagination. Her hand fell slowly down his arm, briefly brushing his hand before letting go.

A soft gasp escaped Miryam as their skin met. "I do not want you to go," she whispered. "I cannot explain it, only… I feel we were *meant* to meet. Do you know the sensation of which I speak?" She bit her lower lip. "I know it is preposterous."

Ved stood a few inches taller, his breath warm upon her cheek when he spoke. "'Tis not foolish. I feel it as well. That is why I fear being near you."

Miryam's lips parted. "You do?"

Ved nodded faintly. "It is easier to show you than to speak. I am not given to many words." He lifted her hand gently to his own. Their palms met, his rough and warm against hers. "Close your eyes. Attend only to your breath. In... out."

Miryam drew a long breath, trying to quiet her fluttering heart. And trying to ignore the very attractive boy standing near her. She strained to focus on nothing else but her breath.

In.

Out.

Her lungs filled and emptied. The world around them hushed, as though time itself stilled. Soon, a warm calm washed over Miryam and enclosed her with a feeling of pure acceptance.

In.

Out.

The wind picked up, circling their bodies, tugging at the hem of her gown, whipping it around her feet. A current of unseen force moved through her, goosebumps prickling her arms. It wove in and out of her and Ved, twining through their joined hands.

In.

Out.

Miryam opened her eyes. All the leaves, tiny branches, flower petals that had once been littered across the forest floor swirled around them in the gentle circling breeze. The forest birds' chirping seemed to amplify. The spring peepers sounded as if they were croaking in her head. She could truly *feel* the forest. The wind its breath, the Earth its pulse. It lived, and she was part of it.

In.

Out.

A steady thrum radiated from beneath their feet. The Sun beamed down warmth that seemed to fill Miryam to her core. Then came the rush of it. An overwhelming tide of love, unconditional and whole, encompassed every part of her being.

This. This is what she had been missing all her life. There was something more to our existence than toil and duty. It was magical, and it was all around her. Miryam smiled, a tear slipping down her cheek.

Ved reached to brush it away, his fingers lingering for a breath before he let his hand fall. At once, the wind stilled, the forest hushed. Only a circle of leaves and petals in the dirt marked what had taken place.

"'Twas wondrous!" Miryam gasped, eyes wide. "What was it? Did you do that? What did I feel?"

"'Tis what you have been seeking, is it not? Something beyond sight. Something greater." Ved's gaze lingered on hers, as if he peered straight into her soul—bare yet wholly accepted.

She never wanted this feeling to end.

"Now," he said, stepping back, "I truly must go. And so must you."

The spell broke. Miryam's thoughts leaped back to the market, her family, the earl's speech. She tilted her face skyward. *Past noon.* How long had she been gone? Minutes? Hours?

He was right. But she pressed on. "Is that what they teach you at the abbey? Can you teach me? I have always known there was more to life than I was told. How can I resign myself to the boring life of a weaver's wife, when I know that life can be so ... *magical*? Now, I absolutely cannot wed! It would utterly stifle me." She let out a large huff.

"You are to be wed?" Ved asked, startled.

"Not if I have any say in the matter." Miryam folded her arms. "I have not even met the man. That is why I ran. And screamed. And cried. And then talked to a caterpillar. At this rate, within one Sun cycle, I shall be the mad bug woman!" She threw up her hands in exasperation.

Ved laughed, and she enjoyed the sound.

"Perhaps you shall like him?" Ved offered.

Miryam sneered. "Are you really rooting for him?"

"Of course not." A soft smile graced his lips.

Miryam longed to sink into that smile and stay there for eternity. But she could not. Her father and Isabella were probably already fretting about her. She stepped toward Ved again, feeling a vibrancy between their bodies. "Until our next mysterious meeting, I suppose?"

"I cannot wait," he replied.

Miryam skipped back to the city market, humming to herself. Seeing that her father and Isabella had already packed up the booth and loaded the cart, she headed toward the square to listen to Lord Amalric's speech and find them. Isabella would scold her about not helping—*yet again*—with the market.

But, as usual, Miryam didn't really care.

Her thoughts drifted to Ved, his warm scent, his bright eyes—when a blood-curdling scream split the air ahead. The sound of flesh tearing, bones breaking, and the shrieks of the crowd followed.

Without thinking, Miryam broke into a run toward the chaos.

CHAPTER 8

LEAH

"Kat, it's an emergency," Hana said through speakerphone, eyeing her mom from across the room.

Leah was sprawled on the bed, motionless, staring at the ceiling like it had personally betrayed her. The afternoon Sun cascaded into their tiny apartment, illuminating the truth of the situation. Clothes were strewn about the floor. The small trash bin by the nightstand overflowed. The now-empty box of wine and a wine-stained cup decorated the table-side. Right now, all she wanted was to drown herself in self-pity and a pint of rocky road. Maybe curse Seth out in her head a few more times. Actually ... didn't Felix get her that voodoo doll one year for Christmas? It might be time to put it to use.

"What happened?" Kat asked after a sharp intake of breath.

"It's bad," Hana said, dead serious.

"I'm fine." Leah rolled her eyes.

"What is it?!" Kat repeated.

"Mom is on her second pint of ice cream today and still in her pajamas. She won't stop asking me about Dad and his girlfriend, Delilah. And this room?" Hana gave it a slow look. "Total pigsty. She desperately needs a friendervention."

"Oh, my goddess, Hana." Kat exhaled. "I thought something *serious* had happened."

"See?" Leah said, sitting up slightly. "No need to come by. I'm just in a mood. And also possibly allergic to my own life." She glanced around her room.

46

It wasn't *that* bad.

Okay, it wasn't great either.

She could see why Hana was concerned. The space did kind of resemble what you'd imagine when someone described an old cat lady who'd lived alone too long, forgot what soap was, and died in her bed. Only to be found two weeks later, partially eaten by her own cats. Leah shuddered at her own disturbed mind.

Hana waved her off and kept talking to Kat. "This *is* serious. Bring Felix. And one of your cute summer dresses. She needs both of you to pull her out of this funk. Even my adorable smile isn't working anymore." She gave Leah a pointed look. "And you *know* the best way to fix this—"

"Is going to the beach!" Kat squealed. "I have the *perfect* idea. On my way!"

The call ended.

Hana walked over to Leah, hands on her hips. "Mom, seriously. You've got chocolate on your sweatpants. Gross."

"Cont ... strop," Leah mumbled, shoving another spoonful of chocolatey marshmallow goodness into her mouth. "It mrakes mre hoppy." She wiped the smudge off her pants and licked her finger.

Hana rolled her eyes and left the room.

An hour later, Leah's friends showed up in full-on rescue team mode. Kat with ibuprofen and a glass of water, and Felix meticulously picking up clothes and trash with each step.

"C'mon," Kat said, yanking back the blankets and handing Leah the meds. "Up and out of bed you go."

Felix wrinkled his nose as he dangled a dirty shirt from his fingertips into the hamper. "Did you even *get* out of bed today?"

Leah set her ice cream aside and gulped down the entire glass of water. "Uh, *yes*. I did *a lot* today, thank you very much. I made an appointment for these bitchy migraines, drank a pot of coffee, mentally plotted all the ways I could murder Seth, and watched six episodes of my favorite medical drama. And how else do you think I got this ice cream?" She held up the pint like a trophy.

Felix crossed his arms and raised one perfectly sculpted eyebrow.

"Okay, okay, jeez. The rest is going back in the freezer," Leah grumbled, dragging herself out of bed. "I can see your judgy eyes."

As she trudged to the kitchen, her gaze landed on a bright green sundress draped over one of the dining chairs. "For the record," she said, pointing at it, "I'm not wearing that."

They all gathered around the kitchen table.

"Mom, you need something to pull you out of this," Hana said, motioning dramatically at Leah's entire being.

Felix and Kat nodded in agreement.

"What's wrong with sweats and a T-shirt?" Leah asked, deadpan.

"Ughhh," Hana groaned. "I have homework. She's your responsibility now." She looked at Kat and Felix, then turned and stomped off to her room.

Kat clapped her hands together with a sparkle in her eye. "Guess what? It turns out that there's this beach party I was invited to. I wasn't sure I was gonna go, but now ... this feels like divine guidance."

Leah cringed. "Please don't say this is a bunch of New Age clairvoyants and mediums. I *really* can't handle that level of toxic positivity right now."

"Even better." Kat beamed. "Yogis!"

Leah grunted.

"Honey, you know we love you, but" — Kat grabbed her hand — "you need to get *out*, out of your head, and out of this apartment. Especially before the whole circus of a custody case starts."

Leah leaned against the counter, arms folded. She probably would have some fun if she let herself. But letting go of negative thoughts wasn't exactly her strong suit. She was practically a professional wallower.

"Felix, what do *you* think? You've been unusually quiet." She narrowed her eyes at him. "Did Seth say something about me? I still can't believe you work with that asshat."

"That *asshat* is the police chief," Felix said, arms crossed. "I don't exactly have a say as a lowly patrol officer. Besides ... Seth's not *that* bad when you're not around."

Leah blinked slowly, then gave him a painfully fake smile. "Oh, thank you for coming over to cheer me up. Please continue to tell me how Seth is great when I'm not around." She slumped into a chair, head hanging. "Maybe Hana will think the same thing when he wins full custody."

Kat shot Felix a look and elbowed him hard.

He yelped. Backpedaling, he said, "Leah, babe, what I *meant* to say is that I think we should go out and have fuuunnnn. Not think about Seth, or the case." He picked up the bright green dress and waved it in front of her face. "So, go put on this sexy little dress before your ice-cream-thighs say otherwise."

Leah shot him a death glare.

Felix grinned and added, "And besides, I gotta agree with Kat. She and I are technically still married."

"That's not how marriage works," Leah said.

"It's how *ours* does. My marriage to Kat ensures no one in the department suspects my *true* identity," Felix said, grabbing Kat's hand and kissing it dramatically. "Mi amor ..."

"Everyone here knows you're gay." Kat laughed, gently pushing Felix away from her. "But thank you for agreeing with me."

She turned to Leah. "You. Dress. Now."

Resigned to defeat, Leah took the dress and headed to her room to change.

She had loyal friends who cared about her, but she wasn't sure why. She tried to put on a cheerful face—for them, for Hana, for the world. *Smile. Joke. Play the part.* But she always kept a piece of herself hidden, tucked just far enough away that no one could truly know her. Because if they didn't know her, they couldn't hurt her.

Leah sighed, wishing she were different.

She and Kat had met Felix in college, before Hana was born. Kat had been working toward her degree in environmental studies, with a human rights minor. Leah, her psychology degree. And Felix—Kat's eccentric roommate and an exchange student from Mexico—was studying criminal justice. That was five years before Kat and Felix's 'wedding.'

After overstaying his student visa, Felix decided to make America his home. And for Kat, there had never been a question. He was their friend. He needed help. So, she married him. He got his green card and then citizenship five years later. Since they were still living together as roommates, the marriage was never officially dissolved. And now, Felix kept up the charade—afraid that if his colleagues on the force found out he was gay, they'd treat him differently.

Maybe he was right. People were cruel.

Leah knew that all too well.

When Seth had found out she was pregnant with Hana, he'd broken up with her. Over the phone. He had even offered to pay for an abortion. But Leah's Catholic guilt—and the flickering sense of atoning for something else—wouldn't let her go through with it.

Nine months later, Seth reappeared, saying he wanted to help raise their daughter, but wanted nothing to do with Leah. To this day, she didn't know what changed his mind. Maybe it was seeing tiny Hana wrapped in her hospital swaddle. Maybe it was pressure from their parents. Maybe both.

Either way, Seth was in their lives, the good—*his finances*—and the bad—*everything else*. For thirteen years, he had made Leah's life a living hell. Between bouts of depression and struggling to make ends meet, she never did finish her degree.

"Chica! What's taking so long?" Felix shouted from the other room.

Leah stood looking at herself in the mirror in the cute green dress. It screamed *Kat* all over—flowy, bold, unapologetically cheerful.

Everything Leah was not.

This week, she'd meet with her lawyer and start the uphill battle to keep her daughter. And also try playing the responsible parent until it finally sunk in, she hoped. But tonight? Tonight, she would be flowing and bright, at least on the outside.

"Coming!" she yelled back. Leah stepped out of the room slowly, tugging at the hem of the dress.

Kat and Felix gasped in unison.

"Oh wow, honey, you're so beautiful. I can see your aura is already looking lighter," Kat said as she messed with Leah's hair a bit.

Leah blushed and looked away. "Don't. It's just a dress."

Felix grabbed her hand and pulled her into an exaggerated tango. She let him lead her body to his steps. *Flowing. That's my mantra tonight. Oh God, I'm starting to sound like Kat in my head. Don't ever let her know.*

Leah straightened, letting go of Felix's hands. "So, when is this party?"

Kat perked up. "Not until eight. Hana told me Seth is picking her up at seven, so we have a little time to kill before we leave." She reached into her bag and pulled out her Tarot deck.

"Oh, yaaayyy!" Felix shrieked, clapping and jumping up and down. "I love your readings."

"Are you *sure* they don't know you're gay at work?" Leah asked him, raising one eyebrow.

Felix pursed his lips in mock offense.

"But seriously," she continued, eyeing Kat. "Can't we leave the Tarot cards at work?"

"You haven't let me give you a reading in over a year," Kat said, pouting. "Pleeeaassee?"

Leah narrowed her eyes. "You sound like you did in high school."

Kat grinned, all mischief.

Leah's mouth twitched into a reluctant smile. "Fine, fine. But Felix first. I'm going to get us some wine for this pre-party."

Leah went to the kitchen cabinet and returned with three glasses and a fresh box of Merlot.

One glass in, Kat had given Felix his reading—dramatic reactions and all—then read for herself.

"Now," she said, turning to Leah, "there's no one left but you."

Leah made a show, glancing around. "We could go get Hana for a reading."

Kat frowned, unimpressed.

"Okay, fiiinne." Leah sighed in resignation, topping off her glass. "Let's get this over with."

"First," Kat said, settling into her 'mystic' voice, "think of a question or situation you'd like to know more about. Let me know when you have it."

Leah leaned back, swirling the wine. She thought about Hana, the custody case, and her migraines. But mostly, she just felt ... lost. *I want to know why life continually gives me shit sandwiches.*

Feeling the effects of the wine, and not knowing quite what else to say, she uttered, "Universe, why are you giving me shit?"

"That's not a good question." Kat wrinkled her nose.

"I don't think it's up to you to judge my question." Leah nodded toward the cards. "Go on."

"You're lucky I'm nice." Kat smiled, then picked up the deck of cards, shuffled, and spread them out in a fan across the table. "Now, pick three."

Leah did as instructed, pulling three cards from the spread and placing them face down.

Kat flipped the first one over. "The first card represents your past."

Five of Cups.

Leah groaned. "Fucking figures."

"What does it mean?" Felix asked, glancing between them.

Kat hesitated. "It means ... regret ... disappointment. Often focusing on what is lost rather than what remains."

"This is fun," Leah muttered, chugging more wine. "I love being reminded of my past mistakes."

"Okaayy, let's move on. The next card represents your present." Kat flipped the second card.

The Tower.

Leah's face went white.

Even though she didn't believe in any of this, her chest tightened. The Tower card was one of the worst cards in the deck.

Kat froze, visibly rattled.

"What am I missing?" Felix interjected.

"This is bullshit," Leah said, shaking her head. "We're done. Time to go."

Kat didn't move. "The tower ... it's not usually good," she admitted. "It means upheaval. Destruction. But it can also mean *revelation*. A breaking down of what no longer serves. Sometimes, things must fall apart so something better can come."

"Right." Leah's voice was flat. Her buzz gone. "Or sometimes things just fall apart."

"Don't you want to finish?" Kat asked gently.

"No."

"C'mon, it's just one more card," Felix said, nudging her.

"The last card is the most important," Kat pleaded softly. "It's your outcome. Your future."

"I said *no*."

Leah stood up too fast, bumping the table. Her wine glass teetered and fell, splashing the cards red, like blood where it shouldn't be.

Kat screamed, "My deck!"

Felix jumped to get paper towels.

"See? This is what I get for doing these silly things." Guilt and annoyance warred in Leah's mind as a migraine scratched its way in. "I'm sorry, Kat. I'll buy you a new one." She grabbed the napkins from Felix and started blotting the wine-soaked cards.

"It's fine," Kat said, voice tight. "I kind of made you do it." She knelt on the floor, frantically trying to salvage the reading. "They're all mixed up now. We'll never know which one was your final card."

"I can already tell you what it said. Something like *yada, yada, life is suffering, blah, blah, blah*. There. Now we can go." Leah wiped the last puddle of wine.

Kat flinched. Felix winced.

"Leah ..." Kat said, barely above a whisper. "I just wanted us to have fun tonight."

"I know." Leah's voice softened a notch. "Can we just go to the beach party?"

Kat nodded silently.

As they packed up, Leah glanced down and spotted a stray card on the floor, face down.

She picked it up.

The Star.

It meant cosmic protection, and even through difficulties, there was meaning and purpose. *All would be well, and there would be good fortune. Destiny was at work.* At least, that's what she would tell a client. She didn't believe in destiny. Or magic. Or alignment.

Still, it made her pause.

CHAPTER 9

KARAIA

The broadcast through the rail speakers was championing the story of New Soteria and how Seromela became the Official Corporation in preparation for the anniversary celebration later that week.

Karaia gritted her teeth as she impatiently rode to work. Usually, she'd enjoy gazing out of the windows, imagining up some pretend scenario where she lived in a forest in a stone castle, or on a beach in the California Keys, or, even wilder, as some sorceress from one of Arjun's favorite holo-games defending her kingdom.

But today, her fantasies seemed far away. And she just wished she could get to work and get back to life with NeuroCredits.

Listening to the news, she was brought back to her primary school days when she had first learned her country's history, but more importantly, to the moment when she had first met Arjun. Right now, the history of the Marshall family gaining prominence and its rise to power barely interested her.

She just needed Arjun to make everything normal again.

Karaia's mind raced as she listened to the broadcast, wondering what her life would be like if her NeuroCredits couldn't be fixed. Her hands shook. Her stomach ached. She tapped her foot on the floor repeatedly. *How the hell did people used to live like this?* Fidgeting in her seat, she adjusted her clothes as she willed herself simply to let the news story distract her.

Hundreds of years ago, they'd said it would never happen. That the United States of America was too great, too big, to fail. But history tells us otherwise.

The Great Fall is what they called it.

In the year 2101, the United States' political divide had become too extreme, and it found itself on the brink of falling apart into smaller, isolated regions. Then, another pandemic hit the world that same winter, shaking the already fragile nation. Worse than the 2020 pandemic, they had said. The virus had stayed alive on surfaces longer than previously thought possible. People had become afraid of each other. Feared leaving their houses. The vaccine was delayed. Millions died.

The last thing to happen between that winter and the next spring was climate change unlike anything the world had seen. Sea levels rose. Coastal cities flooded. Weather patterns shifted. Massive crop failure. Unprecedented forest fires. It was as if the Earth simply gave up on humanity and stopped living. A barren, brown husk of its former green and blue self.

Civil war, a global pandemic, and numerous climate disasters all within one year. How could a country survive? The answer was simple: *it didn't.*

Worldwide economic collapse ensued and led to global anarchy for nearly fifty years. The world population dropped to one billion, where it stood now, a tenth of what it once was.

Karaia had a hard time remembering all the details, and she somewhat appreciated the refresher prior to the 50th celebration in case she had to talk to the press. She hadn't lived through it. She had watched news stories in school—read about it on her tablet. After the Great Fall came the Rebuilding in the late 2100s, led by the world's tech trillionaires. These leaders bunkered underground and emerged nearly unscathed. They built towers and tubes to house people and keep them safe. They reconstructed entire countries within walls, supported by AI and biotechnology. By 2200, tech companies dominated, and a new form of government emerged.

Corporate governance.

Instead of voting for an individual or political party, people voted for their favorite corporation. In New Soteria, Seromela had been that corporation for the last fifty years. Some people worshiped them like the gods of old because they restored life to a crumbling planet.

As the rail slowed to a gentle halt, Karaia noted she only had one more stop until she was at work. *Arjun, please know how to fix this fucking glitch.* The rail sped forward, so she focused on the broadcast again before she let her jitters take over. She picked up on key talking points in case she was called upon to speak at the celebration or beforehand.

Some people rebelled. The Defiers. Our government had called them terrorists. They had waged war against nations, a potential threat lurking in every tube, fighting against everything from AI factories to food preparers to country borders. They claimed they stood for humanity's freedom and individual choice, but all she saw and heard from the news and history was destruction.

In 2257, when Seromela won its first election as New Soteria's Official Corporation, the use of Seromela's coveted NeuroCredits first began as a treatment for people with depression and anxiety. With the ability to release serotonin directly into the brain, people could calm themselves and feel happy almost immediately. Then, they started testing it on offenders in the criminal justice system and found that those using credits didn't re-offend.

Finally, they launched a nationwide marketing plan. NeuroCredits—the answer to all our society's problems. Depression? Take a credit. Have a kid with anger issues? Transfer that credit for them. Anxiety from work or life? Buy a credit now.

And crime numbers went down.

Murder rates. Suicides. Petty theft. It all went down. While stocks soared, and the economy prospered. With NeuroCredits linked directly to every person's NIVA system, it was the most convenient way to instant relief. That was why Seromela was so vital. They provided stability in an insecure world. They provided calm in a storm. They saved humanity from itself.

Karaia's stop. *Finally.* She walked up the steps to the capitol building, through the front doors, and into the three-step process of entering any large commercial or government building: a brain scanner for identification, a metal detector for weapons, and finally a sterilizer to kill any foreign bacteria or viruses.

On her way to the elevator, she pressed her comm. *Contact Arjun Patel,* she said to NIVA.

Connecting to Arjun Patel.

No answer.

Would you like me to continue trying to connect? NIVA asked.

No, Karaia said.

Connection ended.

She dug her nails repeatedly into her skin along her elbow and forearm. She huffed at the reason that barreled through her mind for Arjun ignoring her call. She'd have to find him in person.

The hallways were quiet, except for the faint hum of the steri-bots cleaning. People worked from home most days but were required to come in at least once a week, for meetings and special presentations. Some jobs, like Arjun's, required being in the office more often in case anyone had issues with hard-wired technology. There was always a group of IT people on site ready to help.

Karaia slipped into her office unnoticed. When she sat down in her chair, the holographic screen popped up automatically in front of her. She swiped it away and rubbed her hand on her forehead, closing her eyes.

Good day, Karaia. I notice you are at work now. Would you like me to run through your schedule for the day? NIVA inquired in her head.

Not yet, NIVA, thank you. Please enter privacy mode now, Karaia instructed.

Entering privacy mode now. You have fifteen minutes until I resume my normal functioning. Thank you.

Every time NIVA shut down in her mind, it was like something was missing. No news feed, no email, no schedule, no comm system for fifteen minutes. That's all that was allowed each day. She headed to Arjun's office.

Karaia approached his open door. "Knock, knock."

"What?" Arjun groaned at the sound of her voice.

"You can't ignore me forever." She stepped inside slowly.

"Well, no, *forever* would be impossible, but I can for the rest of the foreseeable future." Arjun twisted a holographic Rubik's cube in his hands, not looking her in the eye.

Karaia waited a few moments, standing there in awkward silence. "You know how much this bothers me."

"I know."

She shifted her weight between her feet, smiling her biggest smile at him.

"What do you need?" He finally glanced up at her, lips pursed.

"Is it that obvious?" Karaia asked, crinkling her brow.

"Why should I help *you*?"

"I know I don't deserve it. But it was three months ago, Arjun. When are you going to forgive me? I'm your best friend."

"I'm over it already. I'm not mad. Credits helped me with that. But I don't want to be your friend anymore. It's the most logical choice," Arjun said.

Karaia's face fell flat. "Can we talk about it?"

"You knew I've liked Raven for years. And you go and sleep with her. What else is there to talk about?" Anger tinged his voice despite his conviction otherwise. "Hold on." Arjun communicated with NIVA in his head. A gentle calm washed over him. "You were saying?"

Shame landed like a rock in the pit of her stomach. She too wished for a credit to quell her mind and her guilt over one stupid decision months ago. "You have every reason not to talk to me again. It was a one-time thing. Raven and I ended up at the same club one night. It was meaningless fun. *Nothing* has happened since. If I could take it back, I would." Karaia's shoulders dropped. She hoped it was enough. "Please, Arjun, I need you now more than ever."

"Fiiiinnne. I will help, begrudgingly," he said through gritted teeth. "But don't be surprised when I make snide remarks toward you."

Karaia wasn't sure if he had truly forgiven her or if it was the serotonin coursing through his brain that led him to agree. "Fair." She gave him a big smile.

"Okay, what is it you need help with? The big presentation?" he asked.

Her eyes went wide. "Oh, shit, I completely forgot."

"What do you mean, you forgot?" He swirled his chair to face her. "This is something you've been working on for months now. I thought you needed help with setup."

"No, I've been having issues with my NeuroCredit system. I need you to run some tests on me." Karaia hesitated to say more. "And I need you to run them *offline*. No one can know about this."

Arjun swiped away his Rubik's cube, looking intrigued. He always liked a good puzzle. "What kind of issues?"

"Well, my NeuroCredit system ... it ..." *Why is this so hard to say out loud?* Karaia tried again. "It isn't working. At all. NIVA still works, but my credits don't. I bought one-hundred NeuroCredits last night and transferred them all. Not a single one took. I didn't feel anything."

She started pacing in his office, rubbing the small of her back with her thumb, feeling the tension rise from the pit of her stomach, the scene from the night before rushing back. Remembering the woman writhing, begging for her life. Then—the blood. She squeezed her eyes shut.

"Man, that is bad," Arjun said, grimacing.

You don't know the half of it, Karaia wanted to reply with. Instead, she opened her eyes and just slowly nodded.

"But not to worry, let me hook you up to my PET, and I can run some brain scans from there." He pulled a small device out of his pocket.

"What is that?"

"It's my PET. It stands for private external tablet. This bad boy runs its own server, Wi-Fi network, and can extract data from outside networks without being noticed or connected to them. It can even send out a dampening field, temporarily blocking comm signals—like this." He swiped up the holo-screen and pressed a few buttons. "I got it last month, and I've had him with me ever since. Aren't you sweet, my little PET?" He mockingly stroked the tablet.

"Only you would have a pet computer." Karaia laughed, then lowered her voice. "Wait, isn't it illegal not to be connected to the New Soterian servers?"

"Hey, a man's got to have his secrets, right?" Arjun winked. "Just kidding, it's mostly got holo-games on it. And yes, ones that might *technically* be illegal. So, I have to keep them off the web, you know."

That's why Karaia and Arjun were best friends. While both were committed to Seromela and New Soteria, they also both bent the rules every now and then when it was harmless. That was even how they had met in primary school.

Young Arjun and Karaia had sat next to each other in a Virtual Reality coding class when another boy in their class started teasing Arjun. "Hey, nerd, you're always going to have to create strong avatars in programs because you're never going to be like that in real life," he snickered at Arjun as he looked to his friends for validation.

Arjun had sat there, tiny tears welling up in his eyes. Children didn't have free rein of NeuroCredits; consent had to be approved by either a parent, teacher, or authority figure, so Arjun couldn't just take a credit to feel better.

Young Karaia could see he was struggling. She felt the urge to correct the wrong that was happening before her. "Hey," she whispered to the bullies, "leave him alone."

They ignored her and ramped up their taunting. "Oh look, your girlfriend has to defend you because you can't even defend yourself. How sad."

"I'm not his girlfriend, and he doesn't need me. Bullies like you shouldn't get away with saying that stuff to anyone."

They shifted their attention to her. "Yeah, what are you going to do about it? You're just a sad little girl with no parents. I heard they left you behind because they didn't want you anymore."

Karaia's anger rose inside, and she knew she should have asked for permission for a credit from her teacher. That's what they taught kids to do. Instead, she walked over to the taunting boy. He wasn't much bigger than she or Arjun. He just *thought* he was bigger and better than they were. She pulled back her fist and punched him square in the jaw.

"Owwwwww!" He burst into tears. "You hit me! Mrs. Deluth, Karaia punched me!"

Karaia's knuckles ached. She had never hit anyone before. Part of her felt righteous; part of her felt bad. Before she could think more about it, teachers and security officers surrounded them. They pulled her out of the room, but not before she saw a huge grin spread across Arjun's face.

That made it all worth it.

This incident resulted in her spending each afternoon for a month in a VR safe room, away from the other kids. The VR room was supposed to help Karaia work out her issues in a safe way that didn't harm anyone. It replayed scenes that ignited her anger, but before she could act in aggression, NeuroCredits were transferred to her brain instantly. It was supposed to help her learn to calm herself down, rather than act out. That's what the counselor said.

On the simulation's last day, Karaia prepared to face a monster in the VR world. Expecting the regular release of serotonin, she didn't even try to fight back, knowing the program would end shortly after. But then—the monster hit her and knocked her down. Stumbling to get away, she picked up a virtual stick and swung it at the monster, striking it in the legs. It winced but kept coming.

The serotonin wasn't being released. *Was this a test? Am I supposed to calm down on my own?* The monster kept coming. There was no stopping it—no calming down.

She had to fight.

Karaia stood tall and swung at the monster, cutting its arm. Blood dripped out. Again, she hit it. And again. Channeling all her rage into each motion. Finally, the monster lay defeated on the ground. The simulation ended.

When Karaia took off the VR headset and exited the room, the counselor congratulated her on finishing her sessions and let her leave. She was confused. How did the counselor not know she had just fought the monster? Why didn't she receive her NeuroCredits in that last simulation?

As she walked down the hallway, Arjun popped up next to her. He whispered, "How many hits did it take to defeat the monster?"

"What?" Karaia laughed nervously.

He winked at her.

"Did you just hack into our school's VR system and change my simulation?" she asked, mouth agape.

"I can neither confirm nor deny," Arjun said with a smirk. "I never got to say thanks for the other day. Those guys have been making fun of me for years, and they haven't in a month because of you."

"You're welcome," Karaia said. "But I have to know. Why would you risk all that for me?"

"You helped me when you didn't need to. And you shouldn't lose all that fight in you. It might be useful someday." He said it with such seriousness, looking down at his feet when he walked.

"Hmm. I never thought of it that way. But you could have gotten in trouble," she said.

"Only if they catch me. I've been hacking into the school's programs since I was six, and they haven't caught me yet."

Karaia burst out laughing. "We have got to be friends." She linked arms with him, and they walked out of the school together.

Now in Arjun's office, waiting for answers, Karaia tried to remember her past conviction and the confidence she normally had. *Or was I ever really confident?* She wanted to feel strong and secure, but having no connection to her credits made her question everything about herself. She wished for the feeling to go away.

Arjun scanned all around her head with his PET, collecting data. "Okay, that's it," he said.

"Really?"

"Yep. Now the analysis could take up to a day, at the most. It'll go a little slower because the tech on this drive isn't nearly as efficient as what Seromela has, but no one else will know." He pocketed the tablet and pulled up the holographic Rubik's cube again. "Also, I really like your hair like that. You should wear it curly more often."

Karaia smiled, sighing, happy to have her best friend back in her life. "Thank you, Arjun, really. This last day has been so crazy."

"What's so crazy?" someone asked from the doorway.

Karaia jumped as she and Arjun both looked toward the door. Raven stood there, a digital clipboard in hand.

"Raven, hi," Karaia said.

Arjun stared down at his cube.

Raven repeated herself. "What's so crazy?"

"Oh, it's nothing, really. I watched some news from the European War on my holo-screen last night, and it really got to me, so I had to buy a NeuroCredit. I was telling Arjun he really shouldn't watch that news segment."

"Oh, that doesn't sound crazy ... but whatever." Raven looked annoyed. "You ready for the presentation? The entire board is going to be there, and we can't mess anything up. Not with the big reveal of Phase Two at the gala this weekend."

"Yeah, of course I'm ready." Karaia smiled wide, hoping Raven would go away.

Raven didn't share the same desire to bend the rules as Arjun and Karaia did. She couldn't find out about Karaia's broken neural link.

"Okay, I'll see you in the conference room in five," Raven said, lingering for a moment.

After she left, Arjun asked, "There's nothing else I should know as I'm running these scans that you can tell me about last night?"

"Not that I can think of." Karaia didn't like lying, but it was safer this way. Arjun could get in trouble just by talking to her about her credit issue, let alone helping her. Yes, it was to protect him. But also to protect herself.

"So, *are* you ready for your big presentation?" he asked.

"You mean, other than the fact that it's in five minutes, and I'm not even set up yet. Yeah, sure." Karaia grimaced as she pulled up a small holo-screen from her wrist and started looking for her presentation notes.

"You'll do fine. I'll help get the screen set up for you in the conference room. You've got this," he assured her.

"Thank you." She nodded.

As Karaia marched down the hall and toward her presentation, NIVA popped back in her head. *Hello, Karaia, privacy mode has ended.*

CHAPTER 10

MIRYAM

Panting from her run, Miryam reached the village square just as the new Earl of Norfolk addressed the throng.

"My loving people, what you have just witnessed here is the work of God." The earl motioned a cross over his chest as he spoke. "By command of my Lord, the King of England, ordained by God himself, it is my honor and sacred duty to protect the good folk of this land."

Miryam forced her way through the frenzied crowd, searching for her father and sister. But her eyes kept darting back to the stage.

Lord Amalric stood high on a wooden platform in the square's center. His knights—Gawain's father among them—ringed the stage in iron. Beside him loomed the bishop, head of the Church in the region. Behind them lay what remained of a man who had been quartered. His body torn and cast in four directions. Blood slicked the platform and spattered the cobblestones below. Servants bent to gather the pieces, while the horses were led away, their harnesses stained red.

Vomit rose into Miryam's mouth. She gagged and clapped a hand to her mouth, turning aside.

Lord Amalric raised his voice. "By this judgement, I condemn the barbaric rituals of paganism, heresy, and witchcraft. Let this man—nay, this heretic—stand as a warning. Do not consort with devils, lest you meet the same fate." He thrust a finger toward the butchered remains. "For I am your new Earl of Norfolk, and under my rule, no heretic shall live upon this land—now, nor evermore. May God have mercy on your souls. Go in peace."

He lifted a hand to the masses, and the people roared in applause.

At last, Miryam spotted her family. Heart pounding, she weaved her way through the mob to reach them.

"Thank God in heaven you are well! Where have you been?" Isabella threw her arms around Miryam. "We feared when you did not return for some time."

"I went to the woods for air, and I ... must have dozed off," Miryam lied. "Father, forgive me?" She batted her eyes.

"Of course, my darling girl," their father replied. "But you shall help unload the cart when we reach home. Your sister did it all alone earlier."

Isabella shot Miryam a glare that could pierce even the thickest wool. Miryam shrugged, offering her most apologetic smile.

As they made their way back toward the cart, Simon spoke again. "You are lucky to have missed that sight. I had to shield your sister's eyes. No woman ought to see such butchery. 'Tis grievous to think heretics walk among us. I pray to God the earl brings them all to swift justice." He sighed.

Miryam's mind drifted to Ved, and to what she had felt in the woods. *Was that heresy?* Could something be sinful but feel so good? Scripture warned about that. Yet the love and peace that had flooded her, the wind swirling like God's own breath, had nearly brought her to tears. How could that not be divine?

"Father," Isabella broke in, "before we head home, may Miryam and I stop by the tavern? Gawain and the other squires plan to gather there after the speech."

Simon furrowed his brow. "Will his father be present?"

"Of course."

"Very well. Do not stay late, and see that Gawain or his father walks you home before sundown to put up the chickens—*and* the cart of wool." He raised his eyebrows at Miryam.

"Thank you!" Isabella kissed his cheek and hooked her arm through Miryam's.

Still lost in thoughts of the woods, Miryam let herself be dragged back toward the square and to the village tavern.

The dark, musty bar smelled of ale, piss, and forbidden acts. As they entered, Miryam stepped in something sticky. A rat scurried along the wall, heedless of the drunken ramblings of patrons and vagabonds. A burly man belched as they passed, while a cluster of squires raised a bawdy song by the barkeep. It was a far cry from Miryam's time in the woods. Yet something about the place excited her just as well.

Isabella wrinkled her nose as she tiptoed inside. "Ugh ... I am here for Gawain alone. 'Tis vile in this place." She lifted her skirts to keep them from brushing the floor.

"I find it interesting here," Miryam said as they approached Gawain and his companions.

"Of course, you do, dear sister. You would find a cave or a dungeon interesting too."

Miryam shrugged in agreement.

"M'lady," Gawain declared. He thrust a pint toward Isabella, which she promptly set aside. "We need to celebrate! There is good news all around."

"What news?" Miryam asked.

"Oh, Miryam, you have not heard." Isabella's eyes sparkled. She promptly retold what had happened at the morning market after Miryam had fled. "... and that was when he asked Father's permission." Her smile stretched wide, eyes brimming with joy. "We're to be wed! Can you believe it? I am the future wife of Gawain, son of Edmund, and soon-to-be-knight himself."

Gawain blushed and took a drink of ale. "'Tis true. She is to be my bride."

"Congratulations, I am truly happy for you," Miryam said, forcing a smile for the beaming couple.

And she was happy for her sister. Yet she longed to talk of her own excitement. Wished she could tell her sister all about Ved. About the forest and the wind. About the feelings she had inside. She yearned to tell someone because the longer she kept it to herself, the more it seemed like a fever dream, each passing moment becoming less clear, like it had never even happened.

"Now we are both to be wed soon, and both to dwell within the castle walls. 'Tis so wondrous." Isabella tilted her head. "Are you not happy?"

The words had only reminded Miryam of her own betrothal. Her heart twisted in its own knots of joy and sorrow, anger and fear, confusion and bliss. The range of emotions she had felt that day left her speechless. Which was a rarity for her. Fortunately, Isabella was so caught up in her engagement that the question faded and was soon lost in the tavern's din of cheers, drunken songs, and the slosh of ale. So Miryam sat in her silence, adrift in confusion, until their time there was done.

The Sun was setting as they arrived home that evening. Gawain bid them goodnight, and Miryam and Isabella slipped inside to find that their father was already putting up the chickens and out finishing the nightly farm chores. They began unpacking the cart what they hadn't sold. Among the pile lay the blanket with the flaw Miryam had made.

"You never answered me earlier." Isabella had not forgotten her question.

As Miryam thought of how to avoid the discussion of her betrothal, Simon hobbled in their front door, arms full of firewood.

"Oh, Father, let me aid you." Miryam rushed to him and carried the wood to the hearth. She fetched kindling from the bucket near the stove, then the flint and iron from the table, and made her way toward the fireplace.

"Thank you ..." Simon eyed her, for Miryam was rarely so eager to tend the hearth. With a groan, he sat down. "Bella, would you fetch me some ale? I need some for my throat."

Bella sprang up at once to oblige.

Simon turned his eyes back to Miryam. "Well. Are we going to speak of it?"

"Speak of what?" Miryam busied herself with the growing flames.

"Your impending marriage."

Both her father and sister, it seemed, wished to talk about it now. Miryam kept her eyes fixed on the fire, prodding the logs with the poker. When she finally managed words, her voice was terse. "What is there to speak of? You have already made the arrangements."

Isabella returned with the ale and placed it in Simon's hand. "See, Father, I told you. She is not content with it."

"How could you have guessed?" Miryam retorted, glancing up from the blaze.

Simon sighed. "Dear daughter, you must know I do this for you. For our family's future. There is no other way for you and your sister to inherit aught of what we have, save through your marriage to Dempsey."

Miryam could see the love on her father's aging face. "I know you believe this is for me. But it is not what I want."

"What do you want?"

There was that troublesome question again.

"I want ..." She rose, gazing upwards as if she could see the night's stars twinkling brightly, and sauntered around the room. "... to explore. To find what truly calls me. To choose my own path."

Simon's expression softened. "My girl, you are your mother's daughter. But even she came to love our simple life together." He shook his head. "I love that you yearn for more, but 'tis—"

"Not our life. *I know*." Miryam's voice cut across his. "I live it daily with the two of you. Between you and Bella, I am reminded often enough of our place in the world."

She sank once more beside the hearth, eyes fixed on the flames as they leaped and danced. For so many days she had wished her mother were still alive. To have grown up with her—someone like Miryam—someone she might confide in, share secrets with.

Someone who understood her.

That was what Miryam wished for most of all in this world. Even more than she longed to travel, to know, or to explore. She wished for someone to truly understand her and love her, in all her quirks and oddities. A small tear escaped her eye, and she quickly brushed it away.

"Miryam," Isabella said gently, "we only wish you to be happy. But you are ever so unsatisfied with life. What if you gave Dempsey a chance? Perhaps you may like him. At least wait until the dance."

There was Isabella, practical as ever.

Miryam hadn't even met Dempsey yet. She had opposed the match on principle alone, that she had not chosen it herself. *Fine,* she told herself. *I will try to be open to it. I shall wait until the dance on Friday. And stop,* stop, *thinking about Ved.*

She tried to push that thought aside, though it tugged stubbornly at the edges of her mind. She told herself she would wait until the dance.

Then, she would decide how to proceed.

Chapter II

LEAH

Frolicking silhouettes of people danced in the hue of the Sun's rays as they pulled up to the beach party. The clouds kissed the ocean, and both were shades of glistening pink, purple, and blue as the Sun faded into the horizon. Waves crashed onto the shore. Salty warm air drifted into Leah's nose. All of it sent her into nostalgic bliss.

It was one of the few places her mother had let her truly be free. Leah's father had hated the salty water, the cool ocean breeze, and sand beneath his toes. So he'd never go with them, and that had probably been why her mother had loved it so much. It had represented her freedom from a controlling husband, for a few hours at least. While the ocean water was far too dangerous for young Leah to play in—so her mother said—she played for hours in the sand while her mother sunbathed. Leah would build sandcastles and pretend she was an all-powerful witch in charge of the kingdom and doling out orders. When her mother asked what she was doing, she'd reply, "I'm playing princess, Mama."

Now as she, Kat, and Felix got out of the car, Leah breathed in the salty air. She scanned the beach party. A bonfire. Live music. People dancing, talking, laughing, adorned by the setting Sun. She tried to remember the last time she and her mom went to the beach. It had probably been decades at this point.

Her mother, Karen, had worked as a secretary, then had become a stay-at-home mom after Leah was born. Her father, Fred, was the police chief, a Vietnam War vet, and fifteen years older than her mom.

Funny—or sad—how Leah had ended up with the next police chief, who was fifteen years older than herself. History has a way of repeating itself.

While her mother had smothered her as a child, her father had ignored her. "Karen, get me another beer!" he'd yell from the living room. Karen would go scampering toward the kitchen. Leah would hear the clink of the can top and then her mother's footsteps clapping back to the living room.

"Here you go, my dear," she would say.

He rarely replied. Just grunted. It was probably for the better because when he did talk, like on Sundays after church, it stung.

Abusive had been the word Leah's shrink used.

"God dammit, woman. Can't you get anything right?" he'd complain about her mother's cooking. "This bread is all soggy, and the tuna smells like a fish threw it up. Make it again," he'd say. "And, Leah, quit hanging around. Don't you have chores to do?"

As Leah would get to her chores, she would hear him quoting the Bible out loud, stumbling over his drunken words. He never quoted the parts about love or kindness. It had always been the lines about a woman's place or how a wife should serve her husband.

To say the least, Leah hated Sundays. She had grown up Catholic. *A recovering Catholic*, as she would say. That alone probably said enough about her neurotic ways. Before she had been born, like all good Catholics, her parents had tried having children for years and had nearly given up. After five miscarriages, they finally had their miracle baby. That's what her mother had called her—a gift from God. However, after reflecting on it as an adult, Leah had concluded her mother invested all her energy in raising her not because she loved her so much but to escape her marriage.

Leah couldn't blame her, but she did resent her for it. Because her mother *cherished* her so much, it led to an overprotected, sheltered childhood. Her mother filled Leah with fear of the outside world. As a toddler, she wasn't allowed to explore. "You could get hurt," her mother told her. As a young child, she wasn't allowed to play outside with the neighbor kids. "Something bad could happen to my little miracle," she'd say. And as a teen, she couldn't date boys. "What if they hurt you?" she would ask.

Over time, Leah learned to keep to herself, observe, and let the world slip by.

Tonight, she wanted something different. Instead of just watching, she wanted to experience life. But the closer she got to having to actually interact with other humans, the more she envied them. They all looked so effortlessly happy. Leah grimaced.

As they approached the party, Kat ran up to a small group of people near the grill, giving them all hugs one by one. Someone had already thrown Felix a frisbee and invited him to play.

Leah stood alone and gulped. *I need a drink.* She made a beeline to a table that had been set up with cups, a small cooler, snacks, and yoga mats. *Because what party wouldn't be complete without complimentary yoga mats?* She laughed.

"What's so funny?" a voice said.

She turned to find a man standing beside her. "Oh, I didn't realize anyone heard me. It's nothing, really."

"Excuse me." He reached across her to grab a beer can out of the cooler.

Leah studied him, as she did anyone she first met. He stood a head taller than her, looked about thirty-five, but he was in good shape, so he could be older. His hair was pulled back in a man bun, and he wore loose linen pants and a plain gray fitted T-shirt, showing the muscles beneath. He smelled of laundry that had been hung out to dry. She was instantly attracted to him. She tried to shrug off the feeling.

He popped the top of his locally brewed brown ale. "Have you tried this brewery before? They're really good."

"No, I haven't. I'm more of a red wine kind of gal myself." She grabbed a cup and poured herself some wine from a box on the table, taking a quick sip. Then another larger swig.

"Hey, do I know you from somewhere?" he asked, narrowing his gaze.

"I don't think so." She looked toward the ocean, trying to act uninterested in the conversation. The two sides of her battling within. One wanting to connect, the other wanting to protect.

"Are you sure? You look really familiar." He took another sip of beer.

Leah replied with a snark, "I think I'd remember someone as pushy as you."

"Ouch," he said, but continued, "So how do you know Raj and Phoenix?"

She had learned they had organized the beach party, based on Kat's details on the ride over. "I don't." She gulped some wine. "My friend Kat does. They all did yoga teacher training together."

"Ah, I see," he said, voice trailing. "Sooo ... do you do yoga?"

"No." *Fuck, Leah, just be nice. Why is that so hard?*

Awkward pause.

"I'm Tate." He stuck out his hand to shake hers. "I was the yoga teacher trainer who instructed their class seven years ago. We all try to get together at least once a year."

His hand hung in the air.

Anxiety gripped Leah's mind, and her brain couldn't make her hand meet his. Tate shook his head and turned to go. At that moment, Leah realized how much she really didn't want him to leave.

"I'm sorry," she blurted out, grabbing a quick glance at his behind. *Of course, he has a nice ass.*

He swiveled back to her. Leah tried to smile but worried it came off more like an awkward, childish grin. She took another swig of her wine.

"I've had a bad couple of days, that's all. Kat thought that by bringing me here, it would cheer me up, but so far ..." She took a deep breath, remembering her mantra for the night. *Flow.* She looked at Tate. "Can I have a do-over? Hi, I'm Leah," she said, sticking out her hand.

"It's nice to meet you, Leah," he said, drawing out her name as he slowly took her hand in his, shaking it.

Firm but gentle. Damn, he was becoming even more attractive to her.

"Wanna walk along this beach with me?" Tate asked, gently biting down on his lower lip. "It's a gorgeous night."

Leah nodded, trying not to ogle his beautiful face for too long. "So, you're one of them?" she asked as they began to walk along the shore, side by side.

"One of who?"

"You believe in all that spiritual, woo-woo shit?"

Tate chuckled. "Well, I wouldn't call it that, but yeah. What do you believe?"

"What I can see, touch, what we can actually explain," Leah answered.

"So, you don't believe we go anywhere after this life?" He turned and gazed at her in the light of the setting Sun.

The depth of his stare made her avert her eyes. "No, I mean ... I don't know ..."

"Don't worry," he assured her. "We can save the deep subjects for a later date."

A later date? That meant he was single, Leah took note.

"What do you do for a living? Because you're not just a yoga teacher." She could feel her buzz coming on, and she was starting to loosen up.

Tate cocked his head. "How did you know?"

"I'm a psychic," she replied with a wink.

"Wait, you just told me you don't believe in any of that 'woo-woo' crap," Tate said with quotes in the air.

"Something has to pay the bills."

He laughed. "Well, you're right. I do yoga as a passion project. My full-time job is—"

Leah held up a hand. "Wait, let me guess. A doctor or a firefighter? Something heroic. I can sense that you like helping people. You probably also own a dog, jog every morning, and volunteer at a soup kitchen on the weekends."

"Why do you do that?" He frowned.

"Do what?"

"You're analyzing me, like you're looking through a lens of a microscope at a specimen. It just feels so ... separate."

Leah wasn't used to being called out. "And here I thought we were having witty banter." She laughed—alone. He just continued to pierce her with his soulful eyes. "I'm sorry. I'm going to start over again and try to be a normal human being." She stuck out her hand once more. "I'm Leah."

Tate smiled. "You don't need to do that. What would happen if you tried to just *be*?"

"Be what?" Leah asked, furrowing her brow.

"Just be, be *here* now, be present. What would that look like to you?"

Finally, she let her eyes meet his, and a wave of comfort washed over Leah, like she had known Tate for years. She wanted to let him in. She wanted to be real with him. She forced the words out of her mouth, even though it went against everything her past programming had taught her to do. "I don't know why I do what I do. It's probably because I feel like I don't deserve happiness, like I need to be punished for something. It's easier to keep people at a distance than let them get close. Because it always ends in disaster. Which is why I usually end it before it begins. I don't even know why I'm telling you all this. I don't even tell my therapist all this. Hell, I don't usually tell people I see a therapist."

"Maybe I'm just a good listener." Tate smiled, and they continued walking.

Leah let out a huge sigh she had been holding in. She was definitely loosening up, and it felt good. Was it Tate's presence or the wine? She slipped her shoes off and nestled her toes in the sand with each step. "Maybe you're too good to be true. I need to know something weird about you. Are you secretly a masochist? Do you have a third nipple? Live in your mom's basement?"

Tate choked on his next drink of beer, laughing. "Wow, you are getting real now. Sorry to say, none of those are true. But my grandma told me I slurped my soup too loudly when I was a kid. I still like to play with Legos sometimes. I pee in the shower most days. And once when I was fifteen, I stole from a pharmacy."

This time, it was Leah's turn to almost spurt out her wine. "At least I know you're human now."

"Well, I actually stole insulin for my mom, who has diabetes."

"So, you're Robin Hood?" she joked.

"You can keep trying to put me in a box, or ... you can come put your feet in the water and check out the full Moon with me." Tate gestured toward the water as he slipped off his sandals.

The Sun had set, and the Moon was rising. It glowed a faint orange just above the horizon. It was a perfect night. Everything Leah loved about the beach. "I can't," she said.

"Why not?"

"Because I don't think I can handle it if you're romantic too."

"That's not a good reason, come on!" He set down his beer and ran toward the water, kicking up sand behind him. He turned to look back at her.

God, he's good looking. And charming. And funny. Ugghhh. This is definitely going to end in disaster. Despite her mind telling her otherwise, Leah walked toward the ocean. The waves crashed against the sand, ebbing and flowing with the Moon's pull. Tate was already standing knee-deep in the water, his pants pulled up around his thighs.

"C'mon," he said. "It's not too cold."

Leah had actually only been in the ocean a handful of times. Her irrational childhood fears crept in. Her mother's voice in her head warned her. *It's dangerous, Leah. Be careful, Leah. Don't get too close, Leah—*

Shut up! she screamed at her inner thoughts.

Moseying toward the water, she let the next tide touch her toes. The ocean's chill ran up her spine. She jumped back.

"That's all you're giving me?" Tate asked.

"This water is freezing," she insisted, her lips curving at the corners.

"You're right, it is." He reached down and splashed her, splattering her dress with saltwater.

"Hey!" Leah playfully shouted.

She stepped forward to kick water back at him, but just as she did, Felix came running by, trying to catch a frisbee. He bumped right into Leah, launching her forward.

"Sorry!" he yelled as he went after the frisbee.

As Leah teetered on the edge of one foot, trying to catch her balance, her arms flailed in the air. The green dress swayed in the breeze.

Tate rushed forward, arms out. "I've got you."

But it was too late. Her momentum plunged them both downward into the frigid ocean.

With a splash, Leah landed on top of Tate in about two inches of water. Then, the tide rushed in, soaking them both. Only a thin layer of clothing separated them. Her body pressed up against his lean muscles. A warmth in her groin begged to be satisfied. She could feel the rough sand beneath her legs as they entangled with Tate's. Her wet hair clung to her skin, and she licked saltwater off her lips. Inches away from each other's faces, they both burst out laughing as cold waves cascaded over their bodies with each incoming tide.

For the first time in a long time, Leah didn't care. She felt happy. She wasn't sure if it was all the wine, or Tate, or the beach and the moonlight, but she couldn't remember feeling this free—*this alive*—ever before.

Tate stilled and then asked, "Can I kiss you?"

Leah held her breath, then nodded.

Pressing his lips hard against hers, Tate's mouth was warm and tasted like a good beer. Leah melted. Her whole being lit up, electrified from the inside. Not remembering the last time she had been kissed like this before, if ever. Tate grasped at her body, pulling her closer to him as if the waves might wash her away if he didn't.

Between tender kisses, he whispered, "I like you, Leah."

She wanted to say it back, but all she could muster was a smile as she slowly peeled herself off of him. She stood, trying to brush the wet sand from her dress and skin.

Tate sat up, still in the water, and grinned up at her. "You intrigue me too. I feel like there's so much more to know about you."

Leah shook her head. "I've done nearly everything to push you away, stereotype you, poke fun at you, and now, you're covered in sand and water because of me."

"You can't reason with the mysteries of the heart."

"Well, I ..." She stopped herself from denying it. Instead, she reached down and helped pull him up out of the water.

He stepped close to her and kissed her again. Leah wanted to melt again and float away in an ocean of bliss with Tate. But this time, she didn't allow it. She thought of Hana and Seth and the impending custody case. She couldn't get wrapped up in some love affair right now. There was too much at stake.

She pushed him back gently, letting her hand linger on his chest. "I have to go, but it was really nice meeting you." Giving him a peck on the cheek, she turned to walk away, resolved to accept it for a good evening and move on before things got complicated.

"Wait, Leah!"

Not turning around to look at him, Leah sped up, grabbing her sandals on the way, and rushed toward the parking lot. If she turned around to see Tate's face again, she might never leave him.

She reached Kat's car. Unlocked, in usual Kat fashion. Leah sat down in the backseat, shivering from her wet dress and hair. She looked around for a sweatshirt or towel, anything to dry herself. Nothing. *Fucking figures.*

The farther she got from Tate, the more Leah felt like her old self. She closed her eyes, head hanging low. *How could I let my feelings drift to some guy when I should be thinking about Hana and doing everything I can to win this custody case?*

The wine's effect was wearing off, slowly being replaced with another migraine. She gazed out the window and watched the party-goers. Some still played beach games. Others splashed in the water. Most huddled around a big bonfire, laughing and talking with one another. One guy was playing the guitar while another played a bongo drum. A few people danced to the beat, their hands up and waving in the air.

Leah was jealous. She had never felt that free, that happy, in her whole life. Except tonight, she had the chance ... but something always ruined it.

This time, it was her.

"Why are you in here?" Kat opened the car door and popped her head in, seeing Leah drenched in her backseat. "Oh no, what happened?"

"Oh, nothing, just my usual self-flagellation."

"Stop it. Your aura is all dark and gloomy. What's wrong?" Kat sat down next to her and closed the car door.

"It's just all *this*." Leah waved her hands in the air. "I shouldn't even be here. I should be preparing for this custody case like a responsible parent for Hana, not partying like I'm twenty-five again."

Kat retorted, "Hana's the one who knew you needed to go out and have fun. She's a smart kid, and she loves you so much. Are Seth's nasty words getting to you again?"

Leah didn't reply.

"Do you want to come back to the party?"

"No."

"Okay, I'll see if Felix is ready to head home. We'll be back soon," Kat said as she scooted out of the car, leaving Leah alone in the dark with her thoughts.

Chapter 12

KARAIA

"Safe. Happy. Healthy," Karaia said, scanning the conference room and taking a deep breath. "These three words have secured Seromela as the world's leading corporate government for the last fifty years. Marketing trends show that fifty percent more Neuro-Credits have been purchased this year over last year. Studies also show that those who grew up with the neuro-link in their heads purchase more credits than those who didn't. However, our population has reached the threshold of what we can sustain in terms of amounts of serotonin in our systems daily. And that's why we're here today."

Holographic projections of each Seromela board member filled each empty chair at the central table. The only other actual people in the room were Arjun for tech support, Raven, who was head of security, and Griffin Marshall, CEO of Seromela and President of New Soteria. He sat smugly at the far end and head of the table, slowly rapping his fingers across the surface as he studied Karaia giving her presentation. She wiggled in place and straightened her dress.

There was a new development in the NeuroCredit system coming soon, but Karaia wasn't privy to that information since she just provided data and marketing trends. The only thing she did know was that there was something coming. *Phase Two*. Each Seromela department had been assigned specific tasks a few months ago, but they weren't able to share across departments what they were working on. Even within the marketing department, they were split into marketing analysis, which Karaia was in charge of, and the Phase Two marketing plan that would be revealed at the 50th anniversary gala by Griffin. He kept his newest projects incredibly secret, so he was heading up the Phase Two rollout himself. No one, not even Raven, knew the details. At least, that's what she told Karaia.

Karaia finished her presentation to the board's light clapping. She answered their questions. One by one, they blinked out of the room.

"Well done, Ms. Pine." Griffin applauded. "Those are just the numbers we need for our next phase. Send that data to me by this afternoon. I'll include some of them in my gala presentation."

Karaia let her shoulders relax. It was the first time since last night's incident she had felt halfway normal again. She accessed NIVA in her mind. *Transfer all presentation data to Griffin Marshall now.*

A pause. *Transfer complete.*

"Already done, Mr. Marshall." She nodded, standing tall.

"I wouldn't expect any less. Thank you again for your hard work. In four days, we are going to revolutionize the world." Griffin smiled wide, leaning back in his chair, his eyes already roving Karaia's figure. His gaze flicked to Raven. "Ms. Ryder, meet me in my office and make sure my lunch is hot on my desk in exactly fifteen minutes. And now, Mr. Patel, Ms. Ryder, give me and Karaia the room," he instructed, motioning for them to leave.

Karaia waved to Arjun and mouthed a *thank you* to him as he and Raven both promptly exited, leaving her alone with Griffin. He greedily ogled up and down her body as he rose from his chair.

"NIVA, put the room in privacy mode and dim the lights fifty percent," he said out loud.

The lights dimmed, and the windows tinted, both to the outside and to the inner hallway. No one could see in or out. A soft click from the doors indicated they were locked.

An electronic voice replied, "Privacy mode enacted, Mr. Marshall."

Karaia was so used to hearing NIVA's voice in her head it sounded strange out loud. But Griffin's NIVA system was actually connected to the entire building, not just in his head. He could lock doors, make coffee, check security feeds, and tint any window, anywhere in the building, all from his neural link with NIVA.

Griffin strode over to Karaia. "God, you're fucking gorgeous," he said as he grabbed her by the waist and hoisted her up onto the table behind her.

The cold table sent a chill up Karaia's spine. She got a flash of the night before in her mind, hearing the shot, seeing the woman's blood exit her body. Slump. Dead. *Did Griffin know about what his officers had done?* The thought frightened her.

Karaia wished for a NeuroCredit, so she could actually enjoy this moment. Instead, she went through her normal motions, and she wrapped her legs around Griffin's waist. He pressed himself against her.

"Just watching you give that presentation, in that dress, I knew I had to have you afterward." He licked his lips as his hands groped at her body. "Even with these messy curls." Pulling her hair aside in one rough motion, he kissed her neck hard.

Goosebumps graced her skin at his touch. Biting gently every now and then, his kisses made their way down to her collarbone, where he pulled down one side of her dress. His other hand made its way in between her legs.

"That's all you got from my presentation?" Karaia gazed up at the ceiling, trying to get into the moment. Normally, she relished a daytime romp with Griffin, or anyone for that matter. Instead, she found herself wishing he'd just hurry up. *Damn, a credit would be bliss right now.* Her panties slipped to the floor.

"Of course not." Griffin's lips moved down to her chest as he pulled her dress collar farther down. "You're a brilliant mind, one of my most dedicated employees, and you're an excellent fuck."

Just before his lips hit her nipples, Karaia pulled him up into a long kiss, feeling the stubble from his chin, his mouth's warmth on hers. She needed things to hurry along. "No more talking," she hushed.

Their bodies took over.

Karaia had first met Griffin as a marketing intern in her third year of secondary school. Every New Soteria student went through rotations of internships to different occupations, assessing their ability at a variety of tasks. In the fourth year, each student was given their Official

Assignment in the appropriate job based on their desire, aptitude, and skill set.

She had just started her Seromela internship a few weeks earlier, never once actually having seen the CEO and president there, until Griffin stormed into the room that day. They had been preparing a sample marketing campaign for Sector Five of New Soteria, the man-ufacturing sector—one of the hardest populations to market to.

"Who is responsible for the latest marketing campaign report sent to me on Sector Five?" he had yelled as he entered the room, his face contorted.

This hadn't been their society's usual charming, smiling leader that Karaia had been used to seeing on the holo-screens. She couldn't tell whether he was upset or excited. *He seriously needs a NeuroCredit,* she thought.

"Mr. Marshall," one employee said, "I ... I'm sorry. Whatever it is, it can be corrected. That was just a preliminary report. I believe one of our interns compiled it."

She looked around the room at the five interns, including Karaia.

Griffin raised his eyebrows and waited.

"It was me." Karaia reluctantly stepped forward, head down.

While they had all worked together on the campaign, it was Karaia's week to submit their campaign's weekly summary, and she had added some of her own ideas to it. *Without* permission.

"See me in the hallway." Griffin stormed out.

Karaia gulped. Her hands suddenly became clammy. All the other interns and employees just gaped at her. The President of New Soteria and the CEO of the richest corporation on Earth just asked to speak with her, Karaia Pine, a sixteen-year-old nobody.

To say the least, she was terrified. She took slow steps forward until she made it into the hallway and faced Griffin. He had a charisma about him that could make someone completely adore him and fear him at the same time. Her curiosity got the best of her, and she peeked up from her sullen demeanor. He was even more handsome in person.

Griffin looked her straight in the eye and asked, "Can you explain this report?"

"What do you mean?"

"I don't have time for this shit. Who are you?"

"Karaia Pine, sir."

She felt like squirming there in her increasingly sweaty blouse but held firm. He continued his stare. She stared back.

"Well, Karaia, was this report your idea or your team's?"

"All the data is from the team, but the idea about the marketing tactic to Sector Five was mine," she said meekly.

Griffin inhaled. She waited for the blow. Would she be demoted to a different internship? Right when she was starting to enjoy this one, she screwed it up.

"It's brilliant, fucking brilliant," he said, clapping his hands together.

Karaia couldn't believe what she was hearing. He didn't hate it. He loved it. *Griffin Marshall loved my work.* She could feel the pride swell inside of her.

He continued, "I haven't seen ideas as fresh as this since ... I don't even know when. It doesn't matter. What matters is *you*. I need you. Now. As my employee. Brilliant. Fuck. What year are you anyway?"

Karaia beamed, suddenly thinking of all the opportunities she'd have working for Seromela. Her grandma would be so proud. "It's my third year. I don't get my placement until next year."

Griffin tilted his head back and laughed, then pulled her close to him. "We can change that. Starting today, you're mine."

That day, Karaia didn't know how right he was, but she did now.

Not only did she get her Official Assignment a year earlier than most students and started work at Seromela, but she also became one of Griffin's mistresses. He was married, but marriage these days meant nothing more than a legal contract based on social status and politics. It was normal for people to have multiple partners, of any gender, and use sex to release tension or have fun. It wasn't anything serious.

This was part of the reason Karaia was surprised when Arjun got so upset about her and Raven. But after thinking about it more, Arjun differed from her in this area. Being extremely shy, he didn't get out much and had probably fantasized about Raven for years. It was insensitive of Karaia to overlook that. Now, she'd stick to sleeping with people she didn't work with.

Griffin, the exception of course.

Mostly, Karaia enjoyed her time with him. He was fit, handsome, and, while almost her father's age, with the latest technology, he didn't look a day over thirty. She enjoyed having a reliable fling with no strings attached. He wasn't clingy or possessive, unlike some guys or girls she had dated who wanted to take things further with her. She wasn't interested in a relationship yet.

Yes, she would probably get married at some point down the road, but most people waited until they were about thirty to do so and usually went to a Wed Right service, that analyzed location, personality, and genetics—if you wanted kids—across New Soteria, finding the perfect spouse for someone. It took all the guesswork out.

Karaia wasn't sure how many women Griffin slept with or had on the side. That wasn't her place to ask, and he didn't ask about her extracurricular activities either.

But when Griffin Marshall wanted something, he got it.

Zipping up her dress, Karaia heard the click of the doors unlocking and saw the windows resume their normal transparent state. Griffin gave her one more slap on her butt before leaving the conference room.

Somehow managing to finish up her work for the day, Karaia headed home. This time, taking Rail 87. As she rode, she tried to concentrate on all the good things in her life, but her brain still couldn't stop spiraling and thinking about the woman in the alley or wondering why her NeuroCredits weren't working.

Arjun is going to fix my NeuroCredits, and I'll be fine. It will be as if I never saw that woman. My life will go back to normal.

It will all go away. She could hear her grandma saying it in her head.

A distant memory flooded her mind. Karaia was young, sitting on her grandmother's couch. She had just been rubbing her eyes and crying about missing her parents, who had left for the Settlement days before.

"It will all go away, my dear. There's nothing to be afraid of," her grandma had said, rubbing her back.

"But, Granma, what if it hurts?" young Karaia had asked.

"It doesn't matter. You won't even remember afterward. Everything will be better after this. Everything you saw, you won't be troubled by it anymore. No more nightmares. No more sadness."

"Otay," was all Karaia said back to her grandma. She didn't understand much of what her grandma was talking about.

"Now, this nice man is going to put something on your head." She motioned to a man wearing a black mask and suit.

Karaia remembered thinking he looked like one of the bad guys from her VR game, *Knights Out*.

"It might feel funny or cold. Don't move now," her grandma instructed.

The man put something on her head. It was cold and heavy and made her neck hurt holding it up. Karaia started to cry again. She missed her parents, and she was scared. Scared almost every night.

"This might hurt a little," the man said. "But then, it will all be over."

Pain shot through her brain like a lightning bolt. Slowly, she forgot why she was there. The laser etched through her mind, erasing the memories, erasing the sadness, then finally erasing the pain.

Karaia winced and grabbed her head as if it were happening to her now as an adult. She glanced around her. She was still on the rail. It was almost her stop. She blinked a few times, straining to remember more of the distant memory, but she couldn't. Why was she suddenly remembering all this now?

CHAPTER 13

MIRYAM

"We aim for a life with our Lord at its center. Yet, do we truly understand what that entails?" The wrinkled priest stood at the head of the village church, behind the altar, posing a question only he intended to answer.

The sisters sat with their father in their usual place, third pew from the front. A wide yawn escaped Miryam's mouth, perhaps a little too loud. Isabella turned with a scowl. Miryam only shrugged at her. No one seemed to notice. Few were listening to the priest, for that matter. Though he now spoke in their own tongue—the sermon being the only part of the service not given in Latin—most had long since learned to sit in silence until the bell released them.

The priest cleared his throat and droned on. "To quote Saint John: *'The next day John seeth Jesus coming unto him, and saith, Behold the Lamb of God, which taketh away the sin of the world.'* Christ came into this wretched world to bear away our sins. *Your* sins."

Miryam's hands curled into fists at those last words. Something in her wanted to rise up and cry out against them. She did not feel sinful. Yet perhaps that was the very mark of sin. That one did not know it.

He went on, "We need to remember our sinfulness every day. Pray on it and repent." The priest traced the sign of the cross over his chest, gesturing to the gathered faithful.

Miryam could not listen any longer. So, her eyes wandered about the church.

By one of the great stained-glass windows, a spider wove its web. A fly trapped within wriggled in vain, awaiting its end. Across the aisle, an elderly man whose name escaped her—though she knew him from the market—slowly let his chin sink toward his chest. Each time his head snapped back upright, only for the process to begin again. In the pew before them sat Hildegarde, who lived down the lane. Miryam was certain the woman was older than Oakeshire itself. Bent with age, nearly bald beneath her wimple, she bore a single long gray hair sprouting from the side of her neck. Miryam's fingers itched to pluck it. Beside Isabella, her father toyed with a loose button on his shirtfront. It dangled by a thread. She imagined he would mend it once they were home.

Then there was Isabella, right next to Miryam.

Dutifully, she sat tall and ever so still, face fixed on the sermon. *She looks so perfect,* Miryam thought. But behind that pious, reserved exterior, she knew Isabella didn't always feel so.

She had first learned that when they were but eleven and twelve. Their father had left for the market, leaving the two of them in charge of the farm and cottage for the day.

"Why do we not go down to the lake? I wager I can skip stones farther than you," young Miryam had said.

"Father told us we must finish the chores before he comes home," Isabella replied, already reaching for a basket to gather eggs.

"That sounds sooooo dull," Miryam had groaned, flopping back on her bed. "What if we do the chores, then go to the lake? A compromise!" She beamed at her cleverness.

"No. We cannot compromise." Isabella's voice was stern as she crossed her arms. "Do you not care for our family? I am the younger sister, yet I am always the one who must tell you what to do."

"Then stop!" Miryam had flung up her hands. "No one asked you to tell me what I ought to do."

"I know. It is... well... I feel... ugggghhh. Will you simply listen to me?" Isabella had shouted.

Miryam had never seen her sister so frustrated. She wasn't sure what to say.

Isabella drew a sharp breath. "I apologize, sister. 'Tis not how a young lady should act. I ought not to raise my voice. 'Tis only—" She burst into tears.

Miryam had rushed to her side and thrown her arms around her. "Bella, I will do the chores and the weaving—and aught else you need. Do not weep. Please."

Between sobs, Isabella said, "I ... feel ... as though I must."

"Why?"

"Because 'tis my fault."

"What is?"

"Mother's death. I was born, and she died. Now I must bear that weight, for she is not here. I must be the perfect daughter, and someday, I shall be the perfect wife and mother that she never could be."

"Oh, Bella." Miryam held her sister until at last she calmed.

Nothing in Isabella's behavior had changed since that day, but it gave Miryam new understanding. For the first time, compassion softened her irritation toward her sister's dutiful ways.

The foolish thing was that Miryam also carried blame. She believed that if her mother had not given her a blasphemous name, or if she had not inherited that same wild spirit, perhaps her mother might still live.

Then Miryam would not feel so different, so alone.

Yet unlike Isabella, who sought perfection, Miryam yielded to her wildness. *If I am already condemned, why not live untamed?* Still, she loved her sister and father and never wished them caught in her mischief. So, she played her part as best she could, biding her time until she found a way to someday be free.

Miryam's attention turned back to the sermon just as the priest issued his final Latin phrase. The congregation rose, shuffling toward the doors and out into Oakeshire's muddy streets, dispersing to their chores and daily labor.

The autumn Sun hid behind a blanket of clouds. Rain was coming, and the air felt damp already, leaving a chill on Miryam's skin. She shivered.

Ahead of her, Simon and Isabella walked arm in arm.

"You're unusually quiet, daughter. Is aught the matter?" Simon asked, slowing so Miryam might catch up.

"No ..." Miryam joined her arm with his other. "Do you know of the monastery outside our village, near the woods?"

"Becoming a nun, are you?" Isabella teased. "Have you at last found a way to escape your betrothal?"

"Do not give her any ideas," their father said with a nudge to Isabella as they strolled.

"I only wondered why the monks seldom come into our village." Miryam thought of Ved and plotted how she might see him again. Perhaps she could make another *chance* encounter take place.

"They have most of what they require within their walls. I do recall, as a boy, they came out once for a—" Simon broke off in a harsh cough, coming to a halt.

"Father, are you well?" Miryam rubbed his back as he bent forward.

A few villagers hurried past, baskets brimming with fresh autumn greens. Still, Simon coughed, unable to catch his breath.

"I shall fetch ale," Isabella said, worry shadowing her face.

She darted off, leaving Miryam to steady their father and guide him onto a straw bale by the path to their cottage.

"Miryam ..." Fits of raspy breaths and grating sounds made their way out of his mouth. His face shone bright red as he tried to regain control.

"Do not speak. Bella will be back soon," Miryam consoled him.

"We ... need ... to talk," he choked out.

"Now is not the time, Father."

"I do not know ... how much ... longer ... I have."

"What are you speaking of?" Miryam frowned.

Isabella returned with a leather pouch of warm ale. "Here, drink." She still panted from her run.

Simon quickly slurped down the ale, and his breathing calmed. His face returned to a normal color once again. Patting his chest, he looked at Isabella. "Thank you, my daughter. Might you fetch me a little more... and an oatcake? Then I shall be well enough to walk home."

Isabella spun around and hurried off again.

Simon turned back to Miryam, his face solemn. "We must talk."

Miryam sat down next to him and held his trembling hand, not wanting to hear what he had to say. "Father, your hand. 'Tis so cold."

"My dear girl ..." His eyes became watery, and his paper-thin wrinkles blanketed his icy hand despite an accelerated pulse.

Miryam thought of Hildegarde and the old man from church whose name she couldn't remember, and the way their frail, old bodies were slowly wearing away. One could see it in their mannerisms, their behavior, and their whole being. Until now she had believed her father *infinite*, an unshakeable force in her life. But when she looked at him now, she saw only the sickly, aging man he had become.

"... there's a reason I have chosen to marry you off so swiftly."

Miryam shuddered. "Must we speak of this?"

Simon shifted, trying to sit straighter on the wobbly straw bale. His bones cracked as he did. He tightened his grip on her hand. "I have lived a long and happy life with you girls. But the time comes when—" He broke off, pulling a small linen cloth from his pocket and coughing into it.

As he pulled it away from his mouth, quick to get it back in his pocket, Miryam caught sight of blood on it.

"What are you saying?" Miryam's breath came shallow. Her eyes searched her dear father's face, frantic, afraid of what he would say next.

Simon's voice wavered, shifting from firm to shaky. "I wish I could tell you otherwise, but I am coming to the end of my wonderful life." Tears welled in his kind, wrinkled eyes. He tried to brush them away to no avail as they were just replaced by more.

Miryam had never seen her father so vulnerable before, and it terrified her.

"Say no more." She shook her head, her chest constricting, each breath shorter than the previous one.

Her father cleared his throat. "I have hidden most of the signs from you and Isabella, but I can no longer. It is phthisis of the lungs. I have been to the apothecary, and even to the priest. They say 'tis a wasting of the spirit. There is naught to be done."

"No, I will not believe it," Miryam cried. "You are the best father any daughter could ask for. You must not die. Not now. Not ever ..." She knew how childish it sounded, but she clung to him tightly, feeling the heave of his chest against her own.

He pulled her back and looked at her again. "Now you see why you must wed. I must know that you and your sister will be cared for before I depart this Earth."

"Oh, Father." Miryam buried her face against his chest, letting her sobs soak into his thick tunic, trying to fix his scent in her memory.

Above them, the clouds gathered, heavy and dark. Just as Isabella returned, the first drops fell. Wiping the last of her tears away, Miryam sighed in resignation. As the rain fell harder, soaking them, Miryam and Isabella rushed to bring their father inside. The last thing they needed was him catching a cold now.

Once home, they settled him in his favorite chair by the fire. Miryam stoked the flames higher, determined to keep him warm. She understood now. It was not about what she wanted. It was about what must be done for her family.

Yet that night, Miryam wept for herself, sobbing into the covers, trying not to wake the others, grieving for the life she wanted but would never live.

CHAPTER 14

LEAH

It had been three days since the beach party, but only twenty minutes since Leah had relived that kiss with Tate in her mind. Sitting at her dining room table, she shook her head, trying to focus on the paperwork in front of her. But it was so hard when she could still taste the sweet saltwater and beer from the first kiss she'd had in ... what, five years? Leah licked her lips.

Focus! The official custody documents had arrived in the mail yesterday from Seth's lawyers. So, for the last few hours, she had been pouring herself into research about custody, planning for what to bring up with her lawyer, and of course, all the ways Seth might 'accidentally' die before the case came to fruition. Taking a sip of black coffee, she sneered.

"Hey, Mom," Hana yelled as she came inside, threw off her shoes and backpack, and scuttled off to her room. "Dad is at the door. He asked to talk to you."

Leah wondered what else he could want. *My kidney?* She rolled her eyes as she made her way to the front door.

Seth stood there, gray suit and tie matching his hair, a phone in hand, and his eyes down. His new Tesla Model S car parked behind him. Leah could only assume that was Delilah sitting in the passenger seat, checking her makeup in the mirror. The entire scene looked like an image out of *GQ* or *Forbes* magazine. The thought made Leah want to puke.

Seth looked up from his phone. "Hey."

"Hana said you wanted to talk to me."

"Yeah, so this custody thing. Just sign the papers and send them back to my lawyer. You know this is best for Hana, and it wouldn't be good to drag her through an ugly custody battle anyway. Plus, I am allowing for some supervised visitation and holiday time with her." He looked back at his phone.

Leah's mouth hung open. *Are you fucking kidding me? My daughter is my life. I will fight until my last breath for her. How dare you try to take her away from me?* was what she wanted to say. Instead, what actually came out was, "I can't do this. Just go."

"Whatever." Seth waved a hand in her direction. "Here you are, making things difficult again. No surprise there. This is exactly why Hana would be so much better off with me and Delilah. She wouldn't have your drama to contend with. See you in court." He left in a huff.

The anger inside of Leah gnarled and twisted its claws, begging to come out, but instead, transformed into one of her pressing migraines. Inhaling, she wanted to scream out loud. But she held it in. She always did. Rubbing her temples, she slammed the door, cursing under her breath. Mostly at Seth. But also at herself, for ever allowing him into her life.

They had met at her dad's retirement party from the police force. Her father had been the police chief, so most of the department was there. The house had felt full and overwhelming. She had been twenty-three years old and had already regretted attending the party. She hadn't seen her parents in over a year, and being back in the home she had left five years prior chafed her.

Her mother, Karen, nagged at her. "Leah, my love, what have you been eating in college? You don't look like you're getting enough. Here, let me make you a plate of food." She scampered off.

Leah's father sat in his chair in the living room, beer in his hand. The TV was on, even though you couldn't hear it over the conversations all around. Leah chuckled to herself. Was her father even aware there was a celebration happening for him?

She scanned the party from a kitchen corner. Her eyes fell on Seth, the force's newest police officer. He looked about ten years her senior. Turns out, it was actually fifteen years. But he always looked good for his age and knew it. *A real go-getter,* as her father described him. He had come from a family with money. And not just rich but wealthy. Old money from generations of English nobility, apparently. However, Seth broke from his family's tradition, switching from a career in business to police work. He said, "I like keeping people safe." Part of that was true. Later, Leah learned he liked to control people too.

At the retirement party though, Seth was charming, smooth, and cocky. Exactly the toxic type that Leah usually fell for. He approached her. "Hey, you're Fred's daughter, right?"

"Yeah. I'm Leah."

"Seth." He shook her hand. "I heard you're going to school for psychology. What do you plan to do with that?" he asked as he began mixing a drink at the bar.

"I want to go into—"

Karen interrupted them with a giant plate of food for Leah. "I got a little of everything. Be careful, the casserole is still pretty hot. Do you want me to cool it off for you?"

"No, Mom, I can handle it." Leah grabbed the food and looked back at Seth, rolling her eyes.

Seth understood. "So ... would you like to show me your childhood backyard?"

"I'd love to. Thanks for the food, Mom." Leah led him outside. She turned to Seth and said, "Thanks for the save. My mom can be *a lot* sometimes. She means well ... never mind, you don't want to hear about my childhood."

"No problem. I grabbed this for you," he said, handing her a drink. "It seemed like it might help take the edge off."

"Thanks." She took a sip. "Yikes, what's in that?"

"Whiskey, mostly." He laughed. Seth's hand had already found her waist, and his charm had already wedged its way into her mind.

"Good." Leah downed the whole glass. The rest of the night was a blur.

Just over thirteen years later, here she was.

It was as if life was playing a cruel joke on her, but when was the joke going to be over? Leah sighed heavily as a migraine slowly invaded her brain, making everything fuzzy and gray. She drank the last of her room-temperature coffee and shuffled through more custody documents, scanning them for clues of how she'd fight this battle, when her phone dinged with a notification.

Mtg with lawyer-DON'T FORGET

Shit! Leah scrambled to gather the papers into her bag and ran to her room to change clothes. Where had the time gone? She knew she was supposed to meet with her lawyer today to go over the case. But how did she only have thirty minutes until her appointment? Between these constant migraines, time seemed to bend and break in her head. She strained to remember the plan for that day. She had asked her mother to stay with Hana while she was gone, not knowing how long this initial meeting would be. *Where is she?*

Zipping up her pants on her way out of her room, Leah popped into Hana's room to see her teenage daughter lying on her bed furiously texting something on her phone.

"Hana, I need to leave for my appointment with the lawyer, but Nana will be here to hang out with you. Would you give her a call and ask her when she'll be here?"

No response.

"Hana?"

A slow realization dawned across Hana's face as she looked up from her phone. "What?"

"Did you hear me?" Leah asked.

"Something, lawyer, something, Nana ..." Hana gently smiled.

Leah huffed as she made her way to the kitchen to pour herself another cup of coffee to go. "Call Nana and ask her when she's going to be here. I need to leave now."

"Sure. But you do know I'm old enough to stay by myself," Hana called from her room.

She was probably right. Maybe it was her mother in her, but Leah was protective of Hana, and she still felt better about her staying with an adult. At least for now. She slipped on her shoes and grabbed her purse. About to head for the door, she first stopped to say goodbye to Hana, who was just getting done texting her grandma.

"Okay, I gotta go," Leah said, giving Hana a kiss on the head.

"Bye, Mom. Nana will be here in less than five minutes."

"Great. I love you, sweetie."

"Love you, Mom."

Thanking the gods of Los Angeles traffic that day, Leah made it to the lawyer's office with two minutes to spare. She frantically pushed the elevator button. "C'mon, c'mon."

The elevator reached the fifth floor. Not noticing the wet floor sign, Leah rushed out onto the slick floor. In one motion, her feet were no longer beneath her. Flailing her arms widely, grasping at air, she was slipping, and there was nothing to stop it.

Leah landed squarely on her butt. The coffee flew out of her hand, splashing the dark brown liquid all over her light blue blouse and the newly cleaned floor. Pain radiated from her tailbone.

"Fuck!" she yelled.

She looked around and didn't see anyone in the hallway. *At least no one saw me fall.* She started peeling herself off the sticky floor, trying to decide what to do—either call and reschedule her appointment or just get it over with, covered in coffee.

"Here, let me help you," someone said as their hand reached down in front of her.

"I'm fine," she replied. She didn't take the hand and pushed herself up, trying to wipe off the coffee from her top. "Just my ego is a little bruised."

Leah looked up to see who had come to her rescue.

"Tate?" Leah said in shock.

"Hey," he said and smiled, his eyebrows raised.

There he was. Tate. From three nights before in real life, but only about five minutes from the last time Leah had thought about him. She looked at his lips and remembered their kiss once again. She couldn't make sense of this. Her migraine throbbed. *Why was he here?*

"I can't do this right now. I need to get going," Leah said, rubbing her head. "I am already late for an appointment." She stepped past him toward the lawyer's office door.

"About that ..." Tate hesitated for a moment, then continued, "... I'm your lawyer."

Chapter 15

KARAIA

"**A**re you sure?" Karaia asked, stretching her arm to its fullest length to reach the back of her cupboard. Feeling blindly for the bottle with her hand, she was sure it was still there. Her fingertip grazed the smooth synthetic glass, and she plucked it from the shelf, kicking up debris on the way down.

"I'm sorry, but I can't find anything wrong with the software problem you are having," Arjun said cryptically over her comm.

Looking at the dust-covered bottle, she tried to remember how old it was. She received it as a gift from Griffin for one of her birthdays, years ago. Most people didn't drink alcohol anymore. Too many negative side effects. But today, it was worth it. Without credits, she needed something to take the edge off. Karaia twisted off the top of the green tea wine. The vinegary smell flared her nostrils.

"I ran the scans twice," Arjun insisted. "The first time, I thought I detected what could be nanobots, but after looking more closely, it was just some extraneous code in NIVA's system. Now, we could run them through Seromela's software analysis, which might give us a more complete picture of what's happening, but you know what that means ..."

She did.

"No, don't do that. I've got one more idea. Thanks, Arjun. I appreciate you checking." Karaia pressed her temple, ending the conversation, and poured herself a drink. Between the incident with the woman and these recent memories about her parents, she wished now more than ever she had a NeuroCredit, or twenty, to feel better.

Instead, she took a swig of the old wine and slumped down on her couch. The spicy burn of alcohol felt strange and foreign in her mouth, making her wince a bit. It tingled going down her throat. Notes of green tea, chamomile, and honey danced on her tongue.

She took another sip, and another, and after a while, she didn't even notice the bitterness of the vinegar aftertaste. It was replaced with a warm belly and fuzzy thoughts. Pulling out the tiny paper with the mysterious address on it again, Karaia flipped it back and forth in her hands. *Where do you lead?*

She wasn't quite ready to go to the address on the paper. It would just be inviting more drama into her life. No, first, she would talk to her grandma. Tonight was their weekly family meal together, and she never missed that for anything.

Karaia and her brother, Cassian, had grown up with their paternal grandmother, Cecelia. While Karaia could remember fleeting moments of her parents, Cass couldn't remember anything about them. He was four years younger than Karaia, and not even a year old when they had left.

Like most people in Sector One, both of her parents had worked for either Seromela or the New Soterian government. Karaia's mother, Mai, had worked in biotechnology at Seromela, and her father, Damon, had worked in the diplomacy department on the government side. His job had demanded a lot of traveling for work. Often, he'd be gone for weeks, sometimes months at a time, and young Karaia would get so excited when she'd hear the beep of the door entry code signaling his return home.

Karaia could see his face now in her mind, entering their house, his smile lighting up as she ran to greet him. She couldn't remember the last time she had pictured him this vividly. Ever since her Neuro-Credits had stopped working, it seemed like her brain, her senses, and her memories were working in overdrive. It almost completely took over her situational awareness, and she felt like she was back in her childhood home.

Her dad smelled like the forest, at least what Karaia's sixth sense told her a forest smelled like. When he'd come home, she'd snuggle deep into his chest. He'd envelop her in his arms and swing her around as they both giggled and smiled until her mouth hurt and belly muscles ached. Then, at night before bed, her dad would sing to her. He told her they were the old songs from before the Great Fall. They didn't exist anywhere except in their heads. That's what made them so special.

While her dad had been warm and cozy, her mom had been practical and smart. Even though she worked a lot, Karaia would peek in on her in the home office. When her mom caught her watching, she'd bring Karaia in, plop her on her lap, and show her a human body projected in 3D on a holo-screen, explaining the different parts of the body and how they interfaced with the implanted technology. Little Karaia would gape at the detailed images floating above her, asking question after question. Her mother patiently answered each one.

Those were her favorite childhood moments. Karaia smiled now as she sipped more wine. For the first time this week, she felt a moment of calm. Even with her credits not working, she thought maybe life isn't *so* horrible without them if it meant being able to remember her parents as vividly as this. She closed her eyes and let one specific memory play out.

"Hi, guys, I'm home," her dad had said as he entered their apartment.

"Daddy!" little Karaia yelled from down the hall as she came running to greet her father, beginning their welcome ritual.

"I'm glad to be back with you," he'd whisper, squeezing her tight.

"Dad, come watch this new video game I'm playing. You get to be a giant creature on a faraway planet. Isn't that sooooo cool?" Karaia tugged at her father's arm toward the living room.

After unpacking, her father sat down next to little Karaia on the couch. "Hey, sweetie," he said, "I have something special for you."

"What is it?"

He had pulled out a small box and opened it. Inside was a necklace. Hanging on a thin chain was a smooth metal piece. It looked like a snake to Karaia. It was about three inches long and made of pure silver.

The top looped around the chain and then came down in a swirl, to a point at the end.

"Here, let's put it on you," her father said as he wrapped it around her neck.

"It's cold."

"It will warm up next to your skin."

"But, Daddy, what is it?"

"Honestly, I don't know," he said, smiling. "I traded for it on my last trip out in the California Keys. It reminded me of you. Every time I'm gone on a trip, you can hold this and know I'll always come home."

Karaia hugged him. "Okay, now let me show you this game."

She missed her parents so much her heart yearned for them as she rubbed the smooth metal snake between her fingers, still hanging from the necklace she wore every day since then. It had been a long time since she had let that pain in and truly felt it. *Why didn't they come back for me?* She had asked that from a logical viewpoint a million times over. But today, she just felt her feelings and breathed deeply.

Stinging abandonment lingered on her lips as she downed the last of her glass. Willing herself to let the effects of the wine overtake her, Karaia stood to gather her things and her swirling emotions. Shaking them off, she grabbed the rest of the bottle of green tea wine and headed out the door to catch the next rail to her grandma's house.

Cecelia had done a fine job of raising her and her brother, but her holo-screen or news feed had often distracted her. Karaia never got the same attention she had gotten from her parents, so she'd become a sort of parent herself to Cass, and to an extent her grandma as well. Always organizing family dinners, outings, and making sure to keep in touch with her grandma daily. That connection was important to her, and if she didn't have her parents in her life, she was determined to be that parent for those around her.

Plus, it made her feel important and needed, and Karaia did like that.

Cass didn't seem to notice. He was just as distracted as their grandma, playing some video game with his friends online. They were the perfect consumers, Karaia would tell herself. Exactly what Seromela sold to the people of New Soteria, and Cass and her grandma gobbled it up.

It wasn't the same for Karaia. Yes, she used NeuroCredits. Yes, she played VR games with her friends. All her 'good citizen' boxes were checked—watch the news feeds, indulge in the senses, keep working, stay safe.

But something felt *off* to her, and she had never told anyone that. That was her sixth sense talking again. Most days, she tried to even keep it from herself. And she succeeded for the most part, with the help of NeuroCredits. But now, without serotonin flooding her brain, that discontent grew.

She got off the rail, wine in hand, and walked up the tube to her grandma's apartment. Karaia, being the responsible one, put it on her grandma and Cass's schedules to have a family meal together at least once a week. Most people ate alone while working, gaming, or multitasking. This was the one time during their week their family still ate together, but something was still lacking. Now more than ever, she wished her parents could be there with them too.

Karaia scanned her hand across the door sensor. "Karaia Pine. Approved," a robotic voice said.

The door clicked, and she pushed it open. The smell of curry and basil hit her nose as she walked in the front door of her grandma's apartment. Cass was sprawled out on the couch with his VR visor on, talking to his friends. Grandma Cecelia was in the kitchen, grabbing plates.

"Grandma, I thought we said no games during family meal?" Karaia raised her eyebrows, looking at Cass and then her grandmother.

"I know, I know. But it makes him so happy. Who am I to take that away?" her grandma replied. "Look, I ordered your favorite curry!"

Normally, she'd get onto her brother for gaming during a meal, but now wasn't the time to start any conflict. She didn't have the energy. Her thoughts and emotions still wouldn't settle. *Just try to enjoy the night.* Karaia forced a smile as she grabbed a plate and started spooning the rice onto it, making hers and one for her brother. "Thanks, Gram. It looks great."

Before heading to the table, she poured herself another heaping glass of her green tea wine. Cass begrudgingly got off his game, and they all sat down and began eating. The blend of sweet and savory spices melded in Karaia's mouth. It was warm and tasted like home. *Things can be good again,* she reminded herself, and just in case, she gulped down some more wine to follow.

"Are you excited for the big 50th anniversary gala this weekend?" her grandma asked, grinning big between big bites of food. "There's going to be a parade in every sector. And free food and drink to all citizens! I heard they may even shoot off fireworks outside the tubes. We can watch them from the bio-dome in person. We truly live in the greatest country in the world. Don't you think so, dear?"

"Yes," was all she could say back. Did she live in the world's greatest country? Karaia had no idea—or did she? Her thoughts raced as she questioned everything she thought she knew. Flashing memories of her father swirled with images of Griffin having his way with her body, twisting and writhing in her brain. Feelings of discontent compounded her desire to feel good again. Something yelled at her from her gut.

Did she want the truth? Or did she want the lie?

Squeezing her eyes shut, she begged her mind—and gut—to leave her in peace. Right then, she remembered something from the night the strange woman had been murdered that she hadn't before. *The prick* when the woman ran by her. Was it connected to why her NeuroCredits weren't working? She looked at her arm where she had felt the prick. Nothing there. Not even a dot.

"Karaia, are you okay?" Cecelia rested a hand on her shoulder. Before Karaia could answer, her grandma went on. "You should take a NeuroCredit or two. It's much better than this green tea wine. Why did you bring this anyway?" Her grandmother held up the bottle, her nose upturned, looking at it suspiciously.

Karaia was gripping her fork with her fist clenched tight. She released the fork. "Excuse me."

She ran to the bathroom, feeling uneasy. Was it the wine or these invading thoughts? Waves tumbled in her stomach. Staring at herself in the mirror, her own eyes penetrated her soul. Except—she didn't believe in souls. Those were just from the stories her dad used to tell her. *Right?* Something still pulled at her from her core, pleading to come forth.

She heaved into the toilet.

After cleaning up, Karaia reemerged into the dining area.

"You okay?" Cass asked, swiping away his holo-screen from his wrist and actually looking up at Karaia.

"Yeah, I'm fine," she lied and sat back down at the table. Both food and drink looked unappetizing now.

"It was this wine, I'm telling you," Cecelia said, grabbing the bottle and holding it an arms-length away from her.

"You're probably right, Grams." Karaia shifted in her seat as another thought popped into her head. "Hey, can you tell me about what it was like for you before NeuroCredits existed?"

Cecelia frowned, pouring the remaining contents of the wine down the drain. "Oh, you know, I don't like to think about that time."

"Please," Karaia pleaded.

"Ughhh ... fine." Cecelia sighed. "Are you done?" She motioned to Karaia's plate.

What was once an appetizing array of food now looked like the contents of the toilet bowl. "Yeah, I am," Karaia said, rising from the table. "But I can help."

"I'm done too," Cass said, jumping up from the table. Without clearing his plate, he returned to the living room to play with his friends.

Rolling her eyes, Karaia grabbed his plate as well as hers and followed their grandma into the kitchen.

"Life was sooooo much more difficult." Cecelia placed the dirty dishes in the all-purpose washer-bot and pressed the 'dish cycle' button. "Your grandfather and I would always get into fights over silly things. Like what to eat for dinner or what to watch on TV. It's just what people did. They fought. They argued. People even *killed* over disagreements."

Karaia asked, "What about when Dad was young? Were there any issues when he first connected NeuroCredits to his brain?"

Cecelia tilted her head in confusion at the question, but continued, "Once when your dad was little, he fell and scraped his knee badly.

He was crying so much. As a parent, you always want to make your child's pain go away, but I couldn't. I felt helpless. But then once he had NeuroCredits, it was so much better! Oh, why are you asking about all this? Just talking about it stresses me." Her grandmother's mood shifted as the serotonin hit her brain. Her shoulders relaxed, and the muscles above her eyes smoothed out as she made her way to the living room.

"One more question, Gram," Karaia said, her head still a little swimmy from the wine. "Can you tell me more about Mom and Dad leaving? I had this memory from after they left. I was crying a lot. Do you know why?"

"I don't know what you're talking about."

Cecelia didn't look at her. Instead, she snuggled up next to Cass on the couch and pressed her temple to tune into her personal holo-screen, the sound only in her head. It was almost time for her favorite nightly news segment.

"Are you sure? Because I think you were there." Karaia inquired on.

Cecelia pressed her temple again to mute her holo-sound and looked directly at Karaia. "No, darling. Your parents left and didn't come back. I'm so sorry for that. But you and Cass have had a great life here with me. I love you, but please no more questions." She was firm but not stressed anymore.

Karaia wouldn't get any more answers out of her, so she headed toward the door to go.

"Are you sure you don't want to stay a little longer?" her grandma asked, not looking up from the screen. "There's a special airing of *On the Verge* tonight in preparation for the anniversary. I can turn it on the main holo-screen if you want to watch with me."

"No thanks. I think I'll go home instead. You were right. That wine is getting to me." As Karaia grabbed the handle, she said, "Goodbye, Grams. Bye, Cass. Love you guys."

But both were already absorbed in their own virtual worlds. She left to no reply.

Stepping out onto the artificially lit tube, Karaia peered outside the tube windows. It was dark, and buildings blocked out most of the moonlight. She imagined what the wind would feel like on her skin and what it would be like to look up at a clear night sky and see the illuminated Moon looking back at her. Something seemed to call to her from out there.

Deep inside, she yearned for a place she had never known. A world different from this one. She wasn't sure exactly what that was, but her sixth sense was on high alert tonight, and she was determined to listen to it. She thought of her grandma and Cass, blissfully unaware and content with their lives. A tinge of jealousy washed over her. She shrugged it off.

That wasn't the life for her.

It never was.

With that, Karaia pulled the paper from her pocket. *NIVA, I need directions.*

CHAPTER 16

MIRYAM

Every year at harvest time, the people of Oakeshire gathered in the church to give thanks to God and to mark the season with a village dance and feast. Dances were always held at the church. It was the only building in the area, save for the earl's castle, that could hold the crowd. And the clergy insisted on keeping watch, to see that all was done with proper conduct and Christian modesty. Usually, Miryam delighted in such an evening. She loved to dance and to be allowed to sway to music with a whimsy that was often frowned upon in society, but at dances, villagers partook in it with joy. However, tonight was different.

Tonight, she was to meet Dempsey, her future husband.

As they readied in their cottage, Miryam exhaled loudly as Isabella pulled at the laces of her gown. The bodice felt tight around her chest, and she tugged at it hoping for more air. Their father had woven the cloth himself, from their finest wool, and he had beamed with pride when he gave it to her. It was to serve as her wedding gown as well. He had even paid to have it dyed for her. The dark green set off the fire of her hair.

She traced her fingers across it, feeling the soft wool, and sighed.

It was beautiful.

She despised it.

Moving to the stool by the hearth, Miryam sat, and Isabella began messing with her hair. "Why have you so many knots? I should not be surprised to find a bird or two nesting in here."

Miryam lacked the energy to reply.

"Cheer up, sister. You look ready for a funeral, not a dance," Isabella said.

"How can you even speak of funerals at a time like this?" Miryam muttered, thinking of their father.

"You know it would gladden Father to see you happy." Isabella finished the braid and tried to smooth Miryam's curls around her face.

"*You know* you will never tame those curls," Miryam said with the faintest smile, hoping to lighten the mood.

"So, there is a smile hidden in there?" Isabella elbowed her. "Now, your turn to do mine. Be sure the braid is straight this time. Last time, it was crooked."

"I can make no such promise." Miryam rose from the stool, and they traded places. Isabella's hair, like her demeanor, was more obedient. The soft blond waves fell neatly beneath Miryam's fingers as she plaited them.

Simon entered the cottage, set down some logs near the fireplace and beamed at his two daughters with pride. "You two look beautiful. You shall have a wonderful time tonight."

"Are you not coming?" Isabella inquired.

"I must rest. But I shall walk you to the church and be there when you meet Dempsey." He nodded toward Miryam. "I may even bring some food back with me." He chuckled and rubbed his belly.

Miryam saw the weariness in his eyes. He did indeed need rest. She tied off Isabella's braid. Then, she walked over to kiss her father's cheek.

"Well then, what are we waiting for? Let us get you both to your future husbands." Simon wrapped his arms around their waists and steered them toward the door.

The Sun hung low in the sky. The clouds had cleared, and the full Moon was already preparing for night. Around the church doors stood baskets of vegetables and fruit, offerings for the harvest feast. The savory scent of roasting pig drifted from the side of the church.

Miryam's stomach growled. She had only tasted pig once before. It was a delicacy more often reserved for nobles. She wondered why they were serving it tonight.

They entered the church to find that it had been transformed. Pews pushed against the walls, leaving a wide floor for dancing. A long table near the entrance sagged beneath platters of food and jugs of drink. In one corner, a small stage had been raised for the musicians: three men played a gentle tune, one with a lute, one with a harp, and one with a flute while a drum thumped beneath his foot. A few trumpets rested idly against the wall.

Ordinarily, instruments were forbidden within the church, but for such feasts, exceptions were made. The priest sat at the head, watching so still he might have been carved of stone.

Villagers poured in, some already dancing in lively circles. Music played, laughter rang out, and the mingling smells of roasted meats and vegetables filled the air. For a moment, Miryam's sorrow and anger ebbed, tugged at by the surrounding joy.

She yearned to join in, dance freely, and to pretend she didn't have a care in the world.

But she did.

And that annoyed her all the more. She turned her nose up at the throng of cheerful people.

"I see Gawain," Isabella said, scanning the crowd. "Father, may I?"

"Go ahead." Simon nodded.

Isabella skipped toward Gawain, who stood beside his father and several other knights at a table laden with autumn desserts. Miryam saw the light in Gawain's eyes brighten the moment Isabella approached.

"It seems Dempsey has not yet arrived," Simon whispered to Miryam.

"Good," she replied without thought.

"Miryam, you promised to give him a chance."

She sighed. "I know, Father. I will." She turned her gaze to the feast. "Are you hungry? I am famished." She headed over to the food and started filling a plate. Her father followed.

But before she could take a bite, the music ceased, and trumpets blared. Miryam looked up with the rest of the villagers as the Earl of Norfolk, Lord Amalric himself, entered with his wife, his son, and an entourage of knights.

As the trumpets quieted, a herald announced, "Introducing the Earl of Norfolk, Lord Amalric de Dunne, along with Countess Adeline and their son, Edwin de Dunne."

Now the pig made sense.

The crowd cheered as the new earl stood tall, chest puffed, and raised a hand. His voice boomed through the church. "Greetings, people of Oakeshire. I know it is uncommon for a nobleman to join such company. Yet I come from a line of brave knights, and I would have you know, I am here to guard this land from evil. It is my honor to celebrate the harvest with you tonight. Now please," — he gestured toward the feast — "carry on."

After a pause, chatter resumed, and the band struck up again. The earl's family were shown to tall chairs at the head of the church beside the priest, from where they could oversee the hall.

Trailing in behind them, to no applause or fanfare, shuffled a snively, little man. He hovered near the church entrance, awkward and alone.

"Come, Miryam, I believe that is Dempsey. He spoke of what he would wear this night. We must introduce you at once," Simon said.

Dempsey was short and thin, especially compared to Lord Amalric, who towered over most men. Miryam imagined him stretching on tiptoe to reach the earl's shoulders for a fitting. Tonight, he wore brown and white wool mixed with linen. The wool was of fine quality; she would grant him that.

As she drew nearer, her eyes swept his pale face. He was not ugly, but neither was he handsome.

With each step, Miryam felt fainter, like life was draining from her. She steadied herself against the wall. *Be strong, for Father.* She forced her feet forward and followed him to Dempsey.

"Master Slye, it is my honor to make your acquaintance," Simon said with a bow. "And to present my eldest daughter—and your future wife—Miryam." He stepped back after speaking.

Miryam stood there, frozen, telling herself, *stay quiet, stay quiet, like a good ... wife.*

"God save ye, Mistress Miryam." Dempsey bowed low. "'Tis a pleasure to meet you at last. You are as fair as your father described." His voice sounded as if he were holding his nose while speaking. And despite the night's chill, sweat beaded his brow.

He reached for Miryam's hand to kiss it.

She pulled away.

"My daughter is modest, sir." Simon hastened to smooth the moment. "Do not take offense. She shall warm to you in time. Come, why not join the dance? See, they begin a fresh round even now." He gestured toward the floor.

"Glad to," Dempsey said and tried to take Miryam's hand in his again.

She took a deep breath and allowed it. His hand was soft and clammy. She remembered the last time she had touched a man's hand. *Ved*. In the forest. His hand had been rough and warm, everything Dempsey's wasn't.

Thinking of Ved, Miryam smiled.

"'Tis good to see you smile," Dempsey said.

Miryam's smile faded at once.

Together, they moved toward the dancers and joined in. The music quickened, light and merry. Isabella and Gawain leapt into the dance as well. For the first time that night, Miryam lost herself in the rhythm. She loved to dance. Here, she was free. Her gown swayed with each turn, her feet skipped to the beat, and she felt the current of energy as the circle moved as one.

After countless songs, the musicians paused to rest. Breathless, Miryam glanced around the great hall. Isabella and Gawain bent close nearby, whispering to each other. Dempsey excused himself to fetch cider. He did not offer her any, Miryam noticed. The earl and his family had already departed, and so had her father.

Then, through the open church doors—she saw him. *Ved*.

Her eyes met Ved's as he left a small piece of parchment rolled up on a ledge and disappeared. She strained to see where he had gone, but the church windows were too high.

Dempsey returned to the dance floor when Miryam said, "I must step out."

Rushing to the note, she snatched it up and slipped out the church doors. The night air struck cold against her skin, giving her goose-

bumps. She blinked, her eyes straining to pierce the dark. A few villagers passed on their way home, torches bobbing in their hands. Aside
from them, the square lay empty. Ved was nowhere in sight.

"Ved," she whispered, "are you there?"

Miryam circled the church, searching every side, but he was gone.
She unrolled the parchment. It was too dark to read at night, yet she
dared not carry it inside. She went around to the back of the church,
where they had been roasting the pig. The fire pit was still hot and
smoldering. She thrust a stick into the embers until it flared, then held
it close to the page, careful not to scorch it. The handwriting was
near-perfect.

Dearest M,

*Words escape me when I am near you. Perhaps my heart
is so full that my mind falls empty. Still, I cannot cast you
from my thoughts. I leave you a poem from a great sage
named Rumi. I pray his words stir you as they stir me.*

A moment of happiness,
you and I sitting on the verandah,
apparently two, but one in soul, you and I.
We feel the flowing water of life here,
you and I, with the garden's beauty
and the birds singing.
The stars will be watching us,
and we will show them
what it is to be a thin crescent Moon.
You and I unselfed, will be together,
indifferent to idle speculation, you and I.
The parrots of heaven will be cracking sugar
as we laugh together, you and I.
In one form upon this Earth,
and in another form in a timeless sweet land.

Destroy this after reading. To be found with such would be deemed heresy. Until our next meeting.

Yours,
V

Warmth spread through Miryam's body as she read Ved's note, despite the chilly autumn evening. Deep within her soul, she knew this wasn't some trivial relationship forming. They weren't just two young people attracted to each other either. It was more than that. She felt it. And so did Ved. What she didn't know was what to do about it.

Would Ved take his vows, committing himself to a life of monastic solitude and celibacy? Would she marry Dempsey and live as a weaver's wife until her death?

She was to be wed, and he was to be a monk.

Was there ever a world in which they could be together? She prayed so.

Miryam did not wish to burn the note. She longed to keep it, to revel in its words each day, to laugh and twirl with joy at its meaning. Instead, she only smiled to herself as she lowered the burning stick toward the parchment.

But before the flicker of flames touched the page, a nasal voice called from behind, "I was beginning to worry."

Miryam startled and dropped the stick. Its fire hissed out on the damp grass. Dempsey would be upon her in moments. And see what she held. Panic surged. With a cry, she threw herself toward the pit, and the parchment caught fire at once, disappearing to ash.

She, however, landed close enough to feel the blaze's heat on her face.

Dempsey rushed forward. "You are on fire!" he cried, though he did nothing.

One of her linen ribbons had indeed caught flame. Miryam clenched the folds of her wool dress and smothered it herself, snuffing the fire before it spread. "How dare you sneak upon me so," she scolded, stomping back toward the dance.

113

He hurried after her, desperately pleading. "I am truly sorry. Pray forgive me. It grew late, and your sister was looking for you. I sent her off with Sir Gawain and his father, and I claimed the honor of escorting you home this night." His lips curled into what some would describe as a smile.

It did seem he was sorry. And Miryam knew it was not truly his fault. "I suppose that will be acceptable," she said with a curt nod.

"Thank you." He bowed and offered his arm.

She kept hers stiffly at her sides.

"Ah, yes, I recall. You will make a godly wife for me. I cannot wait until the night of our nuptials."

Miryam gagged at the thought. Thankfully, he could not see her face in the dark.

As they left the church for the path toward her cottage, Dempsey filled the silence with talk of himself: his family's weaving trade, the generations before him, how he rose to become the earl's personal tailor, and their future life within castle walls. Not once did he ask Miryam a question, nor pause for her reply. At the fork in the road, Dempsey turned the wrong way.

"My cottage lies this way," Miryam said.

"I know well enough where you live, my dear," he answered smoothly. "This way leads there as well. 'Tis but a little farther, yet wondrous when the moonlight kisses the lake at night. I would see it with you."

"I am growing weary." Miryam faked a yawn.

"You would not wish to disappoint your future husband," he said, letting the words hang heavy in the air.

Tempted to walk home by herself, Miryam weighed her options. It was not proper for an unmarried lady to stroll alone at night. Plus, it could be dangerous when most of the village men had been drinking too much ale.

Trying to be the good bride-to-be, she reluctantly agreed. "If you insist."

Chapter 17

LEAH

"You've got to be fucking kidding me," Leah said, stunned.

"Nope," Tate replied. "Why don't we talk in my office?" He gestured to the door that said *Randall, Smith, and Vega Law Firm, LLC.*

She didn't follow. "So, which one are you—Randall, Smith, or Vega?"

"Vega," he answered.

"Is there any way I can see Randall or Smith for my case?"

Leah desperately hoped this was an option. She didn't think she could handle the embarrassment of sitting with Tate covered in coffee, nursing this headache, having to look at those lips and smell that fresh laundry on him. It all made her want to run away and hide under her covers.

"Unfortunately, Gregory Randall is on a year-long sabbatical in India, and Megan Smith is booked solid for the next month," Tate said. "I think you're stuck with me unless you want to cancel and find a different law firm?" His last words lingered.

He clearly didn't want her to leave, and they were by far the cheapest law firm in the area, running on a sliding scale based on income. Honestly, Leah couldn't afford anyone else.

"No, this is fine." Leah stepped forward and into the office door after Tate. She could be professional, she told herself. Focus on Hana and the case. Glancing at the empty front reception desk as they passed, she asked, "You don't have a secretary?"

"Nah, can't afford one. I think we do too much pro bono work." Tate chuckled. "Between Megan and me, she does the billing, and I do the scheduling. We get it all done somehow. Luckily, we love our work and only take cases we believe in."

"Of course you do," Leah said with a huff.

She sat down across from Tate at his desk, which had papers on it organized in neat piles. A large window in his office overlooked the street below. In front of it, an array of tropical-looking plants adorned the floor in pots of all shapes and sizes. On the opposite wall, there was a painting of a giant, colorful mandala. In the corner was a rolled-up yoga mat. He also had a little Bonsai tree with sand around it and one of those tiny rakes. The sand was perfectly raked, with little lines running across it. Leah felt like messing it up.

Tate began, "About the other night—"

"It didn't happen. As far as we are concerned, you are my lawyer and I am your client now, nothing more." Leah couldn't think about her stupid kiss with Tate—*why does he smell so good?*—or being embarrassed about having coffee all over herself. Nothing could get in her way. Not Tate. Not her feelings. Not these damn migraines.

Nothing.

Disappointment flooded Tate's eyes. His smile faded, but he nodded. "You're probably right," he said, straightening the papers in front of him. "To business, then. I reviewed the preliminary documents that you sent in, and honestly, it's not going to be easy, but I think we can win this."

Leah perked up. "Really?"

"Yes, his lawyer is good. Like, really good." Tate scanned the paperwork. "He obviously has a lot of money to throw at this case. But what he doesn't have is solid evidence ... and love."

"Love?" she asked, thinking, *oh no, please don't bring any of this woo-woo crap into the case.*

"Yes, love. Love for your daughter, Hana. His case is based solely on tearing you down and discrediting your character. What he doesn't do is talk about why he wants Hana to live with him, why he believes his house would give her a better home, a better place to grow up, to be cherished and loved. That's why we're going to win. Your written statement was all about Hana and why you care about her needs and security. Honestly, between you and me, this Seth guy sounds like an ass who just wants to win at something." Tate paused. "That last bit is not an official statement from Randall, Smith, and Vega."

They both laughed at the same time.

"No worries, I won't quote you on that one," Leah said.

He continued, "But really, it's clear to me that you love your daughter deeply."

"I do," was all she could say back, without letting too many emotions in.

"So, let's get some more information from you. Then, we'll run through a timeline of the case. Sound good?" Tate asked, flashing a smile.

She matched his grin. "Sounds perfect."

They went over the case and planned to meet again in a week, before the hearing with the judge.

Leah left the building feeling hopeful, which was often a fleeting feeling to her. *Maybe this all won't be as bad as I thought.* The bright Sun beamed down on her as she reached her parking spot a block away. She went to grab her sunglasses out of her bag when the migraine that had started that morning came back with a vengeance. She gripped her head, dropping the sunglasses and yelping out loud in agony. Beginning to get dizzy, she squeezed her eyes shut, trying to regain control. Her head swirled. She tried to reopen her eyes, but the world was a blurry jumble of shapes. She groped for her car to balance herself, missing it. The throbbing in her head consumed her, darkness creeping into her vision from either side. She was headed for the ground.

"I've got you," a scratchy voice said. Someone caught Leah's fall. "Come, come, in with me." They led her inside somewhere. "Sit, sit. I'll be back with some water." They scurried off.

Sitting down, Leah was able to keep from falling over, despite the pounding in her head. She squinted around the room, willing objects to come back into focus. Everything seemed bright and obnoxious. Somewhere along the way, she had lost a shoe as her toes tickled the ground.

An old woman came back with a mason jar filled with water and herbs in it. "Here, here. The mint and rosemary will ease the pain."

Leah took the water, gulping it down. The water soothed her mind as much as it quenched her thirst, and she felt halfway normal again. She was in a bookstore. A very dirty old bookstore, by the looks of it.

"Did *you* catch my fall?" Leah asked, eyeing the strange old woman standing before her.

"Oh yes, you were about to have a big, big tumble. That would have been bad, very bad indeed," the woman said, gently rocking back and forth. "Into the road you would have gone. We couldn't have that, now could we?"

Leah studied the woman's face. She looked ancient. She had wrinkles upon wrinkles. Her beady eyes were barely visible beneath them. She probably needed glasses. The woman's hair was piled on top of her head, messy and gray. Leah couldn't even see how it was held up. A small, white daisy peeked out between the hairs.

Shifting her focus to the woman's clothing, Leah guessed a toddler had picked out her outfit. She wore a pair of mismatched rain boots; one was black with pink polka dots and the other solid red. A green floral skirt hung from her hips and went down to her knees. A plaid, button-up flannel for her shirt topped it off, the sleeves rolled up around her elbows. This little woman couldn't have caught her fall. She couldn't weigh more than a hundred pounds.

Despite the appearance of being so frail, the woman began moving quickly around the store, searching for something.

"How did you catch me?" Leah asked, narrowing her eyes. "No offense, but it doesn't seem possible, given your size."

"*How* doesn't matter. Only the *why* matters." The woman kept searching the store and was now climbing up a wobbly wooden ladder to check the top shelves.

"Who are you?" Leah rubbed her head.

"The name is ..." The woman's shoulders slumped as she cocked her head still atop the high ladder. "... Matilda ... no, that's not right. Is it ... Kylen?" The woman began mumbling to herself, pulling out books, tossing them on the ground. "No, it's Gertrude, definitely, Gertrude, this time around. My name is Gertrude, I think," she concluded with a nod.

A crazy cat lady saved me, thought Leah. *There have to be cats around here somewhere.* She looked around for a litter box or a cat food dish. "Gertrude, do you own any cats?"

"Ha! Cats!" Gertrude cackled loudly. "Cats—that's good. But no, of course not. I'm allergic. Here it is!"

She yanked a book from the top shelf, teetered on the ladder's edge. Then in an instant, she was back down on the ground, holding the book for Leah to see. It looked like she glided through the air, rather than taking the steps down the ladder.

Man, this migraine is making me see things. Leah shook off the thought and asked, "What is that?"

"*This.* This is why you're here, Leah," Gertrude said, a wide, childish grin stretching across her face as she held up an ancient-looking tome.

Leah arched an eyebrow. "I never told you my name."

"Doesn't matter. Doesn't matter. All that matters now is—" Gertrude froze. She looked defeated, her eyes frantically moving back and forth, shaking her head. "Oh dear, oh dear, I've lost it." Rubbing the bottom of her chin, she started pacing the room, talking to herself. One hand still held the book. The other hand's fingers started fidgeting with each other. "Think, think, think. One plus one is two. One plus two is three. Two plus three is five. Three plus five is eight. That's it!" She glanced down at the book she was holding. "The book! It's all in the book." She shoved it at Leah.

Rolling her eyes, Leah slowly took the leather-bound text. Of all the people to help her from a fall, of course it had to be a woo-woo crazy, *catless* lady.

CHAPTER 18

KARAIA

*I*nput *address, please,* NIVA responded in Karaia's mind.

240052 East 85ᵗʰ Tube, Sector One, New Soteria, Karaia instructed, reading from the small piece of paper. Biting down on her lower lip, she hoped it held the answers she was looking for.

Calculating. After a split-second, NIVA continued, *The most efficient route from your location would be Rail Route 5. Would you like turn-by-turn directions from your current location?*

Yes, Karaia said, already marching down the tube. While nerves danced in her stomach, she held fast to the idea that if she didn't get a solution to her credits issue soon, way worse things would be in her future.

NIVA navigated her to the rail station that would take her to her mysterious destination. Taking a deep breath, Karaia stepped onto Rail Route 5 and found a seat by the window. It looked like any other rail in New Soteria. Sleek, efficient, modern, and immaculately clean. Those were the words that the designer had used when describing the new rail features five years ago. Karaia had dated them for a while, right at the time the rails were being retrofitted. Wiley—or was it Riley?—was their name. Mostly their relationship had been about going out, having fun, and occasional sex. She couldn't remember much else about them, but she did remember how excited they were to install the new rail features. It was a good distraction—trying to remember her past lover's first name. Between that and half-listening to a late night reality show through the rail speakers, Karaia made it to her stop without worrying too much about not having NeuroCredits and the fact that her life might never be the same if she didn't get them back.

After exiting the rail and walking halfway down 85th tube, Karaia was standing in front of the address door. It was a business, a hair salon by the looks of it: *Lacy's Nails and Hair.* Frowning, she double-checked that the numbers matched the paper she had. This was *it.*

Part of her felt disappointed, but another part felt relieved.

Maybe that woman had just been planning to get her hair cut or a manicure later? Maybe this wasn't connected at all? Maybe Arjun will find a different answer to her credit problem? *And my life can go back to normal.*

Something gnawed at her gut. But then, why *paper*? No one used paper anymore. There had to be more to this. It *had* to be connected to why her NeuroCredits weren't working.

Karaia peered into the dark windows of the closed salon. The normal cutter-bots and styling-bots were all there on one side. The other side looked like their waiting area and front desk. *What was I expecting?* With shoulders dropping, she stepped away from the window to head back to the rail and go home when a light flicked on inside, coming from behind an interior door.

The door swung open, and a large man walked out into the main salon, heading toward the building's exit.

Karaia ducked away, pressing herself against the tube's wall where he couldn't see her through the windows. *Make a choice—stay and talk to him or leave now.* She twirled her fingers through her hair as she went back and forth in her head about what to do.

The man stepped out, turning down the tube away from Karaia.

"Excuse me," she blurted from behind him.

"Aaaahhh!" he screamed, raising his hands. "Take whatever you want, just don't hurt me, okay."

Karaia raised her brow. "Uh, I'm not here to rob you. I just want to ask you a question."

She inched forward, wondering why his first inclination was to think she was a robber. There was no petty crime in New Soteria ... or at least that's what she used to think.

He slowly turned around, letting his hands drop to his sides. The man was a head taller than Karaia, and she was considered tall. His round belly stretched his pink shirt to its max. But he was also muscular. A mess of dark purple hair hung from his head, flopping in front of his eyes.

He swiped his hair to the side, and said, "Oh good, because I don't actually have anything on me." He laughed nervously, and his whole body shook.

Karaia tensed as she asked, "Any chance you know what this is?" With shaky hands, she held out the paper.

Taking it from her, the man examined it closely. His brow furrowed. "Where did you get this?"

"I found it in an alley tube," she said, feeling her nerves rise from her stomach. Trying hard not to replay the scene in her head, she clenched her fists and closed her eyes for a moment, wishing for a credit, or more wine, to calm herself.

"Uh, are you okay?"

Karaia opened her eyes. "Yeah, I just ... can you tell me anything about it?"

"I should probably get someone else. This isn't my place to decide." He turned to walk back into the store.

"Wait." Without thinking, Karaia stepped between him and the salon door. "Please, I need answers. I did see something. A woman. In the alley tube. I think this paper was hers."

The man tilted his head. "Was?"

"She's ... dead." Karaia gulped.

With her last word, the man's entire demeanor shifted. His body stiffened, and his eyes scanned the surrounding area. In a hushed voice, he said, "I shouldn't be talking to you. You need to leave."

Karaia was nervous, but she could see now that he was *more* nervous. Desperate, that gave her an idea and possible leverage. Taking a deep breath in, she summoned all her charisma and prayed this man found women attractive.

Leaning forward, Karaia batted her eyelashes and slowly twisted a finger through her curls. "You *do* know something about this, don't you?"

"Maybe." He backed up, wiping sweat from his brow.

"You seem like a nice guy." Karaia cat-walked forward, gently pressing a hand to his chest. She could feel his heart beating loudly within. "Why don't you tell me what you know? I promise not to tell anyone." She traced her finger down his belly with her last few words. He watched her, entranced. She licked her lips slowly. "I'd be forever in your debt."

"Uhhh," he stammered, "I'll be right back, promise." He half-smiled as he huffed past her into the salon and through the interior door.

Karaia loosed a huge sigh from her lungs, hoping her flirting had been enough.

Five minutes passed.

Just as she was losing hope and wondering what the hell she was doing here in the middle of the night, multiple footsteps approached from behind the door. This time, an older woman wearing all black stepped out, followed by the man from before.

The woman marched up to Karaia, eyeing her up and down. She was shorter than Karaia but walked with a commanding presence. Her jet-black hair was pulled into a tight bun at the back of her head, contrasting with her pale skin. She shoved a finger hard into Karaia's chest and asked, "What the fuck do you know about the woman who had this paper?"

With all her previous confidence draining, Karaia choked out, "That's what I came to find out from you."

The woman scowled. "How 'bout you tell us what you know, and we might do the same?"

"Okaayy," said Karaia, swallowing hard.

"This way," the woman commanded as she spun back toward the salon.

Karaia stepped forward, then hesitated, weighing her options. Telling these strangers what she saw that night in the tube was an enormous risk. They could turn her in to the authorities, and she might be kicked out of New Soteria for what she saw or not being connected to her credits. Or worse, they could be dangerous, and she might not even return if she followed them into the salon. She shuddered at the thought.

But at the same time—Karaia's sixth sense whispered to her from the pit of her stomach—she felt that they knew something that could help her.

"We don't have all day," the woman said, tapping her foot impatiently.

Karaia took a deep breath in and out and then followed them inside. "It started when I was walking home from work a couple days ago ..." She proceeded to tell them everything that had happened that night: getting hit by the woman running by her in the tube, the prick in her arm, the officers, seeing the murder, and ending her story with her lack of NeuroCredits. By the end, she could feel the tears welling up in her eyes again. "It was the next day that I found the paper with this address on it, right where *it* had happened."

Karaia wiped her nose and looked at the woman, expecting her to be shocked, surprised, scared, but she seemed unfazed by the story.

"Thanks for that. We don't have any answers for you," the woman said curtly. "But now we know you have something we need. Ziven, grab her."

The man, Ziven, crept toward Karaia, his hands out. "You can make this easy." His voice was shaky. "I don't want to hurt you."

"No! What are you doing?" Karaia asked frantically as she backed up until she hit the wall.

NIVA, call—

Zap! Ziven held a strange device up to her neck, shooting a quick electric jolt through her brain, interrupting her thoughts.

NIVA, call emergency services.

No response.

NIVA? Adrenaline coursed through Karaia's veins as she racked her mind for any trace of NIVA, nowhere to be found.

"What did you do to me?!" she shouted.

Ziven grabbed hold of her arms with a firm grip on each side, dragging her farther into the salon. He was clearly much stronger than she was. Soon, her hands were pinned together behind her back and tied in a restraint. She could not escape.

Just like the woman from the alley.

Karaia didn't want to end up like her. She couldn't. So she kicked and writhed in his grip, to no avail. Struggling to break free, she screamed out repeatedly for help, but the front door was closed behind them, and now, her ragged voice just echoed against the empty salon walls. Soon, tears began to flow from her eyes, and heavy sobs took over her screams.

Ziven whispered to her, "Just come with us, and it will all be okay, I promise. I don't want to hurt you." His eyes were still kind, but his actions said otherwise as he pulled Karaia toward the interior door at the far end of the store.

A knot twisted in her stomach. This is not what she had thought would happen when she had listened to her sixth sense. It had now betrayed her twice in one week.

"You can't just take me wherever you want," she pleaded. "There are laws. Someone will come looking for me. They'll find you! This kind of thing isn't supposed to happen here, not in New Soteria."

The woman whipped around to face her. "Oh yeah? Just like they weren't supposed to kill that woman in the alley? She was my friend." Her eyes pierced Karaia's like a laser gun.

Karaia sniffled. "Then, you shouldn't be like them."

The woman huffed, shaking her head. "Sometimes, we don't have a choice."

Heat rose from the pit of Karaia's stomach. This wasn't right. Her face flushed, and she clenched her jaw. Letting the anger fuel her, her tears quieted, and a fire raged in her belly. She wouldn't let them take her. Not like this.

"No!" she yelled back, her voice clear, surprised by her own bravery.

The woman stepped close, only inches away. Karaia could feel the woman's hot breath on her cheek.

Throwing her head back and laughing, the woman asked, "What the hell did you say?"

"I said *no*." Karaia didn't flinch, keeping her eyes locked onto the woman's. "You're not going to take me anywhere until I know why. I risked everything in telling you what happened."

The woman laughed again and looked at Ziven. "Who the fuck does this girl think she is?"

Ziven shrugged his shoulders, sweat decorating his shirt under the arms and around his neck, as a heavy knot formed in the center of his eyes as he stared at the situation, unsure of what to say or do.

The woman shifted back to Karaia. "You messed with the wrong people, little lady."

She pulled her fist back.

Karaia braced herself.

"Blaze, stop!" Ziven interjected.

"What are you talking about, Z? She'll be easier to deal with if she's unconscious," Blaze said with a snark.

Ziven leaned over and whispered in Blaze's ear. Karaia strained to listen, thinking she heard Ziven say the words *key* and *prophecy*.

Blaze cocked her head and raised her eyebrows at Karaia. "Fine. What if we told you we could help get your NeuroCredits back up and running? Would you *willingly* come with us then?" She rolled her eyes.

"How do I know I can trust you?" Karaia asked.

"You don't, but what other choice do you have?" She gestured toward Karaia's current situation.

Blaze had a point. Karaia gazed down at her arms tied behind her back. In all her struggles, she had ripped one side of her pants and was missing a shoe. She didn't even know when that had fallen off. "Tell me something now so I know you're telling the truth."

Ziven interrupted, "That prick you felt, when the woman ran by, it was her injecting you with nanobots. They are disrupting your NeuroCredits system. When we take them out, your link should be re-established."

Karaia furrowed her brow, trying to think clearly, despite the onslaught of emotions she was feeling. *How did anyone ever make a logical decision before NeuroCredits?* What they were saying could be true, but then, why didn't Arjun find any evidence of nanobots?

"Little lady," Blaze said. "Make a choice. Come willingly, or I can punch you? Personally, I prefer the latter, but Ziven here seems fond of your pretty face." She stroked Karaia's cheek.

Karaia tried to shake off her hand, and said, "I'll go. And my name is Karaia, not little lady."

"Don't care. Follow me." Blaze opened the interior door to reveal a long flight of seemingly endless stairs down into darkness.

"Good choice. I didn't want to carry your limp body the whole way down." Ziven grinned and held out his hand. "After you."

Karaia forced a smile back as she took her first step down into an unknown future.

CHAPTER 19

MIRYAM

An owl hooted in the distance, and crickets chirped as Miryam followed Dempsey along the wooded path. This way wound through the village forest, past the lake, and at last back round to her family's cottage.

Dempsey droned on about his family's inheritance. Or so Miryam thought. She had tuned out most of his words. A great yawn escaped her lips. She longed to be home, warm in her bed, drifting into dreams of Ved. Instead, she was here, trudging through the woods with the dullest man alive. *Is this what marriage will be?* She groaned aloud.

"What was that?" Dempsey asked.

"Uh ... sorry, I am pondering what you said ..." Miryam stalled.

"I was speaking of my late mother's death."

"Yes, and how utterly dreadful that must have been for you." Miryam groaned more softly this time and rolled her eyes, knowing he couldn't see her.

They had almost reached the deepest point of the forest, where the trees grew so thick their canopy swallowed even the Moon's bright light.

Dempsey cleared his throat and resumed his tale. Miryam began counting her steps until she was home. It seemed infinitely more interesting than listening to *Dempsey*. Even his name irked her. *Ugghh!* She tried to resign herself to marriage, for her father's sake, for her family.

But sometimes, accepting one's fate was so hard.

With every footfall, Miryam's path darkened. She strained to focus on each movement, the feel of the moist ground beneath her, the autumn leaves' crunch, and her stride's pace. It took all her will not to run. Run home. Run from Dempsey. Run away from the life she was doomed to live.

As a child, she had roamed these woods a hundred times, light and free. Why did they stifle her now? A stiff breeze swept through the trees, raising a chill up her spine. Gooseflesh danced across her skin.

Ahead, Dempsey halted so suddenly that Miryam stumbled into him, colliding with his bony frame beneath his clothes.

Out of nowhere, a hoarse, phlegmy cough seized him. "I fear I must rest for a moment. My lungs are weak."

His wheezing grew worse. Miryam's mind flashed to her father and his sickness. Though she cared little for Dempsey, she could not help but feel compelled to aid him. "If we go a little farther, there is a bench by the lake. You may rest there."

"I only need to catch my breath." He rasped and bent over, wobbling.

Miryam rushed to his side, steadying him. A stench of smoked fish and body odor made her wrinkle her nose.

"Thank you." Dempsey cleared his throat.

He straightened, standing tall. The frailty Miryam had felt a moment ago seemed gone, replaced by sudden vigor.

"You truly are a sweet girl. So trusting. So pure," he said.

Shuddering a quick breath, Miryam let go of him and took a step back, bumping into a tree behind her. "We should go," she said, her heart thundering in her chest.

"Why? When at last we have some privacy." He whipped around, facing her.

While she couldn't see his face, she could feel an unwarranted smile creep upon it.

In one swift movement, Dempsey seized her wrists and slammed them above her head against the tree, holding them fast with one hand. With the other, he dragged her dress and chemise upward.

Miryam gasped for breath, the wind stolen from her. The bark tugged at her hair; scrapping her legs and bare thighs. Her mind reeled.

Everything was happening so fast. Too fast. She tried to grasp what was unfolding, but her thoughts blurred and jumbled. His movements were too fluid, deliberate. Calculated.

He's done this before.

And then she knew what he meant to do.

What he meant to do—*to her.*

Miryam squirmed, thrashing against his grip. Her legs kicked, but he pressed his body hard against hers, pinning her to the tree. He was stronger than he looked.

Tears spilled down her cheeks. "Please ... do not do this. You can stop now. I ... I shall not tell a soul. Let me go, I beg of you." Her lips quivered between sobs.

"Be a good girl and do not scream too loud." His free hand slid downward.

Miryam screamed. Loud.

But it didn't matter. Dempsey had planned his trap perfectly, and Miryam had stumbled into it. Her screams faded to whimpers with each thrust of his hand, and she retreated further inside herself. She clenched her eyes shut and fled in her mind, imagining she was far, far away.

Then came the sound of a belt unfastening. Dempsey was preparing to draw down his stockings. "Now for the true sport," he hissed.

Miryam saw her opening.

As his buckle distracted him, she gathered all her strength and drove her knee straight between his legs.

He let out a strangled cry. Clutching himself, he crumbled to the forest floor.

Her dress fell back down, and she jumped over Dempsey.

Then, she ran.

She ran harder than she ever had in her life. Wind rushed through Miryam's knotted hair. Twice she stumbled, crashing onto the damp ground. Mud squelched between her fingers and smeared across her dress. *Just run,* she told herself. *Run.* Anything to be free of him.

Time seemed to play tricks on her. She strained her eyes wide on the dark path, unsure of which way to turn.

She ran on.

"Miryam, get back here!" Dempsey's voice rang through the trees, echoing and taunting her.

He was still on her, in her mind, his touch clawing at her skin.

Digging her heels into the ground, she pressed toward home. That was when she realized it. Dempsey would know to look for her at her father's cottage. She could not go there. He would find her. There was but one place she could think of that might keep her safe.

Turning to head deeper into the woods, her lungs burned, but she ran still. And prayed she was right about its location.

At last, the abbey's stone walls rose before her, looming larger than she had ever imagined. Only a single entrance pierced them: a tall wooden gate.

The night air lay stagnant as Miryam approached. All she could hear was her own pulse pounding in her ears. Somewhere in the woods, she had lost a shoe.

She knocked gently at first. "Hello ..." Her voice broke into sobs. "Is anyone there? Please."

She knocked harder.

The gate creaked, and a small, stooped man in a black robe peered out. Without a word, he gestured for her to come inside.

Miryam opened her eyes and blinked a few times in confusion. She lay on a narrow cot in a bare chamber, its walls the color of earth. A single wooden cross hung above her. Candles flickered around her, causing the room's shadows to dance about in strange, horrifying shapes.

A woman tended her. *Sophia*. Miryam remembered her from the orchard.

There was no hearth, yet layers of blankets covered her, and her soiled clothing had been changed for something clean and dry. Sophia pressed a damp cloth to her brow, scented faintly with lavender.

Miryam was warm for the first time since—

Her heart froze. But her mind raced through the nightmare she had endured, wishing it were just a nightmare, knowing it wasn't because of the dull ache between her legs.

She tried to speak, but no words came.

"Do not speak, my dear," Sophia murmured. "You fainted at the gate. Rest now. I'll be close by if you need me." With that, she slipped from the room.

Miryam's eyes darted to the exits. One door, one small window. Surely Dempsey would not dare breach the monastery walls? Still, fear gnawed at her.

She balled up her legs into her chest and released her lungs, feeling like she had been holding her breath for the past hour. With that, her body shook uncontrollably. She pressed her blanket to her mouth, muffling the waves of sobs that broke from her.

Don't let anyone hear you. Don't scream.

It was his voice echoing in her mind.

Rocking herself back and forth, Miryam could not rest. Instead, the scene replayed repeatedly in her mind. *Why did I follow him into the woods? Why had I walked home with him?* She felt stupid, ashamed and—sinful.

The thought of tomorrow seemed unbearable. She wished to die in her sleep rather than wake to the fate of marriage with someone as vile as Dempsey.

CHAPTER 20

LEAH

T he ancient book was bound in dusty leather, fraying at the edges.
Leah took the book from Gertrude, flipping it over. It looked
like it could crumble in her hands. There was nothing on the front
except the initial, M., carved in the bottom right corner.

Leah went to open it, but before she could, Gertrude placed her
hand over it.

"Before you do" — she looked Leah straight in the eyes — "be
prepared for a world anew."

"Okaaay." Leah looked away from Gertrude and rolled her eyes. She
opened the book. The first page had just two words handwritten in
calligraphy on it:

For Leah.

She closed it.

"What is this? A prank? Kat, Felix, are you hiding back there?" she
yelled toward the back of the store, expecting to see her friends come
out, and they could all have a big laugh at her expense. No one came.
She gaped at Gertrude, who was just staring at her in all seriousness.

"Is no prank. This is true," Gertrude said.

"Why did you put my name in this book?"

"Not I." Gertrude held a hand to her heart. "Yes, I have held this
book in my store, but this book is yours then, and yours now, and yours
to come."

Leah squinted her eyes at the old woman. "How old is it?"

"Turn the page, turn the page." Gertrude nodded toward the book on her lap. "Of time stood still, this book."

She smiled wide at Leah, simultaneously looking as innocent as a small child and as wise as an ancient sage. Leah slowly opened it again. *What am I doing going along with this mentally ill woman and her games? She probably forgot to take her meds. Should I alert someone? I should just leave.* But she found her hands turning the page in the book, past the one with her name on it.

At the top of the second page, it read,

One week after the harvest feast, in thy year of our Lord 1307.

"Seven hundred years old?" Leah exclaimed.

"Yes, yes, yes. Blood, ice cream, an owl, green tea, a scream, the tube, salt water, tree. It's all coming together, isn't it?" Gertrude raised her eyebrows.

It looked like she expected Leah to understand, but Leah wasn't sure if she had just heard the woman's shopping list or the ramblings of someone who should be in a mental institution.

Ignoring what Gertrude had just said, Leah asked, "Where did you get this book?"

"The book traveled across a sea."

"You got it from overseas somewhere?"

"The bay. Where all are connected."

Leah wrinkled her brow. "What?"

"eBay," Gertrude said flatly.

"Oh, and here I was starting to imagine something ... never mind." Leah shook her head and looked at the rest of the page:

> *I dreamt of a woman last night. She was alone in a great village with towers as high as the heavens. She held a babe, a girl. The babe grew and turned into a flower. The woman tried to hold on to the flower, but the petals began to fall off when she held it tight. She planted the flower back into the Earth. Then a great beast came, trying to take the flower away. The woman knew she could distract the beast, so she ran. Far, far away.*

Leah closed the dusty book. While the account of the dream was a bit disturbing, the migraine that had been plaguing her all day had gone away sometime while reading the passage. Clearly, this book was a journal of someone who had lived during the Middle Ages. It seemed impossible that it had survived this long intact.

She flipped through the rest of the tender pages, careful not to rip them. Some had dates on them; some didn't. *This could be very valuable. Even if not for the monetary value but for the insight into the life of someone else, especially from so long ago.* And she did love analyzing people and finding out what made them tick. She told herself she was interested in the journal for purely intellectual reasons, but something deep within her knew it was more than that.

"How much for this book?" she asked.

"Oh, it's always been yours. I was just holding it until it found you again." Gertrude nodded.

"Sooo ...?"

"Free for you."

"Thank you." Leah eyed the woman, still skeptical. She stood to leave, feeling one hundred percent better than when she came in. "I had an interesting time here."

"Glad to be of service. Helping those who call. Yesterday and tomorrow. Enjoy your world anew. It might be full of magic. Toodle-oo!" Gertrude said as she snapped her fingers together. A tiny spark lit between them. A blue flame danced on her fingertips for a second before she blew it out and waddled into the back of her store.

Leah stood there for a moment, mouth agape.

Then, she turned and left the store, clutching the book in her arms. As she stumbled out onto the sidewalk, she turned once more and looked back at the bookstore.

Baba Yaga's Books and More.

Finding her lost shoe on the ground, Leah scooped it up and climbed into her car. Her head felt clearer than it had in months. She whispered to herself, "What the fuck?"

CHAPTER 21

KARAIA

It was like stepping back in time. At least, what Karaia imagined the world used to look like before the Rebuilding. Only one dim yellowish light bulb lit the dingy hallway that led down, a stark contrast from the tube's brightly lit corridors. On either side of her, worn, dusty walls hugged the tight hallway, so different from the polished metal she was used to. She tried to peek past Blaze to see where they were headed, but the stairs were playing tricks on her mind. She couldn't tell how far they went down, straining her eyes in the low light.

"Watch your step," Blaze said.

They turned abruptly, and Karaia stumbled. A bead of sweat dripped into her eye. Frantic, she went to brush it off and was quickly reminded that her hands were still tied behind her back. Ziven caught her.

"Can you untie me now?" Karaia asked. "You've already got me in the creepy stairway."

"B, thoughts?" Ziven asked.

Blaze stopped. "Fine. But you know that Ziven here can overtake you if you try anything." She spun, and with a flick of the wrist, she had a small blade in her hand. "Turn around."

Trying to focus on her breathing, Karaia did as she was told, allowing Blaze to untether her hands. She flexed her fingers, twirling her wrists from side to side, enjoying the tiny bit of newly found freedom and willing herself to remain calm despite her situation. One step at a time, she continued down the steps, with Ziven's heavy breath behind her and the back of Blaze's head in front of her.

Down, down, they went, turning and twisting through long halls and endless stairs, spiraling deeper. They had to be past ground level by now, but Karaia had no idea how that was even possible.

Something small scurried past their feet, and both she and Ziven shrieked.

"Don't mind our neighbors. They're more afraid of you than you are of them." Blaze chuckled, unflinching.

"Speak for yourself." Ziven shivered. "Rats give me the creeps."

Rats? Karaia vaguely remembered hearing about them as a child. *Weren't they extinct?*

As they descended farther, Karaia lost all sense of direction. Every little shadow and sound made her jump. And with every step into the unknown, her prior confidence and conviction waned. Without good sight, the rest of her senses were working in overdrive. *What was that smell?* Wrinkling her nose at its pungency, a memory surfaced. *Urine and ... mildew.* Once when she was young, she had peed her pants. Out of embarrassment, she had shoved them under her bed, out of reach from the steri-bot. When her mother finally found the clothing weeks later, they reeked of rancid urine mixed with mildew. But now, in this stairway, there was one distinct smell she couldn't quite identify.

Earth. She had never actually touched the ground, so she wasn't sure, but her sixth sense told her so. She smiled at the thought.

Finally, they hit bottom, literally. The ground beneath Karaia's feet was solid, uneven rock. As she stepped forward across the wobbly terrain, a nearly uncontrollable urge made her want to reach down and touch the cool ground. An overwhelming sense of nostalgia hit her, and she imagined herself walking into a cave entrance.

Jolted back into reality, Karaia ran right into the back of Blaze. "Sorry. I'm sorry," she said, holding her hands up.

"We're here," Ziven whispered from behind her.

"Where's here?" Karaia felt the pit of her stomach drop, wondering how many flights they had traversed, how far away she was from every-one and everything she knew.

Ahead of her, Blaze opened a door. Light cascaded in and pierced Karaia's eyes, causing her to squint. They stepped forward into a large room. The historic hallway disappeared into the past; they were back in the year 2307. High-tech computers and holo-screens lined a row of desks to the left of her. Five people worked diligently at them, not looking up from their workstations. In front of her was a wall of books encased in protective fiberglass. Karaia had only seen one physical book ever, and that was from her father when she was a child. He had brought it back from one of his trips. No one needed physical books now, not with holo-shows, movies, news feeds, and the internet connected directly to their brains. To her right was a wall with two closed doors and a hallway. In the middle of the windowless room sat a large table with a couple of people working there.

"Where are we?" Karaia repeated herself.

"You do realize that if we tell you, we'll have to kill you," Blaze said bluntly.

Karaia couldn't tell if she was serious or joking.

Blaze continued, "All you need to know is we are a group of people dedicated to preserving the world's knowledge and to empowering people with that knowledge."

Ziven chimed in, "Basically, we're nerds and hackers. Blaze here likes to think she's a warrior." He laughed.

"Wait. Are you Defiers?" Karaia asked, her jaw dropping.

"What about the 'we'll have to kill you' part did you not understand?" Blaze asked.

There were always rumors that the Defiers kept bases within New Soteria's walls, but she had never thought that was actually true. There hadn't been an internal attack in years. That kind of stuff only happened outside the walls, or so she thought. She decided she would alert NIVA to her location, just in case. In the event that anything did happen to her, the authorities would know where to find her body. The thought made her stomach turn. *NIVA, save my location.*

No response.

Karaia pursed her lips and remembered Ziven had disabled her connection to NIVA.

Blaze said, "Don't even try to connect to the net. Even without the temporary injection we gave you upstairs, this entire area is surrounded by an electromagnetic dampening field. The only internet connection down here is hard-wired through those computers and holo-screens."

"I wasn't," Karaia lied.

"Whatever."

"Sooo ... what *do* you do here?" Karaia felt desperate for answers.

"What I can tell you is this." Blaze waved her hands in the air. "Up there in those tubes, that's all a fucking dream—or nightmare—however you want to look at it. Do you know how most of the world lives, even right here in New Soteria?"

"What do you mean?"

"My kid sister was one of the ones who the NeuroCredits didn't work on. She kept it a secret for a long time, but do you want to guess where she ended up?"

Karaia could hear the anger in Blaze's voice. She kept silent.

Blaze continued, "First, she was sent to a factory to work as a sorter in Sector Five, but she couldn't keep up with the long, hard hours, complained too much, so you know what happened?"

"What?"

"She 'ran away.' That's the official story, at least." Blaze looked Karaia in the eye, and for the first time, Karaia could see the raw sadness, masked by anger, in Blaze's expression. "But they killed her."

"They wouldn't ..." Karaia thought of the woman in the alley and shivered. "That's what people do outside of New Soteria, not here." She rubbed her temples, racking her brain for answers that made sense of any of this. "Aren't the factories run by AI, not people, in Sector Five?"

Blaze chuckled, shaking her head. "You're a fucking newborn, baby sheep. You're right, you're not a little lady, you're a little lamb. Believing all the shit stories they tell you. Z, hook her up, and let's get this over with." She motioned for Ziven to grab Karaia again.

"I will go willingly. No need to manhandle me again," Karaia said, holding up her hands. "What do I need to do?"

"First, we need to verify that the nanobots are actually there. Follow me," Ziven said, leading Karaia down a hallway to a closed door.

Blaze followed closely behind them. Once inside, there was a metal chair in the middle of the room with all sorts of wires and devices attached to it. Ziven put his hand out, motioning for Karaia to sit down. Tentatively, she sat down in the chair, feeling the cold metal through her clothing. Ziven pulled up beside her.

"Okay, I'm just going to connect this" — he held up a small wire — "to your neural network." He placed it at the base of her head.

After a few minutes in silence and staring at a nearby holo-screen, he said, "Yep, they're definitely there. The nanobots have an Avani signature on them. Ha! And they're hidden in NIVA's code and inaccessible until disconnected from NIVA. So, there was no way for them to be detected until now. Brilliant!" Ziven beamed.

"There's a message inside of me?" Karaia asked. She couldn't join him in his elation, still worried about her own safety.

Blaze clapped her hands together. "Yeah, we were waiting for a message from Avani. And now, we know why we didn't hear anything. We just need to get them out of you and send you on your merry fucking way."

"What's Avani?" Karaia asked, tilting her head.

"You know it as the Settlement," Ziven said.

"Z, no more info," Blaze retorted.

Karaia's eyes lit up as she thought about her parents. "You know people there?" For the first time that night, she felt a little hopeful and that maybe, just maybe, her sixth sense hadn't led her astray.

"We're getting off topic. We can't talk about Avani," Blaze said through tight lips.

Karaia interrupted. "But my parents left for there when I was four and never came back. Do you know how to contact them?"

"We can't. Hence, the super-secret nanobots' communication," Blaze said.

Ziven added, "I'm sorry about your parents, but Blaze is right, we can't do that."

"Oh, I thought ..." Karaia's gaze shifted down.

"The answer is no," Blaze said.

Karaia felt desperate. Nothing about this night made any sense, until now. Maybe it was adrenaline. Maybe it was her sixth sense. Maybe it was the emotional mess of not having access to her credits. Maybe it was just sheer delusion at this point, but she pressed on. This was the first time in her life she had had any sort of way of contacting her parents. What were the chances she would ever be this close again? "But haven't I helped you, and now, you can help me?"

"No."

"It could be a trade."

"Still no."

"Maybe there's something else I can help you with?"

"What could you possibly do for us, little lamb?"

"I work at Seromela. I have access to their information systems. I could be useful," Karaia pleaded.

"Wait, what?" Blaze narrowed her gaze. "You work at Seromela? Fuck, Z, we need to scrub her brain ... like, yesterday."

Ziven whispered, "What if she could be our inside person, you know, for that piece of tech we're looking for, the one hidden in the you-know-where?" He was motioning with his eyes toward Blaze, trying to hint at the thing he was thinking.

"Too risky. We can't trust her." Blaze eyed Karaia suspiciously.

"C'mon, she must be here for a reason! Don't you see? It's all connected." Ziven was getting animated, waving his hands in the air. "You've seen her necklace. It's not a coincidence that she's the one who showed up with the nanobots."

Blaze pressed her lips together, deep in thought.

"What?" Karaia's brow furrowed as she grabbed hold of the silver piece adorning her neck. "What does this have to do with my necklace?"

"Could you get access to Griffin Marshall's vault by any chance?" Ziven stared at her, gears turning in his brain.

"Shit, Z, why did you have to go and say that?" Blaze glared at him. "Now, we really need to scrub her."

"Despite your tough act, B, I know you believe in this prophecy just as much as I do. You've got to see that she could be important to our cause, even the *key* to it." He winked.

"That's not important now. Get the bots out of her. I need to think." Blaze stomped out of the room.

Suddenly, all of this seemed like too much to process. Karaia desperately wished she had a NeuroCredit and could just melt into her couch with her favorite holo-show right now. What did she and her necklace have to do with a prophecy and Griffin's vault? Clearly, these people were up to some weird, possibly illegal stuff, but that wasn't Karaia's business.

That wasn't *her*. Or was it?

Her sixth sense gnawed at her. If she helped them, it would mean risking everything, even her life, for what? Information about why her parents left her and her brother behind? No, it was too risky. She could try to find a legal way to contact the Settlement. It had been years since she had tried, to no avail. But maybe there was a way that didn't include teaming up with the Defiers.

"Never mind. Blaze is right. Let's just get this over with." Karaia nodded at her decision. Then, why did she still feel uneasy?

Ziven said, "Let's get you into the BBP for nanobot removal."

"What's the BBP?" asked Karaia.

"The Binaural Beat Pod. It's actually kind of relaxing and where we go to meditate or chill. But the beats can also be used as a tool if the pod is set to the same frequency that the nanobots are attuned to. Stay in there for about thirty minutes, let them do their work, and pee in this cup when you're finished. They'll come on out." He handed her a small, clear cup.

She arched an eyebrow. "Seriously?"

"Yup."

He led Karaia through the other door that housed a giant pod. She stepped inside. Ziven closed the lid and left the room.

It was pitch black in the pod. At first, Karaia resisted the enclosed space and immediately wanted out. But the soft inside conformed to her body's shape and hugged her. Then, the sound waves began. They were all around her, radiating through her and within her. Soon, she surrendered to their murmurs, and the thirty minutes passed effortlessly. She felt more at peace than she had in days. Maybe ever.

When she exited the room, Ziven and Blaze stood huddled together whispering near the large table at the center of the main room.

Karaia began, "That was—"

"Totally enlightening." Ziven popped his head up to finish her sentence.

"Yeah," Karaia agreed, not really knowing what he meant. She held up the small cup of urine awkwardly. "Does this mean I get to leave now?"

"Is that what you want?" Blaze asked, looking halfway nice for the moment. "We discussed it and will extend an offer to you."

Ziven put on some gloves from a drawer and took the cup from Karaia, handing it off to one of the people who had been working at a nearby computer. He said, "If you help us with an infiltration mission into Griffin's vault in Seromela, we will give you information about how to contact Avani. But ... we can't guarantee your safety."

"Or alternatively, you can choose to forget we exist," Blaze added. "Your NeuroCredits will be reestablished once you return to the tubes above, and you can go back to your life. It's your choice."

"I ..." Karaia's eyes shifted back and forth while she processed her choices. *Go back to your normal life.* That's what her rational mind said and what she had been wanting this whole time. Wasn't it? Then, she rubbed the necklace she wore, the one from her father. Something told her there was something that brought her here tonight. To this very moment. She bit her lip.

"Little lamb, we don't have all day," Blaze said, tapping her foot.

Karaia thought about her life, her grandma, her brother. She couldn't risk their safety and their being tied to her if something went wrong on this 'mission.' All for what? The possibility of contacting her parents? Ultimately, her current family and friends mattered most to her. Not what *she* wanted, or what she hoped for.

"I'll do the brain scrub and go home." She nodded, but as she said the words aloud, part of her already wished she hadn't.

Ziven and Blaze led her to another room with a single metal chair.

"You guys really know how to decorate." Karaia chuckled, not necessarily at the joke but at herself and her ability to joke at a time like this.

She sat down in the chair as Ziven placed a metal contraption around her head.

"There's no way to say this nicely," Ziven said, brows pinching, "but scrubbing your brain and erasing your memories ... well, it's going to hurt. Luckily, when you wake up tomorrow morning, you'll have completely forgotten the pain and us. It's too bad. I kind of liked you."

Before being able to think much more about it, Karaia felt a cool tingle light up at the base of her head as the machine whirred to life.

Ziven grimaced and said, "It was nice knowing you. See you ... never."

Then, a lightning bolt of energy blasted its way through Karaia's mind.

PART TWO

"One does not become enlightened by imagining figures of light, but by making the darkness conscious."
— Carl Jung

CHAPTER 22

MIRYAM

B irds chirped outside as Miryam awoke. The air held a chill, but she was warm and snug beneath the layers of wool. Tiny dust specks drifted through a shaft of sunlight from the little window, making her smile. Still lying in bed, she stretched her arms high above her head.

Dempsey's face flashed before her. *Don't scream.*

She yanked her arms back under the covers, curling her legs tight to her chest. *Get out of my head.* She could feel his hands around her wrists. The slimy touch of his icy fingers on her skin. *Get out!*

Fear gnawed at her, but the anger burned hotter. Angry at Dempsey. Angry at her father for binding her to him. Angry at herself for letting it happen. She squeezed her eyes shut, trying to stop the tears that kept coming.

A knock at the door startled her. Her heart pounded as she froze, listening.

"Miryam, are you awake?" Sophia's voice.

She exhaled in relief. "Come in."

Sophia entered, carrying a tray of food and radiating warmth from her, as if she brought the Sun with her everywhere she went. "Good morrow, dear."

Miryam wiped her eyes, red and swollen, and slowly pushed herself upright. "Morning," she whispered.

Sophia set the tray on a small table and handed her a bowl. "'Tis not much, only porridge with chopped apples. But it will fill you."

"Thank you." Miryam took the bowl, though her hands trembled. Her stomach turned, but she forced a bite anyway.

Eating in silence, she could feel Sophia's gaze upon her as her hand went through the motions of feeding herself. Before she realized it, the bowl was empty. Perhaps she had been hungrier than she thought.

"Shall I fetch you more?"

"No."

"Would you speak of what brought you here last night?"

Sophia's voice carried quiet sincerity. She cared. But Miryam knew if she tried to utter a word now, it would only erupt as a scream of rage. It was as though a fiery coal had replaced her heart. Its heat radiated through her body, threatening to consume her.

"No."

"'Tis natural not to want to speak of it. A grievous incident has befallen you. Yet keeping it buried can do more harm than the act itself." Sophia reached for a small leather-bound book on the tray. "Can you read and write?"

Miryam nodded.

"Then I would bid you write your feelings if you cannot voice them. Here." She handed the book to Miryam.

Miryam turned its cover and let her fingers linger across the blank, smooth pages. She had never held parchment so fine in all her life.

"There is ink upon the table if you choose to write. And a bell, should you need aught." Sophia gathered the tray and paused near the door.

"Please ... leave me be," Miryam muttered.

Sophia inclined her head, then slipped out, taking the blanket of warmth with her.

Outside, heavy clouds swallowed the Sun, and the chamber dimmed. Shivering, Miryam pulled the covers over her face and drifted back to sleep.

It took a full week before Miryam found the courage to pick up the little leather journal and begin writing. At first, she wrote of her father and Isabella. She missed them so dearly that simply writing their names brought tears to her eyes. She could not imagine what they must be enduring, not knowing where she was. Yet she knew she could not face them. Not like this.

Guilt battered her thoughts. *I partook in heresy in the woods, and look at what has befallen me.*

She felt selfish for not returning home, but she felt frozen, unable to face them, especially if it meant seeing *him* again. Dempsey. Just the thought of him dried her tears and set her body ablaze with rage. Her teeth ground together as she seethed. She shook her head, trying to rid herself of his image.

Instead, Miryam turned her pen to what surrounded her. The wood-carved crucifix of Christ upon the wall. Outside, a small nest made a home in the crook of the stone wall. A mother cardinal brought worms to her fledglings. Monks chanted as they passed by in the courtyard, their slow, sullen tones reverberating through her bones.

In time, she began writing her dreams. Often, they were nightmares, horrid ones of Dempsey, where she tried to flee but could never escape his reach. Other nights she dreamed the new earl was quartering those she loved in the village square, forcing her to watch them die repeatedly, powerless to stop it.

At other times, her dreams were stranger, full of vivid colors and swirling lights. In these, she saw faces unknown, and yet, she could sense their thoughts, their feelings, their longings. There were a mother and daughter. Yet the girl would change into a flower, or the mother into a serpent. The forms shifted endlessly, but the feeling remained. An aching bond of love and protection, shadowed by the mother's fear that she was never enough.

Then, there was a different woman, all alone in a busy world. Her mind was clouded and torn. She wondered about her parents and where they had gone. She felt it was her fault they had left her. In one dream, she swam in a vast ocean searching for them, only to discover an anchor was bound to her foot. She had never moved at all.

Why am I dreaming of strangers? Part of her did not mind. It was easier to dwell on their feelings than to face her own.

Miryam had yet to write what had happened to her, or how she felt about it. By now, her family must have scoured the village for her, only to resign themselves to her absence. Did they think her dead or run off? And what of Dempsey? He had been the last to see her. What tale had he spun? Did he feign innocence or weave a convenient lie? She assumed the latter.

Even if she could get over what happened to her, forgive herself, and face Isabella and her father again, what did that mean for her future? She was still betrothed to Dempsey, and she would rather die than marry him.

She picked up the quill, dipped it in the ink, and waited for the excess drops to fall off. Opening the journal, she pressed the quill to the page. The rage inside her built again. The coal burned brightly where her heart should have been.

Snap! The quill broke into two pieces, and an ink blot dropped on her page. Miryam shoved the book across the table. She was not ready. Not yet.

She needed a distraction. Something to carry her mind away from her pain.

Miryam stood and looked out the window. Night had fallen, and the Sun's last glow was long gone. The abbey courtyard lay bare, save for one monk snoring softly against the gatehouse wall. A few scattered candles dimly lit the paths, their flames flickering in the breeze. From somewhere deeper within the abbey—or was it in her mind?—chanting carried faintly through the air. She could hear the sound echoing against stone walls, unable to tell its source.

Her curiosity stirred.

Pulling on a robe Sophia had left for her, Miryam took the small candle from her wall and stepped out of her chamber for the first time since her arrival. Glancing in both directions, a narrow corridor stretched before her, rows of doors on either side. Beyond that, she thought she glimpsed gardens and a small orchard, and what looked to be the edge of a pond glimmering in the dark.

Following the sound of the chanting, she sauntered down the corridor, her steps slow and deliberate. The stone path led her to the main courtyard. A crescent Moon shone bright in the sky above, and bats swooped low, darting after insects. Before her stood the monastery's church, plainer than the one in the village but tall and solemn. On one side lay the infirmary and kitchens, with another row of cells. On the other, an open entryway marked by two tall candles. Vibrations resounded in Miryam's skull, coming from the dark portal.

She edged forward, and the chanting grew clearer. With each step, the steady thrum seemed to seep farther into her bones—beckoning her.

Now, upon the threshold, she held out her candle to see that a stairwell led downward into an unknown darkness. She placed one foot on the first stair. Then her other. And another. Waves of chanting reverberated off the walls around her as she descended. It pulsed all around her—in her—becoming louder with each step down.

Miryam's feet touched a dirt floor. In the pale candlelight, she glanced around and saw she stood in what seemed to be a natural cave, likely older than the abbey itself. The monks must have built directly atop it. Her fingertips traced along the smooth stone wall, finding a thin sheen of moisture on its surface.

The cave curved ahead. She followed the bend and entered a chamber stacked with root vegetables, baskets of apples and pears, and shelves lined with jars.

A root cellar, naturally.

But the chanting. Where was it coming from? She seemed to be right on top of it, within it, and yet, its source still escaped her. Her eyes swept the chamber for another way forward, but none appeared. *It must be here.* She set her candle down and began rummaging through the vegetable boxes and shelves, searching the cool stone walls behind them for a door or another chamber, anything.

After rearranging nearly the entire root cellar, Miryam huffed, realizing just how absurd she probably looked, digging around in a dark cave in the middle of the night. *Imagine what Bella would say.* She chuckled to herself. It felt good to laugh for the first time in a while.

Moving the last of the shelves, she was about to resign her search when her hand brushed against fabric.

A hidden passage. Her heart swelled with excitement.

Miryam tugged the cloth aside and stepped through the opening. She had found the source of the chanting. Inside this new chamber, monks and nuns sat in a circle, legs crossed, eyes closed, their voices woven together in chant. Candlelight flickered against the walls, shadows leaping and shifting as though they moved with the rhythm.

They didn't seem to notice Miryam, so she inched closer to the circle—and froze.

The monks seemed to hover inches above the ground.

That cannot be, she thought.

A wind began to stir inside the circle, lifting dust and tugging at the hems of their robes.

Just like in the forest with Ved.

Enrapt, Miryam let the sound of the chant fill her ears and reverberate throughout her body. The air spun faster and faster, buzzing to the steady beat until the very center of the circle glowed. At first, it was only a pinprick of blue light. Then it flared, swelling into a pulsing orange flame.

She gasped. The sound echoed sharply through the cave and broke the chant. One monk's eyes snapped open. In an instant, the flame vanished, the wind died, and those in the circle collapsed to the ground with a thud.

Every face turned toward Miryam. She stood frozen, eyes wide, trying to speak, yet no words would come.

Chapter 23

LEAH

Tilting her head, Leah picked up the tomato seedling, twisting and turning it in her hands. Trying to forget about the weird bookstore encounter and the embarrassing meeting with Tate from a few days ago, she intently gazed at the small plant. A thin, fuzzy stem emerged from a red plastic cup of soil. The plant's leaves poked out, and a few tiny, yellow flowers graced the top of it, future tomatoes in the making. "Did they give you instructions?" she asked.

"No," Hana said, taking the tiny plant and placing it on their kitchen counter. She flung her backpack onto the floor. "We're supposed to learn how to take care of it ... on our own."

"Hmm ..." Leah tried to focus on the plant, but there was something else she felt she needed to do today. But she couldn't remember what it was. That's how these days had been for the last few months since her migraines had started.

Remembering things were as fuzzy as the tomato stem.

"Mom, it's not rocket science, but if it were, it might be easier for me." Hana scrunched her face and narrowed her eyes. "I've never actually grown anything before, but I have built a small rocket."

"First, we need to get it into a bigger pot. This cup will not hold it much longer," Leah guessed, still trying to rack her brain for the other thing she was supposed to be doing today.

She really needed to write things down, keeping a calendar like responsible adults. But remembering things had never been an issue for her before now. She grabbed a large plastic tub from under the sink. "Will this work for a pot?"

"Yes!" Hana beamed. "And we should put it outside on the patio where it can get sunlight. Do we have more soil?"

"No, we'll need to get some from the store next time we're out. Let's just give it a little water for now," Leah said, shuffling to the kitchen sink.

"See, Mom, we got this." Hana stroked the little plant's leaves.

Leah filled a small cup with water and brought it to Hana to give to the seedling. "What happens if it dies?"

"We can't let it die." Hana's voice went down an octave. "This is a huge part of my grade in biology. We *have* to keep it alive."

"Okay, okay, we will," Leah agreed.

"Plus, this tomato plant is now part of our family. And we don't let family die. Let's name it, so it will be officially a member of the Webb clan." Hana nodded her head as she drizzled water over the tender leaves, watching it soak into the soil.

"What do you want to name it?" Leah had pulled out her phone, scanning the calendar app, hoping she had given herself a reminder of what she had going on today, to no avail.

"How about Hermes?"

"Hermes? Like the Greek god."

"Yeah, but before he was the messenger god of the Greeks, he was known as a god of fertility, farming, and luck. We're going to need all of those to keep this lil guy alive," Hana said as she picked up the plant and rubbed the flower to her nose, like it was a new puppy. "Right, Hermes?"

"Hermes it is," Leah said. "And you've got pollen on your nose now."

They both laughed as Hana wiped her nose.

Leah looked at the time. Then—she remembered.

"Shit! I mean, shoot, my doctor's appointment is today, and I need to get you to your dad's before that." She sprinted to her room.

"Mommmm," Hana groaned.

Leah could hear the eye roll in her daughter's eyes.

Grabbing a shirt from the floor, she sniffed the armpits. Still clean ... enough. She threw it on. Then, she started pulling on some pants when her phone rang from the kitchen. The *Addams Family* theme song played throughout the small apartment.

"Hana, can you" — Leah hopped to her doorway, pants still undone — "get my phone?"

"Got it," Hana yelled back. "Hello?"

Leah strained to listen as she sucked in her belly to button her jeans. *When did these pants get so tight?*

"No, she's not here right now," she could hear Hana say over the phone. "I'll tell her you called. Bye."

Hana walked into her mom's room frowning.

"Who was it?" Leah asked.

"Bill collector. Mom, that's the third one this week. Are we going to be okay, like, financially? I can ask Dad for some money if you need me to."

"We're fine," Leah said bluntly. "And we don't need your dad's help. I just had to divert some of my money to pay for the lawyer, so we might get a few calls from our utility companies until I get paid again."

"Mommmm ..." Hana's eyes doubled back in her head.

"Stop with the eye rolls. Don't worry, you'll still be able to text your friends and watch your favorite shows." Leah tried to joke, but she could see the worry on her daughter's face, something no parent ever wants to see in their child. "I'll pick up more clients at the store. Just things like custody cases and doctor appointments keep getting in my way." She let out an exhausted sigh.

"Okay." Hana nestled into Leah's chest, squeezing her tight. "But I think you're going to be late for that doctor's appointment."

Leah glanced at her phone's time. *Fuck.* She was right. "Why am I perpetually late?"

They pulled into the long driveway at Seth's mini-mansion. Hana got out and turned to wave goodbye to Leah. "Love you, Mom."

"Love you too," Leah said.

She started backing out of the driveway when Seth came out the door and flagged her down. She rolled down her window. "I'm already late for an appointment. I don't have time."

"It will just be a minute."

Leah hated his commanding presence and how he just expected everyone to conform to him. "Fine, what?"

"No need to be snappy. I just heard that you might be having some financial struggles. It's understandable with your inability to manage, well, anything. It's amazing you're not living on the streets." Seth smirked.

Heat filled her cheeks. "How did you—"

"C'mon, Leah, you know I have my connections. I have friends in the city utility department who alerted me to your late water bill, which I paid for you."

He paused, waiting for her reply.

Leah just seethed, wondering if she could 'accidentally' run him over in his own driveway.

"You're welcome," Seth added.

"Seth ..." Leah couldn't find the right words to say anything back. He always managed to get one over on her.

She felt defeated, again.

"I believe it's 'thank you' that you're trying to say," he said.

"I have to go. I have an appointment." Leah pursed her lips, willing herself not to say anything he could use against her in court.

"One more thing, I need the contact info for Hana's music teacher." Seth pulled out his phone. "Delilah and I are thinking of starting her on piano lessons, but I thought I'd talk to her teacher first and get her opinion on Hana's ability. You know, to make sure it was worth our investment."

The investment? On our daughter?! Leah wanted to scream and rage, but she squeezed her mouth shut this time. How the hell Seth thought he was the better parent astounded her. He viewed everything through the lens of how it would benefit or hurt him. Whereas Leah loved Hana and would do anything for her.

She took a deep breath in and out. "First, Hana can do *anything* she sets her mind to. You'd know that if you spent any actual time with her. You don't need to check with a teacher. Second, can't your police connections get this information too?"

"I could have, but I *thought* this would be easier. I see I was wrong." Seth stared at her, unflinching.

"Oh, wow, I think that's the first time you've ever admitted being wrong about something," Leah retorted.

"The contact info ...?" Hand on his hip, he tapped his foot on the ground.

She snatched her purse from the car floor, searching for her phone. When she pulled it out, the leather journal came out with it, dropping in her lap.

A small silver object fell out with it.

"What's that?" Seth perked up, eyeing the piece of metal.

"None of your business," Leah snapped back, quickly stuffing the metal object and journal back in her purse.

"Whatever." He shifted in place, furrowing his brow.

While Seth sounded irritated, what was more interesting was that he sounded *uneasy*. And that was rare. Leah racked her brain to explain the sudden change in demeanor. He was the last person in the world with whom she wanted to discuss the journal. She hadn't even told Kat yet. Even so, it made her pause, and Leah made a mental note for later.

Scrolling through her phone contacts, she said, "I'm sending her contact info to you now. Bye, Seth."

Before waiting for a reply, she pulled out and onto the street. In the rearview mirror, she could see him still standing there watching her drive away.

Fifteen minutes later, and twenty minutes late for her appointment, Leah sat in the waiting room, anxiously biting and fidgeting with her fingernails. Part of her had hoped the front office staff would force a reschedule because of her tardiness, but they said they'd still get her in.

The truth was, Leah hated going to the doctor.

She avoided it at all costs and hadn't been to one in nearly a decade. But these migraines were getting worse, along with her memory ... and her sleeping ... and that weird dizzy spell she had the other day. Even she couldn't justify not going anymore. Plus, she promised Hana.

Everything in the office smelled like the inside of disposable gloves mixed with disinfectants. A child across the way from her was crying and pulling at his mouth. The young mom looked frantic as she tried to soothe him. An older man sat next to Leah, practically hacking up his lungs. She tried to sit on the edge of her chair, farthest from him. *You never know when the next pandemic might hit.*

Leah closed her eyes for a moment, wishing she had a magical way to calm herself instantly, when she remembered the journal again. She hadn't opened it since the day at the bookstore.

The leather-bound mystery addressed to her still sat in her purse, unexamined.

Tempted to read it, she still couldn't get past the idea of reading an old journal addressed to her from the 1300s. It seemed wildly irresponsible and impossibly silly at a time like this.

Between the custody case, bills, Tate, Seth, and now that strange journal—*what was that silver piece?*—it all seemed like too much. Maybe Seth was right. Leah sniveled at the thought. What if his house was the better, more stable choice for Hana? Everything in her life just seemed to go wrong, and she was grasping to find some semblance of peace in it.

Nevertheless, Leah reached into her purse and opened the journal to the first page. There was her name again. It was so strange. She shook her head and thumbed through the pages. Between the writing, there were little doodles — a lavender here, a red cardinal there. She stopped on a page with an inkblot on it. *What happened here?* She traced her fingers across it.

To Leah, the inkblot looked like a cup. And in the cup, there was a tiny person. They were trying to get out, but the liquid was swirling around them, keeping them from escaping, as their little ink blob arms stretched out for help.

Turning the page again, Leah found what appeared more like a regular journal entry, written in exquisite handwriting. It read,

Sophia said I must write what happened to me in the woods. To release my anger, I must forgive, especially myself. Then why doest that seem more difficult than believing 'tis possible to float above the ground or create fire out of thin air?

The strange woman in the bookstore had created fire from her fingertips too. At the time, Leah had shrugged it off as a trick on her eyes, but what if it was real?

She continued reading only to discover the journal's author had been assaulted by a man in the woods and that she had run to a monastery for safety, the place where she was writing from. Leah could feel her own anger rise as she read the account of the attack. The woman was now feeling sinful and ashamed of herself. Leah wanted to console her and tell her it was going to be okay.

God, is this how I sound sometimes? Sinful. Shameful. Feeling like the world had done something to me, but it was all my fault too. A victim of life. So many times, she had said similar things.

Sighing loudly, she exhausted herself. The man next to her grumbled something at her, bringing her back to the present moment in the doctor's office.

"Leah Webb," a nurse called out, scanning her clipboard.

Leah looked up, closing the journal and closing her curiosity with it. Back to reality, she followed the nurse.

Chapter 24

KARAIA

The sting of a thousand tiny needles pricked Karaia's cheek as a dull, searing pain reverberated through her jaw, jolting her out of her slumber. "What's going on?!" she asked in a panic, blinking repeatedly as she scanned her living room.

Raven and Arjun stood over her, looking down.

Karaia's head ached, and her brain felt foggy. She rubbed the sore spot on her face where she had been slapped. "Was the slap *really* necessary?"

"You weren't waking up. Plus, I've always wanted to do that," Raven said, smirking. "Griffin sent me over here personally to see if you're okay."

"I came because I was bored." Arjun gave Karaia a weird look. "And because I care about you." He twirled a new holo-puzzle in his hands.

Karaia couldn't remember what day it was or why she was sleeping on her couch and not in her bed. She looked down to see that she was wearing an outfit she didn't remember putting on. She hadn't even changed into pajamas. Her tongue felt around in her mouth to realize she hadn't brushed her teeth either.

Groaning, she asked, "What time is it?"

"Eleven o'clock. You're three hours late for work." Raven eyed Karaia. "This isn't like you."

"I'm exhausted." Karaia dragged herself into a seated position. "I must have slept through my alarm."

"Have NIVA run an internal diagnostic on you, and then, we need to get to work," Raven said, pulling up her holo-screen from her wrist and scrolling through her schedule for the day.

Karaia rose and walked toward her kitchen to get some water. *NIVA, please do an internal diagnostic of my health and of your alarm system. I didn't wake up this morning.*

Right on cue, NIVA responded, *Yes, Karaia, running a diagnostic now.*

Arjun cleared his throat and spoke up. "Do you think it had anything to do with *the problem?*" He winked at Karaia as she chugged an entire glass of water. "You know, the one that you were having for the last couple of days?"

"What problem?" Raven furrowed her brow.

NIVA alerted her in her mind. *Diagnostic complete. All internal systems are within normal ranges. You are dehydrated and have slightly elevated blood pressure. Suggestions include drinking water and enjoying a NeuroCredit. I detect no issues with my alarm system.*

Karaia sighed as she poured herself another glass of water. *Buy one NeuroCredit and transfer now.*

The credit soothed her mind, and the water quelled her stomach.

Turning to Arjun, she said, "I just checked with NIVA, and she isn't detecting any issues."

"Oh, never mind. There's no *problem*," he said, winking again.

"Why are you winking?" She couldn't understand why he was acting so strangely. She racked her brain to figure out what this could be about. Raven? The upcoming gala?

"You know, *the thing* you told me about."

"Arjun, stop emphasizing certain words. I don't know what you're talking about," Karaia asserted.

He cocked his head, looking equally confused. "You really don't?"

"No."

Karaia and Raven both intently stared at him, waiting.

Swiping away his holo-puzzle, Arjun cleared his throat. "Okaaay, but you can't be mad at me for saying something. You came to me a couple of days ago ... because your NeuroCredits ... weren't working. How do you not remember this?"

"What?" Raven took a step back. "Your credits aren't working, and you didn't report it?"

Karaia held a hand up. "No, my credits are fine. Arjun, what are you talking about?"

"I'm so confused." He plopped down on Karaia's couch. "Are you saying they are working now?"

"Of course. I just transferred one." She narrowed her eyes at him. "Why would you think they weren't working?"

"Because *you* told me that," he replied, putting his head in his hands.

Karaia walked over and sat next to him. "When?"

"Tuesday at work."

Further confusion spread across Karaia's face, and she scrunched her nose. "Isn't ... today ... Tuesday?" Her eyes went wide. "Shit, my presentation! It was this morning with the board. Do you think they rescheduled?"

"What the hell is going on? You already gave your presentation." Raven waved her hands at the three of them. "We were all there. Today is Friday. I'm reporting this to Seromela."

"Wait. Just wait. Please." Tension rose in Karaia's stomach. Her head still ached. "We can figure this out. Just give me a minute."

She closed her eyes. *NIVA, buy and transfer one credit.*

Transfer complete. Enjoy, NIVA replied.

The serotonin hit Karaia's brain and calmed her. She let out a deep breath, racking her brain for answers. Only to be met with none. Opening her eyes, she looked from Raven to Arjun and back, lips pursed.

Silence engulfed the room.

Arjun's eyes lit up. "I think I know what happened."

"What?" Karaia and Raven both said at the same time.

Looking right at Karaia, he said, "You were probably abducted by aliens, and now, they've wiped your memories." His serious expression slowly turned to a grin.

Karaia knew he was trying to lighten the mood, but she didn't feel like laughing just yet.

"I really can't remember a single thing from the past three days." She furrowed her brows, trying to remember anything about the week, but the last thing she remembered was leaving work Monday evening.

Then, blank.

Now, she was here.

Arjun stood up and started pacing the room. "Okay, for real. The simplest solution is most often the correct one." He pulled out his holo-puzzle again and started fidgeting with it unconsciously. "If your memories *were* wiped, then whoever did it must have also fixed your NeuroCredits. It's the only thing that explains everything going on." He nodded, looking smug.

Raven rolled her eyes and grunted. "I think you've been watching too many conspiracy theory shows."

Karaia rose, stretching her achy muscles. Her mind and body were finally waking up. Glancing down at her arm, she saw that she had a few bruises near her wrists. *Where did those come from?* Shaking her head, she asked, "No one knows anyone who has actually had a brain wipe done, right?"

"Reminder, brain wiping is illegal," Raven added.

Karaia ignored Raven's last statement. "Assuming this is a possibility, who even has that kind of technology?"

"It could have been Seromela, for all we know," Arjun said.

"No way, I would have known about it," Raven said.

Arjun raised his eyebrows. "Your brain might have been wiped too."

They sat in silence again for a few seconds.

Raven spoke up. "This is all speculation. I'm late for a meeting. Karaia, I'm going to submit you for a psych eval later today, and if that comes back clear, we can all move on from this. See you at work soon?" Without waiting for a reply, she headed toward the door, checking her holo-feed one more time.

Karaia nodded slowly in agreement. "Sounds like a plan."

The words escaped her mouth before she really believed them herself. There was just something she couldn't yet move on from. But she couldn't let anyone else know.

Before leaving, Raven swung around, facing Arjun and Karaia again. "You know what we need to do tonight to shake this off?" She asked, a mischievous grin spreading across her face.

Karaia had only seen that look on Raven when she was out partying, not usually during work hours. She tilted her head. "What?"

Raven slowly nodded. "Remember what tomorrow is?"

Karaia was putting it together. "If today is Friday, that means that tomorrow is—"

"The gala, bitches! And this whole weekend, Seromela employees get free admission into any nightclub or bar, including free drinks and food, to celebrate the 50th anniversary." Raven eyed Karaia and Arjun both. "Tonight, we are all going out."

Arjun tensed up.

Karaia averted her eyes. And for the first time, she shared some of his socially awkward feelings. She didn't feel like going out tonight. *Just act normal. Like nothing is wrong.* However, something was off inside of her. And she was afraid to speak that out loud.

"Oh, and Arjun," Raven added, "there's a new combat club that just opened. Supposedly, they have the latest VR tech. What could be better than games, fighting, and clubbing all in the same place?" She winked at him.

He blushed.

Karaia was jealous of Raven's ability to move on so quickly. To not question. To not wonder.

"That sounds great. We'll meet you there," Karaia said, putting on a smile as Raven left her house, hoping she wouldn't hear the doubt in her voice.

After double-and triple-checking with her she was okay, Arjun left shortly after, leaving Karaia alone with her thoughts.

She tried to be okay. She wanted to be. But something gnawed at her core, and she couldn't shake it. Heading to her bedroom, she took two more credits, letting her muscles relax again. Then, proceeded to let her body go through the motions of readying herself for work.

With a psychological evaluation and full scan of her NIVA system complete, Karaia had been cleared by Seromela's AI psychiatrist to return to work. Whatever was happening to her, it wasn't physical or mental. She tried to be thankful for that and go about her day. But the hours crept by, taunting her.

Arjun stopped by her office multiple times, checking on her like a mother hen. She convinced him she was still fine, and he seemed satisfied ... enough. Until the next time ... when she convinced him to take a few more credits and promised not to dance with Raven at the club tonight.

Finally, she made it to the end of what seemed like the longest day of work ever. She called her grandma on her ride home and listened to her drone on about the upcoming parades and festivities.

Now, Karaia was alone with her thoughts again.

She exhaled as she looked in her bedroom mirror, smoothing her straightened hair and donning her cutest clubbing dress. She looked fucking hot. But she didn't feel that way. Unconsciously, she tugged at the silver necklace she wore. *Shake it off, Karaia. Go out and have fun.*

"Incoming delivery," she heard a robotic voice call out from her home system.

Karaia walked to her mail delivery chute in her living room. She lifted the lid and pulled out a box. A small digital note hovered above it.

> *Karaia,*
> *Glad to hear you're okay.*
> *Wear this tomorrow at the gala.*
> *Griffin*

She opened the box and found the most luxurious dress inside. She held it up in front of her. Bold red and made from the finest synthetic silk.

Griffin *knew* what he wanted.

Normally, she would have been excited to wear a new dress from him, but something about the way he expected her to wear it irked her this time.

Shrugging off the feeling, she took a credit and headed out the door to meet her friends.

Entering the club was like entering another world. Completely decked out with the latest in holo-projections, the club's walls looked like waves of crashing blue water mixed with colorful electric streaks running through them. The music pumped to the same beat as the waves on the walls, while holo-images of the latest VR game characters walked around the room.

"Karaia!" Raven waved from a corner table of the nightclub as she approached.

"Hey," was all she said back.

"You've got to check out this new game," Raven exclaimed. "I'm going up against Arjun in the next round. You can't miss it!"

"I won't. Let me grab a drink first," Karaia said, trying to sound like she was having fun ... when really, she had taken ten credits before arriving and still felt uneasy.

Raven and Arjun took off toward the gaming area as Karaia headed toward the bar. She scrolled through the holographic drink menu. Instead of alcohol, most drinks were made with synthetic pharmaceuticals now. They produced a similar effect without alcohol's negative side effects. The drinks were also made with bio-bots, tiny organic nanobots that could instantly turn off the drugs' effects in your system. This way, no one ever left a bar intoxicated. Bar fights could cease immediately, and people could be cut off within seconds.

Safety first in all aspects of life in New Soteria, Karaia chuckled to herself as she went into marketing mode in her own head. She held her fingerprint over the button for a Dragon-slayer Xantini.

"Thank you, Karaia Pine. Enjoy your complimentary drink this weekend," the machine replied.

After a few moments, a drink appeared in the dispenser, and she took it.

As Karaia turned away from the bar, she scanned the club. It was packed with people celebrating the 50th anniversary of Seromela. *Keep them happy and distracted. It makes for better consumers and citizens.* So much of what she had learned in her marketing classes growing up had to do with the psychology of the human mind and what people wanted.

Make people comfortable and content, and almost all the world's problems go away. At least they did in New Soteria.

But what was life like outside the walls?

Trying to shake off her intruding thoughts, Karaia took a sip of her iridescent green drink as she headed for the gaming area.

In the center of the club, people congregated around a large combat ring, chatting, drinking, and waiting in anticipation. On either side were two VR holo-suits and platforms. Each player would use their suit to enter a virtual world to fight their opponent on the opposite side. Then, spectators would watch what the players were seeing in their virtual world in a holographic projection in the combat arena.

It was the only time fighting was allowed in New Soteria.

Karaia stepped closer and could see Raven and Arjun getting into their respective holo-suits, attaching their emitters and preparing for their match. Once inside the virtual world, each contestant had to choose an avatar to fight with—along with a weapon.

A few minutes passed.

First, on Arjun's side of the arena, a three-dimensional, tall blue alien appeared. In his hand was a glistening white staff. At one end of the staff, there was a fiery blue and green ball of electricity, crackling and snapping, as he whipped it through the air in a figure-eight motion around him.

Then, on Raven's side, a huge, gnome-like warrior came into existence, holding a giant sword. She tossed it back and forth between her rough, warty hands.

People gathered closely around the arena. The music quieted, and a hush of silence fell across the club.

They were ready.

A speaker called out, "5 ... 4 ... 3 ... 2 ... 1. Let the battle begin!"

The crowd roared with excitement.

First, Raven's avatar charged at Arjun's, sword held out in front of her. He easily deflected it with his staff, swirling around to a different side of the arena. He shot a lightning bolt out of his staff, hitting Raven's side. Fake blood trickled out of her avatar's skin.

Karaia glanced up at the scoreboard. Raven's health had gone down.

Quickly, she recovered and slashed her sword at Arjun, hitting one of his legs. Bluish-green liquid oozed out of his wound. His health score dropped drastically. People started screaming louder as the battle edged closer to its finale. Spotlights flashed all around, following each avatar, and dramatic battle music added to the excitement.

Normally, Karaia would be up front yelling with the best of them, but instead, she found herself stepping back, watching it from a distance.

Just then, a spotlight flashed in her direction. Squinting, she closed her eyes.

She was back at her childhood home. A memory she had forgotten. It was nearly pitch black, but lights flashed around her. *Flashlights.* She ran because she thought it was her dad playing a game at first. Scurrying under their table, she thought, *Are we playing hide and seek, and he forgot to tell me?*

"Mai, you can't let them do this!"

It was her father.

He wasn't playing. She could hear his heavy breathing. And shuffling of feet as he cried out to her mother, Mai.

Little Karaia strained to see in the intermittent darkness. Men wearing black suits had her father by the arms, dragging him toward their front door.

Her mother sobbed. "Damon ... I'm sorry."

Bursting from under the table, Karaia ran into the room and yelled out, "Daddy!"

She could see now that the lights were gun lights and held up toward her father, while some men kept a hold of him. Her mother just stood there, crying to herself.

"Don't take my daddy!" she bellowed.

Mai grabbed her and held her back.

As they pulled her father out of their house, he called out, "Karaia, I love you. Keep your necklace close to your heart."

Then, he was gone.

"Are you okay?" Arjun loomed over her face.

Karaia could feel the cold of the hard floor beneath her skin. Her butt ached. Something sticky covered one of her hands. She was back in the nightclub.

"What happened?" she said, lifting herself to a seated position.

"You fell." Raven reached down to help Karaia up. "*And* you missed the most epic win against Arjun."

She mock-punched Arjun in the arm.

He flinched.

"It wasn't *that* epic," Arjun groaned, helping hoist Karaia to her feet and getting her to a table. "You really didn't miss much."

"What happened to you?" Raven asked, sipping on her drink.

Karaia thought for a moment, seeing the flashing lights in her memory and her father being taken away. It wasn't the story she had been told. Her grandma told her that both of her parents had left for the Settlement ... willingly. A sudden urge to cry bubbled up inside her. She squeezed her tears back inside.

"I don't know," she lied as she wiped away a stray tear from her eye. "I think I slipped ... and hit my head. Where's my drink?" She looked around before she remembered the wet, sticky stuff on her hand. "Oh, never mind."

Arjun rubbed her back, but he wasn't *really* there. Karaia recognized the familiar blank stare on his face. He was taking a credit. His shoulders instantly relaxed.

Raven rose from the table. "Well ... take a credit or two. I'll get us fresh drinks and a sani-towel for your hands."

Coming back to, Arjun turned to Karaia. "So, do you want to hear about that match? I almost had her."

Karaia was staring off into the distance.

"Hello, Karaia? Where are you?" He waved his hand in front of her face.

Karaia crooked toward him, her mind still racing, refusing to take a credit yet, the memory fresh in her mind. "Arjun, do you wonder what life is like outside the walls? Do you know anything about the Settlement?"

"Not really."

"Do you think if someone left for the Settlement, would they be allowed to return to New Soteria?"

He slurped the last of his faux-tini. "Um, is this a rhetorical question?"

"I was just thinking about my parents. They left for the Settlement when I was little. At least, that's the story my grandma told me. They were supposed to come back for me, but they never did." Tears welled up in Karaia's eyes again. Her throat tightened. Tempted to transfer a credit now, she still chose not to, letting herself sit in the discomfort.

She didn't want to forget how she felt.

Arjun bit down on his bottom lip. "I'm sorry about your parents. Maybe they had their reasons for leaving. You've lived a good life though, right? You've got your grandma, your brother, your friends. I mean, like I'm probably the most important person in your life." He elbowed her, trying to make her laugh.

Karaia smiled. "Thank you. I needed that." She took a moment to physically shake off her feelings. "I'm not sure why I'm thinking about all this."

"More drinks are here!" Raven sat down, handing Karaia and Arjun two drinks. "A spicy Fire Serpent for you, Karaia, and a sad Blue Alien for you, Arjun."

"Ha ha," Arjun said dryly, "I'm laughing on the inside."

"Thanks." Karaia took a sip of her new drink. A hint of what tasted like habanero pepper hit her tongue as it went down her throat.

"Wait, wait, let's make a toast," Raven said as she held up her glass. "In honor of the 50th anniversary of Seromela and living in the happiest country in the world. Cheers!"

They clinked their glasses together.

Karaia forced a smile.

Raven took a huge sip of hers and looked directly at her. "Now, we need to get serious. What *are* you wearing to the gala tomorrow?"

Knowing she couldn't keep this up all night without more credits to calm her mind, Karaia transferred ten NeuroCredits, let the waves overtake her, and smiled widely as she described the dress Griffin had picked out for her.

Chapter 25

MIRYAM

Ved rose from the chanting circle and rushed to Miryam. Dust danced in the candlelight as the hem of his robe brushed against the cave ground. His hand gently closed on her forearm.

She flinched.

He swiftly removed his hand and whispered a hurried, "I'm sorry."

The last time she'd touched Ved, she'd longed for his hand against hers. To let it linger on her skin. To feel its warmth. He had made her feel so safe and so *seen*. But now? She was not sure what she felt, only that it was different. *She* was different. The word 'spoiled' echoed in her mind. Dempsey had ruined her. And now, even standing this close to Ved, all she could feel was the lump of coal in her chest, where her heart should have been.

Miryam desperately wished she could turn back time and run away with Ved that day in the woods beneath the midday Sun. Far, far away from it all, just the two of them. Like a pair of birds going south for the winter. But never coming back. Much had changed since then. And that world seemed so very distant now.

Yet here she stood, confronted with another seemingly impossible truth. So, maybe not all was lost, and there was still a world in which her dreams could come true. Miryam had to hope.

It was all she had left.

"Is this ... *magic*?" The word slipped out in a whisper.

"'Tis ..." Ved's eyes darted to the others still seated in the circle. "... a meditation of sorts."

Soft murmurs rippled through the monks and nuns, flustered whispers bouncing against the cave walls.

"Miryam," Sophia said quickly, rising to her feet, "how about you and I speak in the kitchen? There is an herbal tonic there—'tis good for the soul."

Miryam hesitated, her eyes fixed on Ved. "Can Ved join us?"

Sophia looked from her to Ved, then back to the rest of the group. "That would not be wise. Come now," she said, turning toward the cave's exit, expecting Miryam to follow.

Ved opened his mouth as if to speak, then closed it again.

Miryam searched his eyes, desperate for answers.

"Follow Sophia. She shall explain everything." He gave her a small bow and returned to the circle. "I will find you later. I promise."

Miryam nodded and trailed after Sophia.

They made their way up the stairs, through the courtyard, and into the main hall without a word being spoken between them. Miryam pressed her lips tightly closed, waiting, trusting what Ved said, that all would be explained soon. But the questions bombarded her mind regarding what she had experienced in the cave. She wondered if her eyes had been playing games with her? Or if she had really seen people floating above ground and creating fire out of thin air? She speculated whether even more was possible than what she had seen?

She hoped for the latter. With each step, her anticipation grew, and the lump in her chest softened.

Smells from the kitchen greeted them as they entered—fresh bread, roasted rabbit, and chamomile blossoms. Miryam inhaled deeply, her shoulders relaxing. A small fire burned in the stove. Sophia lifted a kettle of hot water, set out two wooden cups, and pinched herbs into each. She poured the sizzling water over them, releasing a sweet steam. Sitting down at the long oak table in the center of the kitchen, Miryam cradled her cup in both hands, letting the warmth seep into her palms.

Sophia sat across from her. "What do you ponder you saw in the cave?"

Miryam thought for a moment, her eyes shifting back and forth. How did one begin to explain what she had seen? It had looked very much like Benedictine monks and nuns practicing *far more* than their daily prayers and silent study of scripture. Deep down, the thought thrilled her. But should she admit that? What if she was wrong, and it wasn't magic at all—simply some monastic ritual she didn't understand? If she revealed her interest, would Sophia brand her as a heretic? She took a sip of her drink, praying the right words came to her. But none did.

Sophia had been the one to tend her after her fall, the one who watched over her after the attack. The lines on her face spoke of years of patient wisdom, and her eyes shone with kindness, not judgment. Miryam felt she could trust her.

"Was it ... *magic*?" she whispered, biting her lip as she waited for the answer in both trepidation and a tinge of excitement.

Sophia smiled.

At once, Miryam's fears waned. And the questions she had been holding in tumbled out. "First—are not monks and nuns meant to live apart? Are you truly a nun? Is this truly an abbey? Are you *witches*? And if so, do you not tremble with the new earl hunting down heretics? And how did you float so? How did you create flames out of nothing?" She stopped to catch her breath, eyes bright. "I always knew magic was real ... Can you teach me?"

Sophia chuckled softly. "Ved did say you were full of questions. I see he did not speak in jest. I shall answer, but best I begin at the first."

Miryam nodded eagerly, taking another sip.

Sophia cleared her throat. "For hundreds of years, the cave you saw served as no more than a root cellar to the monastery above. Then, an abbot unearthed a jar buried deep within the stone, filled with old parchments. They bore teachings said to be from our Lord Christ, yet not the same as those preached in the village church. These teachings were more ... *esoteric*. Do you know this word?"

Miryam shook her head.

"The teachings taught of hidden prayers and secret chants. Some—not all—of the abbots began studying these texts and so began our practice."

"Why must they be secret?" Miryam furrowed her brows.

"Once, our brethren sought to share these teachings with the Church. We were near cast out for it and swore we would destroy the texts." Sophia glanced around as if they might be heard. "We did not. Since that day, we have kept our silence. Were the earl or bishop to learn of our practice, we would be condemned to death."

Miryam shivered in her seat at the thought. How was it that Sophia stayed so calm speaking of her potential death?

"Most who live here at the monastery, and across the creek at the convent," — Sophia nodded in the direction — "do not know of these teachings. Yet, those of us who do, gather *as one,* both men and women. For we believe both man and woman are equal in the sight of God."

Through wide eyes, Miryam said, "How wondrous it must be to stand equal with men."

"Outwardly, we are but an abbey. Yet below, in that cave, we practice what some would call sorcery. We call it *pleroma*. It means the fullness of Spirit." Sophia laid a hand on her chest. "And it dwelleth in every human soul."

Miryam's heart swelled.

"You must tell no one." Sophia steadied her gaze. "We trust you to guard our secret."

"Why would you trust *me*?" Guilt weaved its way into Miryam's heart, overshadowing her excitement. She desperately wanted to be a part of everything Sophia was mentioning, but ... she felt unworthy now. As Dempsey's face flashed before her, she squeezed her eyes shut, trying hard not to let him win. Not to let his grip upon her mind change her—mold her—into something she wasn't.

Or have I always been unworthy?

Sophia must have seen her inner turmoil, as her gentle hand reached across the table and softly pressed to her shoulder. Warmth coursed through Miryam like a soothing balm.

Sophia said, "I *know* we may trust you. That is the gift of such sight."

Miryam gave a nod in reply. Breathing in deeply, she allowed the warmth of Sophia's being to enwrap her. And she allowed the thought to enter her mind that maybe she was not in fact bad, or spoiled, or unworthy, despite her conflicting emotions. The thought of holding such a precious secret—and knowing magic was indeed real—enticed her. She had always felt there was more to life, and perhaps this was what she had long missed.

Plus, it might mean she got to spend more time with Ved.

"I promise not to tell a soul." Her eyes flicked nervously, hesitation battling with curiosity. At last, curiosity won. "So ... can everyone use pleroma?"

Sophia laughed gently. "I see your hunger to learn. But these teachings are not to be taken lightly. You have suffered a grievous wound. Your first work must be healing."

It was not the answer Miryam wished to hear. She loathed being reminded of what had happened, or being told what she could and could not do.

"No, I am ready. I can feel it. This is what I am meant for." Desperation sharpened her tone.

Sophia remained resolute in her answer. "'Tis possibly true. But you must face what was done to you first. Have you written in the journal?"

The memory made Miryam burn with guilt, shame, and above all, powerlessness—a feeling she swore never to endure again. And yet, her longing to wield pleroma outweighed them. "If I do the work ... if I face my feelings ... then, will you teach me?"

Sophia sighed and finished her brew. "I sense great power in you, child. Your spirit is strong; your heart is eager. But hear me—light and darkness dwell in every soul. Pleroma may be turned to good or ill. Those with strength such as yours tempt the darker path most, should pain or anger sway them." She held up a finger and pointed straight into Miryam's soul. "'Tis why you must learn forgiveness foremost—for thyself and for others. Only love and goodness in your heart shall make it safe for you to hold such power. Tell me, is that truly what you desire?"

It was so much to take in. *Pleroma. Spirit. Light. Darkness.*

Miryam did not yet understand it all, but she knew one thing. She wanted to do good in the world. "I do. I shall do the work you ask."

"Very well." Sophia inclined her head. "Then I welcome you, Mistress Miryam ... to the Mystery School for the Order of the Tree of Life."

Chapter 26

LEAH

"You're kidding, right?" Kat sat across the booth from Leah and Hana, sipping her oat-milk chai latte, gently flipping through fragile journal pages.

"Have you ever known my mom to joke about something like *this*?" Hana said, motioning toward the ancient text.

Kat passed it to her.

Hana examined the book from all angles as if it were one of her science projects. Then, she picked up the wiggly silver piece that had been tucked inside. She bit down on it.

"Be careful," Kat snapped.

Startled, Hana gently set down the silver piece along with the journal and immediately pulled out her phone and started texting friends.

"It sounds crazy. I sound crazy. This whole thing *is crazy*," Leah said, rolling her eyes at herself. "But what if it's *real*?" She whispered the last part.

The only thing that seemed normal about any of this was their usual booth in the coffee shop, which they met at weekly. Leah took a sip of her bitter black nectar, trying to let it soothe her. At least Leah had that to rely upon. Whereas nearly everything else in her life was crumbling.

"Honestly, Leah, I can't believe this didn't end up in the trash," Kat said. "That's a step in the right direction for you."

Leah snorted. "Well, I did throw it in the trash *once* but then got it back out again. Then, it sat in my purse for a week. Until I was bored in the waiting room. Now, I've read at least a quarter of it, and I don't

175

know ... what to think." She took a big gulp of her coffee. "You're my all-things-supernatural person. Thoughts?"

"You're right, I am. And we'll figure this mystery out." Kat beamed as she pushed the book toward Leah. "How did your doctor appointment go?"

"Not much to tell yet. I have to go in for an MRI in a few days."

"Good, I'm glad you're taking care of it." Kat nodded. "Let me know if there's anything I can help with."

"I *am*. That's why you're here—to look at this." Leah eyed the journal in front of her like it was a frightening creature she was afraid to touch.

"Of course." Kat put her focus back on the journal. "But you realize you should know as much as I do about this stuff. We own a shop together."

"But I didn't believe any of it, until ..." Leah chugged the rest of her drink, feeling the grains of the French press pour lingering in her mouth. "... this journal. It just feels so *real*. I can't explain it." She threw her hands in the air. "This is so *weird*. I'm going crazy, right?"

"Mom," Hana said without looking up from her phone, "*weird* is the best!"

"Well, it's possible. Not the you-being-crazy part, but that this journal is an authentic account from the 1300s. There were actual mystery schools in the Middle Ages. Some very well-known mystics came from that period. Margery Kempe, Hildegard of Bingen, Catherine of Sienna."

Hana and Leah gaped at Kat.

"Am I the only one studying Christian mysticism in my free time?" They all laughed.

"Apparently," Leah replied. "What do you think it means? Not the content, but my connection to it. Why is *my name* in it?"

"Maybe a coincidence?" Hana chimed in.

"Coincidences happen rarely ... in my opinion." Kat straightened up in her seat. "Leah, sweetie, I think you are connected to this journal—this woman—but I don't know why. I'd ask your spirit guides for guidance and hold that silver piece while you do. It should strengthen the connection," she instructed.

"My spirit guides? Oh, my godddddd." Leah slumped in the booth, not believing she was entertaining such thoughts. "Until yesterday, I didn't believe any of this crap." Glancing at the time on her phone, she said, "Tate should be here soon. Let's leave the mystery of the magical journal for later."

She shoved it, along with the silver piece, into her purse.

"Mom ... too late," Hana said, pointing to the door.

Tate had just walked in, spotting them immediately.

"Maybe he didn't hear me." Leah tried to slide down farther into her seat—into oblivion—in the noticeably quiet, empty café.

She thought about the last couple of weeks. Her visit with Gertrude at the bookstore. Her increasing migraines. This strange connection to this ancient journal. She didn't know what was real and didn't trust to do much of anything by herself at this point. Luckily, Kat offered to drive them today.

Tate approached the table and winked at Leah. "Hey. Don't worry, I heard nothing about a mysterious journal. I'm just going to grab a coffee. Did you need another one?"

Leah nodded slowly. "Plain black coffee, please."

After she was sure he was distracted with ordering, she placed her forehead on the table and covered her head with her arms. "How embarrassing." She whispered under her breath, "Why does he have to be so handsome *and* my lawyer?"

"Mom, eww." Hana looked up from her phone.

Leah regretted saying those words out loud. Hana didn't need to know about her love life, or lack thereof.

Kat's eyes lit up, and she clapped her hands. "I completely forgot about the whole beach party meeting! And now, he's your lawyer. Ooooo, this is going to be so interesting. What do you think—"

"Sshhh!" Leah nodded toward Hana.

"Mom, what don't I know?" Hana fixed her eyes on Leah. "I *need* to know."

"It's nothing, sweetie. I'll tell you later." The last part Leah said between her teeth, smiling.

Tate was headed back to the table.

"I think this is my cue to leave," Kat said, gathering up her things and having one last peek at the journal in Leah's bag. "I'll just be at that table over there when you're ready to go." She got up and settled at another table across the café.

Tate took her place.

He reached out his hand toward Hana. "Hi, I'm Tate. You must be Hana. I feel like I know you already from your mom's account."

Hana blushed and shook his hand. "Nice to meet you."

"You too. I only wish it were on different terms. Today, we need to go over your part of the custody case." Tate took out his laptop and some folders. "I've already gotten your mom's information. I need to ask you some questions, okay? It will probably be very similar to what you went over with the Guardian ad Litem."

"Sure, anything to help my mom," Hana said as she leaned in toward Leah and gave her a side hug.

"You're a strong young woman already, but this custody battle could get ugly. Can you start by telling me what your relationship is like with your father?" Tate asked, ready to jot down any notes.

"He's not that bad, at least with me, always making sure I have what I need—*and want*—most of the time. He's different with Mom though." She cast her eyes down. "They've never gotten along since I was little. It seems like he's always getting back at her for doing something, even if she didn't. I love spending time with both of them, but *separately*. I don't want anything to change."

Leah could tell from the strain in Hana's voice that she really meant what she said, and it saddened her that Hana even had to go through this.

"Thank you," Tate said, taking a sip of his coffee for the first time.

Leah watched him as he licked a drip off his bottom lip. She imagined hers on his again. The way he tasted salty and sweet at the same time. A warmth settled in her groin. She shook off the feeling as quickly as it came.

Fuck, focus, Leah.

Tate continued, "It's going to mean a lot to a judge that you don't want things to change. That will help your mother's case immensely. Do you have any idea why your father would try for full custody now?"

"Not really." Hana scrunched her face. "I can guess it has something to do with the fact that Delilah is moving in, and they're getting married."

Leah gasped. "They're getting married too?"

"Ohhhh ..." Hana grimaced. "I thought I told you."

"It doesn't matter." Leah sighed. "He's always been obsessed with having the perfect family and perfect life, and I don't fit into that. Hana does."

Leah's second coffee had gotten cold, and she was just finishing up the last, this time avoiding the gritty bits at the bottom.

The conversation continued like this, with Tate asking Hana questions that might be helpful to their case for another thirty minutes. He nodded between sips as he jotted down his notes.

"Next is the hearing with the judge in a few weeks. As long as nothing new comes up between now and then, we have a solid case." Tate turned to face Leah, smiling. "We just need to go over the logistics of the actual hearing day before we're done here."

Leah smiled back at him—longer than she should have.

Damn those lips and that smell.

"Mom, it's almost five, and I promised Savannah I'd help her with biology tonight. Can I get a ride from Kat to her house?" Hana batted her eyes at Leah, grinning wide. "Pretty please?"

Flustered, Leah smoothed out her shirt and looked at Hana. "You've got to check with Kat, but it's fine with me. I just need to figure out how I am going to get home ..." Leah's sentence trailed off because Hana was already up and walking toward Kat's booth.

Kat nodded in agreement as she began packing up her things.

"You're okay with this?" she asked, walking up to their table. "How are you going to get home?"

"That's what I was trying to say." Leah raised her eyes at her daughter. "Can you just wait another half hour? This shouldn't take—"

"I can take you home," Tate interjected.

A mischievous grin spread across Kat's face. "I think that sounds like a wonderful idea," she said as she already began leading Hana away. "See you later!" She waved her hand behind her head as they exited the cafe.

Silence filled the space for a moment.

Leah awkwardly looked at Tate. "You really don't have to."

"I'm pretty sure your ride just left. And L.A. isn't exactly known for its public transit," Tate retorted.

"I ..." Leah thought about paying for an Uber home and cringed at the thought of the charge she couldn't afford. "... okay, fine, you can drive me home." She conceded.

The rest of the meeting with Tate went smoothly. They were focused on the case. And Hana. And the facts. This, Leah could do. As long as she didn't look too long at his gorgeous face. She even started to feel confident that they would win. And she could put all this custody shit with Seth behind her. Life could be good again. And maybe, just maybe, she could even be happy with someone like Tate.

Or Tate himself.

With that thought, Leah dared to peer up at him across the table. Tate wore a buttoned-up shirt, with the top two buttons open, exposing a bit of his smooth, tan chest. He bit down on the end of his pen as he talked and scanned his notes, switching between his notepad and his laptop. Lines creased between his eyes, wrinkling his nose and making him that much cuter. Now and then, he'd have to brush a long strand of hair that escaped from his bun out of his face, letting Leah see his eyes clearly. She wanted to gaze into them forever.

Tate glanced up and caught her staring at him.

Their eyes locked onto each other for a moment. Leah felt exposed, raw, but completely understood at the same time. She had never felt that with anyone else—ever.

"Leah ..." he uttered through those soft lips.

"Yes." Leah swallowed hard.

"Do you ever wonder ..." He stopped himself and leaned back in the booth, taking a sip of his now-very-cold coffee.

"What?"

"... why we met on the beach, and then again in my office? I just can't shake the feeling that I know you, but I can't place it." Tate rubbed his face, shaking it. "Never mind, it's silly. And not what we're here to do."

Leah wanted to agree. Leah wanted to say yes, she felt it too. She wanted to join him in exploring her ever-growing feelings toward him.

But he was right. It wasn't the time. At least not yet. So, she stayed silent.

Tate tucked his hair behind his ear. "Anyway, back to the case."

They continued going over the last of the details. Finishing up, Leah felt hopeful. With Tate by her side, she could do anything.

They packed up their things and shuffled out of the café.

But now, it was time for them to be alone in a car together. With no case to keep them distracted. Leah could feel her pulse rise. *Why am I so nervous? Gah, just talk to him like he's a normal person, like you don't want to rip his shirt off and bury your face in his chest.*

Leah got in Tate's passenger seat and put her address into the navigation system as he pulled out of the parking lot. It was an older model Prius. Moderately clean, no trash, though some dust on the dash. *He's not a neat freak, but not a slob either.* His car's back seat held the same yoga mat from his office, along with a duffle bag, probably for changing clothes for yoga. Between the seats, in a cup holder, there was a receipt for a Thai restaurant dated two days ago. *Yum.* She realized how hungry she was. Hanging from his rearview mirror was a string of Mala beads, often used in meditation.

"Where did you get those?" she blurted out.

"What?

"Your Mala beads."

"Oh, I picked those up when I was traveling in India a few years ago." Tate said, keeping his eyes on the road. "I got them at this little flea market by the sea."

"Oh," was all Leah said back. *Why am I being so awkward?!*

Tate filled the lull as he drove. "Soooo ... earlier at the café, you mentioned something about a magical journal. That sounds interesting."

Leah didn't know what she should say. Did she tell him about the journal and the silver piece that came with it? The woman from the bookstore? Her budding spirituality, despite her mind and all logic telling her she was crazy?

"Oh, it's nothing," Leah said flatly. "Just a silly old journal I found. Probably the ramblings of a crazy woman from the medieval times."

Tate's shoulders slumped a bit. "I see ..."

Think of witty banter, Leah, you're usually so good at it.

He merged onto the highway. Awkward silence.

"So did you grow up around here?" Leah asked. *Worst question ever.*

"Yeah, I did," Tate answered, perking up again. "My parents were both professors at Cal State Fullerton."

"Are they retired now?"

"No," he said, a frown spreading across his face. "They were both killed in a car accident last year."

"Oh my gosh, I'm so sorry." Leah wanted to grab his hand in hers and squeeze it. She looked over at Tate, focused on the road, but she could hear the strain in his voice.

"They both lived happy, long lives." He nodded slowly. "And I am grateful I got to be their son. My sister is now a professor there too. She just started last year in the philosophy department, just like my mom."

"How do you do that?" Leah narrowed her eyes at him. "Stay so positive in the midst of tragedy? You must think I'm overreacting to all this stuff with Hana and Seth. It's not as bad as someone you love dying."

"Well, I wasn't like this last year. I was a complete mess. But I try to really *feel* all those crappy emotions and grieve at what I lost. Only then, can I truly let them go." He switched lanes.

"That sounds so mature and *Zen* of you," Leah nudged him. "I can only wish to be as wise as you someday."

Tate wrinkled his brow. "You shouldn't do that."

"Do what?"

"Judge yourself all the time."

Leah wasn't used to someone else watching her, *seeing* into her. That was her job. She tried to deflect. "Oh, look at you now, Tate the Great, the town's newest psychic," she said in a mocking voice.

Silence filled the car once again.

Tate exited the freeway.

"I do," Leah said, shifting her eyes down, "and when I feel vulnerable, I judge others and push them away. Like right now." She huffed audibly in exasperation.

She stole a glance at Tate. He was smiling. Letting her shoulders relax a bit, she let out a little giggle.

"Thanks," he said, matching her laugh.

Leah tilted her head. "For what?"

"For being honest with me, and with yourself. When you do, your whole being lightens up. I noticed it the first time on the beach ... when you finally let go and had fun," Tate said.

They pulled up at Leah's apartment and came to a stop. The evening Sun cascaded into the car, leaving everything with a warm, soft glow.

Tate turned to her. "Like right now, you look radiant."

"Tate ..." Tension rose inside of her, pulling her in two directions. She couldn't look at him or else she might kiss him and fall madly in love, so she looked out the window instead. A migraine loomed on her mind's horizon. "Please don't. My life is too complicated right now, with the case, with the—"

"The case is going to be over in a few short weeks. A blip on the radar. I won't be your lawyer much longer. Then, we can explore what *this* is." Tate said it so firmly, so certainly, yet so gently.

Leah exhaled, jealous of his confidence. Whereas she wasn't certain about anything. "It's not just a blip on the radar for me," she asserted. "This is my life. I can't let my mind go there with you ... yet."

"You're right, it was insensitive of me to say. What I meant was, the time until this is over is just a blip. Then we have our whole lives ..." Tate trailed off, that cute crease between his eyes deepening.

Leah bit down on her own lip, sighing again.

"What else is weighing on you?" he asked.

"Nothing," Leah lied, thinking about the journal in her purse, her migraines, what the doctor might say, and how the heck it was all connected. But she had to brush those aside too. "Once the case is over, maybe we can see where this goes?"

He smiled. "Of course."

She could tell Tate wanted more from her now, but he respected her boundaries. *Damn.* That only made her like him that much more.

CHAPTER 27

KARAIA

Trumpets blared through the tubes' speakers outside and startled Karaia awake. It heralded the beginning of a celebratory weekend for New Soterians but mostly for those who lived in Sector One, where Seromela was located. For them, it was a celebration of a lifetime. No corporation had ever been elected for 50 years in the history of New Soteria.

To Karaia, it was—hopefully—something to keep her distracted from wondering about her parents and the strange memories that kept surfacing.

She pulled up the holo-screen from her wrist.

9:17 a.m.

She had overslept—again. Luckily, it was the weekend.

Typically on a Saturday, she'd be up around six, get in a quick workout, eat breakfast—and have coffee, of course—and be ready, all before nine. But today? She rubbed her forehead. Today, she didn't know what was going on with her. She shuffled out of bed and toward the bathroom.

However, she did know that she wanted—*no, needed*—a distraction from the gnawing in her sixth sense that told her something was *off*. She just didn't know what that was yet.

After brushing teeth, taking a quick sani-shower, and getting dressed, Karaia headed into her kitchen. Her stomach rolled at the thought of food. *Guess it's just coffee this morning.* Settling in with her Americano on the couch, she pulled up her schedule. The entire day was filled with events, press conferences, and preparations, all for the gala tonight. Just what she needed to keep her mind busy. Then why didn't she want to do any of it?

Parades, Parties, and Phase Two. That was the title of the memo that Griffin had sent out to Seromela employees about the anniversary celebration. It included information about all the sector's officially sanctioned events, as well as a reminder to enjoy oneself and indulge in all the festivities. But the most important part of his memo was about the rollout of Phase Two, which he would personally introduce at the gala. His exact words were, "It will be history in the making. You won't want to miss it."

Incoming call from Cecelia Pine, NIVA announced in her head.

Connect, Karaia replied, pressing her temple.

"Good morning, Karaia," her grandmother said cheerfully.

"Morning, Gram."

"Do you want to join me and Cass for the parade? It starts at ten!"

Karaia didn't. But she could hear the thrill in her grandma's voice, and she didn't want to disappoint either. Plus, as head of her department at Seromela, she'd need to be seen in public today making her rounds. "Sure, I'll meet you guys in front of the fountain on the square."

"Oh, you know that's my favorite place to sit and watch the parades. I used to take your father when he was young. He would root for every float that went by, waving his little hands in the air. He and your mother would have loved to be here with us today, I just know that," Cecelia said.

At the mention of her parents, the flash of the memory from last night at the club came back. Karaia frowned and took a sip of coffee.

Would Mom want to be here with us? After she stood and watched them take away her husband, and saw her family torn apart. *Where was she now?* She wondered how much of the story she had been told was true. If any of it was. Her grandmother had lied to her since she was young. How could Karaia face her grandma today and not ask for the truth about her parents' leaving?

The multiplying questions swirled in her head. She took a credit. Her neck muscles loosened. *That's better. Now, get out that door and have some fun.*

Nausea crept over her. She pushed it away.

Or at least, try to.

Karaia left her apartment and took the rail to the Sector One Square. It was the closest thing to an old-fashioned downtown as you got in a city made of metal and glass. At least, that was what she was told downtown squares used to look like. Here, four main tubes converged and opened into a large, clear bio-dome. Stepping into it, the air felt fresher, unlike elsewhere in the tubes, where Karaia always thought it seemed a little stale. Probably because it was one of the few places with actual live greenery in the sector. The actual Sun shone on nice days, like today, and a holo-screen of a false sky would replace it when the weather turned bad, ensuring it was always pleasant in the square.

As they readied for the festivities, people laughed and chatted as they perused the merchants' shops that lined each side, the foot traffic abuzz with activity. VR and gaming centers bustled with excitement over the latest games. Vendors sold food and drink at the corner stalls. It all ensured a complete atmosphere where no one had to leave for lack of any need or want.

In the square's center, tall trees and blooming flowers scattered throughout a large, grassy expanse, beset with benches, a kids' play place, ornate fountains, and occasional tables and chairs. In the center of everything stood a large, gleaming statue of Gulliver Marshall, the founder of Seromela, inventor of NeuroCredits, and grandfather to Griffin Marshall. It made for the quintessential spot to watch the national parade.

As she scanned the crowd, Karaia inhaled the scent of the fresh leaves. Some people were already finding spots to sit along the tube walkways for the parade. She spotted her grandma and Cass in a couple of chairs, with their backs to a small fountain. As she walked by, she ran her hand through the water, feeling the cool liquid skim across her fingertips. The sound of running water trickled in her ears.

"Hey, Gram. Hey, Cass," she said as she approached.

Cass nodded his head toward her. His eyes glazed over, clearly in the middle of a VR game with his friends.

"Karaia! I'm so glad you're here," her grandmother said, smiling wide. "We saved a chair for you. Oh, and here's a synth-drink. I think it's blueberry acai with added vita-bots. Did you know they're free all day today ... for everyone?!"

Karaia took the drink and sat down in the empty chair. Music blasted through the tube speakers. A few children splashed in the fountain nearby. Gram was talking her ear off about the gala tonight. It was all very festive and ... normal. But she couldn't shake the feeling that something was *off*. It wasn't just about her parents. Or the missing memories. Or the feeling that her grandma had betrayed her. It was something else. Her sixth sense was on high alert. She took two NeuroCredits, knowing they wouldn't help.

Cecelia flagged down someone selling churros on the tube. "Kar, Cass, want one?"

Probably not what Karaia needed, but she hadn't eaten yet. "I've got this, Gram." She ordered, "Three, please."

"That will be $324," the man said as he handed them the churros.

Karaia swiped him the digital money from her wrist.

She handed one churro to her grandma, who grasped it eagerly. Then another to Cass, who reached out his hand and took it without looking. Karaia just stared at hers. Her stomach turned.

Shifting her attention to the sounds of trumpets and roars, the parade had begun. The first float came down the tube, and the crowd erupted in cheers. It was the lead Seromela Corporation float. The Official Corporation always led first in any parade, which would then be followed by the floats of different government branches, other sectors, and various businesses.

Seromela's artistic and engineering team had designed this float, probably with Griffin's guidance, and then built it with a 3D printer. The float's primary colors were gray and blue, New Soteria's colors. A massive holo-projection of a lion roaring adorned the top. It looked so real, you couldn't even tell except it wasn't jumping off the float to devour its prey. Of course, Karaia had never actually seen a real lion either, but she imagined that's what it would do. Its front paws were placed on a spinning globe of Earth. Behind the lion, people danced, each wearing a colorful masquerade mask signifying tonight's gala theme.

Karaia bit into the churro in her hand. Her stomach protested. *Not a day for churros either, I guess.*

"Gram, do you want this one too? I can't eat it."

She handed her grandmother the churro, avoiding eye contact. Afraid if she did, she might blurt out the words, *why did you lie to me my whole life?*

The distractions were not working. She took another credit.

"And I'm not feeling well," Karaia said, rising from her seat. "Gonna rest before the big night tonight."

She knew she needed to re-calibrate herself before the gala. She could hardly stand to be around people right now, especially her grandma. There was no way she'd make it through an entire day of parties and press conferences. She pulled up her schedule and deleted every event from her calendar. She'd deal with the backlash at work next week.

Going home sounded like the best idea. *I can't keep going like this. I've got to get back to my normal self.*

"Okay, sweetie. Feel better. Bye!" her grandma said between churro bites.

~◡~

One nap, a home spa treatment, and a double espresso later, Karaia stared at herself in her bedroom mirror. It felt like she was looking at someone else. Flawless makeup. Perfectly sculpted hair. The synthetic red silk she wore had a way of forming around her skin in just the right places. She smoothed out the short dress, pulling and tugging at its hem. *Griffin is going to love this dress on me,* she thought as she turned around, checking herself out. She picked up the matching feathery mask and held it up to her face, giving a fake seductive smile. *Then, why do I feel like I'm pretending?*

Karaia set the mask down, loosing a huff of frustration.

As she fixed the last bit of her makeup, she glanced in her closet and spotted a long blue and green sequined dress toward the back. A warm tingle ran up her spine.

Being a little rebellious might be exactly what she needed.

An hour later, the greenish-blue sequins shimmered and reflected the tube's lights as Karaia approached the Grand Hall, giving the appearance of hundreds of tiny scales on her skin.

"Karaia, is that you?" Raven called from the entrance. Her jaw dropped as Karaia neared.

Karaia smirked from under her mask. "Hey, Raven."

Raven was working security for the event, so she was dressed in her normal work attire—a slim black suit. "Didn't you say Griffin got you a red dress to wear?"

"I had a change of heart." Karaia shrugged. "This one just seemed more 'me' tonight."

"Well, you'd look hot as fuck in anything. I'm sure Griffin will notice that you didn't wear his dress." Raven raised her eyebrows.

"Thanks." Karaia's cheeks flushed a light pink. "And Mr. Marshall will just have to deal with it. Have you seen Arjun?"

"Yeah, he just arrived and looks as nervous as a kid getting their first Official Assignment. You should probably save him from himself. Enjoy tonight."

Karaia stepped into the hall, through the security scanners, and found Arjun hiding near a wall, his hands fidgeting with a holo-Rubik's cube, occasionally looking out at the crowd. She sneaked up behind him. "Boo."

"Aaahhhh!" He threw his hands up and turned to find Karaia, donning her mask. "Why did you do that? You know I have social anxiety. I already took ten credits on my way here. I wish I were home playing the newest version of the *Immortal One*." He paused for another credit. "Did you know that game has the highest-res graphics of any game released this year?"

"Please, no boring me with talk of holo-games tonight. I'm trying to enjoy myself." Karaia teased him, linking arms and pulling him gently toward the main hall, where glittering lights cascaded across the floor and music echoed off the walls.

"Okay, but only if we hit the buffet first," Arjun said.

"Deal." Karaia knew she needed to eat.

They headed toward a massive row of tables, all lined with extravagant appetizers and desserts. Some Karaia couldn't even recognize, and she'd been to a lot of these types of functions. Arjun grabbed a plate and started placing food on it.

"Did you hear that the *elusive* Stellan Marshall is going to be here tonight?" Arjun asked as he popped a cheeseball in his mouth.

"Griffin's son?" Karaia asked, eyes wide.

"Yeah."

Karaia was shocked. No one had seen Stellan in public for what, *ten years*? Not since the Defiers kidnapped him and his brother when they were teenagers. "What was his brother's name? The one they killed."

"Kai," Arjun said as he stuffed his face full of random treats. "They say Stellan went into a massive depression after the kidnapping. Even NeuroCredits couldn't fix him. He apparently hasn't left their house since."

"So do you know what he looks like?" Karaia selected a few tiny appetizers, hoping her stomach would allow it.

"Nope," Arjun smacked. "But I heard he's *handsome*."

"Of course you did." Karaia took a small bite of what was called The Marshall Surprise. She shuddered at the name. It tasted of mild vanilla and a hint of something she couldn't identify.

"I need a drink," she said, already heading toward the drink station. Arjun followed.

Everyone who was anyone in New Soteria was here tonight. Karaia sipped her drink and scanned the crowd. Though it was harder to recognize them in masks, she picked out the European Ambassador, the media relations secretary, and the defense secretary. Even the education director was attending, and she was notoriously reclusive.

Surrounded by their personal bodyguards near the main stage, she easily picked out Griffin Marshall, handsome in a dark gray suit and cobalt blue tie, and his wife, Rhea, elegant in a jet-black gown, the neckline plunging to her belly button. A giant white feather with diamonds protruded from her mask. While Griffin was the charismatic one, always charming those he talked to, especially in public, Rhea often looked like she wanted to murder someone.

When Griffin caught Karaia's eye, he lifted his mask and smiled, but he raised an eyebrow at her dress.

She shrugged her shoulders back at him and gave him a mischievous grin.

"I'm going to go mingle," Karaia said, grabbing a glass of synth-champagne off the table. "Wanna join?"

"What do you think?" Arjun gaped at her.

"Fine." She laughed. "I'll find you back here before Griffin's speech starts."

Karaia wove her way through the crowd, bumping elbows and brushing up against others' dresses and suits. She downed her drink and set it on a table. Determined to relax and enjoy tonight, she took another NeuroCredit and tried to lose herself in the music. Arms up, she let the beat flow through her body. Swaying back and forth, Karaia tried to push down the gut feeling that told her something was going on—bigger than her own problems. Bigger than why her parents left.

It seemed impossible to imagine what that could be.

Dance, just dance.

The rhythm carried her away. She imagined she was a bird and could fly high in the sky over the walls of New Soteria, letting the air lift her nearly weightless wings. Higher and higher. Soaring above the clouds. *Free.*

That's what she wanted to feel.

And for a moment, she did.

Until the feeling in her gut returned with a vengeance, almost doubling her over. Holding her stomach, she stopped mid-dance, feeling a pool of saliva collect in her mouth. She closed her eyes and tried to focus on calming her breathing. Why weren't the drinks or the credits helping?

As she waited there, begging the uneasiness to pass—hoping not to puke on the dance floor—someone brushed past her. Too close.

A sharp jolt slammed into her side.

An image of a dark-hooded figure running flashed before her eyes.

"Hey, watch where you're going!" Karaia shouted, spinning instinctively.

Except ... she wasn't in the tube. This was the gala. And it wasn't a hooded stranger. It was just a man. Dressed in a perfectly tailored suit.

He raised both hands in apology. "Sorry. I didn't mean to bump you."

Realizing she'd *actually* yelled—out loud—Karaia froze. "Shit. No, I'm sorry. I didn't mean to snap. I thought you were ..." Shaking it off, she said, "Long week. Forgive me?" She offered her hand to shake.

He didn't take it. His eyes cemented to the floor.

Karaia let her hand drop and studied him instead. A velvet navy mask obscured the upper half of his face, matching the deep blue of his suit. His brown hair was cropped short on one side, but the other side hung longer, artfully disheveled, draping over one eye. Clean-shaven, with a sharp jawline and a mouth that could smirk and ruin you. And if he let the stubble grow in just a little? Dangerous.

Something about him felt ... familiar. Like a dream she couldn't quite remember. She licked her lips. Maybe *he* was the distraction she needed.

Still, his gaze didn't lift.

"Hey," she breathed. "You okay?"

He nodded. "Yeah. Just taking a couple credits." He turned as if to go.

But just before he did—he glanced up.

Their eyes met.

And the air between them shifted.

Something ancient stirred from deep within Karaia's belly. She couldn't look away. The longer she melted into his dark eyes, the more she *felt*.

Awakened. Connected. Aroused.

A depth—in her soul?—that she had never felt before. And yet ... there was a deep, unspoken sadness there too. Something hidden beneath his surface. She craved to know more.

"Actually, *do* I know you?" She wished she could peek under his mask.

"There's no way you could."

"Oh, I thought ... never mind. Do you want to dance?"

Karaia grabbed two drinks from a passing server-bot and handed one to him. She leaned in, pressing her sequined body lightly against his. His muscles tensed—then slowly relaxed with the familiar release of feel-good chemicals in his brain.

He must have worse social anxiety than Arjun. That was hard for Karaia to imagine. She wondered if she shouldn't press him to dance. Maybe she was coming on too strong. But she felt a pull toward him—one she couldn't ignore. And right now, she wanted a distraction. Dancing—and maybe more—with a mysterious stranger might be exactly what she was looking for.

"I would like that," he said slowly. Then, he flashed a devilishly handsome half-smile—the one that could ruin her.

"Then, cheers," Karaia said, raising her drink.

They clinked glasses.

After finishing their drinks, he held out his hand. She took it and pulled him closer, resting her arms across his shoulders. He placed one palm gently on the small of her back, and a warmth tingled up from her core. Their bodies swayed together, their hearts pounding in sync, to the beat of the music. She could feel his body heat next to hers. Hear his breath in her ear. His scent filled her nostrils—cedarwood and orange blossom.

For the first time that day, she didn't feel uneasy at all.

This Karaia could do. She knew how to flirt. How to be seductive. She was used to it with Griffin and other partners. But something now ... was different. And she relished it. Every touch. Every little movement. Every stolen glance.

She melted.

Above them, sparkling lights shimmered across the glass-dome ceiling, mimicking the night sky. Shooting stars streaked across it, drawing occasional gasps from the crowd. Song after song, they danced. Only taking momentary breaks for a drink or to catch their breath.

Over time, the music slowed, and Karaia and her mystery man matched the new rhythm, their bodies still moving as one.

"You haven't told me your name," she whispered.

He nudged her gently. "*You* haven't told me yours either."

"It's Karaia." She chuckled. "And you?"

"Isn't that part of the mystery of the masks?" he replied, avoiding the question. "We get to be whoever we want with them on."

"Or are the masks hiding who we really are?" Karaia asked. "Shouldn't we take them off to see our *real selves*?"

He stopped dancing as he considered her question.

She could see his eyes shifting behind the mask—searching, pacing, thinking. She held her breath.

Finally, he spoke. "I see your point. But tonight, I choose to be someone else. So, I'll keep my mask on—and my identity a secret."

There it was again. That devilish side grin. *Fuck.*

Karaia went with it. Leaning in, she whispered, "If that's how you want to play, I can play too." Her fingers gently found the nape of his neck, twisting a strand of hair. "So then ... who are you tonight?"

"A guy who works in software and enjoys going clubbing on weekends."

They started swaying again.

"Boring," she teased. "I need something more. Why am I dancing with *you*?"

This time, he leaned into her ear, his breath sending an electrifying chill up her spine.

"Ah, yes. Good question," he said, his voice low. "Let's instead imagine we don't live here at all—but on an island in the California Keys."

Karaia perked up, wondering where he was going with this.

"We get by on fish from the sea and a scrappy vegetable plot we've managed to grow in the sweltering heat. But," — his eyes went wide — "a mighty neighboring tribe is trying to take over our tiny island plot, and we must defend ourselves and our land."

"Sounds a bit terrifying." She pressed herself against his chest, feeling the thud of his heartbeat against hers. "Also ... thrilling. What's our island called?"

"Aeon," he said. "It means—"

"A long or indefinite period of time," she finished for him.

He pulled back slightly to meet her gaze.

They were searching. *For what?*

Then, with a sudden twirl, he spun her on the dance floor and wrapped her in his arms again, this time with her back to him, their hips moving together.

"Back to our imaginary life," he breathed in her ear. "The neighboring tribe tried to take Aeon. To make it theirs. But we won—and held our ground against impossible odds."

"Then what?"

"And then we live. That's it."

"That's *it*?"

"Yeah."

"Your second life was more interesting, I'll give you that," Karaia said, nudging him gently with her backside, feeling heat rise between her legs.

"I hear a *but* coming," he replied, giving her another twirl.

This time, they ended up face to face.

Karaia nestled in and told him something she hadn't told anyone. "No *but*. It's just ... something I never would've thought of. Living outside the walls. Or at least, I never would've considered it before this week."

"What happened this week?"

"I'm not sure—"

But she didn't get to finish.

The lights in the great room brightened abruptly, cutting her off. The music quieted. A spotlight beamed onto the stage. Karaia, along with the rest of the crowd, looked up toward it.

In that instant, her mysterious stranger let go of her.

She twisted back. But he was already gone, swallowed by the mass of people.

And just like that, her fantasy—along with any hope of taking him home—disappeared. Her shoulders slumped, and she let out a deep sigh.

Griffin Marshall was stepping into the spotlight, music swelling—suspenseful, triumphant. The official announcement of Phase Two was about to begin.

Karaia weaseled her way back through the throng and found Arjun near the buffet table, alone.

Raising her eyebrows at him, she asked, "You didn't eat *all* the desserts, right?"

"Of course not. I saved one for you." He smirked, handing her a small chocolate truffle. "How was dancing?"

"I met someone," Karaia said between small bites. "He was so ... interesting. Sexy, but soft. Gentle. Alluring. The opposite of Griffin. Honestly, it was a welcome change."

"Who was he?"

She didn't answer.

After a beat, Arjun repeated himself. "Karaia ... who was he? You're keeping me in suspense here."

She was gawking at the stage.

"Welcome, everyone," Griffin's voice boomed, "and thank you so much for being here with me tonight. It is truly a special and momentous occasion." He waved at the cameras and videos rolling. "Thank you, thank you. But first, before I go any further ... I'd like to introduce you all to my son—Stellan Marshall."

He gestured to the man beside him, dressed in a dark navy suit.

Stellan lifted his mask.

Chatter erupted.

Karaia stared, mouth agape.

"There he is," she whispered. "*That's* my mystery man."

"... Oh, shit," was all Arjun said back.

CHAPTER 28

MIRYAM

The pile of books landed on the table with a heavy thud, startling Miryam so that she nearly leapt from her chair. She turned to see Sophia eyeing the closed notebook resting on her bedside.

"I trust your journaling goes well," Sophia said.

Miryam had been gazing out the tiny window, daydreaming of what it might feel like to wield pleroma, wondering when she could finally try it for herself.

Reading a heap of old texts was not what she had in mind for today.

"The true work begins now," Sophia went on. "You shall help with the daily chores and the evening meal every other night. That is the price of your keep here. And as for our order ..." She rapped the books. "... this is the first step. To become one of us, you must first learn our history and gather knowledge."

"'Tis what I'm ready for." Miryam nodded. She exhaled, reminding herself that the excitement of powers and pleroma would come later.

She could wait—or so she told herself.

"Good. Can you read English?" Sophia asked.

"Yes," Miryam said, silently thanking her father for teaching her, unlike most girls. She drew her chair up to the table.

"Most of these are transcribed into English," Sophia explained, opening the first book. "Yet some remain in Latin or Greek. Can you read those tongues?"

Miryam sighed. "No, I cannot. What shall I do with those?"

"We will pair you with a more advanced student."

"Can it be Ved?" The words slipped out before she could stop herself.

Sophia paused, eyes narrowing with thought. At last she said, with a touch of resignation, "I suppose so. He knows the texts better than any. But ..."

"But what?"

"'Tis hard to explain." Sophia stretched her back and sat on the edge of Miryam's bed, facing her squarely. "You see, each soul has a unique way of working with pleroma."

"I heard that word once in church," Miryam said, flipping through a page. "They told us only Christ was filled with pleroma."

"That is what they would have you believe," Sophia replied. "Jesus sought to teach us that we all hold the same potential. But the Church would not suffer it, so they slew him and warped his message." She leaned forward, lowering her voice. "Pleroma exists in *all* things—you, me, the flower in that vase, the birds outside, even the very breath we draw. Yet it shows itself uniquely in each."

Miryam rested her hands on the table, watching Sophia carefully.

"I, for example, can sense pleroma in others. I see it flowing, and I read what it means," Sophia tapped her chest, then pointed gently toward Miryam. "With you, I sense something thick, concentrated. Brighter too. I felt it from the first moment we met. It worries me as I've never seen such pleroma before. It grows even stronger when you are near Ved."

Miryam's face scrunched. "Why would that be?"

Sophia hesitated, lips pursed. "That, I do not yet know."

A bitter dread swept through Miryam. What if it meant she was ... sinful by birth? She was her mother's daughter. Her name had cemented that truth. Was this her fate? Doomed to atone for a sin she had yet committed? Dempsey's face flashed in her mind, stoking rage in her chest. Then Ved's face followed, stirring a different storm in her altogether. The clash of feelings made her fists clench tight. *I will not believe it. I am not sinful.*

Sophia must have seen the turmoil on her face. "Just because we do not understand something does not make it dangerous." She paused, tilting her head. "Miryam, are you well?"

Miryam forced her hands to loosen, pushing the anger aside. She thought of Ved again. Being near him always carried a strange, undeniable fervor that stirred in her core. *But I think 'tis a good thing.*

She nodded to Sophia—and to herself. *I can be a force for good too.*

Her mind leapt ahead, hungry again to know more about pleroma and its magical powers. "When shall I learn what my unique gift is? What abilities are there? Can any among you fly? I have ever longed to fly away like a bird. What is it that Ved can do?"

Sophia rose and grinned at Miryam. "Your questions will be answered in time. First, you must learn. This first lesson is of knowledge and persistence. We must know that you are committed. The reading is much, yet all of it is needful. These texts tell our history, our beliefs, and shall give you a view of Christ much unlike the one you were taught in church. You have three days to read all."

"Three days?" Miryam gasped, staring at the mountain of tomes.

Sophia's smile lingered. "Best get to reading." She slipped out of the chamber, shutting the door behind her.

Miryam lifted the first book, *The Secret Book of John*, and began to read.

~ ∿ ~

Outside of her new chores and the hours for meals, Miryam read without ceasing for nearly three days straight, one book flowing into the next. She surprised even herself with her resolve. Occasionally, she would take a slight break to write in her journal. Sometimes, she'd draft a letter to Bella or her father. The thought of him dying before she returned pained her deeply. Though she never found the courage to send the letters. Still, unsure how to communicate what had truly happened to her.

But mostly, she read.

In all honesty, the texts enthralled her. They presented Christianity in ways wholly new to her, painting a portrait of Jesus unlike any she had ever heard. They spoke of pleroma as this mystical substance that made up all existence. While the content was foreign, the concepts rang true, deep in her bones. She had long felt there must be more to life—now she had glimpsed it.

And it was a relief to be caught up in ideas instead of her own gnawing feelings.

She read on.

However, her eyes said otherwise. With each turn of the page, the words and letters blurred more. She squeezed her lids shut, blinked hard, then marked her place with a ribbon from her hair. Standing up, she stretched her arms above her head, her stiff muscles loosening with a few sharp pops. A huge yawn escaped her lips.

Through the small window, Miryam spied the courtyard. Dusk lay heavy, and the Sun was sinking low. Monks were finishing their chores, soon to retire for silent prayer or rest. Slipping on her boots, she quietly stepped from her chamber and drifted down toward the pond. Of late, it had become her favorite place, where she could sit in peace and scratch down her secrets onto her journal's waiting pages.

The calm water helped Miryam finally put words to the attack in the woods. She was beginning to accept what had happened. Though she still felt angry, each day in the monastery carried her farther from that night and farther from Dempsey. The rage within her softened, and her feelings toward herself eased as well. She could finally see life beyond the attack.

Even her habit of talking to bugs had returned. And they were plentiful by the pond, always faithful listeners—never judging, never interrupting. She still could not picture going home, but this, at least, felt like progress.

As Miryam neared the pond that day, she noticed someone already sitting in her usual spot. Dark, wavy hair—so unlike the other monks. Ved.

He sat cross-legged, utterly still, palms upturned on his knees. With his back to her, he gave no sign of seeing her approach. Miryam crept closer, holding her breath.

"I know you are there," Ved said, without turning.

Her mouth fell open. "How did you know?"

"I could sense you. That, and your feet are rather loud. Has no one told you?" Ved chuckled softly and turned to face her. His blue eyes locked on hers, sending a warmth rushing to her cheeks.

"My feet are not *that* loud," she scoffed, hands on hips and lips firm. She tried holding her stance, but with every second, she melted further into Ved's gaze. Finally, she gave in and skipped toward him. "What are you doing?"

"Meditating."

"Is that similar to praying?" She plopped down on the grass.

"A little. Fewer words, more listening."

"What are you listening for? Does it have to do with pleroma? Sophia told me we all have natural gifts. What are yours? Also, she said I'd need help with the texts in Latin and Greek, since I cannot read those. I asked her if you could help, and she agreed." Miryam's eyes brightened, hopeful. "If you want to?"

Ved drew a deep breath and looked down.

"I did it once more. Rambling and asking too many questions, didn't I? I do that when I am nervous, or excited ... or both." She gave him a wide grin, trying to ease the air between them.

"You *do* ask many questions, aye—but 'tis not you. I am simply unaccustomed to speaking much at all. And with you ... it is as if something enwraps me so, clouding my thoughts, and I cannot find the words."

Miryam chuckled softly. "I feel it too. Only I chatter when it happens. Perhaps we can balance each other. You try speaking, and I shall practice listening."

She fell silent then, letting the quiet settle heavy between them.

After a moment, Ved nodded. "I would be honored to help you with your texts."

Miryam pressed her lips together tightly.

"You may as well ask what you like, one question at a time," Ved said, glancing at her. "'Tis written all over your face."

"I must know. How did you end up here at the monastery?" Miryam asked, stopping herself before another deluge of questions could escape her lips.

Ved gazed out at the pond, where a pair of ducks drifted lazily across the water. "I have lived here nearly all my life."

He paused.

Miryam shifted, willing herself to match his stillness. Every word seemed carefully measured, each one chosen with intention. So unlike herself, who blurted out whatever thought came first. Perhaps this was good practice ... for something, she just didn't know what yet.

"My parents brought me here when I was but a babe," Ved continued at last. "I was born in France. My parents were Jewish. In 1290, when the king issued the Edict of Expulsion, all Jews were ordered to leave England, else be slain by the crown."

Miryam clasped her hands over her mouth.

"Uprisings followed, and Christians were free to kill Jews without consequence. Fearing for their lives—and mine—my parents left me with the Benedictine monks here until they could find safe passage back to France for us all." His voice faltered. "They were slain the very next day."

Miryam's chest tightened. She wanted to pour out words of sorrow, to tell him how deeply sorry she was. Instead, she swallowed them back, breathing in deeply. For once, she forced herself to wait.

Ved twirled a blade of grass between his fingers. "I remember none of this. It was told to me later by the monks who raised me."

The vulnerability in his eyes told her he rarely shared this story. Miryam's hand twitched with the urge to reach for his, but she held back. "'Tis horrible. I am truly sorry you never knew your parents."

Ved still gazed out at the pond. "That is why it is hard for me to grow close to others. I never had a mother or father. Sophia is the nearest I have to kin. Though life here was not the same as a home. I learned to meditate before I ever played a game. By ten, I was reading in five tongues, yet I had never been around other children." He wrinkled his brow and, for a moment, looked decades older than he was. "Later, the monks took in students nearer my age, but ... they came to learn pleroma, not to make friends."

"I cannot imagine my life without Bella to play with, or my father to hug when I am ..." Longing washed over Miryam, and tears pricked at her eyes. "... sorrowful."

Ved turned to her again, and her heart swelled.

"I was going to ask why you are here as well," he said. "Sophia has only told us you are staying with us for now."

Miryam took a deep breath in and out. She wasn't ready to talk out loud about what had happened to her. Not yet.

"I want to tell you, I do." She shut her eyes for a moment. "Only, I do not have words yet, as surprising as that is. I know I cannot go back yet. Even when I wish to. Whenever I think of it, my whole body either wants to burst with rage or curl into a ball and never open up again."

"I know what you mean. Not about what happened to you." Ved breathed in, his eyes shifting, searching for words. "But about the warring feelings within. Before I met you, I thought I knew my path. I would live as a monk, study our teachings, and die in quiet service. But now ..."

His blue eyes pierced through Miryam, and a flutter rose up her spine.

"... now, I do not know what I want. With you here, I feel things inside me I did not know existed." He exhaled loudly. "It is as though you opened a whole new world, and it utterly confounds me. In less than one Moon cycle, I must take my vows to become a monk ... or not."

Miryam's pulse quickened at Ved's last words. "Are you saying you might not take your vows?"

"I know not what I am saying. I am ... a fool." He shook his head, brushing a hand through his dark hair.

Miryam wished it were her hand.

She bit down hard on her lip.

"No, you are not." Before she could stop herself again, she reached out and placed her hand on his.

Ved's hand tensed beneath hers, but he didn't pull away.

It was the first time she had touched someone since the incident in the woods. *Maybe I can feel safe again.* With Ved, she thought it was possible.

"I never had the chance to speak with you after you left me that poem in the church. It was so beautiful. Where was it from?" she asked.

"It was written by a poet named Rumi. He was a Sufi from Persia. One of our monks traversed there and brought back his works. I've read them all. They stir the soul. That one I translated into English for you. I can only hope my own verses reach even close to his." He smiled.

"You write your own poems as well? May I read one? And ... what is a Sufi?" She caught herself, smiling sheepishly. "One question at a time."

Ved's lips curved faintly. "Yes, I write verse, and I shall share one with you. As for Sufism—it is mystical Islam."

"Is that where your name comes from?" Miryam leaned in. "It does not sound Jewish or Christian."

"My given name is Joseph. But in the order, we may choose a name that fits our spirit. I chose *Ved*—meaning 'sacred knowledge' in Sanskrit. It came to me at the same time as I discovered my gift with pleroma. I can access the Akashic realm—a spiritual plane, like a magnificent library that holds the knowledge of the world, both past and future."

Miryam tried to take it all in. It sounded impossible. "Let me see if I understand correctly—you are a Jewish boy with a Sanskrit name, living in a Catholic monastery, who reads Islamic poetry, and practices magic?"

Ved chuckled. "Put it as so, I sound like quite a conundrum indeed."

They both laughed, loud enough to startle the frogs and crickets around the pond, leaving a hush in their wake.

"I think ... I like conundrums," Miryam whispered as she edged closer.

"I think" — Ved gulped — "I like you."

His hand gave hers a gentle squeeze. He moved toward her as well, their faces only inches apart. Heat rose between them. Miryam's heart pounded in her chest.

"I do not know what I am to do," he said, voice unsteady.

"Nor do I," Miryam breathed.

Desire spread through her body. She licked her lips, waiting for his to meet hers, imagining her hands finding his body—gripping him—feeling his lean muscles under his tunic and tracing her finger-tips along his warm skin.

"But I cannot." Ved pulled back.

Stunned, Miryam's shoulders fell. "Why not?"

"Not yet. If I am to take vows as a monk, this … what stirs between us … is forbidden." His words faltered, though his eyes betrayed the same longing.

"Why is *this* forbidden when all this monastery does would be condemned beyond its walls?" Miryam threw her hands in frustration, startling the ducks in the pond.

"Miryam, I do not set the rules," Ved said, clearly torn. "Please grant me time. I must know my own mind before I speak my heart. I swear I will tell you once I know."

Miryam swallowed her protest. She often rushed headlong into things, but perhaps patience was wisest now. "I understand," she huffed. "For now, you are my tutor, and I, your student. Nothing more." She gave a small nod.

"For now." Ved squeezed her hand once more before letting go.

CHAPTER 29

LEAH

I need one day to be normal, Leah told herself on her way to work. *Make money, pay bills, eat, drink, sleep, repeat. Why is that so fucking hard?*

Leah pulled into the small parking lot that the shop shared with two other businesses, a smoke shop and a dry cleaner. The man who ran the cleaners waved at her, smiling, as he checked his mailbox. She smiled back. *One normal day, here we go. No migraines. No Tate. And no magic journal.* She pushed all those thoughts to the back of her head, but they seemed to push right back, bubbling to her mind's surface, as she walked in the front door.

"Good morning," Kat said, chipper as a bird early in the morning. "How are you doing today?"

"I don't have a headache, so that's good," Leah replied. She checked the time. Her first appointment was in five minutes.

"I made a new batch of Kombucha. Ginger-blueberry flavor. It's in the fridge in the back if you want any."

"Thanks, but I'll stick with my black coffee."

"Okay, let me know if you need anything," Kat said.

Leah headed to the room where she did her readings. It was in a quieter, private space, separated from the rest of the store. There was a large wine stain in the corner and a huge, slightly blurred painting of the beach on the wall. No crystals, no mantras, no fluff. And it didn't smell like patchouli.

The room felt perfectly *Leah,* and she liked it.

Sitting down in her chair, she drew a deep breath in, cracked her knuckles, and prepared for a day of psychic readings. Not before the last sip of coffee, of course.

The front doorbell chimed as her first appointment entered.

Dave. One of her regulars. Forty-seven, balding, and an avid Los Angeles Angels fan, he often wore sunglasses and a baseball hat to nearly every appointment. His wife had left him for a twenty-three-year-old surfer from Oxnard named *Bentley*. He groaned every time he said his name. At his first appointment with Leah, he had told her life was meaningless. He needed to glimpse his future and get some direction. Despite considering himself a devout Christian, he was desperate for answers. That was over a year ago.

He knocked on her door.

"Come in," Leah said, sitting up straighter and more confident. "Hey, Dave, how are you?"

"Honestly, not well." He slumped down across from her.

No hat. No sunglasses. Instead, he donned a buttoned-up shirt, disheveled and un-ironed. His hair was greasy. And he wore a little stubble on the chin, unlike his normal smooth-shaven appearance. Leah smelled a faint whiff of cologne.

Not from today though—yesterday's cologne.

"I was worried you would say that." She shifted her gaze to his mannerisms.

Fidgeting hands. A deep crease in his brow. A tapping foot under the table.

"You were?" Dave reeled.

"I knew it before you walked in," she said plainly.

"Oh, maannnn." His brow deepened. "I thought I was on the right path, and then, I don't know … things just feel *off* … in my life. Do you know what I mean?" He tossed his hands in the air.

Leah wanted to say, *I feel it too. I have no fucking clue what I'm doing in my life right now.* Instead, she said, "I understand. There's someone new in your life. A woman?"

"Yeah, there is. Man, you're good at this."

Leah kept her head up, her gaze locked on Dave, as she smoothed out the tablecloth in front of them. "I can sense there's some discord between the two of you."

"Oh my gosh, yes." Dave slammed a hand down. "She's so amazing one minute, but the next, she's toying with my emotions like I'm a yo-yo or something."

"Have you tried talking to her about it?"

"That's the thing. Every time, something interrupts us." His eyes went wide. "This morning, the pipes in my second-floor bathroom flooded my entire closet full of clothes. I didn't have time to shower, shave, or even put on new clothes today."

Leah scanned his outfit. "Well, mercury is in retrograde right now, and that's going to interrupt communication. Probably why you're feeling like you can't talk to her. Wait until after the 24th of this month and give it another go." She leaned in and winked. "And Dave, she's the real deal."

"I knew it. I knew she was the one." He beamed. "Thank you so much."

"It's why I'm here," Leah said, smiling. *You're a fraud*, said the voice in her head. It sounded like her mother. And so it was going to be a normal day for her after all. "Is there anything else I can answer for you?"

The appointment continued. And then the next and the next.

Leah took a brief break for lunch. Well, *kind of* lunch. She ate an old, slightly stale granola bar she found in her purse that filled her up enough. It was good Kat didn't see because she would have given Leah crap for not treating her body like the divine temple it was.

One more reading was on her schedule for the day. This one, however, had no name attached to the appointment in her calendar. *How was that even possible?*

Quickly checking her phone to see if the doctor's office had gotten back to her with the results from her tests, a knock rapped on the door.

"Come in." Shoving her phone away, Leah glanced at her last client.

The cooky, old woman from the bookstore crept inside and sat down in the chair across from her.

Leah was stunned for a moment. "You?"

"Hello," she croaked through thick wrinkles that surrounded her mouth.

"It's *you*." Leah gaped.

"Do I know you?" the woman asked, staring blankly, no ounce of recognition in her eyes.

"Yes, we met at your bookstore a couple of weeks ago," Leah insisted.

The woman shrugged her shoulders, a few bones popping along the way. "That is odd because my bookstore hasn't been open in ten years," she said in the most serious tone. "And I don't remember meeting you."

She's not the looney bin she was the other day, Leah thought, brows pinched together. "You *really* don't remember? You gave me this old journal. It had my name on it. Wait, let me show you." Leah rifled through her bag, found the leather book, and held it out for the old woman to see.

The old woman peered at it with her tiny eyes, squinting. "Interesting."

"So, you remember it?" Leah's eyes widened.

"Oh, no. I've never seen this in my life, but it looks very interesting." She brushed her frail fingers across the front of the journal, tilting her head as she did. "I'd guess from around the Middle Ages?"

Leah felt like the Universe was pranking her. *How does she not remember?*

"Dear, are you going to give me my reading or not?" the woman asked.

Coming back to the appointment, Leah shook her head and put the journal back in her bag. "Of course, sorry. I must have mistaken you for someone else. My name is Leah Webb. What type of reading would you like today? I can do Tarot, a palm reading, or a general reading using the aid of my crystal ball."

"Do you do past-life readings?"

"It's not my specialty."

"Would you do one for me?"

"I can try." Leah put on a fake smile. "What's your name?"

"Gertrude."

"You *are* the woman I met in the bookstore!" she exclaimed.

Gertrude, wide-eyed as an innocent baby, had no reaction.

Huffing, Leah closed her eyes to start her reading. But once she did, she realized she had paid no attention to what Gertrude was wearing or how she looked. She had been too distracted by the woman not remembering her in the first place. *Think, Leah, think.* Even without her observation skills, she had done hundreds, maybe thousands of readings. She should be able to say something vague enough that Gertrude would fill in the rest for herself.

"Give me your hands," Leah said, reaching out her palms on the table. "As I get in touch with your past lives, be thinking of an intention for this reading. What message do you need to hear from a past self? What questions do you have?"

Gertrude placed her hands in Leah's. They were light and fragile but warm to the touch.

"I sense a woman coming forward." Leah made it up as she went, eyes still closed and her ear tilted up as if receiving messages directly from the sky. "She's wearing a uniform of some kind ... a nurse. There are soldiers around her in beds. It appears you may have been alive during a war in one of your lives."

"That's not right," Gertrude said bluntly.

Snapping Leah out of her normal routine, she opened her eyes. "What do you mean, *not right*?"

Gertrude stared her down. "You're making this up. Tell me something *real*."

Leah didn't know what to do. She felt naked and exposed for the fraud she was. Closing her eyes again, she said, "Oh, I see now. She's not a nurse. She's wearing an apron. A wife." *Geez, is that vague enough?* She hoped Gertrude would fill in the blanks.

"Nope, you're still not telling the truth," Gertrude drilled her.

Fuck, fuck, fuck. Leah could feel her pulse rise and her palms sweat.

"Let the image come to you, dear." Gertrude cleared her throat. "Don't make it up in your mind. Take a deep breath and just *wait*."

Who is the psychic here, lady? was what she wanted to say but didn't. Leah drew in a deep inhale and waited.

An image of a young woman flashed before her mind's eye. With wild curly hair and crystal blue eyes, the girl pranced through a field of lavender, laughing.

Leah was taken aback and held her breath.

"Don't push it away," Gertrude instructed. "What do you see?"

"A red-haired girl in a field. She's wearing a long green dress, as they did in medieval times."

"What else?"

Leah focused again. Now, the young woman sat in a cave surrounded by what looked like monks in a semicircle. *Miryam*. The name just popped into her head.

The journal.

Miryam was—Leah pushed the thought away.

It was too crazy.

Leah opened her eyes, angry with Gertrude, her nails pressing hard into the table. "Why are you doing this to me? You *do* remember. You gave me that journal, and now you're putting these thoughts in my head."

Gertrude's eyes twinkled. "Not my doing, no." She waved a finger. "But don't you see? It's all connected so."

"No," Leah retorted. "You're doing this. I don't know why, but you need to stop. I don't need anything else in my life to deal with," she said with a grunt. "And I need you to leave now."

Gertrude held firm, her eyes piercing Leah's. Goosebumps ran up Leah's spine. And for one moment, she felt like she *knew* Gertrude. More than just from the bookstore. More than from this reading. From another ... *life*? She shook her head, laughing at the thought, and looked away.

Gertrude sighed and slowly made her way out of the room.

Leah sat there in disbelief.

A migraine pricked at her, sending a shooting pain throughout her head. Covering her face with her hands, she begged it to go away. The migraines, the journal, the custody battle. It all felt like too much.

There was a knock at the door.

Kat peeked in. "Hey, I saw your last appointment leave early. Everything okay?"

"No."

"What is it?" Kat sat down. "You can tell me."

Leah hesitated at first, not wanting to face it. "I think I had an actual vision of something *real*," she choked out.

"Whaaaatttt? That's so exciting!" Kat clapped her hands together, bouncing up and down. "You're a real psychic now."

"One vision hardly makes me a real psychic." Leah rolled her eyes.

"Soooo, what did you see?"

"The girl from the journal. Her name is *Miryam*."

"Oh my gosh, that's amazing." Kat leaned forward, eyes wide. "What do you think it means?"

"I don't know." Leah pressed her thumb hard into her temple, massaging her head, pleading for relief she knew wouldn't come. She grabbed her bag and began looking through it for some ibuprofen.

"What did you see? Describe every detail, even if you think it isn't important," Kat said. "It will help us figure out why you're seeing her."

"Stop pressuring me!" Leah blurted.

Kat's whole body stiffened. "Sorry, I didn't mean to. I'm just trying to help."

"I just have another migraine, and I can't do this" — Leah waved her hand in the air — "woo-woo shit right now. Just leave me ... alone."

At the bottom of her purse, she found an empty bottle of ibuprofen.

Of fucking course.

"Oh, I just thought ... never mind." Kat pursed her lips.

"Kat, wait—"

"No, you made it clear." Kat stood to leave. "But you know, if you keep pushing your friends away, you might actually be alone someday." She rushed out of the room without looking back.

Leah had just wanted a normal day.

She packed up her things, said goodbye to Kat to no response, and headed out the door. As she made her way through the parking lot, she saw Seth's police car parked next to hers. Seth stood there, looming by her car.

"This is not the day," Leah said through her teeth.

"I need to see that leather journal you had the other day in my driveway," Seth said curtly.

"No," she hissed. *Why the fuck does Seth want to see that?*

He stepped directly in her path.

"Get out of my way." She reached for her car door.

"Just let me see it, and I'll let you go home," Seth insisted.

"It's none of your business."

He grabbed her arm. "It's official police business."

Normally, his aggressive behavior worked with Leah. It was too much effort to oppose it. But then ... she thought of Miryam in the woods with Dempsey. He had thought he could control her and bend her to his will, but Miryam fought back.

She was finding her power, and Leah could too.

"I don't care," she said, "and take your hand off me."

Seth's grip tightened. "What did you say to me?" He wasn't used to her speaking back to him. His chest puffed up.

"Take your hand off me," Leah growled, her eyes shooting daggers at him. "Or I am going to—"

"What? Call the police?" He rolled, letting out a vindictive laugh. "I can destroy you. Here, and in the courtroom. Hana will be mine, and you'll be left all alone."

Rage coursed through her being as Leah struggled to get out of his grip. She reached across Seth to open her car door with her other hand. When she did, he blocked her with his palm, enclosing her fist in his. He was strong. Much stronger than Leah. But she didn't feel like giving in. Not this time.

Not ever again.

Leah pushed forward with her hand with all her might, pressing against Seth's, unable to budge.

Suddenly, he released his pressure, allowing her hand to surge forward.

Her fist collided with his nose.

Blood spurted out, spilling onto Leah's hand and blouse. She quickly pulled her hand back in surprise.

"Assaulting an officer, and right before the custody case." Seth grinned, his teeth bloodied. "What do you think the judge will say?"

Chapter 30

KARAIA

"You danced with the infamous *Stellan Marshall*?" Arjun said, bouncing slightly from one foot to the other. Lowering his voice—as he remembered gala guests still surrounded them—he added, "Do you think Griffin saw you two? That would be ... awkward."

"It's no big deal. Really," Karaia said, trying to convince herself as much as him.

Something in her gut said otherwise.

To distract herself, she grabbed a small plate from the nearby buffet table and began piling appetizers on it. She still hadn't eaten for most of the day. She shoved an unknown morsel into her mouth. "Plus, you *know* Griffin. He's not exactly known for exclusivity." She raised her eyebrows. "He can't expect the same from me."

"True." Arjun nodded eagerly as he whispered. "But it's *Stellan*, his only son."

"I'm very aware of that," Karaia muttered between chews. Her head swam, buzzing from her earlier drinks. Or maybe ... from Stellan. She just wanted to forget about the whole thing and get on with her night. Then why couldn't she get the sweet smell of cedar and orange blossoms out of her mind?

Arjun pressed on, biting his nails like she was the star of his favorite daytime holo-show. "Now that you know who he is, are you going to talk to him again?"

"I'm not sure about anything," Karaia snapped. "I just want to enjoy the rest of the night, okay?" The tone of her voice hit the air sharply. Regretting it immediately, she added, "I'm sorry, Arjun, it's just—"

"No, *I'm sorry*," he cut in. "I only live out my social life vicariously through you and sometimes get carried away."

"Maybe you should try talking to people yourself?" Karaia teased, nudging him lightly with her elbow. She popped the last bite into her mouth and, finally, felt slightly better.

"You're probably right," he admitted. "Do you think I should leave this buffet table at some point?"

They both laughed, drawing irritated glances from those around them.

Karaia and Arjun turned their attention back to the stage as the entire country watched and waited for the big reveal.

"Connection. Freedom. Safety. At Seromela, we're always striving to give our citizens the very best technology." Griffin, still building toward his Phase Two announcement, paced confidently across the stage as he spoke. "But it's not about the money for me. It's personal." He stopped and faced the camera head-on. "When my two sons were kidnapped by Defiers, I made it my mission to see that no parent ever goes through what I did. To lose a child" — he wiped a tear from his eye — "is the hardest thing in the world."

Griffin walked toward Stellan and put his arm around him. Stellan's back went taut.

Karaia wondered if it was nerves—or something else.

"I am lucky to have Stellan here with me today," Griffin continued. "After the kidnapping, he tried the normal NeuroCredit treatment for PTSD. But it wasn't enough. That's why I've devoted the last ten years of my life to finding something better to help him. And to help *you*."

Karaia wrinkled her nose.

"That's what Phase Two is all about." Griffin let go of Stellan and began walking the stage floor again. "Imagine the best of virtual reality paired with NIVA and NeuroCredits, right at your fingertips. A fully immersive experience, unlike anything you've seen before, to truly 'be' *and* 'feel' anywhere in the world—all inside your mind."

The crowd erupted in whispers. Camera lights flashed. News reporters scrambled to react at the edges of the grand hall.

Karaia stood gaping at the spectacle, face scrunched. She should have been excited, if not for technology, then for the next phase of her own career at Seromela. But she wasn't. At all.

Arjun leaned over to her ear. "I can't wait to play *The Tides of Gasmia* with this level of immersion."

Karaia nodded mindlessly. Her gaze stayed fixed on Stellan. He was fidgeting with his hands. His eyes darted from side to side. *He's nervous. But why?* A twinge tightened low in her abdomen.

"But that's not the exciting part," Griffin said, his voice lingering as he took a slow, deliberate sip of water.

He knew how to hold a crowd. A hush fell over the hall as people waited for what came next.

"You're probably thinking, we've always had this type of VR technology. What's new about this?" Griffin smiled, pacing again. "Yes, we've had VR vacations for years. Whether at home, or in clinics with food and hydration drips, we've been able to escape for hours—even days. But then what happens?"

Stellan cast a glance up at the ceiling for a second.

Karaia narrowed her eyes.

Griffin continued, "You come back. You're behind at work. Your house-bot needs repairs. Your apartment's a mess. Real life kicks in. But what if I told you there was a way to end all that unnecessary *post-vacation stress?*"

Soft music began to play as a huge holo-screen lit up behind the stage. On screen, a series of polished, beautiful people moved through their lives—riding the rail, going to work, eating dinner, each with a small glowing white light beside their left temple.

To Karaia, they looked like hollowed-out shells of humans.

The screen zoomed in on one woman's eye—then transitioned to her lying in a beach cabana, sipping a tropical drink as the Sun dipped behind the ocean.

"Let me introduce you to NeuroTryp." Griffin gestured toward the screen. "Where you can go on your dream vacation *and* tend to all your physical needs at the same time. The best of every world. NeuroTryp gives you *total freedom* while also remaining a productive member of society. Paired with the latest NeuroCredit enhancements, each Tryp releases perfectly timed doses of serotonin when you need them most—right inside the simulation." He winked at the cameras.

A roar of applause erupted.

A faux-champagne bottle popped somewhere behind them, making Karaia jump, causing her to knock into Arjun. "Sorry," she whispered.

"It's okay," he yelled above the chaos. "I can't wait to try it. Can you?"

Karaia didn't respond. Something was *wrong*.

Trying to listen to her gut, she scanned the surrounding area.

Griffin's voice rose. "Each individual on a NeuroTryp will display a small white light on their temple—so others know they're 'away.' Think of it like autopilot. Your body keeps functioning, but you won't be able to engage with others on a higher level until your Tryp ends. Now, of course, there are safety features in place—"

All the lights in the hall went out.

Gasps escaped the crowd.

Karaia blinked a few times, straining to see in the pitch darkness. *Something's coming.*

"It appears we're having some technical difficulties," Griffin's voice called out. "Where's the top tech company when you need them?"

The audience laughed—nervously.

Those on stage shuffled furtively, most likely Raven and the security team, trying to figure out what caused the blackout. Around Karaia, people stirred, anxious voices rising and worried murmurs echoing through the hall.

Then Griffin yelled again from the stage, "Don't worry! We're working to restore the power. In the meantime, please enjoy five free NeuroCredits—on me. They're available ... now."

A hush fell over the crowd as people immediately accepted the offer.

Inside Karaia's mind, NIVA spoke calmly. *Karaia, you have five NeuroCredits purchased and awaiting transfer. Would you like to transfer now?*

Karaia didn't answer.

A crash rang out in the hall. Then, another crash. Glass shattered, and shards rained down from above.

A slice hit her cheek, and Karaia dropped into an instinctive crouch, arms shielding her head from the rest of the falling debris. Her mind scrambled as she reached out with her free hand for the buffet table. *Where's Arjun?*

A sharp, acrid scent filled the air.

Smoke. Which meant ... fire.

As if on cue, sparks from a fiery blaze lit up the darkness.

Similar light shows—except it wasn't a show—danced throughout the gala hall. The thickening smoke burned in her lungs. She coughed hard, eyes stinging. She had lost Arjun in the mess. Her heart pounded—not just for him, but for everyone. A sudden burst of light near her illuminated the devastation.

The hall was in ruins.

A steady fire danced where people and tables once stood. Bodies—injured, bloodied, groaning—lay scattered across crumbling tables and server-bots in heaps.

Then, like a bell inside her gut, the truth rang out. *This is an attack.* They all needed to get out. *Now.* But why wasn't anyone rushing toward the exits?

Fuck ... NeuroCredits.

Everyone else had just transferred a blissful serotonin elixir directly into their brains.

But not me.

A distant memory flashed like disjointed scenes before Karaia's mind's eye. A woman running. A struggle. A flash of the laser gun. And Blood. So much blood.

Shaking it off, she shouted in the crowd, groping in the dark, "Arjun?"

"Karaia?!" his voice croaked from somewhere nearby.

She followed the sound of his voice and found Arjun dazed, crouching near a broken table. "Are you hurt? We need to get people out of the building before something worse happens," she said, coughing between words.

"I'm okay." But Arjun didn't move.

"C'mon." Karaia grabbed his arm and yanked him toward the main doors. "We need to get out!" she screamed to others around her, pushing them forward. Some obeyed. But most didn't have the sense of urgency they needed. "Hurry!"

A gigantic explosion went off near the stage. A fire engulfed it in hissing flames. Karaia peered through the smoke, eyes scanning, shoulders tense.

Griffin—*Stellan*—and his family were already gone.

She exhaled—relieved.

"Out the doors. It's an attack!" Karaia yelled over the barrage of flames and crashing metal and glass.

After the stage explosion, more people snapped out of their stupor. Panic rippled through the hall as others began running toward the exit.

Karaia felt like she was moving in slow motion as she pushed toward the tube entrance. All her senses sharpened. She could see that the fallen glass had sliced through several people—much worse than the cut on Karaia's face. The fires had burned others. Some were sobbing, clutching their wounds. Some hunched over, coughing violently. She tried her hardest to help as many people as she could, hoping it was *enough*.

A woman nearby stood in shock—blood splattered across her elegant gown from a blast injury. Her hands trembled at her sides.

The woman in the alley.

No, she was at the gala. And the woman wasn't dead.

Karaia ran to her. "Are you okay?"

"I ... I need ... more credits," the woman whispered, eyes confused. "NIVA won't give me more. Why?"

"You need medical attention," Karaia said gently. "Let me call you an Ambu-bot."

She pressed her temple. *NIVA, I need to report a medical emergency. Please send an Ambu-bot. No—send as many Ambu-bots as you can to the Seromela Grand Hall.*

NIVA replied, *Your report has been filed, and help is on the way. Thank you, Karaia.*

"Help is coming soon," she said to the woman.

Karaia made it out to the tube. It seemed safe enough out here. *But where is Arjun now?* She scanned the crowded tube. He wasn't here. She had lost him again. A sharp ache twisted in her core at the thought of losing someone else from her life. Part of her wanted to take the free NeuroCredits, sit in safety, and wait for emergency workers to arrive.

But her gut screamed at her, telling her otherwise. It didn't take long to decide which voice to follow.

Karaia ran back into the hall, pushing past the stream of people pouring out.

"Arjun!" she shouted.

Smoke thickened the air, ripping painful scratches into Karaia's lungs with each ragged breath. It was impossible to see more than a few feet ahead. She stumbled through the chaos—tripping over dropped glasses and crushed food. The fire by the stage had grown, and now the overhead sprinklers kicked on. Water poured down on her. Nearly falling over a broken table, she caught herself just in time—throwing out her hands. A jagged shard of glass sliced her palm. She winced, pain flaring. Blood oozed from the cut.

But there was no time to tend to it now.

Karaia's eyes roved the surrounding area, burning as they strained to see through the destruction. Few people remained in the hall, but visibility was too low to be sure. She made her way back toward the food table where she and Arjun had been standing. Except there wasn't a table anymore. An explosive device must have landed on the table, sending it into a million tiny pieces. Food splattered all over the ground and wall.

Arjun was *not* here.

Karaia turned back toward the main doors. "Arjun!"

"Hellllp," a scratchy voice called from the ground.

"Where are you? Keep talking," she shouted, changing direction. It wasn't Arjun. But it was someone who needed help.

A few feet away, she found a man lying on the ground, his body twisted and covered in blood. The sight triggered the same invading memory—a splash of blood hitting an alley tube wall and oozing down a lifeless body.

Karaia stiffened, resisting the urge to take a credit.

"Help me," he crackled again.

Stay focused. This man needed help.

Karaia couldn't tell what color suit he had been wearing. Now, it was just a dark-red puddle. Where his legs should have been was a grotesque mess of muscles, bones, and tendons. It looked like a jigsaw puzzle for body parts—except one no one should ever have to put back together. Her stomach lurched, and she held a hand to her mouth.

Kneeling beside him, she placed a hand gently on his shoulder. He was surprisingly calm.

"I need to find my wife," he said as blood dripped from his lips. "She's here with me. Can you help me find her?"

Karaia gaped from his ruined body to his face and back again. Hot tears streamed out of her eyes, and her face sweltered. Her breathing came in shallow bursts. She didn't know what to do—if there was anything she could do. She felt helpless. But she still had to try.

Trembling, she asked, "Why don't you tell me about your wife while I pull you out of here?"

"Why are you going to pull me?" His voice shook, more blood bubbling from his mouth. "I just need help finding my wife."

It was too much to handle. Karaia wanted to shrink back, get to safety, run away. *Just take a credit. Feel better.* The escape from this terror was so close.

Yet ... she didn't.

Breathe through it. She fought to stay present, curling her arms under his. "We'll find her, I promise. I just need to get you out first."

Karaia pulled with all her might.

"Aaaahhhhhh!" he yelped in pain.

She *wanted* to lift him, to carry him out of this hell. But he was too injured to move. *Where were the emergency workers?* Her eyes paced frantically in her head. They should be here by now.

Karaia gently lowered him back to the ground. Her hands and gown were soaked in blood. Quiet sobs escaped her as she tried to stay strong amidst the chaos.

Then, just a couple of feet away, she saw a woman's body lying still.

Squeezing her eyes shut, the memory flashed again—two officers hauling a body down an alley tube. Shuddering, she tried to pull herself back. There was no time for strange visions, or memories, or whatever they were. She looked again at the lifeless woman. The blast that injured the man must have hit her too ... and done even more damage.

"I don't think I can move you," Karaia whispered to the man, choking on her tears. "Tell me about your wife. What's her name?"

"Liona—the most beautiful woman in the world. Love at first sight." He coughed. "They say that doesn't happen anymore. People don't get married for love. But we did." He paused and gazed up at Karaia, then asked again, "Can you help me find her?"

"What does Liona look like?" she asked, wiping her nose.

"She has long gray hair with one turquoise streak in it," he said. "Green eyes like the trees in the bio-dome. It was our favorite spot in the evenings, right next to the fountain."

Karaia nodded solemnly, salt tingling her lips. "What did she wear tonight?"

"A turquoise dress to match her hair," he said, his voice weakening. "With white sparkles."

Karaia looked at the woman's body lying next to them and let out a little yelp. She covered her mouth, trying to stifle the sob.

"Why are you crying?" he asked softly.

She didn't know how to say it. That she had found *his wife*. Tightness gripped her chest, sharper than anything she'd ever felt before. But she knew what she had to do.

"I found her. Your Liona," Karaia said, swallowing hard. "I just need to pull you a little. Do you think you can handle that?"

"You found her?!" He cried tears of joy. "Oh, thank you. Thank you."

"Don't thank me," she managed, gently scooting him up next to the woman's body. She placed his hand on Liona's.

"Why isn't she moving?" the man asked as he rolled over to face his dead wife. "And she's cold. Honey, wake up?" He began shaking her to no avail.

Karaia rested her hand on theirs. "She's not going to wake up."

"No, no, no ..." he said, his cries echoing on the room's high walls. "Liona ..."

Karaia took a step back from the couple, giving them one last private moment. She swiped the hot tears from her cheeks, only for more to replace them. A pit of sadness filled her belly. Doubling over, she buried her head in her hands, closing her eyes. So much of her wanted to take a credit and feel better. It was what she had been taught to do.

But something else told her it was more important to feel this pain. Really *feel* it.

So she did. Waves of sadness coursed through her body. Sobs rose from deep within her core. She wailed out loud. Echoes of her pain rang off the shattered and broken hall.

After an unknown stretch of time, Karaia returned to the man and his wife, kneeling beside them, only to find that neither was moving now. She reached down, felt for a pulse on the man, finding none. She closed his eyes. They were holding hands and looked peaceful.

They had found love in this life.

And for that, Karaia smiled.

Stumbling out of the hall, she finally spotted Arjun near the entrance. He had made it out safely.

"Karaia!" he exclaimed, running up to her. "I'm so glad you're safe."

"You too. I didn't know where you were, so I went back in and ..." Karaia felt raw and exposed as she stifled back the tears she knew were coming again. "... and I found a man. Arjun, he died. Right in front of me." She collapsed in Arjun's arms, releasing a deluge of wet sobs into his shoulder.

Rubbing her back, he said, "You need to take a credit."

"No." She lifted her swollen eyes to his. "I know what I need to do."

"What's that?"

Karaia straightened her stance. "I need my memories back."

CHAPTER 31

MIRYAM

Tracing her fingertips along the stairwell's damp stone walls, Miryam hop-skipped down into the hidden cavern beneath the monastery. With each step, she felt safer, stronger, more alive than ever. At last, she was *living*—finally part of something greater than herself—and it thrilled her.

She found a place on the cool ground within the circle of monks, nuns, and other students. Right across from Ved. She stole a glance at him and bit down on her lip. Nearly a week had passed since he had squeezed her hand by the pond, yet she still imagined the warmth of his touch on her skin.

"Congratulations on completing your first lesson," Sophia said, standing in the center of the cave. "I trust Ved was a suitable tutor for you."

"Yes, he most certainly was," Miryam answered.

Her gaze slipped across the circle to Ved once again. She gave him a quick smile, though she tried to keep her focus on Sophia's words.

Still, she felt the invisible thread—the pull—between the two of them.

As if sensing her wandering thoughts, Sophia cleared her throat sharply, bringing Miryam's attention back. "Now, you are ready to meet the rest of our order."

Miryam snapped her head back toward Sophia.

"As you know already, not all who dwell here belong to the Order of the Tree of Life. Some live simply as monks and nuns," Sophia explained. "We live both as religious servants in this abbey—*and* as order members. Meaning, we still abide by the monastic rules, keeping a strict regimen of silence, study, and service. We practice celibacy and do not marry."

"Never?" Miryam interrupted, a deep frown blanketing her face.

Sophia arched a brow, then continued, "Now, for introductions." She stretched out her hand toward the circle. "All, please welcome Miryam, the newest initiate of our order."

The introductions began on the left. "This is Father Thomas. He is elder abbot here, and after me, the longest practitioner in the order. He maintains and protects our sacred texts. He can also call upon Earthly spirits for our aid."

Miryam's eyes widened. "What doest you mean, *Earthly spirits*?"

Thomas's voice was steady, his smile knowing. "You call them fairies or elves. They dwell in another realm, oft unseen—though not always." He gave her a wink.

Elated, Miryam started to ask, "And how do you see—"

Sophia nodded at her, indicating there would be time for questions. But now wasn't it.

She turned to the next person, a young woman near Miryam's age. "This is Matilda, also a student, like Ved, like you will be. Her gift is still awakening, yet she shows a natural talent for herbal cures and tonics. She brewed the mead you drank when first we met."

Matilda straightened proudly at the mention, her chin lifting just so.

Beside her sat Ved—and at once Miryam's attention wavered. The candlelight teased the shape of his shoulders beneath his wool robe, hinting at the strength beneath. She remembered the spark of his touch and longed to feel it again—to feel his skin against hers, warm and rough. Biting down on her bottom lip, she shifted in her seat, heat spreading low in her body. Her eyes traced his form all the way up to the dark curl that fell perfectly onto his brow. She imagined brushing it aside and pressing her lips to his.

Then Ved's eyes met hers.

Caught, Miryam stiffened, remembering she was in a circle of monks and nuns—her thoughts far from the order's vows of celibacy.

Quickly, she tore her gaze away and fixed it back on Sophia, who was still speaking.

"Here is Catherine." Sophia introduced another elder. "She commands sound vibrations. With her chant, she may lift and move objects."

Miryam blinked in wonder.

"Next to her is Fern," Sophia continued, gesturing to a young boy with big eyes. "He communes with the natural world—plants, beasts, even the smallest of creatures. He tends the stables and often works with Matilda to craft remedies."

Fern waved softly at Miryam.

At last, Sophia reached the young man seated beside Miryam. "And this is Will. His gift is still growing, but already he can step into another's mind and hear their thoughts. So," she added with a faint smile, "mind what you think in his company."

Miryam's cheeks flushed pink.

"Don't worry, I will not tell a soul." Will smirked.

Across the circle, Matilda let out a soft chuckle.

Miryam's face turned a deeper crimson red. She wanted to sink into the dirt floor. She dared not lift her eyes to Ved—or to anyone for that matter.

"Will, you cannot do that to everyone," Fern chided. "'Tis rude."

"William," Sophia said firmly, "we have spoken about respecting others' privacy."

He only nodded, still grinning to himself.

Pop! A sharp sound startled Miryam from her shame back into wonder as Sophia had walked to the cave wall and pressed against the stone, opening a hidden compartment. From within, she lifted a rectangular object wrapped in linen and set it at the circle's center. With careful hands, she unwrapped it to reveal a small wooden chest.

"What is it?" Miryam whispered.

"This is the heart of our order," Father Thomas explained. "The Chest of Immortality. 'Tis why we keep our work hidden from the world. When our sacred texts were found, *this* was with them."

At first glance, the chest looked plain—dark, smooth wood, no markings or adornments, only a single keyhole. Yet the longer Miryam gazed, the more it seemed to shimmer, not with light, but with an unseen force. A quiet breath, a pulse. *Pleroma*. As if the chest itself were breathing—a living artifact—maintaining itself throughout time.

"I am certain you have heard of the Ark of the Covenant?" Thomas asked.

"Yes," Miryam replied. "Moses built it to hold the Ten Commandments."

"'Twas not its sole purpose."

Miryam cocked her head. "'Twas not?"

"No," he continued. "The Ark was crafted of sacred wood, imbuing it with immense pleroma. Some claim it was cut from the Tree of Life and bore the power to grant men—"

"And women," Sophia interjected with a raised brow.

Thomas smiled, inclining his head. "Yes, and women—the power of gods."

"But we cannot prove all this," Matilda chimed in. "Not yet, at least."

"Correct," Sophia agreed.

"Wait," Miryam interjected, "you mean the Tree of Life in the Garden of Eden?"

"Yes," Father Thomas said. "We believe the Tree of Life was fashioned into the Ark, along with other sacred relics. What remains to us now is only this chest. When the Babylonians conquered Jerusalem, most were destroyed in fire."

"But this chest endured," Sophia added softly.

Miryam's mind spun. "How did it come to be here? How does the wood hold pleroma? Does it make one immortal? And where is the true Garden of Eden? Are there still trees that—"

Ved cleared his throat. Miryam flushed, lowering her eyes with a small, sheepish grin.

"We do not have all the answers," Sophia said, "Yet we believe an ancient Jewish sect—the Essenes—kept it safe for centuries. From there, it passed into the keeping of Jesus and his disciples. Later, the Gnostics buried it here—in this very cave—nearly six-hundred years ago."

"I remember reading about the Gnostics in the texts you gave me," Miryam said, eager to add her bit of knowledge. "Their teachings spoke of the divine spark within each of us. They believed every soul held God inside, but that the rulers feared such knowledge."

"Yes," Sophia replied, nodding slowly.

"So ... are you Gnostics?"

"We are ... and we are not," Father Thomas answered.

Miryam's brow furrowed. "Then pray, what is it you believe?"

Sophia leaned forward, her eyes warm. "We believe God reveals Himself—or Herself" — she gave Miryam a quick wink — "in many forms, to all people, in every corner of our Earth."

"To us, God is not one man upon a throne in Heaven," Thomas said.

Sophia nodded. "Rather, God is ... pleroma. 'Tis within us, around us, in all things. It matters not whether one calls oneself Gnostic, Jew, Saracen, or Pagan, we all hold pleroma the same."

"In short, 'tis why we can all do magic," Matilda said proudly.

"All humans?" Miryam asked, eyes wide.

"Yes," Sophia answered. "But most have no sense of it."

"Then why do we not tell them? Should not the world know of such wonders?" Miryam's voice rose with excitement, as did her pulse. Her mind raced—if all people understood this, the burdens of daily drudgery might vanish. Perhaps they could be free.

She could be free.

"Because those in power would never allow it," Father Thomas replied gravely. "That is why we practice in secret. 'Tis our duty to protect the Chest of Immortality. In the wrong hands—especially those of the Church—it would be twisted for control."

Miryam hesitated, then smiled faintly. "I have but one more question."

"Only one?" Sophia teased.

Miryam laughed, the sound bouncing off the cave walls. "Why would the authorities wish to keep the truth from people?"

Sophia looked around the circle. "An excellent question. Maybe one of our students would answer?"

Matilda's hand shot up at once. Fern, slower, raised his as well.

Sophia said, "Fern, go ahead."

Matilda gave a small grunt.

In a timid, quiet voice, Fern spoke. "It began in the Garden of Eden. The gods saw that after Eve ate of the Tree of Knowledge, if she and Adam also ate of the Tree of Life, humankind would become like them—like gods. So, they barred the way, lest we discover our own pleroma. Since that day, they have done all they can to keep humans separated from their true power."

"That is not the story taught," Miryam interjected.

"When last did you read the Bible, child?" Sophia asked.

"Well, I ... I have not," Miryam admitted, her brows knitting. "But in church, we were told God punished Adam and Eve for heeding the serpent. That is why they were banished—was it not?"

"Matilda," Father Thomas said, "fetch a Bible, and let us read Genesis together."

She ran off and soon returned with a leather-bound book, placing it in Miryam's hands.

Miryam read silently.

There it was.

She set the book down, her nose scrunched. "But I do not understand. Was the serpent good? Who were these gods? And why would they not want mankind to hold the same power as they?"

"More excellent questions—ones we shall answer in due time," Father Thomas said with a warm chuckle. "I knew we made a wise choice in welcoming you into our order."

Miryam began. "But—"

"All in good time, dear." Sophia gently cut her off. "Fern, would you continue the tale of the Tree of Life?"

Fern swallowed, his voice soft but steady. "The Demiurge—one of the false gods—slain the tree, so none could ingest its fruit. He then used its wood to fashion sacred objects for himself and the other gods. When people beheld the power within those relics, they began to worship the Demiurge as the one true God instead."

"Thank you, Fern." Sophia inclined her head.

Father Thomas added, "It is no small matter to guard this chest—or wield pleroma. Before you may move further in your lessons, we must be certain you can carry the weight of such power, as not all can."

Miryam drew a sharp inhale. "How can one be *sure*?"

"The chest holds a great store of pleroma," Thomas explained. "Across the ages, similar objects steeped in such power have allowed those unwilling to labor at their own inner work seize these artifacts, and too often, they have turned that magic toward greed or destruction."

Her curiosity peaked. "What kind of objects?"

"Some minerals, like quartz, or even certain flowers and herbs may be used. On the darker side, some have turned to sacrifice—animals, even humans. A human soul holds great amounts of pleroma." Father Thomas's voice deepened, heavy with warning. "That is why it would be most perilous should this chest fall into the hands of those who seek harm or control."

"And so, your next lesson begins this day," Sophia said. "You shall be given a fraction of the chest's magic. What you do with it shall be your choice."

"What?" Miryam froze, her mouth hanging open. Surely, she was too new, too untested. Yet even as doubt rose, a slow wave of exhilaration followed. She was going to touch *pleroma*—even if but for a moment. Her heart pounded. Her palms grew slick. She nodded, perhaps too quickly, and smiled wide.

Sophia gestured her forward. "Ved, the key."

Ved reached beneath his tunic and drew out a leather cord. A small wooden piece hung from it—shaped like a writhing snake. He removed it and went to the hidden drawer in the wall, where another piece lay waiting. This one was silver, yet identical in form. Pressing one to the other, the halves clicked together, forming a single key.

Miryam stared in awe. "Why doest Ved wear one half?"

"Another day, dear," Sophia interrupted gently.

Ved knelt by the chest, placed the key within the lock, and lifted the lid just a finger's breadth. From the opening, a wisp of sparkling smoke unfurled. It curled upward, glimmering, then drifted straight toward Miryam.

"Now, step forward and breathe it in," Sophia instructed.

Miryam's heart raced, but her feet would not move. Fear and wonder warred within her, a thousand thoughts surging all at once.

At last, her excitement won.

She stepped closer, lifted her chin, and drew in the shimmering cloud. Warmth tingled through her nostrils, then rushed down through her chest, into her lungs, filling her. Power coursed outward to her limbs, buzzing like a hive of bees under her skin. Her spine straightened as a surge rose from its base up to the crown of her head. And the world slowed. Her senses sharpened. Every sound around her amplified. Every breath. Every heartbeat. The candle flames swayed in rhythmic waves. Soft colors bloomed into geometric patterns, radiating from each soul in the chamber.

And Ved. His energy was the brightest, swirling and pulling at her new senses. She could not fathom how she had failed to see it before. Holding her hand out before herself, she watched as her fingers threaded near-invisible lines of pleroma in the air.

"We will convene again tomorrow," Father Thomas said. "Everyone, save Miryam, silent meditation and prayer for the next two hours. Then attend to your daily chores. We shall see you at the evening meal."

"Wait," Miryam exclaimed. "Am I not to receive any guidance?"

"Simply think and it shall be so," Sophia replied before she, Thomas, and the elders left the cave, leaving only the students in silence.

Miryam turned toward Ved, eager to pour out everything she was feeling. But he, like the others, had already closed his eyes for meditation.

She stood for a moment, still gazing at her hands. The strange pulse of energy thrumming beneath her skin, flowing down into her fingertips. She clenched one hand into a fist, focusing all her thoughts on *fire*.

Opening her palm, a tiny orange flame leapt from the center of her hand.

Fern gasped. Matilda cracked an eye open, leaned toward him, and whispered something before returning to her meditation.

The flame extinguished.

Heat rose in Miryam's cheeks. If she were to test this gift, she wanted to do it without watchful eyes. Leaving the cave and stepping into open air, Miryam felt lighter. Her stride carried a new confidence—one she had yet to experience. This power made her feel like anything was possible.

And it felt good.

Skipping to her spot by the pond, Miryam stretched out her hand above the water, and she circled her fingers. The surface rippled and spun, forming a tiny whirlpool. She pulled her hand higher, and the water rose, following her command, before she flung it outward in a spray across the pond.

The world was truly alive around her. The sky was bluer, the grass greener. Insects and birds moved in rhythm, as though breathing with the Earth. Miryam drew in a deep breath. She felt pleroma pulse through her, weaving its power into every fiber of her being, surging through her heart.

And in its wake, the hard coal in her chest—once thought extinguished—ignited.

Her nostrils flared, her brows pulled tight toward the center of her eyes. Catching her by surprise, Miryam thought she had dealt with her feelings around Dempsey and what had happened to her in the woods. *'Twas not my fault. 'Twas Dempsey's.*

The hard coal swelled to a simmering fiery ember, rage fueling it from within. But this time, her anger was not directed toward herself. *Dempsey needs to pay. And I mustn't let him do this again. Not to me. Not to anyone.*

Clouds began to churn above, thunder cracking in the distance. Miryam clenched her fist, then opened it. A flame leapt up in her palm, stronger this time, and she grinned. How had she not seen it before? What needed to be done. It was so obvious now. What Dempsey deserved.

What *she* could do to him.

She rose to her feet and strode through the courtyard toward the gates, where a monk stood idly watch there.

"Good day," he said with a sleepy nod.

"Step aside. I must leave," Miryam commanded.

His eyes blinked a few times. "Perhaps we shall ask Father Thomas—"

"No one tells me what I can or cannot do." Her voice rang out.

Another clap of thunder shook the sky. Rain began to fall, dark drops splattering on the courtyard stones. With a thrust of her hand, the gates burst open, the wood cracking as though struck by lightning.

Miryam gasped at her own power, stumbling back. *What are you doing?* A steady, quiet voice whispered from within.

Nearby monks stopped their sweeping, staring at the shattered gate, then back at each other, unsure what to do.

Rain poured down, soaking her hair and dress. Miryam pushed the strands from her face, chest heaving. The pleroma within roared, fueling her feelings and clouding her thoughts. The red coal burned hotter than ever. *Dempsey must be stopped.*

She turned back to the monk at the gate. "Move. Now!" she shouted over the storm's heavy patter.

His hesitation lasted only a breath. "Very well," he said, stepping aside.

Miryam crossed the threshold, but at the cusp of the doorway, the still voice rose again. *This isn't you.*

She froze. Spinning around, Miryam looked at the monks in the courtyard. Worried expressions blanketed their faces, and murmurs echoed against the stone walls.

Then, she saw *him*. Ved.

Disappointment swept across his face as their eyes met.

This isn't me. Miryam's shoulders eased. A wave of calm washed over her. The fire inside settled, and for a moment she felt in control again. If only she could turn back time, erase the scene that had just unfolded. Her anger ebbed as the storm above softened to a drizzle. Her gaze clung to Ved's like an anchor, desperate for safety, fearful of what might have happened had she let herself go further. Worried about what might have happened had she truly been set *free*.

She breathed—slow, steady—*in and out*.

What would she have done if she had passed through the gate? Confront Dempsey? Make him pay? How? By hurting him? *Killing* him? But she had not. She had stopped.

She had not abused her power. Not ... yet.

Her head spun, and her heart made silent pleas to Ved's eyes, praying he would tell her she was still good. Not lost. Not sinful.

But his eyes broke from hers, and he let out an audible sigh.

A cry escaped Miryam's throat, soft as a whisper. "I am sorry," she said, fleeing down the stony corridor to her room.

CHAPTER 32

LEAH

A well of tears rose through Leah's throat to the cusp of her eyes, heat coursing through her body as she stood frozen in her work's parking lot—besot with disbelief and anger that even Seth would stoop this low. How could she let herself fall right into his trap? And this close to the custody case. She squeezed her eyes shut, willing her tears to hold off.

Seth rolled his head back and laughed, face bloodied. "This is better than seeing that damn book. I'll get it anyway." He wiped his mouth with his sleeve and winked. "See you in court."

Leah shoved her way past him, got in her car, and drove off.

Throughout the entire drive home, she kept her sobs at bay. The last thing she needed was to get into an accident because she wasn't paying attention. Still, she cursed Seth in her mind. Her thoughts kept replaying the same potential custody case scene.

The one where Seth wins, and she loses Hana.

Bubbling up like a pot about to overboil, her feelings edged the surface, begging to spill out. She tried to contain them, shove them down, to the furthest reaches of her mind. But with a pot on high heat, they just kept coming, pushing back harder.

The house was quiet when she entered. Hana was still at robotics club.

Alone, Leah let the pot overflow. She screamed out. *Loud.* Hoping her neighbors wouldn't hear, knowing they would. She didn't care. She dropped her purse, its contents cascading across the ground. Her voice echoed off the walls, reverberating throughout her body. She let the waves take her to the floor as well, where she rested her head on the cool linoleum, heaving in gnarled sobs.

For the first time in years, Leah didn't hold back.

She cried. Messy, ugly tears. All the pain and anger she felt towards Seth. All the frustration of barely making it by. All the feelings of being a fraud at work. Disappointing those she loved—repeatedly. She wailed.

Until there wasn't a drop left in her.

Then, peeling herself off the floor, she dragged her heavy body to the kitchen. On autopilot, she found a bottle of red wine in the cabinet and poured it into the nearest cup, taking a huge gulp. Then another. And another.

When her cup was empty, she poured more.

Within an hour—or was it minutes?—the bottle was empty.

Leah hunched over the dining table, disheveled. The swimming buzz of alcohol blurred her thoughts and numbed her feelings. She half-smiled.

Click. The front door opened, and Hana bounded in.

Scrambling, Leah quickly rose, knocking the chair down from behind her. In one sweeping yet clumsy motion, she tried to smooth out her hair and simultaneously hide the wine, all while stumbling toward the kitchen. As she made her way, she tripped over her purse's contents.

She tilted her head. *How did those get there?*

Luckily, she saved the bottle from shattering but kicked something in her drunken mess.

"Mom!" Hana yelled, dropping her backpack and rushing toward her. "You killed Hermes!"

Leah looked down at her feet to see Hermes, their tiny tomato plant—broken with soil falling out—exposing his roots.

Hana knelt and scooped her plant from the ground.

"What is he even doing inside?" Leah's face contorted as she held back a burp. She choked out, "I thought he was supposed to be on the porch."

"Our neighbor's cat kept coming over and messing with his soil, so I moved him in here where I thought he'd be" — Hana shot a glare at Leah — "*safer.*"

Hermes' main stem had snapped right in the middle. His top half flopped over like a limp rag-doll. One almost-ripe tomato lay on the ground.

Hana tenderly held Hermes as she pushed dirt back in and tried to scrape up more from the floor. She looked back at Leah and wrinkled her brow. "Aren't you going to say something?"

Leah gaped at the sad plant, a haze swirling in her head. "I didn't see him."

She reached down to help.

"No." Hana pulled Hermes close to her.

"I think he'll live." Leah went to touch the broken part of Hermes's stem. "We just need to cut off this part, and he'll bounce back."

"Don't touch him," Hana snapped at her. She narrowed her eyes at Leah closely for the first time since getting home. "God, Mom, are you drunk?"

Leah stared at her daughter. She wanted to hold her, hug her, and tell her how she was feeling. How she had been wronged. How life kept throwing her punches, and she didn't know how much more she could take.

But she didn't say a word.

Instead, she stepped back, swaying in place.

"Ewww, you are." Hana sniveled her nose. "I can smell it on your breath."

"I'm sorry," was all Leah could edge out.

"That's not going to work this time." Hana shook her head. "Now, I'm going to get a bad grade in biology because of *you.*" She stood to go, clutching the plant like a baby. "And I'm taking Hermes to my room where you can't hurt him."

Leah huffed, the beginnings of her usual migraine pressing on her skull. "Honey, let's talk."

"There's nothing to talk about. I don't want to see you right now. Don't" — Hana held up a finger — "follow me."

She left, slamming her bedroom door behind her.

Leah closed her eyes, lips quivering. *First, Kat is mad at me. And now Hana.*

I am a fucking mess.

A throbbing pain in her head was starting to replace the wine buzz. She wasn't sure if it was from the alcohol wearing off or her normal daily migraine inching closer.

She had almost gotten used to them now.

I need something to make me feel good. Anything ...

Her mind wandered to Tate. Leah imagined him with his cute, goofy smile, his light-hearted laugh, and his lean, tall body. Pressed up against her. Waves crashing on them. The feeling of being free. A deep desire surged in her groin.

Grabbing her car keys, she packed up her purse contents. Her entire body craved to feel better, and she knew exactly how to do that.

At least, her tipsy, uninhibited brain thought so.

Leah arrived at Tate's office just before five. She checked her makeup in the mirror and popped a breath mint into her mouth before getting out of the car.

The elevator dinged when it reached Tate's floor. She leaned forward, peeking out into the hallway, and checked for a wet-floor sign before stepping out. The coast was clear. *Good.* She confidently—albeit a little wobbly—strode toward the door of Tate's law firm and opened it. As usual, there was no front-desk person to greet her. It was quiet except for the tick of the wall clock. Maybe he had already gone home for the day. Her shoulders slumped, and she wondered about backing away. That thought depressed her, and she frowned.

She kept marching forward, rounding the corner that led to his office. A light was on, and the door was slightly ajar. He was still there.

Leah smiled as she slowed her pace, inching toward the door. Leaning in close, ear forward. The steady sound of his fingertips on a keyboard meant everything. It was perfect. No one else was in the office. She gently knocked as she peeked in.

"Leah?" Tate's spine stiffened, then relaxed almost at once.

"Hi," she breathed back. She licked her lips, her mind and heart racing as she thought about what she wanted to do with him.

He threw her an enchanting smile. "What are you doing here?"

She wanted him even more now than ever.

"I was driving by and thought I'd stop in," Leah said. *Starting with a lie. Great job.* Her inner voice told her to leave while she still could. But another part of her kept her unsteady feet in place. "I wanted to see you."

"About what?"

Leah stepped closer to him, carefully placing each foot down, as if being tested for sobriety. The voice in her head got louder, asking her what the fuck she was thinking. But her body led, making its way to the side of the desk where Tate sat.

"About us."

With that, one of Leah's hands stroked his face. The other grabbed his chair, turning it to face her.

"I thought—"

She straddled him.

His spine hardened. That—and something else.

"I got to thinking, why wait?" She leaned forward. "Why does it matter that you're my lawyer? There's no rule that says we can't date."

Tate, wide-eyed and flustered, gaped at her briefly before looking away.

Leah bent down and kissed his neck. He still smelled of fresh linen. Leah inhaled and kissed again.

He pushed her away for a moment and gulped, loud enough for her to hear. "Actually, there are rules about what I can and I cannot do when you're my client."

She laughed, ignoring him, and kissed his neck, moving her way up to his face. "Fuck those rules." Leah pulled him into a long, hard kiss. Her fingers ran through his hair and down his arms.

He finally gave in and kissed her back, pulling her deeper into him. *This. This is what I wanted, what I needed.*

Leah's mind focused on one thing. To feel good. And all the other stuff magically faded away. It had been so long since she'd been with a man.

Way too long.

Tate's arms cupped the nape of her neck, sending a shiver of goosebumps along her skin. She pressed against him, feeling the heat between their bodies, sweat building. Their tongues danced with one another. His lips felt perfect on hers. Leah reached down to unbutton his shirt.

"Wait," he said between short, ragged breaths. "As much as I want *this*." His hands continued to explore her body. "We really shouldn't."

Tate pried his own hands away and lifted Leah off him.

"You don't want me?" she asked, doe-eyed.

Between another deep breath, he choked out, "Of course, I do. I have since the first day I met you, but this isn't the way ... or the time."

Embarrassment flooded Leah. Her cheeks reddened, and she could feel all those pesky feelings bubbling up inside of her again. "What's different now from the other night in your car?"

"You were right then. We need to wait until after the trial. I could lose my license. You could lose ..." Tate's voice trailed off, and he began shuffling with papers on his desk.

Leah's lips pursed together. She wanted to be mad at him and push him away. Protect herself. It's what she did. What she *always* did.

But something about Tate was different, and something couldn't quite let him go.

Tate spoke up. "Maybe we should talk somewhere less private. Have you eaten dinner? I know a great little taco stand down the street. Best street tacos in L.A., I promise. What do you say?"

"Fine," she said through tight lips.

They walked outside in silence, ordered food, and found a small table to sit at under a gazebo in the nearby park. The Sun was low in the sky, and the air had a slight breeze around them, cutting the day's heat. String lights illuminated the space. A few kids and their mom played on the small playground equipment. Their giggles filled the silent void.

It would have been a perfect first date.

"Leah?" Tate said between bites of taco. "You haven't said anything since leaving my office. What's on your mind?"

Oh, just that I sabotage everything good in my life ... because I don't think I deserve to be happy. I feel like my whole life is some repentance for something I did wrong. But what I desperately want is to be loved, but I keep screwing that up too.

Leah stared out at the busy street of cars flying by.

Because I don't actually love myself.

She knew her issues. She had analyzed the crap out of herself. But she couldn't say that out loud. Not to Tate. Not to anyone. Because then if she did, it would become real, and she'd have to deal with it. And honestly, ignoring it was easier.

At least, it used to be.

Finally, she said, "I'm sorry. I need to go. I'll see you next week at the hearing."

She set down her uneaten taco and left in a flurry.

"Leah," Tate called to her.

Go back! Go back and talk to him. The voice in her head screamed at her.

She didn't turn around. *If I talk to him, I'm just going to get hurt in the end. Why do I always feel like something bad is going to happen?*

Leah answered her own question.

Because it always does.

CHAPTER 33

KARAIA

Lying on Arjun's couch, eyes red and throat sore, Karaia gaped as a news segment of *On the Verge* with Brian Holster and Vee Maddox played on the massive holo-screen. They—along with every news outlet in the country—ran the story of the century: *The first Defier attack within New Soterian walls in a decade.*

It had only been a few hours since the events of the gala. Her dress smelled of fire and ash. She still wore others' blood on it. At some point after, her own cuts had been bandaged and tended to, but she didn't remember when or by whom. Her head ached, her stomach groaned, but mostly, her heart tightened with the weight of a hundred bloodied corpses.

Everything felt like a blur.

And Karaia still hadn't taken a single credit.

Next to her, Arjun scrolled through his socials, which ran parallel to the show, displaying on-screen as well. Questions arose on every media channel and social feed. It was all anyone was talking about.

> *"How did they breach our security walls?"*
> *"Will they attack again?"*
> *"How is Stellan coping after another encounter with the Defiers?"*
> *"What will President Marshall do to retaliate?"*
> *"Will NeuroTryp save us all?"*
> *"When did Stellan Marshall get so handsome?"*

Images of the night played back in Karaia's head. Cries of pain. Blood. And death. She squeezed her puffy eyes shut. Her mind begged for a credit. Or ten. But her gut stayed resolute. The time for erasure was over.

She had to get her memories back.

Opening her eyes, it was as if she were seeing reality for the first time. Everything around her seemed slightly off, like it was part of one of Arjun's VR games. The holo-screen wasn't real. The steri-bot that cleaned the already pristine room mocked her. Even the couch she lay on felt *too* comfy, like it was made of clouds, not actual material. Close to real life, but not quite.

Karaia narrowed her gaze at Arjun next to her. Eyes glazed over, a shell of himself, he tinkered with some holo-game while simultaneously watching the news and scrolling. She envied him, wondering how many credits he had taken.

"I knew it! I knew it," Brian barked from the screen.

"You knew what?" Vee asked with her usual shocked expression.

A steady yet building soundtrack played music behind the newscasters on the holo-screen. Karaia had never noticed that before.

"I knew there was going to be an attack." He slammed his fist down. "We have not done enough to keep our citizens safe. The only way is to take the fight to the Defiers, rather than wait for them to come to us."

Vee visibly shook in her studio chair, and the gaudy diamonds around her neck sparkled in the spotlight. "It is horrifying to think about this happening inside New Soteria. I can't imagine being at that gala when it happened. Can you?" She sipped a bright pink faux-tini.

Another fake thing. Karaia grimaced.

"Absolutely not." Brian solemnly shook his head. "I almost hit my daily limit of credits simply watching the footage. I heard that those in attendance will receive a free download of the latest NeuroTryp technology by Seromela."

"Speaking of that. Have you bought your copy yet?" Another sip of her faux-drink. "I can't wait to go on a NeuroTryp."

"I already *have*. After seeing that footage, I had to ..." He shuddered. "... get away. Just before this show, I was relaxing in a spa in the Tibetan mountains, all while I physically got ready to go on air. Multitasking at its finest."

He winked at the camera.

A false vacation.

"Wow, that's amazing!" Vee beamed. "How did it compare to normal VR? Do you remember what you did physically while you were on your Tryp?"

"This is the best VR tech I've *ever* experienced. It was so real. Physically, sort of like a dream. Blurry. But I still did a good job picking out a nice suit," Brian said with a chuckle as he looked at himself.

A false reality. Is anything real?

Karaia peeled herself into a seated position on the couch, rubbing her arms, shivering. She was cold despite the temperature being perfectly set. The crease in her brow deepened. She *had* to move. *Had* to do something. But her body protested, still shaken from the night's events.

Even listening to her sixth sense felt far away right now.

"Wow, just wow. I can't wait to take a NeuroTryp tonight." Vee clasped her hands together, looking directly at the camera. "How about you, viewers? Who is taking a NeuroTryp soon? Make sure to tag us and tell us about your experience at *On the Verge* with Brian and Vee. See you soon!" She gave the camera a small wave.

"Arjun," Karaia croaked out, unsure if her voice was even real.

No reply.

"Arjun," she repeated, glancing at him next to her.

A small white light sat on his temple—a NeuroTryp.

Not thinking, she shook his body. "Arjun!"

The light blinked off.

"Whoa," he said, looking all around the room in a daze.

"Were you seriously on a NeuroTryp right now?"

"Maybe," he said sheepishly. "I wanted to see what it was like."

Karaia exhaled loudly, willing herself to keep moving forward in her determination to get her memories back. But so much of her just wanted to sleep and fall into a deep blissful state. The two sides of her warred within. "I need your help. Can you get into the Seromela tracking system from your home office?"

"Is that even a question?" Arjun smugly replied, already getting up to walk to his home workstation.

She followed him, stretching her achy body as she made her way across the room. "I need to see where I got my brain wiped last week."

He pulled up the Seromela software on his computer.

Karaia leaned over his shoulder, watching his swift motions on-screen. "Have you ever heard of someone reversing one?"

Mouth agape, Arjun swiveled and looked directly at her. "Wait, what? You want to reverse it?"

With lips pursed, she nodded.

"I've heard it's super painful and can cause a mental break." He turned around and started typing again. "One guy who had his memories restored could never figure out *when* his memories happened. They all got jumbled up in his brain."

"I have to try. So ... can you help me?" Karaia said.

Arjun pulled up a three-dimensional map of Sector One.

Locate Karaia Pine, he typed.

Locating ...

The screen zoomed in, and a target popped up on the map. It hovered over Arjun's apartment.

"Well, at least we know this is accurate. Okay, now we copy your brainwave signature and sneak in the backend ... like this ..." He typed some code. "... and now we just need to get the last week of map data ..." Some more typing. He pulled up another screen. And then, another.

Karaia tried to follow, but this was beyond her coding skills. Plus, he was crazy fast.

"Anything yet?" she asked, tapping her foot.

"Not yet. Seromela doesn't really want anyone doing this unless directed by security ... wait, let me try something else." Arjun typed away. "Dang! It's restricted to those in senior management of Seromela's security department. We need a passcode."

"Can't you get past it?" Karaia bit her nails.

"I'm trying, but I helped design this system, and the second someone tries to break in, it triggers a security breach. There's no way of getting past it without that code. I'm too good even for my own hacking," he said, laughing a little to himself.

"What do we do? Arjun, I need to remember," she stressed. "I keep seeing flashes of this woman killed in an alley tube. There was a prick in my arm. And then something with my parents. Did I tell you about any of this last week?"

"No, sorry. Wait, your parents?" He turned, cocking his head to the side. "How are they connected to this?"

"I don't know," Karaia said as she rubbed her necklace. "That's why I need my memories back."

"Well, we do know someone in security ..." Arjun raised his eyebrows.

"Raven."

"Yup."

Could she trust Raven to keep this big of a secret? Karaia didn't know her that well. True, they had slept together and worked together, but beyond the superficial social events, Karaia didn't really *know* Raven. But she was desperate.

"Okay, let's call her. Do you want to do it?" she asked.

Arjun's eyes got big.

"I'll take that as a *no*." Karaia laughed for the first time that day. "I'll call her then."

An hour later, there was a knock at the door.

Arjun began frantically pacing, smoothing his hair and clothes. "I haven't changed since the gala. I'm all gross and dirty."

Another knock.

"We don't have time for this," Karaia said as she marched to answer the door. "Just take a credit."

She immediately regretted telling him to do so. But his shoulders already slumped with instant calm.

Karaia opened the door. Raven stepped inside, fresh and dressed for the next workday that hadn't even started yet. She was alert and scanned the apartment, then looked Karaia and Arjun up and down, still in their gala attire. Arjun bashfully excused himself to change clothes.

"Thanks for coming," Karaia said, biting down on her lower lip.

"I don't have a ton of time," Raven said curtly. "There's a ridiculous number of security measures we're working on as we speak. But rest assured. We, in collaboration with the New Soterian military force, have the tubes and borders secure now. We are safe once again." She nodded, reciting company lines.

Karaia clutched her stomach, a feeling of sickness overcoming her. She gawked as Raven spoke with such certainty. She was so *composed*. No, that wasn't the right word. Distant? Aloof? Sterile?

Content. That was the word.

It wasn't right. People had just died. How could she be so normal? Bile rose from Karaia's stomach. She gulped it back down. "I really appreciate you coming," she said, trying to appear calm.

"You sounded cryptic on the comm," Raven said through tight lips. "You need help with a security clearance ... for what?"

Karaia opened her mouth to speak. Then shut it again, drawing a deep breath in and out. *Now is not the time to back out.*

"Hey," Arjun said, returning in fresh clothes. He stood there awkwardly between the two of them.

Karaia finally said, "Uhhh, Arjun, would you pull it up?"

He didn't move.

"Arjun?"

"Oh sorry, was taking a credit. I'm good now." He strolled to his computer, pulling up the map.

"Is this for a work project?" Raven asked, leaning over him to get a good look at the screen.

Arjun tensed up.

"Not exactly ..." Karaia answered, joining them by the computer. Her voice was still shaky, but she was determined. "So, it's actually *personal*, not for work."

Raven straightened her spine, arching a brow.

Karaia stared into her eyes, hoping to find some semblance of emotion behind that tough exterior.

"Okay ..." Raven crossed her arms, matching her gaze.

Karaia could feel Raven studying her, trying to figure her out. She edged out a small smile, hoping it wouldn't seem too fake.

"Remember last week when we think I got my brain wiped?"

"Yeahhh."

"I need to go there again to get my memories back."

"Why?" Raven laughed.

Karaia held her breath.

"Oh, fuck, you're serious?"

Karaia started pacing the room. "I keep getting flashes of memories, not just of last week, but also from my childhood. I think they're connected somehow, and I just need to piece it all together. It's hard to explain. But I need your help."

Raven, narrowing her eyes, looked from Karaia to Arjun and back. "Fine," she said.

"You will?" Karaia exclaimed. "You will!"

"But," Raven interrupted her excitement, holding a finger in the air, "I'm reporting your brain wipe to Seromela in forty-eight hours. It is illegal under Section 45 of the New Soteria Constitution unless authorized by the government. Most aren't punishable by jail time, but you'll face a heavy fine and restricted travel access."

Karaia knew she was right. It was illegal.

She didn't care, but Raven did. On the other hand, she didn't even expect Raven to help them, so she wasn't about to argue.

"Deal." Karaia stuck out her hand, and they shook on it. "Now, we just need your security passcode."

Another smile forced.

Raven huffed. "Pull up Seromela's security portal."

She typed in the magical code, and now they had access to the entire country's past actions and movements.

Seromela tracked all of this.

Arjun began typing furiously. "This will just take a moment. The computer is scanning last week for your specific brain waves. It's not continuous, though. Scans are sent to the main server every fifteen minutes. Any more frequently, and it'd be too much data. Any longer and you might miss a location," he explained.

As they waited, Karaia realized she might finally get her answers. Her stomach quelled, and for the first time that day, she had a moment to reflect on more of the previous evening. Specifically, earlier in the night.

Her mystery man.

Stellan.

The memory of dancing with him warmed her from the inside, and she smiled for real. She wondered where he was now, hoping he wasn't hurt in the attack.

"Raven, did everyone in Griffin's family make it out safely tonight?" she asked. "After the first bombs, I saw the stage was empty."

"Yeah, they did," Raven answered. "In situations like this, we are prepared to get them out immediately. There's always a back door to escape through."

"Oh, of course, glad everyone is okay. Where are they now?"

"I think at ... home."

"And how is Stellan?"

Raven cocked her head. "Why are you asking about *him*?"

Before Karaia could answer, an icon beeped from Arjun's holo-computer.

It started moving around the map as the timestamp on screen went backwards in time—*Karaia* in reverse: The Grand Hall. Home. Work. Home. The combat club. Home. Grandma's house.

"Wait, go back a second. I mean, forward, whatever. Right after my grandma's house, I go somewhere that's not on my normal route," Karaia said, pointing at the map. "There. What's the address?"

Arjun paused the screen and zoomed in. "It says: 240052 East 85th Tube. Do you know it?"

"No," Karaia asked, her clammy palms beginning to sweat. "That's got to be the place. Can you see whether it's a home or a business?"

Arjun typed some more.

"It appears to be a ..." Arjun's brow creased. "... hair salon?"

"You got your brain wiped at a hair salon," Raven joked. "Maybe the style-bot accidentally fried your memories while doing your hair."

Karaia wasn't in the mood for jokes.

"I need to go there now," she said, resolute.

"What? No," Arjun insisted. "It's like two a.m. and you haven't even slept. Or showered. And terrorists just attacked us."

"I have to," Karaia retorted.

Arjun stared at her in disbelief.

"Looks like my work here is done." Raven nodded, checking the holo-screen on her wrist and heading for the door. "I need to get back to work, but remember, *forty-eight hours*, and I'm reporting that address."

The front door clicked shut.

Karaia let out an enormous sigh and shook her body, trying to let go of the whirlwind of anxiety it contained.

"Have you *still* not taken a credit?" Arjun gaped. "You're crazy."

"Yeah, maybe I am," she said, parading into his bedroom.

She gasped as she peeled the scaly, green dress off, being careful not to scrape her existing bandages or bump any of the growing bruises on her arms and legs. Next, she shuffled through Arjun's clothes for something that would fit her. She called out to him, "I need to go there—*now*."

"What? No, you can't go there *by yourself*. What if it's dangerous?" Arjun pleaded. "Why don't we do a little more digging first? See if that address pops up on any dark servers."

She returned in a fitted gray shirt with a serpentine creature on the front and some of Arjun's pants on, held up by a belt.

"You heard Raven. We don't have time. So yes, I'm going—alone," Karaia said as she laced up a pair of shoes she found by the front door. "Unless you want to go with me?"

The look on his face told her he hadn't even considered that option.

Arjun's words stumbled out of his mouth. "I can't. I get scared just thinking about a crowd. These are potentially dangerous people with crazy technology."

"You're right, but I'm still going," she said firmly, standing at the door.

"Karaia ..." He squirmed in his chair.

"Arjun ..."

"Fine. I'm going with you," he huffed and then paused, taking a credit.

"You will?" She was taken aback.

"Of course. You're my best friend," he said, striding toward her. "And we protect each other, remember?"

Karaia pulled him into a tight hug. "Then, let's not waste time."

"Ugh, did you know you stink?" He turned up his nose.

"I do now," she said, elbowing him hard.

They both chuckled and strode out into the dim, early morning.

The hair salon was dark inside, and the tube surrounding it—while always brightly lit—was empty. Most citizens were probably still at home asleep or consuming the latest media about the attack.

Karaia tried the doorknob. Locked. She peered through the window. The place had a sense of familiarity. Had she really been here before?

"Stand back," Arjun whispered to her.

"What?" She gaped, shocked again at his confident attitude.

"Let me see the door lock." He took out a small device from his pocket. His PET. He pulled his holo-screen from his wrist and typed a few things. Then, he held up the PET to the door's sensor.

Click! It opened.

"How'd you know how to do that?" she asked, slack-jawed.

"I've told you before. A guy's got to have his secrets." Arjun smirked.

They tiptoed into the empty store, each flicking a small flashlight from their wrists and scanning the area.

It appeared like any other salon. *What am I looking for?* Karaia strained to remember when she had been here. But everything was hazy.

She closed her eyes, listening inward. And waited.

A man grabbing her flashed before her mind. There was a struggle. Another door. And a winding descent. Snapping her eyes open, she glanced around. And at the very back of the store, there it was.

"Arjun?"

"Yeah."

"I found something," she whispered. "Come here."

They crept toward the narrow door.

It looked so plain, so ordinary. Yet, Karaia knew it wasn't. Her sixth sense confirmed this would lead to answers. To exactly what she didn't know. She reached for the handle and opened the door.

Arjun clung to her back as they stepped across the threshold. And went down.

Down through a winding labyrinth of dimly lit halls and endless stairs. Down into depths that seemed impossible knowing the lowest tubes were only thirty feet from the dusty brown Earth. *Down.* They had walked for what seemed like minutes—or hours. Karaia's mind began playing tricks on her. Shadows danced on the walls, and tiny scurrying claws echoed around them. She could hear Arjun's rapid breathing on her neck as he dug his fingernails into her side. Just as she wondered that maybe, somehow, they had made a wrong turn, they arrived at another door.

Arjun gripped Karaia's arm tight. "If we die here tonight, I just want to say—"

The door swung open.

Arjun let out a squeal.

Karaia jumped.

Two people stared back at them from inside a large room.

A short but tough-looking woman spoke. "How the fuck did *you* find us again?"

CHAPTER 34

MIRYAM

The knock at the door startled her. Miryam burrowed deeper beneath the wool, curling her legs tight and pressing her face to her knees. She wished she could undo the last hour. Rid herself of the pleroma that still hummed beneath her skin. Sink farther into this bed—into a deep abyss—where no one could find her. She had failed her second lesson; she was sure of it.

"Come in," she mumbled, praying it was not Ved.

"Miryam, dear?" Sophia's voice was soft as she slipped inside and sat on the bedside with a long exhale.

Keeping her face buried in the damp wool, hiding from the world, Miryam did not move an inch.

Sophia said nothing. She simply waited.

The silence grew heavy.

At last, Miryam dragged the blanket away, peeked out, and let the words fall from her mouth, thin and raw. "I erred."

Sophia nodded. "I heard."

"I cannot bear having such power. There is something wrong with me. I do not deserve to be here. The power—it nearly consumed me." The pleroma still whispered in Miryam's veins, its temptation like honey on her tongue. Shame bent her shoulders inward.

"Nearly," Sophia echoed.

"After but an *hour*? I shall pack my things and leave at once." Miryam's gaze stayed on the blankets. She imagined facing her father and Bella, and the thought of Dempsey returning to claim her.

She pictured giving up this chance at something magical; her old life pressed around her like a too-tight bodice. But perhaps a weaver's daughter—and wife—was all she was destined to be. She peered up at Sophia through wet lashes. "Why doest you say so little?"

Sophia lifted a brow but still did not answer.

Miryam answered her own fear. "You knew this would happen. You expected this." She shoved her face back under the blanket and let out a deep, guttural howl.

Sophia's smile was gentle. "Who said you must leave?"

"I failed, did I not?"

"Did you?"

Miryam felt as though she were trapped in a dark storm cloud. Unsure if she would ever break through the fog. Slowly, painfully, she sat up, wiping the tears from her face.

Sophia spoke softly, but firmly. "What I saw was a young woman *nearly* consumed by a great power—yet she stopped herself. That, my child, shows true strength. You did not let anger rule thy actions. Still, that anger lives in you, and soon you must face it."

"What say you?" Miryam whispered, eyes widening, clinging to the hope of blue skies beyond the storm.

"You may stay," Sophia said. "So long as you refrain from any more outbursts today." She chuckled softly, not in mockery but in warmth.

Relief broke through Miryam's clouded heart.

She smiled widely. "Thank you, thank you, thank you! I promise I shall not." She leaned forward and embraced Sophia. The power still surged within her, but she vowed not to let it—or her anger—take control again.

She had learned her second lesson.

A chilly autumn week passed. The leaves, once a blaze of orange, had dulled to brown, bowing to the coming winter. During that time, Miryam kept mostly to herself. She did her chores, helped with the last of the harvest, and filled her journal with words she could not yet speak aloud.

This morning though, it was time to face what she had feared. Miryam, painstakingly slow, made her way down into the cave, where once she had looked forward to going to, but now ... she didn't know what to expect. Would they shun her? Cast her out of their circle?

She had silently avoided interacting with the order members after her outburst at the gate. But now, here she was, back in the cave, surrounded by all of them, with Father Thomas and Sophia standing at the head. Miryam sat right across from Ved. Every part of her longed to sink into his dreamy eyes, to find in them the forgiveness she so desperately sought. Yet, fear held her back. She remembered too clearly his look of disappointment in the courtyard.

Instead, she stared downward, tracing small circles in the dust.

Sophia's voice drew her attention. "Now that you have completed your first two lessons, Miryam, 'tis time for your third—and final—lesson as an initiate. However, many find it to be the most difficult."

Miryam lifted her eyes. "And what is it?"

"The lesson," Father Thomas answered, "is to surrender."

"Surrender?" Miryam leaned her head to the side. "And what do you mean, *final lesson*? What happens after that?"

"Once your lessons are complete, you shall face the last rite of passage—your initiation," Father Thomas said. "You must descend into the underworld, confront your inner demons, and retrieve your power—your own unique way of wielding pleroma. After this, you shall be counted as a true student, though your training will continue for many years to come."

Sophia raised a finger. "But first, you must learn to surrender, else you will never pass the initiation. Would one of our students explain why surrender is so vital to our practice?" She glanced around the circle.

Matilda's hand shot up, wiggling eagerly.

Sophia nodded to her.

"When we surrender," Matilda explained, "it allows us to use pleroma for the highest good, not merely for our own desires."

"Why should not we use it for our own desires?" Miryam asked.

Father Thomas answered, "At times, our desires may be righteous. Yet even when they are, our vision is narrow. When we surrender to something greater than ourselves, we gain the chance to see from a higher vantage. We cease to cling to trivial matters—wealth, influence, earthly hungers. Then comes the possibility of merging with pleroma wholly, becoming one with the fullness of existence—with God itself."

"'Tis what I meant to say," Matilda added quickly.

Miryam's face scrunched. "If we are meant to merge with *all*," — she waved a hand in the air — "why are we made separate in the first place?"

"Ah, yes. You do ask good questions." Thomas smiled. "Yet that is an answer one can only find within thyself."

Her face fell in disappointment. "Then, how doest I learn to surrender?"

"You simply tell God you wish to surrender," Sophia said, "and you shall be given the lesson you need."

"'Tis so plain?" Miryam asked, exhaling in relief.

"Yet not so simple," Sophia cautioned.

"When you ask for a lesson," Thomas said, "be ready for resistance and trial. We humans are persistently stubborn learners by nature."

"So, after I ask ... then pray tell?" Miryam tilted her head.

"You wait," Sophia stated. "Until that time, students, resume your daily meditations. Miryam, once you have finished all your lessons and your initiation, you shall be welcome to join us. For this morn, however, I ask you to tend the garden and help prepare our afternoon meal."

Miryam longed to remain with the group. Most of her time at the abbey had been spent in the kitchen, the garden, or bent over a washbasin. She ached to practice magic with the order, not do trivial chores. The work was starting to remind her of the dull life of a weaver's daughter.

Home. A twinge pulled at her heartstrings. Home wasn't always *so* dull. She missed her father and Isabella deeply. However, she wasn't sure if she could ever go back to a life of such repetition and drudgery, now that she knew pleroma existed in the world—and in her.

No, she was determined to complete her lessons, even if it meant enduring these chores for now.

"Very well. Thank you." She bowed and left the cave.

God, she said in her head, *if you are listening, I ask to surrender.* The thought felt foolish, but she clung to it, regardless.

In the garden, she set to digging carrots. The first frost had already come, and now was the time to pluck the last of the roots from the ground and pack them in sand for the winter cellar. She bent low, parted the leafy tops, pressed her fingers into the damp Earth, and tugged. A long purple carrot came free, still clotted with dirt. She brushed it off and laid it in her basket, then reached for another, and another. Soon seconds slipped into minutes, minutes into hours, until two baskets brimmed full.

High above her head, the winds shifted, and the sky darkened. Where the morning had been clear, now gray clouds gathered. A gentle rain fell, wetting her hair and forming droplets on her wool dress. Yet, the water felt comforting against her skin. She had been carrying tension since that day in her chest, and now, as the rain soaked her, it slowly washed away.

Each day, she thought, *a little more of my anger subsides. Perhaps this is surrender.*

"Hurry, girl, get those carrots inside before the storm breaks!" one nun shouted from the kitchen.

"Coming!" Miryam called back. She carried the baskets in just as the clouds opened and heavy rain poured down.

Lightning splintered across the sky, followed by a long roll of thunder.

"Is there aught else I can do to help today?" Miryam asked.

"Not now. You may spend the rest of the day in silent prayer or study," the nun replied, grabbing the carrots from her.

Miryam hurried beneath the thatched canopy, keeping as dry as she could until she reached her room. There, she opened her journal and wrote as the storm roared beyond her window, words of letting go, of loosening her grip on the anger she still held, of becoming a truer version of herself.

She smiled.

Sophia would call it *progress*.

Hours passed before the storm eased to a soft, misting rain. Beams of sunlight pierced through the thick clouds, glistening on the wet stones. From her small window, Miryam watched as the members of the order filed up the steps from the cave. Ved came last. His expression, usually solemn, carried a deeper weight that day. A crease set firm between his brows.

Miryam's heart stirred at the sight of him. She longed to hear his calm, measured voice, to lose herself in his soft oceanic eyes, to feel that pull she could never quite resist.

But she had not spoken to him since *that* day.

She could keep hiding from him ... or she could be brave. Drawing a steady breath, she chose the latter.

Stepping out of her room, she pranced down the stone path that led around to the main courtyard.

With eyes set on the ground, Ved didn't see her approach.

"Hi," she said, stepping in front of him, biting down on her bottom lip.

He halted, meeting her gaze only momentarily. While his mouth did not smile, his eyes softened, and the crease between them eased. "Hi."

"I was thinking ..." Miryam twirled a finger in one of her curls. *Be brave*, she reminded herself.

"All very pious thoughts, no doubt," Ved replied, the corner of his mouth lifting.

She enjoyed making him smile.

"Of course," she said quickly. "I would not want Will to overhear aught." She cast a sly glance at the other students, then winked. "Would you walk with me?"

Ved gave a small nod.

Together they slipped away from the group, down one of the quieter corridors. Miryam lifted her skirts slightly and danced from stone to stone, careful to skip over the puddles left by the rain. A light hum escaped her lips. It felt good to be playful again. She had missed it—missed *herself*.

And she liked that Ved brought that part of her back.

"So," Ved said at last, "what was it you were thinking?"

Miryam spun toward him, eyes bright. "Let us go somewhere—beyond the walls. Only for an hour or two. I want an adventure. Some excitement."

He fell silent.

"I promise—*nothing* romantic." She held her hands up innocently. "Do you never wish to go beyond these walls and be free to do as it pleases you?"

"I feel free all the time," Ved answered. "Though I seldom leave these walls, my mind and spirit have wandered the heavens and beyond. I do not feel constrained. In time, you shall see."

Miryam strode ahead of him, arms up and twirled. "Ugh, but what of surrendering? Are not you meant to be open to what God presents?" Rushing back toward him, she stopped mere inches from his body, breathing him in. "And here you are, presented with the chance for a little spontaneous fun. How can you deny God?" She lifted her chin, satisfied with her clever turn of the argument.

Ved's lips quivered. "I do not believe that is what surrendering means."

"I am serious." Miryam tried her best to look solemn and wise, though the sides of her mouth twitched and betrayed her. "You told me once that you never played as a child. Sometimes life need not be so rigid. It can be messy—or even wet!"

With that, she leapt into a nearby puddle, splashing rainwater across both their feet.

Ved shook his head, but there was laughter in his eyes. "You make a fair point."

Miryam did not know if he truly believed her—or if he simply wanted a reason to stay near her. Either way, she did not care. For their eyes met, and her heart swelled.

At last.

It had been far too long.

Ved's lips curved into a grin. Leaning in, he whispered, "I know a way out that will draw little notice. Come."

He led her to the back wall of the abbey, where a narrow wooden door opened onto the woods and the path toward the creek.

They stepped through the opening into a glistening forest-scape. The mossy floor lay heavy with water, and droplets clung to bare branches and the last fading leaves of autumn. The rush of a creek called nearby. Birds flitted from tree to tree, their chirps echoing through the damp air. And as shafts of sunlight pierced the clouds, the forest seemed to glow, every color deep and alive.

"'Tis so magical," Miryam exclaimed as she skipped ahead of Ved, stretching her arms wide and breathing in the sweet scent of rain and flowers. She spun around to face him, walking backward with a playful grin.

A smile lingered on Ved's face, soft and untroubled. Whatever had weighed upon it before was now gone. "It is," he replied.

Was he speaking of the forest—or of her? She hoped for the latter.

"This reminds me of the day we met in the woods, when you startled me," she said, still marching backward.

"Miryam—"

"The whole forest feels alive," she went on, swaying her arms from side to side. "The birds, the trees, the water—everything."

His voice rose. "Miryam—"

"Can we do another meditation, like that day?" she asked, lost in her own delight.

She took another step back.

"Miryam, watch out!" Ved shouted.

But it was too late.

Her heel slipped on a rain-slick stone at the creek's edge. Swollen waters churned beneath her. She caught one last glimpse of Ved's hand reaching for hers—before she toppled backward into the rushing stream.

Most days, the spring-fed creek drifted in a gentle, lazy current, barely a foot or two deep. But today, with the recent storm, the waters surged high and fast.

Miryam plunged into the frigid water. The rushing current seized her, pulling her under in its icy grip. Needles of cold pierced her skin like a thousand pins. Her back slammed against the rocky bed.

She tried to scream, but only a gurgle escaped as a stream of liquid forced its way down her throat, choking her, flooding her where no water belonged.

Panic overtook her. Thrashing, arms flailing, her hands clawed at nothing as water rushed through her fingertips. She couldn't tell which way was up or down. The wool dress twisted tight around her legs, holding her, dragging her deeper.

The cloudy water blinded her.

Her lungs burned, begging for air.

Time blurred into one long endless ache in her chest, and the thought struck—she could not hold on much longer.

Then—her fingers brushed against something.

Reeds.

She clutched at them desperately, yanking herself upward. Her head broke the surface. She coughed, sputtered, gasping ragged breaths. "Ved!" she cried hoarsely, but her voice was drowned in the roar of rushing water.

The current still pulled at her—clawing—beckoning her to bend to its will. Her grip on the reeds was weakening, her fingers stiff from the cold.

The stream tugged harder, relentless.

She was slipping, losing strength.

"Miryam!" Ved shouted as he sprinted along the bank, stretching his arm out over the tall grasses. "Take my hand."

The ceaseless current tugged at Miryam's body as she strained to keep her head above water. She clung to the plants with one hand and reached with the other, but their fingers couldn't meet.

"Ved, I cannot hold much longer," Miryam gasped out. Water lapped against her face. The icy whisper of submission called her. Her grip was slipping.

"Do you trust me?" he asked, eyes resolute.

"Of course, I do."

"Then, let go."

"What?"

"I promise," he said, holding a hand to his heart, "you shall be all right."

Fear plagued Miryam's heart—fear of losing Ved, fear of dying before she truly lived, fear of never learning to know her true power. "I cannot let go."

Ved's blue eyes locked with hers. "Miryam, do you not see? 'Tis your lesson. You can surrender to the current pulling you—or you can fight and try to control it."

His words rang true.

She had always thought herself free, someone who let go and had fun. But she'd always been in control of her actions. Despite her dull existence as a weaver's daughter, Miryam had still maintained control of herself. Until ... Dempsey had taken that from her, leaving her terrified of powerlessness.

The fear of losing control was greater than any fear of sin or death.

"I do not think I can let go," she muttered through the rushing waters.

"I believe in *you*, Miryam," Ved said, his voice steady, unbreaking. "You have made me question all I thought I knew—in the best way possible. I cannot imagine my life without you in it."

His words wove their way through her, settling in her heart, and her panic ebbed.

"Trust," she whispered as she released the reed.

Then, the current swept her away.

CHAPTER 35

LEAH

I am in this place again. The place where the fog blurs my vision so greatly. I can't see past my history or the story I've told myself. I want to tell myself that life's not fair. That no one wants to be around me. And if they do, it always ends badly.

I tell Hana that I'm feeling this way again. She doesn't take the bait. I try to justify my story by telling myself that even she doesn't want to be around me.

Why do I keep pushing people away?

Why do I keep telling myself the same story?

Why is it so hard to change?

I should tell Tate how I feel about us, about the journal, but letting myself be vulnerable is so hard. It's because I want to be strong, to be tough, to hold my own. But here I am, alone again.

That's what I'm most afraid of. Being alone. There, I said it. Well, technically, I wrote it. And now, I've gone and pushed everyone away. It started with my mother. Then, Seth. Now, it's Kat and Tate. Even Hana is mad at me. What if that changes what she says at the trial? I can't imagine not having her to snuggle with or laugh with. I feel like I haven't even lived my life yet.

But my life isn't over.

So why do I keep telling myself lies? This isn't the right place or time. I have too much to do. I can't be happy. I'm not good enough. I don't deserve love.

Because I don't love myself. That's the big one.

Love. Why does it have to be so tricky and complicated? What would it look like to allow love into my life? Could I love others if I loved myself? Why can't I just stop thinking all the time and just go do it?!

These migraines are a bitch.

Leah set her pen down and crossed out the last line in her journal. This was her therapist's latest assignment. To journal her thoughts and feelings. It might work, except Leah didn't have a problem knowing what her thoughts and feelings were.

She just didn't listen to them.

A migraine pressed upon her skull.

Leah pushed her own journal away and glanced at Miryam's tattered one. It had been a few days since she had last read it. Miryam had just written about her second lesson in the order. She had almost failed, consumed with power. Now, she was preparing for her third and final lesson. It made for an interesting story, at least. *But could it be real?* Leah shook her head. It was hard to believe that Miryam really could be the woman she had seen in her vision. She picked up the leather-bound book. Her migraine's dull pressure faded away.

She set the book back down. And the migraine returned in full force.

She quickly picked it back up. Migraine gone.

Leah tested it one more time to be sure. Set it down. Migraine. Pick it up. No migraine. *What the fuck?* She traced back through her memories over the last few weeks since she had the journal in her possession. She went all the way back to the time at the bookstore when she first saw it. Her migraines always went away when the journal was in her hands.

A quiet voice in her head said, *It's all connected.* Leah rolled her eyes and opened the journal. Her fingers slowed before turning the page.

Miryam was talking about a chest with two interlocking pieces—one silver, one wood—that formed a single key. Leah gazed at the silver piece sitting on the table. Was this one half of the key? If so, where was the other half?

She read on.

As she let the journal's words sink into her mind, the feeling of déjà vu overtook her. She had experienced this before. Not reading the journal, but ...

Leah brushed it off. *That's crazy.*

But the words wouldn't leave her mind now that they were there.

Not reading the journal but *writing it.*

An overwhelming feeling of love—like a warm blanket—overtook her, and she couldn't contain herself. Gentle tears flowed from her eyes.

Surrender. That's what Miryam had been writing about, and Leah could feel the message deep within her bones, too. *I've never surrendered to love. I've always kept it at a distance, even from myself. Out of fear. Fear of being hurt. Fear of being vulnerable. Fear of truly living.*

Leah didn't want to push it away anymore.

Big, wet, ugly sobs exuded from her being, allowing herself to truly feel her feelings, for the second time that week. But this time, she wouldn't numb them with alcohol or find something to make her feel good. This time, she just let them wash over—like a stream of water washing over her.

The last bit of salty tears smeared down her cheeks, and Leah stood up to get a glass of water from the kitchen. Setting down the journal, she fully expected her migraine to return in full force. But the migraine didn't return this time.

She had learned her lesson. Just like Miryam. *Now, I really do sound like a woo-woo hippie,* she laughed to herself. Not sure what she believed anymore, she was okay not knowing.

After gulping down two glasses of water, she knew what she needed to do. She grabbed her phone and texted.

An hour later, there was a knock at her front door.

"Come in," she said, taking a deep breath and brushing her newly showered hair behind her ear.

Felix and Kat walked in. Both hovered in the entryway. Kat fiddled with her purse string, not looking up at Leah. She wasn't her usual cheerful self.

Leah cleared her throat. "There's lemonade on the table. Sit, have some ... I'm just waiting," — she poured herself a glass — "well, hoping, for one more person to show up."

"Oooo, lemonade? Is it spiked?" Felix helped himself to some as well.

"No," Leah said plainly.

"What have you done with my friend, Leah, and who the hell are you?" He waved his finger in her face.

Leah's shoulders slumped at Felix's assumption. "No alcohol this time."

Kat, still standing in the entryway, asked, "What's this about? You sounded so cryptic in your text."

"I'm sorry. For everything." Leah's eyes pleaded.

Kat nodded, and she sat down at the table, giving Leah's hand a gentle squeeze.

Leah yelled down the hall, "Hana, would you come out now?"

Hana emerged from her room, dragged herself slowly out, and sat at the table, arms crossed. "This doesn't mean I forgive you for what you did to Hermes, Mom. It just means I'm willing to listen," she huffed.

"That's all I'm asking," Leah replied. She glanced at the time on her phone. *He said he would be here.* "I promise I'll explain more about why you're all here in a moment."

The seconds ticked on in silence.

Finally, a knock at the door perked Leah up, and she ran to the door to answer it. Grabbing the handle, she slowed down, taking one last deep breath in and out.

She turned the handle.

Tate stood a few feet away from the door, checking his phone. It reminded her of Seth. She'd never seen him on his phone. *Is he just doing that to seem uninterested in being here?* Then, she caught herself making up a story and feeling bad about herself. *Stop that.*

"Thanks for coming. Come in. If you want, there's lemonade on the table," Leah said, holding out her hand.

"No thanks," he said as he ambled in slowly. He stood next to the table instead of sitting down. "Hey, Kat, how are you?"

"Good, thanks," Kat said, then turned to Leah. "Now, can you explain why we're all here?"

Leah took a sip of her drink and addressed her friends, daughter, and Tate. "I asked you all here today because ..." She closed her eyes and drew in a large steadying breath. "... I have been a total bitch to all of you. Sorry, I mean I've been a butthead."

Hana rolled her eyes. "Mom, I'm thirteen, not three. And yes, you have been a bitch lately. But honestly, we're kind of used to it."

Leah's defenses shot up.

For a moment.

Then, she breathed again and let the pain in.

"But you shouldn't be used to it. You are my favorite people in the world, and I shouldn't treat you the way I do." Tears welled up in her eyes, and a boulder seemed to have lodged itself in her throat as she tried to speak, but she continued, "I push you away when you try to help, and I'm sorry for that."

"What Hana says is true, but it's not the whole truth." Kat grabbed a box of Kleenex and handed it to Leah. "Can you be cold sometimes? Sure. But you're also caring, protective, and loyal."

"I want to be better, though," Leah said, wiping her nose. "My whole life, I've guarded myself. And that negative programming won't go away overnight. So, what I'm asking you today is to forgive me, but also to be *patient*. Know that I'm working on being a better mom, friend," — her eyes drifted to Tate's — "and well ... I'll probably need a reminder, or twenty."

She looked from her daughter to Kat to Felix and finally to Tate again, lips pursed, with hope in her wet eyes.

"Of course, I forgive you, honey," Kat said first as she stood up and gave Leah a huge hug. "I'm proud of you."

"Me too," said Felix, squeezing her hand. "I wouldn't be who I am today if it weren't for you. Plus, you know I don't take things personally."

Leah looked at Hana, a grin spreading across her face.

"Mommmm, it's about freaking time!" Hana jumped up from the table and joined in the embrace. "And don't worry, I'll hold you accountable."

"I know you will." Leah smiled back.

Then Hana whispered, "Oh, and you need to call my biology teacher to explain why Hermes is broken."

"Deal."

Tate still hadn't spoken.

Leah let her gaze drift to him. She narrowed her eyes, wishing she could read him right now, but she couldn't. His face gave nothing away.

Kat interrupted the silence. "Hey, why don't I treat Hana and Felix to some ice cream? There's that little place a block away. Their sign said that their special today is mocha chip."

"Mocha chip. That's my favorite!" Hana exclaimed. "Mom, can we?"

"Of course," Leah said.

The three of them rose, shuffled to the door, and exited.

Silence fell across the room.

Leah finished her glass of lemonade.

"Tate ..." Leah's brow knit together. "Would you tell me what's going on in your mind right now?"

"Why should I?" Tate snapped back, throwing his hands in the air. "A few days ago, you didn't think it was important to do the same for me."

"I know." Her head hung low. "You're completely within your right not to tell me. I ran away from you at the park. I showed up at your office drunk. Tried to seduce you." Burying her face in her palms, she added, "I've screwed up a lot of things lately."

"Yeah."

"How do you feel about a do-over?" She peeked out from under her hands.

Tate grunted and rolled his eyes. "I'm done playing games, Leah. Past that phase of my life. I want to be with someone who wants to be with me. Not this back-and-forth shit. And I'm not sure that's you."

The words stung like needles in Leah's heart. She wanted to wallow. Wanted to sink into her own misery. Wanted a pity party of one. Instead, she took ownership.

"I understand. I haven't been fair to you." She nodded. "And for that, I'm sorry. But I can only try to be different in the future. And for the first time in my life, I really feel like I can do that."

Tate's eyes darted back and forth, thinking. He took a large inhale and exhale before meeting Leah's eyes. "Why the sudden epiphany?"

That was a good question.

Leah's first thought was to make something up. But things were going to be different now. She told the truth.

The *entire* truth.

"So, this is going to sound crazy, but it started when I got this old journal in a bookstore ..."

Leah told Tate everything—about the journal, Gertrude, her migraines, the vision of Miryam, and the strange metal piece.

"Whoa," he said, leaning back in his chair.

"It's insane, right?" She tossed her arms up. "Like, how can I be connected to this woman from the 1300s? I don't even believe in all this woo-woo stuff. And now ... I don't know. But I think I'm supposed to figure it out."

"I don't think you're crazy," Tate said, smiling at Leah for the first time that day.

It made her heart leap.

"When I was in India," he explained, "I stayed with these Buddhist monks and experienced things that modern science just can't explain. Levitating, astral projecting, things like that. So yeah, I believe it's possible, and you should explore what it all means."

"Thank you." Leah reached for Tate's hand across the table. Tiny sparks danced on her fingertips as she touched him, sending goosebumps up her arm.

"However," he said, pulling his hand away from hers, "we still shouldn't be together."

And her entire day of healing, of journaling, of forgiving herself, evaporated like a storm on a horizon that never passed over but lingered and haunted Leah from a distance. She wanted to get better. She really did.

But damn, life could really suck sometimes.

Chapter 36

KARAIA

Her mind scrambled to process what she was seeing. Karaia's eyes fixed on the two figures in the doorway. Her logical brain hadn't expected to find anything—had maybe even *hoped* not to. If nothing was here, she could slip back into her normal life, return to her job, and bury this entire ordeal under the comfort of a NeuroCredit or two. She could feel comfortable again.

Safe. Happy. Healthy.

She exhaled, the weight of all of it sinking in. Those feelings weren't possible. Not now. Not for her. Deep in her gut, something insisted she had been here before. And whatever lay beyond this door was tied to her missing memories.

She had to know.

"Do I know you?" Karaia blurted.

"Well ... fuck, you're not supposed to," the woman standing in the doorway snapped. She grabbed Karaia's wrist, yanking her forward. "Get inside. And great—this time you brought a friend. Ziven, take him."

The man, Ziven, seized Arjun as the woman dragged Karaia inside.

Squinting against the sudden light, Karaia scanned the space. Empty except for the two who had brought them in. A circular table sat at the center, high-tech consoles lined one wall, and across from them stretched a dark hallway with a pair of closed doors. But it was the far wall that arrested her attention—or maybe her memory.

Books. *Actual books.*

˙ She had never seen so many in one place. Or had she?

Arjun hovered awkwardly beside Karaia, gaping at the surrounding bunker. He closed his eyes, the familiar motion of someone about to take a credit, then snapped them open again, panicked. "Why aren't my credits working?" He squeaked, wincing. "Please don't kill us."

The woman rolled her eyes and stomped off down the hallway.

"Hey, I'm Ziven—call me Z," the broad-shouldered man said, offering his hand. "And that's Blaze. She's rude to everyone. Don't take it personally. Oh, and credits don't work down here."

"I see," Arjun muttered, wide-eyed.

"It's good to see you again, Karaia," Ziven said.

Her stomach dropped. "So ... I know you?" She took his hand, and to her surprise, the contact eased the storm inside her. "I've been getting flashes—memories that don't make sense. I think my brain was wiped. Did I do that *here*?"

"Clearly the wipe didn't stick," Blaze shouted from the other room. "Z, hook her up again. And this time, be thorough."

Karaia raised her hands. "Wait—no. I don't want to forget again. I came here to remember. Can you help me get my memories back?"

"No," Blaze said bluntly, striding back into the main room until she stood directly in front of Karaia.

Blaze was shorter than her, but her presence radiated so much authority that Karaia fought the urge to shrink back.

"And now we'll need to wipe his too." Blaze jerked her chin toward Arjun. "Get them set up, Z."

Ziven hesitated.

That was her opening.

Karaia turned to Ziven, chest forward. She bit down on her bottom lip and pleaded, "Ever since my memory wipe, nothing has felt right. After the gala attack, I just can't go back to pretending it is. I *need* to remember. Please—help me."

Doe-eyed, she batted her lashes.

Ziven's eyes darted from her to Blaze, and back, as he shifted in place. He clenched and unclenched his fists. "B, maybe she'll help us with the other *thing* now." He gave Blaze a small, pointed nod.

"No," Blaze shot back.

Getting desperate, Karaia interjected, "What do you need?"

"It's too late," Blaze said flatly. "You made your choice the last time you were here."

Karaia pushed forward anyway. "What if I told you this place will be reported to the authorities in less than forty-eight hours? But if you leave sooner, you can escape." Her face tightened as she braced for impact.

"You reported us?!" Blaze roared, jabbing a finger hard into Karaia's chest. "You little fucking—"

Karaia locked her muscles, every nerve waiting for the blow.

Surprisingly, Arjun stepped between them. "We had to use Seromela tech to get us here. But you can still get out in time. Karaia didn't have to tell you, but now ..." his voice quivered, "... now you have a choice." He looked as if he might pee his pants standing up to Blaze, but he held his ground.

Pride swelled in Karaia's chest, and she smiled. She'd always known this side of Arjun existed—quiet strength beneath his nerves—but rarely saw it surface. His courage sparked her own.

She would not leave without her memories.

"Let's all calm down for a sec." Ziven slowly pulled Blaze away from Karaia and Arjun. "You're right. We have time to pack up and get to safety. And we thank you for that." He turned to Blaze. With a hushed tone, he said, "What if we use this chance to move forward on the mission? You know we need the key. The sooner, the better."

"It's way too dangerous, especially if Seromela's on our trail," Blaze retorted.

"That's why Karaia is going to get it—not us."

"I am?" Karaia blurted. She caught herself and straightened. "I mean, I am. What exactly am I getting?" Her stomach fluttered, but she forced her breath steady, anchoring herself to her goal.

"Fine," Blaze huffed. "First things first, you'll be getting your memories back." Her stare lingered on Karaia, lips pursed. "Then, we talk mission."

Karaia nodded firmly. "Tell me what I need to do."

Ziven guided them into a stark room with a single metal chair at its center.

Once they did, Karaia's sixth sense flared, a rush of familiarity slamming into her. The tang of metal coated her tongue. The acrid sting of burnt flesh filled her nose. A sizzling sensation needled her brain. And a flash of unbearable pain seared through her body.

This was where her memories had been taken.

And now, she was about to get them back. She wondered if they'd come with more of her childhood memories—of her parents—or if it'd just be the recent fragments she had lost.

She hoped for the former.

Ziven began setting up the equipment. Arjun gaped, caught between fear and fascination.

"Sit down," Blaze hissed. "This is going to hurt. A lot." A smug grin tugged at her lips. "And there's no guarantee your memories will come back correctly."

"I still want to do it," Karaia said, trembling. Despite her fear—and the echo of the pain she remembered from before—she lowered herself onto the cold metal chair. She glanced toward Arjun. "Will you hold my hand?"

"Of course." He clasped her clammy palm as she leaned her head back into the heavy headpiece, while Ziven fastened straps and connected wires around her temples.

"How are you doing without credits down here?" Karaia asked Arjun.

"Oh, you know—only living out every worst-case scenario in my head, having mini-panic attacks every minute, and I'm pretty sure I peed my pants earlier." He let out a nervous laugh. "But I couldn't do this for anyone else. You make me braver than I am."

Karaia squeezed his hand, steadying herself. "You make me braver too."

"It helps that this is some of the coolest tech I've ever seen." Arjun's awe grew as he watched Ziven power up the console linked to Karaia's chair. His voice slipped into full-on geek mode. "Whoa, you're connecting directly to her neural pathways. I didn't think anyone outside Seromela even had this kind of tech. Is that ... a map of her brain?"

"Yeah, isn't it so beautiful?" Ziven grinned at his own work.

"How do you bypass NIVA's system to access the memory files?"

"Since NIVA and NeuroCredits don't function down here, we can tap straight into the brain without firewalls," Ziven explained.

"And the memories themselves," Arjun pressed on, more relaxed than he had been all night. "Are they still stored in her brain and you just unlock them, or did you copy them onto an external drive and now you're reinstalling them?"

Talking tech was his comfort zone.

Clearly, it was Ziven's as well.

The two bounced back and forth for another minute.

"Umm, are you almost done?" Blaze cut in, tapping her boot on the floor sharply.

"Oh, sorry, B. It's just nice to finally have another techie who appreciates my work," Ziven said with a smirk in her direction.

Blaze's expression didn't budge.

Ziven turned to Karaia. "Getting your memories back will be more painful than the first time. Twice as bad. Because you'll remember the first wipe in full—while feeling this one too."

Karaia hated the constant reminders of the pain that awaited her. She was already tormenting herself with those thoughts. Steeling her voice, she said, "Do what you need to do."

As Ziven keyed commands into the holo-screen, Blaze leaned in and murmured something in his ear.

"You sure?" he whispered back.

Blaze gave a curt nod, and Ziven's brows knitted.

"What did you say?" Karaia asked.

Blaze pursed her lips, not answering immediately.

Karaia felt the silent tension ripple through the room. It brought back memories of primary school, when she used to ask too many questions. *What does the Earth feel like? Why can't everyone travel to the California Keys or the other sectors? Why do we take Neuro-Credits?* Her inquiries had often been met with canned responses or worse—VR therapy sessions. Over time, she had learned to stop asking out loud.

Blaze finally said, "I told Ziven to add more than just your memories. If you're going to complete the mission, you need to know what we know."

"And what's that?" Karaia asked, eyes wide.

"Besides your own memories, you'll get a download. New Soteria's true story."

Karaia tilted her head. "True story?"

Blaze shot back, "We don't have time to explain. It's *this way*, or not at all."

"Go ahead," Karaia said. She'd come this far. There was no turning back now.

"Wait." Arjun's voice cut through, startling them. All eyes swung to him. "If Karaia's getting the true story, then I want it too."

Karaia blinked at him, stunned. Maybe Arjun was braver than she'd ever given him credit for.

"You sure?" Blaze asked, one eyebrow raised.

"Yes ..." Arjun's voice cracked, but he forced the word out.

Blaze smirked, patting his cheek. "I knew you liked pain." She winked. "Z, start with her—then my boy Arjun is next."

"Here we go." Ziven hit the final command on the console.

Karaia squeezed Arjun's hand. *Be brave,* she told herself as the machine lit up, its whirring hum filling the room.

Then pain struck—sharp and instant—lightning coursing through every muscle, every fiber, every nerve, of her body. Like a laser gun searing through her brain tissue, the metallic taste and the bitter stench of burning flesh returned—only this time, not as a distant memory. The pain, so intense, canceled out the world around her. The room vanished. Arjun was gone. Ziven and Blaze dissolved into nothing. All that remained was blinding, searing pain, consuming her, splitting her skull apart, ripping a scream from her throat. She begged for it to end.

Something had to be wrong.

This pain was unbearable—too much. She couldn't survive this. She couldn't do it. She would go back. Back to her old life. Back to forgetting. Anything, if only this would stop.

Then—the memories poured in.

It began with her parents. The night her father had left. Her mother's voice, cold and unyielding, as she turned him over to the authorities. They had hauled him out of their home, screaming, crying, "Mai,

Mai, how could you do this?" Then his eyes had locked on Karaia. His voice broke as he pleaded, "Hold on to your necklace."

Her necklace. The memory snapped into focus.

Ziven and Blaze had mentioned it the last time—something about a prophecy. They wanted her to steal Seromela tech in exchange for information about the Settlement and possibly, her parents.

Another flash, another memory.

The woman in an alley tube—the one who had started it all—smashed into Karaia, leaving a prick in her arm, and the nanobots that left her creditless. Then, there was blood. And a murder that shouldn't have happened.

More scenes bled through in jagged succession—war, riots, soldiers with weapons raised against civilians. Karaia wept as her mind filled with images of children starving, bodies in the streets, crowded factories choking with filth, and the fist of a tyrannical government crushing lives.

Then—all went still.

Karaia's heart thundered in her chest. She tried to steady her breath, to quiet her sobs, but the effort only wracked her body harder.

"The truth hurts, doesn't it, little lamb?" Blaze said, cutting through the haze.

Gasping through tears, Karaia managed, "I don't understand. Why did you show me all that? I already knew what happened in our history."

Ziven gently removed the cap from her head.

"No," Blaze said sharply. "You don't understand. Those weren't from a hundred years ago during the Great Fall. Everything you saw is happening *now*—inside New Soteria."

"What? No." Karaia's voice trembled. "I know there's some shady stuff with Seromela and the government, but *this*? Letting children die? I can't believe it."

"Believe whatever you want. That's the truth," Blaze replied. "Those in power have perfected the art of keeping us divided, distracted, and comfortable."

"It's how they control us," Ziven added, his eyes heavy with resignation as he helped Karaia out of the chair. "Just think about the most recent attack at the gala."

Karaia's mind raced, trying to piece everything together. "The attack ... but that was Defiers ..." Her brow furrowed as she took a slow step backward.

"Wait—are you Defiers?!" Arjun's voice pitched higher as panic set in. With sweaty palms, he tugged her toward the exit.

Blaze rolled her eyes and blocked their path. She nodded at Karaia. "You've already asked us this before, remember?"

Karaia nodded slowly. Her new—no, old—memories were still hazy, but she remembered asking that the first time she'd come here. "Arjun, I think we're safe," she said, trying to steady her tone.

"Are you sure?" He writhed in place, glancing at the door as if to bolt. "Where did you bring us? We're going to be murdered in this tiny, filthy underground bunker and become the next interactive crime drama for the masses to consume."

Blaze stepped closer, a sneer spreading across her face. "Oh, little lamb's friend," she murmured, "if I wanted to kill you, I would've done it already."

"B, stop messing with him," Ziven chimed in.

"But it's so much fun." Blaze's lips curved—predatory—like she could devour Arjun in a single bite. Then her gaze flicked to Karaia. "For real, do you honestly think that attack came from the Defiers? And before you answer, *really* think about it."

Ever since the gala, Karaia's sixth sense had been going off. The timing had been too precise, too convenient, hitting the exact moment Seromela unveiled Phase Two. And afterward? NeuroTryp sales had exploded.

"You're saying ... it was staged?" She couldn't believe the words coming out of her mouth. "But why? To sell more product, or keep people in line?"

Before Blaze could reply, Karaia knew the answer, the truth settling in her gut. And at that moment, she knew she could never return to her old life.

"You're smarter than you look," Blaze said with a sly smile.

Karaia caught Arjun's frightened gaze and gave him a firm nod. "We'll be okay, Arjun. You'll be okay."

"I trust you," he said. Then, with a shaky attempt at humor, added, "And if I die, my only hope is they make me into an epic character in a video game someday." He stepped toward the cold metal chair. "Wish me luck."

Ziven worked quickly, strapping Arjun in for his download.

The next few minutes were agony as Karaia watched her best friend squirm and cry out under the procedure. She held his hand, whispered comfort, and stayed with him until it was done.

Then, she turned to Blaze and Ziven and asked, "So, what is this mission?"

"One more thing. Follow me," Blaze instructed.

Karaia noticed her shoulders were tense, and she consciously let them drop as she exhaled. *One step at a time,* she told herself.

"Stay quiet," Blaze whispered.

They followed Blaze down the hallway until she stopped midway, in front of what looked like a blank wall. She pressed a single spot, and a hidden door slid open.

The air hit Karaia immediately, thick with the smell of body odor. A steri-bot hummed futilely across the floor. Inside, four narrow beds lined the windowless room, lit only by a faint nightlight. A girl and two boys slept in three of the beds. As the door opened, one boy stirred awake.

"What is this?" Karaia whispered, trying to breathe through her mouth.

"This is ..." Blaze faltered. She glanced at the children and then spun away. "I can't. Z, you explain." And she marched off down the hall.

Karaia remembered the story about Blaze's little sister.

"Karaia, Arjun," Ziven whispered, leaning closer, "this is Cella, Zane, and Kiron. We rescued them yesterday from a Sector Five factory. They were working nearly twelve-hour shifts." He softened his voice. "Kiron, I'm sorry we woke you."

"Oh, you didn't," Kiron said, rubbing his eyes. "I was ... just thinking."

"What do you mean, *rescued them*?" Karaia asked, crouching down so she was at eye level with the boy. He looked about nine years old. "Is that true?"

He nodded.

"Where are your parents?"

"I don't have any," Kiron said.

"The New Soterian government takes orphans and puts them to work in the factories," Ziven explained, his head bowed. "That way... no one notices they're gone."

"Would you tell me about working in the factory?" Karaia asked.

"It was hot and smoky, and we got really dirty every day. I didn't like it. But they fed us, and I got free credits whenever I wanted. The government told me my parents had left for the Settlement. But Blaze tells me that maybe ... maybe they didn't leave me by choice. Maybe they are dead, I don't know. I just want to ..." His words broke into a well of tears.

"I'm so sorry." Karaia's heart ached with the urge to pull him into her arms, to hold him tight and promise he'd be safe. She longed to give him what had been cut short when she was young—someone to hold her when she had been afraid.

Kiron wiped his eyes with the back of his hand. "I wanted to go on a NeuroTryp. The people at the factory told me last week I could—even while I was working." For a moment, his eyes lit, but then his shoulders sagged. "But now I'm here. And I'm glad I'm not working anymore. These people are nice. But ... Blaze says NeuroTryp is bad for us. Credits don't even work down here." His voice cracked. "I just feel so sad. I don't want to feel sad anymore."

When he finished, he threw his arms around Karaia's neck and clung to her in a tight embrace.

She hugged him back. His body felt so light, so fragile, she worried she might crush him just by holding on. *What is happening here?*

Karaia looked from Kiron to the other children. "I know it seems hard now not to have credits in your brain, but I think Blaze is right."

Kiron yawned.

"You should get to sleep now," Karaia said.

He gave a small nod, curled into his blanket, and they left him to rest.

Back in the main room, Blaze stood over a holo-screen projection of the city tubes, her face lit by its faint glow. Karaia, Arjun, and Ziven joined her.

Humbled, Karaia asked, "What's going to happen to them?"

"For Kiron and Zane, they'll get new identities here in Sector One. We can place them with families who can't have children. There's a black market for that," Ziven explained. "As for Cella, she's too old for adoption, so she'll stay with us."

"Speaking of that, we need to discuss the mission." Blaze's voice cut through the room, her gaze still locked on the holo-screen. "We have little time before we need to clear this location and move—especially the kids."

Karaia drew in a long breath. She had gotten her memories back, and now she had to hold up her end of the bargain. "I understand. Tell me what I need to do."

Blaze turned to face her, a slow smirk curving across her lips. "Oh, little lamb ... you're not going to like it."

CHAPTER 37

MIRYAM

The creek's current enveloped Miryam, and she let it take her. Wet, silvery fingers closed around her skin, pricking her with their icy touch. Yet instead of fighting, she released her grip and surrendered. As the waves lapped against her body, one word resounded within her—*trust*.

With arms stretched wide and palms up, she floated.

The current tugged at her in every direction. At times, it dragged her beneath the water, forcing her to hold her breath until her chest burned. At others, jagged rocks scraped her flesh—an elbow here, a calf there. But the more she yielded, the less it stung.

Miryam lifted her eyes to the drifting clouds. They floated with such ease, untroubled, open to every turn of the wind. She imagined herself among them, carried wherever the sky willed. For a moment, she thought she saw a horse in their shape—no, *a dragon*, fierce yet wondrous, like the tales she had read as a child. Only this dragon was not meant for slaying. Instead, she rode upon it, soaring with the waves and the clouds alike.

Before she knew it, a laugh burst from her lips.

It started as a small giggle but soon grew into uncontrollable laughter that welled up from deep within. She tried to keep her head above the water, sputtering between gulps of air. Yet she could not stop. Joy spilled out of her, wild and unrestrained. How had she been so terrified only moments before? The freedom of surrender was sweeter than she had ever imagined, more fulfilling than anything she had known. She prayed she might hold on to this feeling forever.

The current carried her around a bend in the creek. Sunlight broke through the thinning clouds, and Miryam beamed, her heart soaring with the river.

Then—suddenly a hand seized her arm, wrenching her from her bliss.

Ved hoisted her onto a small embankment. She collapsed onto the sandy ground in a heap, coughing up mouthfuls of creek water, shivering as the chill nipped at her skin. Yet even as she gasped for air, she could not stop smiling.

She threw her arms around Ved, clinging to him in gratitude. For a moment she felt the solid warmth of his body, until he stiffened, and she released him.

Ved's normal composure was completely gone. Panic flashed across his face. "Are you cold?! How do you feel? You need dry clothing—look at you, you're shaking." He ripped off his outer robes and swiftly wrapped them around her shoulders.

Miryam glimpsed his toned body beneath his undershirt. Heat flared in her cheeks, and she quickly averted her eyes.

"Wait—were you *laughing*?" Ved asked.

"I was!" Miryam's voice trembled with excitement. "I had the most surreal, peaceful experience. You won't believe it—or perhaps you would. You were right about trusting." She paused, searching his eyes. "Thank you for saving me. I am happy to be on dry land now." She gave him a small smile as she inhaled his scent on the surrounding robe.

"I am glad you are safe," he said, settling himself beside her on the sandy bank. "You saved me too. Well ... in a way." Ved inched closer to Miryam. His hand found hers and held it tight. He cleared his throat, opened his mouth to speak, but no words came. He tried again, his voice low. "What I mean is ... you have saved me from living a life I was not meant to live."

His eyes rose to meet hers.

Miryam's heart leapt in her chest. "What are you saying?"

"I am saying ..." He took a deep breath in and out. "... I cannot become a monk. Because I love you."

Warmth coursed through every fiber of her being, her heart thundering as if it might burst from her chest. Miryam hadn't known until that very moment how much happiness and love could bloom within her.

Their eyes locked.

Ved leaned forward, slow and deliberate.

Miryam trembled, her gaze dropping to his soft lips, wondering what it would be like to taste them—feel them—pressed against hers. A tingle crept up her spine, goosebumps danced across her skin, and her body felt more alive than ever. She leaned in to meet him.

The tension encased them, thick and intoxicating.

Everything else faded away.

"Miryam?!"

The voice shattered the moment like a stone through glass. And for the second time that day, she was jolted out of her bliss.

Miryam jerked upright, scanning the surrounding forest. From the thicket, two figures broke into view.

Her eyes widened. "Bella?"

"Where have you been?" Isabella stormed toward her, her face fierce with worry and anger.

Trailing a step behind, Gawain tensed, his hand resting near the hilt of his sword as his eyes flicked between Ved and Miryam.

"Uh ..." Miryam pulled away from Ved, stammering as words deserted her.

"I thought you were *dead*," Isabella screamed. "Everyone thought you were dead. We had a funeral for you! And all along, here you are, about to kiss a boy in the woods. What the bloody hell?!"

Miryam blinked. She didn't know her sister had the word 'hell' in her vocabulary.

"You two should speak privately," Ved interjected, looking to Miryam and sliding away from her.

Miryam realized how it must look. An unmarried man—let alone *a monk*—and a young woman caught alone together. It wasn't just improper; it was sacrilege.

Her cheeks burned hot. "Bella, I can explain—"

But Isabella ignored her, pinning Ved with a deathly glare. "Who are *you*, and what have you done to my sister?"

"Miryam can explain—" He rose, offering his hand to Miryam.

"Do not touch my sister," Isabella asserted as she rushed toward Miryam to help her to her feet.

Ved gave her a polite nod and added, "You must be Bella."

Isabella was irate. She jabbed her finger toward Ved. "Oh, you know who I am? How marvelous. Then tell me—why are you alone with my sister in the woods? Did you kidnap her? Bewitch her into love? Who are *you*?!"

She marched up to him, fuming.

Then, realizing she was shouting at a man, she caught herself, straightened, and stepped back with forced composure. "Gawain, help me free my sister from her captor."

Gawain moved instantly, drawing his sword. The steel tip pressed against Ved's chest. "Sir, step away from this maiden. We will take her home now."

"My name is Ved," he said calmly, hands up. "I did not kidnap Miryam. I assure you there is no need for your sword."

"Do not tell me what to do. I am a knight of the Earl of Norfolk," Gawain snapped, pushing the blade harder against Ved.

Only a thin linen cloth separated the piercing metal from Ved's toned chest.

Yet he did not flinch.

Miryam's heart swelled, butterflies fluttering in her belly. He was so very brave. And that made him all the more attractive. She bit her lip, frowning at herself for such thoughts at such a dire moment.

"Let us find a common place where we may speak plainly and answer your questions," Ved said, nodding slowly.

"We're taking her now," Isabella snapped. "And if you try to hinder us, Gawain will arrest you." She strode forward and seized Miryam's arm, tugging her toward them.

"Bella—please don't!" Miryam cried, planting her feet beside Ved.

"There is no explanation for this," Isabella retorted, steadfast in her grip. "We will speak when we are safe at home. You know not what I have endured without you, my sister ..." Her voice shook, tears spilling from her eyes. "I thought I lost you."

Miryam pulled her into a long embrace. "I am so sorry, Bella. I missed you and Father dearly. But I could not return home, not yet, because ..." She dropped her arms and took a step back next to Ved.

She reached for his hand.

Gawain stepped forward and swung his sword at Ved's arm.

But before the blade struck, Ved flicked his other hand, and Gawain's feet flew out from under him. He tumbled hard to the ground, his sword clattering beside him.

"How did you do that?" Gawain shouted, scrambling up to his feet.

"I believe you tripped upon that stick, sir," Ved replied coolly.

Isabella rushed to Gawain's side. "My dear, are you hurt?"

He grunted, more from embarrassment than pain, brushing dirt from his armor.

Isabella returned to Miryam and held her hand close, then whispered, "I do not know what you are up to with this man and his 'tricks,' but come—now. We must return home before dark."

"No." Miryam's chin lowered, her eyes locked on her sister's.

Silence fell over them all.

"Please—let me explain," Miryam said firmly, giving Isabella's hand a squeeze.

A deep crease formed between Isabella's eyes. "Very well, if you insist. But we speak ... alone." She cast a sharp glance toward Ved.

"Agreed. Let us take a walk, sister. Gawain, please do not kill Ved whilst we're gone," Miryam said, glancing between the two men.

Ved grinned. Gawain nodded curtly.

Miryam and Isabella turned down a narrow path that followed the bend of the creek.

When they were well out of earshot, Isabella spoke first. "Where have you been? Father has hardly slept since you vanished. We thought you dead."

Miryam began with the day she followed Dempsey into the woods—telling the whole truth, save for the part about magic and her place in the secret order—and ended with her tumbling into the creek.

It was the first time she had spoken aloud of what Dempsey had done to her the day she went missing. And though the words burned in her throat as she said them, it felt good to have her sister beside her again.

"I am truly sorry you endured that." Isabella hugged Miryam tightly, both with tears streaming down their cheeks. "And Dempsey?! I cannot believe it." She clenched her hand into a fist. "He told us that three men had attacked you—that they struck him senseless and carried you away. He even wept as he told the tale."

Miryam was grateful Bella did not question her words. "Thank you for believing me. Please do not tell Father yet. I would have him hear it from me."

"Very well. But what of this Ved? That is a strange name. Is he not a monk? And are they not forbidden to ..." Isabella trailed off, blushing.

Miryam's face tightened. "'Tis complicated. He is not a monk—not yet. He is but a novice, and was training to become one."

"Was?" Isabella tilted her head.

"Oh Bella, he told me he loves me!" Miryam clasped her sister's hands, her face alight. Giddiness rose in her chest at the thought of a future with Ved. "And I love him too."

Ever the practical one, Isabella asked, "So you shall be wed? Then you will not have to marry Dempsey." She smiled widely. "And ... you can come home."

Miryam had not thought this all out yet.

The questions flooded in.

Would they live in the village? Would Ved simply refuse his vows? Could they remain part of the order if they were together? She did not know the answers, but it hardly mattered.

She knew they would find a way.

"I do not know if I can yet face Dempsey. I cannot bring myself to report him to the earl, for no man would believe me." Her jaw tightened, heat building in her chest. "What if he tries to finish what he began?"

Isabella sighed. "But you must come home sometime, must you not?"

"I will, I promise, sister," Miryam assured her.

"Oh, I haven't even told you!" Isabella straightened, her eyes beaming. "Gawain and I are to be wed in two days' time."

"'Tis wondrous news!" Miryam said, truly joyous for her sister. Maybe they would both get their happy endings?

"You must be there." Isabella gripped her hands. "For I cannot wed without my sister beside me. Promise me—come home for that?"

Miryam looked at her pleading sister. She couldn't let her down. "How could I miss your wedding?" She nodded, smiling along, though her heart quaked at the thought of leaving the safety of the abbey and facing Dempsey once again.

She glanced at the low Sun in the sky. "Though now, we should return before those two men kill each other."

"Oh my," Isabella said with a snort, "you're right."

They walked back to where Ved and Gawain stood a few feet apart. Neither spoke. Ved stood still and calm, hands folded, while Gawain shifted restlessly from foot to foot, breath huffing through his nose.

The moment Isabella came into view, Gawain rushed to her. "Well? Did she explain why she abandoned you and your father?"

"She did." Isabella's eyes flicked to Miryam, uncertain how much to reveal.

Miryam gave a small nod.

"It was not strangers who attacked her that night in the woods," Isabella explained. "It was Dempsey. Miryam ran from him, and she has been safe at the monastery ever since."

"Oh ..." Gawain's shoulders dropped. He turned to Miryam, his face softened with regret. "I am sorry, M'lady." He bowed to her and to Ved. "And forgive me for drawing my sword, dear sir. A knight must always defend a lady's honor. But now I see—you are no captor, but her savior. For that, I thank you."

Ved's solemn expression had returned. He turned to Miryam. "I should return. 'Tis well past the hour for our afternoon meal. They shall wonder where I am."

"You keep saying *I*, not *we*." Miryam nudged him with her elbow. "Are you so eager to be rid of me?"

"I thought ..." Ved looked down at the ground, his voice barely above a whisper. "I thought you would return home now that your family is here."

"Ved." Miryam reached for his chin, lifting his gaze to hers. "You are my family now, too." She searched his eyes, sensing there was more he longed to say, but would not.

Turning to Isabella and Gawain, Miryam said, "I will be returning to the monastery this day, but I promise to come for your wedding. After that ..." She glanced between them, "there will be much to decide." Grabbing her sister's hands once more. "And remember—*only* tell Father that I live. Let no one else know."

Isabella nodded in agreement.

Miryam hugged her one more time and then curtsied to Gawain. At last, she faced Ved. "I think I am ready."

His brow furrowed. "Ready for what?"

"My initiation."

CHAPTER 38

LEAH

It was as if all the air had been sucked out of the room, and Leah gasped for breath. Grabbing a tissue, she fought hard to keep her tears from pouring out. She had bared her soul to Tate, and it wasn't enough.

She wasn't enough.

"What I mean is we can't be together *right now*," Tate corrected himself, grabbing her hand and holding it steady against his chest. "You were right. I'm your lawyer, and you're my client—at least for another few days. After the hearing, I'm ready to see where this goes, if you are." He smiled.

Her palm reverberated with his heartbeat. It was fast, like hers.

Leah exhaled. A wave of relief washed over her, and a little tickle of joy ran up her spine as she tried to compose herself. She smoothed her hair, laughing. "Look at me. I'm a mess. Of course, that makes total sense."

"A little mess is okay," Tate said with soft eyes, squeezing her hand tight.

Sighing, Leah wished for more. But he was right. Focus on the case for now. Everything else can come after.

Just then, the front door swung open, and Hana ran in giggling while trying to lick up her dripping ice cream cone, followed by Kat and Felix.

Leah let go of Tate's hand.

"Well, this is probably my cue to go, but I'll see you in a couple of days," Tate said as he rose to leave. But not before he turned and smiled once more. "We've got this."

Leah's head buzzed, and she grinned back. He had said, *we*. That would be enough. Until then, she would focus everything she had on winning her case.

~๑๑~

Two days later came the custody hearing. Leah had smoothed things over with the people who mattered. Small victories she could feel good about. But now she had to face Seth. Her entire world was on the line. This would be her biggest battle yet.

Outside the small courtroom, she stood with Kat, Hana, and Tate at her side.

Breathe, just breathe.

Leah repeated her latest mantra as she tugged at the hem of her button-up jacket, trying to ground herself in the neat lines of her most responsible-looking outfit. She checked her bag—for the third time since arriving. There lay her case notes, a water bottle, a stick of deodorant, a granola bar, and ... Miryam's journal and silver piece. She reached down and placed a hand on it. Just touching it calmed her and gave her the confidence she needed.

Plus, it kept her migraines at bay.

Kat pulled her into a tight hug. "I will be right outside spiritually cheering you on and sending you all the positive vibrations. Seth has nothing on your love for Hana." She pressed something into Leah's hand. "Also ... take this. Just in case."

Leah glanced down, brow furrowing. "What's this?"

A cool blue gemstone glinted in her hand.

"It's blue kyanite," Kat said. "Helps with clarity and communication. And assertiveness. You'll need it going up against Seth" — she wrinkled her nose — "and his slimy ways."

"You know, for the first time," Leah said, tucking the rock in her pocket, "I will not make fun of you and your crystals. Can't hurt."

Kat beamed. "Wow. I really am proud of you."

Leah smirked faintly. "Thank you." She glanced toward Tate. "Is it time yet?"

He checked his phone. "Yeah. Looks like we can head in."

"Good luck, Mom. I love you," Hana said, throwing her arms around Leah.

Leah hugged her back, holding tight for a beat longer than usual. She whispered, "Love you, too."

Then she stepped into the hearing room behind Tate.

It was smaller than she had expected. More like a classroom than a courtroom. Childhood memories flashed—chalk dust, harsh lights, her mother's voice at the back of her mind: *Be quiet. Be good.* Leah inhaled sharply and straightened her shoulders. She shook it off. She was done playing small. And so, she marched into the small room with her head held high. Ready for the battle ahead.

The setup was simple: one raised desk at the front for the judge, facing two long tables in the center, each with a pair of chairs—one for the lawyer, one for the client.

She and Tate entered first. They sat at the farthest table, near the row of windows. Tate immediately spread his documents across the table, rifling through folders, double-checking every little detail. Leah pulled out her notes too—a jumble of messy notebook papers shoved into one of Hana's old school folders. She rolled her eyes. God, she appreciated Tate's level of organization.

Closing her eyes for a moment, she refocused on her mantra. *In. Out.*

She opened her eyes at the sound of the door opening, and Judge Betty Scarborough stepped in.

Leah's mouth parted. *What the hell?* This wasn't the judge they were supposed to have. Her pulse raced as she clenched and un-clenched her fists, shaking her head.

Seth. He had to have pulled strings. *Fuck him.*

Betty and her husband lived in the same gated community as Seth and Delilah. Maybe they weren't friends—but they definitely *knew* each other. Leah's throat tightened. If Seth had orchestrated this, it could only mean one thing. He clearly thought it would give him an edge.

And she worried he might be right.

Betty's outfit was flawless—a pale pink pantsuit with black trim, not a wrinkle in sight. Leah made a mental note. *Polished. Organized. Likes things neat.* Her fingernails gleamed with matching polish. Hair pulled into a tight bun. Feminine, but no-nonsense. A woman who could hold her own in a man's world. Leah guessed she was in her mid-fifties. The not-so-subtle work on her face gave her away. She pictured Betty at the yacht club, sipping a martini under a canopy, never once stepping into the pool. Her husband manning the grill, beer in hand, laughing too loudly with the other husbands. Seth probably among them, making crude jokes or ogling the younger women.

Leah's eyes flicked down to the paperwork spread across their table, scanning for anything she could scribble on. She had to tell Tate about the judge.

"Ms. Webb."

Her head snapped up.

Judge Scarborough's voice carried across the room. "Did you hear me?"

"Sorry—can you repeat that?" Leah asked, heat crawling up her neck. *Damn it, Leah, focus. Not a good start.*

"I simply asked how your day was," Judge Scarborough repeated, voice stern.

"Very well, thank you," Leah said quickly.

In her desperation, she reached under the table and grabbed Tate's hand. His warmth steadied her for a moment, but comfort wasn't what she needed. She needed a pen and paper. Some way to tell him about the judge.

The door creaked open again. Seth strode in with his lawyer at his side.

For a second, Leah blinked—because the resemblance was uncanny. The man could have been Seth's brother. Same square jaw, same smug posture, even the same taste in expensive tailoring. Both looked like bodybuilders trapped in business attire. She sniveled. *Where the hell does he find the time to work out that much?*

But the difference was Seth's mouth.

The cut on his upper lip. The bruise blooming around it.

Right where Leah had hit him.

She hadn't heard from the police, which meant he hadn't reported it. But she was sure he would still use it against her in the hearing.

"Good afternoon, Mr. Barclay," the judge said as she nodded at Seth's lawyer. "Mr. Gray." She nodded at Seth.

"Good afternoon, Judge Scarborough. You're looking lovely to-day," Seth said smoothly as he slid into his seat.

Betty blushed.

Leah rolled her eyes.

Tate nudged her elbow. A quiet reminder: *don't take the bait.*

He was right. This was exactly what Seth wanted. She had to keep her focus. Leah shuffled through the stack of papers on the desk until she uncovered a blank legal pad. She scribbled quickly, *Seth knows the judge personally*, underlining the last word repeatedly. Then, pushed the note toward Tate.

"Well, let's get to business," Judge Scarborough announced.

"Excuse me, Your Honor." Tate raised a hand politely.

"Yes, Mr. Vega. Proceed."

"It's just been brought to my attention that you and the opposing party are personally acquainted. That may be considered a conflict of interest in your judgment of this case," Tate stated, calm but firm.

Judge Scarborough folded her hands. "It's true, Mr. Gray and I know each other. But I can assure you, it will not affect my decision. However," — she glanced between Leah and Seth — "Ms. Webb, if you wish to reschedule with a different judge, that can be arranged." Her gaze lingered.

Leah felt the pressure mounting.

The truth was, there probably wasn't a judge in the entire Los Angeles metro area that Seth couldn't reach with his family's money and influence. Switching judges would only delay the inevitable.

She drew a breath. "No, Your Honor. Please proceed."

Tate turned, his eyes wide. *Are you sure?* he mouthed.

Leah nodded, trying to convince herself as much as him.

Judge Scarborough adjusted her glasses and explained how the hearing would proceed. Both parties would make their statements, followed by the judge's questions. After the hearing, she would review all documents, evidence, and witness testimony, along with the recommendations from the guardian ad litem.

Then, the following week, they would reconvene for the final decision.

"Mr. Gray," the judge said, "we'll begin with your statement, since you filed for an amendment to the custody arrangement. As it stands, you currently share a parenting agreement granting fifty-fifty custody. Is that correct?"

"Yes, it is."

"And you are now filing for full custody?"

"Yes."

"Thank you. You or your attorney may explain why you have initiated a proposed change to your current parenting agreement."

Seth's attorney, Mr. Barclay, rose, buttoning his suit jacket like he was stepping onto a stage. "Thank you, Your Honor. My client, Mr. Gray, is deeply concerned about the wellbeing of his daughter, Hana Elizabeth Gray."

Leah could already feel her fumes rising. Her fingers dug into her knees as she forced herself to breathe, in and out, and not explode.

Mr. Barclay continued, "Mr. Gray believes that Leah Webb, Hana's mother, poses a danger to their daughter. As you can see from the submitted documents, Ms. Webb has a history of depression, alcohol abuse, and attempted suicide."

The judge glanced down at her files.

Leah wanted to yell, *this isn't fair*! *That was years ago.* Her lips parted, ready to argue—then she clamped them shut.

"Objection, Your Honor," Tate interjected. "My client's history is irrelevant to this hearing. The original parenting agreement was formed after these alleged incidents, and Mr. Gray had no objections then."

"Noted, Mr. Vega." Judge Scarborough turned her cool stare toward Seth's attorney. "And I have to agree. How is Ms. Webb's past relevant now?"

"Because," Seth's lawyer said smoothly, "my client believes Ms. Webb has resumed her substance abuse—possibly pharmaceuticals, certainly alcohol. We've provided witness testimony of her excessive drinking in recent months, along with evidence of erratic behavior that has led to irresponsible parenting."

The words hit like a punch.

"Who's the witness?" Leah blurted.

"Ms. Webb," Judge Scarborough said firmly, "please refrain from speaking unless asked, or until it's your turn."

Leah bit the inside of her cheek and nodded.

The judge turned back to Seth's attorney. "Mr. Barclay, can you provide examples of parenting behavior that support this conclusion?"

"My client has documented five separate occasions on which Ms. Webb failed to pick up their daughter within the last month—either from school or from Mr. Gray's residence." He flipped to the next paper. "Ms. Webb has always been *somewhat* tardy, but recently, her lateness has become consistent. In addition, he has witnessed her taking pills on multiple occasions. Just this past week, Hana herself reported finding her mother intoxicated in the middle of the day."

Leah squeezed her eyes shut.

Her worst fears were coming true. *I can't lose Hana, I can't.*

"Ms. Webb," the judge said, turning to her, "is this true?"

"Yes, but—"

"Thank you for your honesty," Judge Scarborough said. "Go on, Mr. Barclay."

Barclay nodded. "Besides these behavioral changes, my client has noted financial instability. Ms. Webb defaulted on her utility bills, one of which my client had to cover through the city water department."

"Thank you." Without pause, she turned to Seth. "Mr. Gray, do you have a statement prepared regarding your case?"

Seth cleared his throat, his voice heavy with false gravity. "Yes, Your Honor. I'm deeply concerned about my daughter's well-being. Living in a tiny apartment with a drunk, irresponsible, financially unstable mother is not the life I want for her. It's not the life any child deserves." He paused, then added with a quiver, "I've given my life to serve and protect those who can't protect themselves. Why should my daughter be excluded from that?"

A single tear slid down his cheek.

Ugghhh, how fake! Leah wanted to barf. She fumed, forcing her mouth closed as she listened to this shit-show. Just as a dull throb began at her temples—her migraine creeping in right on cue. She stole a glance at her purse, wanting to grab the journal out to ease the pain, but knew she couldn't. Not right now.

Seth pressed on. "I can't sit back and watch my daughter suffer. If I do nothing, what happens next? What if Leah drives Hana home after drinking or mixing pills, and she falls asleep at the wheel? What if Hana goes without meals? What if—"

"Objection," Tate said, his tone controlled. "This is speculation."

"Agreed," Judge Scarborough said. Her eyes cut back to Seth. "Please stick to the facts."

"Of course, Your Honor." Seth drew in a breath, straightening. "As you may have noticed, my lip is bruised and cut. Just a few days ago, Leah and I had an altercation that ended with her punching me in the face—leaving me bloody." He showed off his newly adorned cut.

"Ms. Webb, can you confirm this?"

Leah swallowed hard. "Yes, but it was an accident—"

"You will get your chance to explain soon," the judge said. "Mr. Gray, Mr. Barclay, do you have anything further to add?"

"No, Your Honor. Thank you for listening." He flashed his most charming smile. "All I want is what is best for Hana."

"Very well. We'll take a five-minute recess. When we reconvene, we'll hear from your side, Ms. Webb. Don't leave the building," — her brows lifted pointedly at Leah — "and don't be late."

Fuck, fuck, fuck, Leah said to herself.

Everyone rose as the judge exited. Then, they followed.

Out in the hallway, Hana and Kat were waiting on a bench.

Seth strode up first, sweeping Hana into an exaggerated hug. "Hana, so good to see you, sweetie." He kissed her cheek, loud and performative, making sure Judge Scarborough was in earshot.

"Dad, come on," Hana muttered, pushing him back, her cheeks pink. "You're embarrassing me."

"See you after the hearing," Seth said warmly to Hana before strolling off toward his lawyer, smugness radiating from every step.

Leah stood frozen, shooting death glares at Seth.

Hana turned to her. Her expression fell. "Mom ... are you okay? You're all pale. What happened in there?"

Leah's pulse throbbed—in her ears, in her throat, in her fingertips. She regretted that third cup of coffee this morning. She opened her mouth, but no words came out.

"Leah, honey?" Kat said, rubbing her arm.

It was all too much.

What had she been thinking—believing she could win against Seth? He had destroyed her in there.

Leah gulped and whispered, "I can't."

"Tate, what happened?" Kat's eyes widened, darting frantically between the two of them.

He shook his head. "I'll be honest. It was worse than I had expected. They went hard on her past, twisting it to make her current behavior look like ..."

"Like what?" Kat pressed.

"Like I'm an irresponsible drunk, not fit to parent," Leah said, her voice cracking. She flung her hands in the air. "And that's putting it *nicely*. Seth accused me of substance abuse, erratic behavior—everything he could think of. And the thing is ..." Her throat tightened. "He's right. Most of what he said was true. Maybe I don't even deserve Hana."

She dropped onto the bench, burying her face in her hands, and prayed—to a god she didn't believe in—for a miracle.

Chapter 39

KARAIA

B laze leaned against the center table of the bunker and eyed Karaia. "First things first, little lamb—"

"No," Karaia hissed, matching her gaze.

Blaze blinked, eyebrows lifting. She looked more impressed than offended.

"*Don't* call me little lamb anymore," Karaia said, her voice unwavering. "And tell me about the prophecy." She had lost too much already—her memories, her childhood, the truth about the government. Too much had been kept from her for far too long. She wasn't sure how much of her life had been real until this point. That ended here.

Blaze gave a curt nod, respect flickering across her face. "Fair enough." She turned to Ziven. "Go ahead, Z. This is your specialty. I'll start packing. Once I'm done, we'll go over the mission before we all head out."

Ziven cleared his throat, gesturing to the chairs nearby. "You might want to sit for this one."

Karaia sank into the soft cushion. The moment her body hit the seat, a heavy wave of exhaustion threatened to drag her under. Her determination battled the fatigue, anchoring her in place.

NIVA, what time is it?

No response.

Oh yeah, never mind.

She scanned the room until she found a clock.

3:33 a.m. No wonder she felt so drained. Her stomach growled on cue.

"Hungry? We've got protein shakes and bars in storage. I can grab some," Ziven offered.

"No, it's fine, go on."

Ziven began. "Okay—"

"Thank you for saying something," Arjun blurted. "I'm dying of thirst. And food. Please. Sorry, Karaia, I know this is important to you, but I seriously need something." He looked rattled, fear etched on his face.

"Oh my gosh, of course. I should've thought of that," Karaia said, nodding quickly to Ziven.

He slipped out to fetch their refreshments.

Karaia turned back to Arjun. "How are you holding up?"

"I've been better." He tried for a smile, but it barely made it halfway, looking more like a gnarled grimace instead.

"Seriously?" She raised a brow.

"Okay ... I'm trembling inside. My mouth is dry. My pits are drenched. These people freak me out. But what freaks me out even more is that we had to rescue children from factories in our own country. And those images—people dying, riots, war—what is happening *here*?" Arjun's voice broke as he started rocking in his chair. "I desperately want to take a credit—or twenty—and just make it stop."

Karaia pulled him into a hug. "I know it's a lot. But I'm thankful you're here with me. I know it's scary, but it matters. I can *feel* it." She gestured to her stomach. "And now, I know I need to see what answers lie outside the walls."

Her dad had called it her sixth sense, but Karaia knew it was something deeper—more ancient.

"You're right," Arjun said after a moment. "But do you really think you could *leave* New Soteria?"

"I need to know if my parents are at the Settlement and how I'm connected to all of this." Her gaze drifted toward the far wall of books. She thought of her dad—he would have had some wise words for her right now. Rolling the necklace between her fingers, she longed for his guidance.

"That is insanity. You're talking about leaving the safety of the walls," Arjun said.

"But how can you keep living here, working for Seromela, knowing what we know now?" Karaia thought of Griffin and shivered.

He'd known all along. Heck, he was the one calling the shots. She wondered if Stellan knew too.

"As scared as I am living here, leaving these walls freaks me out even more," Arjun said. "I'm not cut out for that kind of adventure. But you are, Karaia. You always have been. Plus, you might never know when you'll need a guy on the inside again." He gave her a quick wink.

His fear hadn't disappeared, but seeing him pull himself together eased Karaia's own nerves.

Ziven reappeared, carrying protein drinks, handing one to each of them.

Then, smiling wide, he rubbed his hands together. "So, you two ready to have your minds blown?"

"Isn't that the theme of the night?" Karaia chuckled, her voice quivering.

Ziven only grinned wider. "But for real. This is the stuff I live for. Well, this, my tech ... and my nana's tacos. Those are fucking amazing."

Karaia wished for a taco instead of whatever this protein sludge was, but her exhaustion didn't care. She sipped it anyway.

"It all started about a thousand years ago ..." Ziven said. "In the early fourteenth century, all the magic that normally lives in every human was bottled up and locked inside a chest."

Karaia blinked.

"Ancient texts call it the Chest of Immortality," he continued, "because it's said to have been crafted from the same wood as the Tree of Life in the old Bible story of Genesis. We believe the silver piece around your neck is one half of the key needed to open that chest and release humanity's magic back into the world."

"Whoa, whoa, hold on." Karaia set her drink down and held up a hand, trying to process. "This sounds like one of Arjun's epic story video games. Back up. You're telling us *magic* is real—and we all have it inside us?"

"Technically," Arjun said, draining the last of his protein drink, "he said we *should* have it inside us. We don't anymore."

"Exactly," Ziven confirmed.

Karaia narrowed her eyes. "Rightttt. So, we don't have magic because someone locked it all up in a chest—made from fancy wood from a Bible story. You remember the Bible? That ancient document we proved wasn't factual centuries ago. You sound insane. And now you think I have a magical key?"

"Technically," Arjun interjected again, holding up a finger, "*half* a key."

"Everyone knows magic isn't real. Arjun, how are you even entertaining this story?" Karaia shot back. But even as the words left her mouth, something deep in her gut twisted in disagreement.

"That's what they *want* us to think," Ziven said, his gaze steady on her. "I know it sounds absolutely bonkers, but magic *is* real. Humans just can't access it anymore. We lost our direct connection. It doesn't come from within us now—but through magical objects or the Earth itself, it can still be reached."

"Prove it," Karaia challenged.

Ziven's eyes flicked side to side as if searching for an answer. "Wellll ... I don't actually know how to *do* magic," he admitted. "All that knowledge was lost over the years. But if we could restore our natural magic, then maybe."

Karaia pressed her lips together, her forehead creasing as she tried to force this into logic. Some part of her knew she was connected to something—that all of this had led her to this exact moment. But this? This wasn't what she was expecting.

Not at all.

"I'm losing you again, aren't I?" Ziven asked, pulling up a small holo-screen.

"Yeah ... but go on." Karaia forced herself to stay focused. As outrageous as his claims were, her curiosity was piqued. "So, what is this prophecy?"

"Let me show you what we have." His fingers flew across the keys, fast and fluid—reminding Karaia of Arjun when he was on one of his research binges or buried in a new game.

Images flickered across the screen in rapid succession. Karaia leaned in, trying to catch each one. A crumbling stone castle. The coiled body of a serpent. A sunlit beach, waves rolling in.

"Okay, here it is," Ziven said at last.

A three-dimensional image materialized—an ancient sheet of parchment, tan and worn, suspended in the air. The handwriting was so faded and jagged, Karaia couldn't make out a single word. But beside it, a neat translation glowed in crisp digital text. She read it out loud.

"Bound within these walls, a power so great.
Only time will tell if it is our fate.
For in this chest, pleroma resides.
For all to see, and all to abide.
What once was ours, now away it be.
A silver serpent, a broken key.
Alas, a thread of hope for mine.
Humanity's magic, woven in time.
When keys unite, all will be free.
But pay the price, and you will see.
For if released—"

"If released, what?!" Arjun cut in, throwing his hands up.

The prophecy echoed through Karaia's chest like a memory half-remembered. It felt carved into her very being. "What happened to the rest of it? It looks like it was torn," she said, leaning closer to study the ragged edges of the parchment.

Ziven shook his head. "We don't have the rest. We've been studying this fragment, along with other ancient writings, for years at Avani, along with—"

"Avani?" Arjun crinkled his brow. "Now, this really sounds like one of my games."

"The Settlement, as you know it," Ziven clarified. "It's where I was born—and where my nana makes those amazing tacos. Man, now I'm hungry too." He chuckled, rubbing his stomach.

"Wait, are you even a New Soterian citizen?" Karaia asked.

"That's for you to wonder." Ziven winked before scrolling through more images of ancient documents. "Combining this prophecy with additional texts we've uncovered over the years, we've concluded that we need the two halves of the key to open the chest and release humanity's magic back into the world."

"But why believe any of this? Why pour years of research into the words of a thousand-year-old scrap of paper?" Karaia pressed, feeling torn in two directions—logic battling instinct, skepticism pulling against trust.

Ziven's tone shifted, and his eyes were serious. "Because if people knew what they truly were, what they held inside, what they were capable of ... then maybe we could create a more beautiful world. A world not ruled by fear. A world that doesn't abuse its power. One with depth, feeling, beauty, and love. One worth living—and sometimes dying—for. Governments may call us Defiers, but we are the people of Avani. And we won't stop until humanity is free."

His gaze locked onto Karaia and Arjun. The weight of his words hung in the air.

Something struck a chord in Karaia's mind.

Or was it her heart?

Either way, the realization hit her. Staying safe, staying alive, and staying comfortable all the time wasn't what life was about. She wanted to believe Ziven. Wanted to join their cause. Wanted to be part of something bigger than herself. But ... it was still such a stretch.

"I won't lie. I don't believe in magic or prophecies. Not yet ... at least." Karaia laughed out loud. "But I want to help you. People deserve to be free. And if I can find my parents too, it's a win-win." She nodded. "I'll get what you need from Seromela."

Ziven's stern expression broke into a wide smile, reminding her of the gentle giant he was.

"There's one more thing," he said.

"What?"

"We'll need your necklace."

Karaia's hand instinctively went to the silver piece at her neck, and her stomach dropped. She thought of her father while her fingers traced the smooth metal. Taking a steadying breath, she said, "Fine. It's yours." The thought of giving it up twisted something inside her, but if it meant finding her parents, it would be worth it. She reached for the clasp at the back of her neck.

Ziven raised a hand to stop her. "We don't need it yet. After your mission, you'll trade it to us for directions to Avani. For now, let me get Blaze to explain the plan."

Blaze returned as Ziven clapped his hands, pulling up a blueprint of Seromela Corporation on the holo-screen.

"This is where things get interesting," Blaze said sharply. "I've been waiting a long time for this mission. Honestly, I didn't know if we'd ever find someone who could get inside, but I think you can. First though, you must sever your neural link—permanently."

Karaia sank into her chair.

Arjun's jaw fell open. "How is she supposed to do that?"

Ziven looked at Karaia. "We'll shock your brain with enough electricity to fry the neural connections—then jump-start you fresh."

The room seemed to narrow around her, the holo-blueprint glowing too bright. Karaia shifted in place, a tremor of unease running through her as she thought about life without NIVA or NeuroCredits.

Arjun broke the silence. "You're saying she'll be brain-dead. For how long?"

"About a minute."

Karaia blurted, eyes widening, "What happens if I don't come back?"

"That's probably not going to happen," Blaze said curtly.

An awkward silence followed.

Karaia squeezed Arjun's hand. "I'll be fine. I'm sure they know what they're doing." She nodded to Blaze and Ziven, seeking her own reassurance. "So how do I get into Seromela if I don't have my neural link? They check that at the entrance scanners."

"There are maintenance hatches we can get you into," Blaze said.

Ziven zoomed the holo-map of Seromela's headquarters and pointed out a few sparse locations.

Blaze went on. "Once you're inside, no one will suspect you—because you *work* there. Then, get into Griffin's private vault in his office.

Wait until he's away, then temporarily deactivate the safe door with a localized EMP—"

Arjun shot up a hand. "Wait, wait. That won't work. Security sensors will pick up an EMP blast in ten minutes—maybe less. That's not enough time."

"Do you have another plan?" Blaze raised a brow. "As she said, she can't very well walk through the front doors."

"Give me a minute. This is just a gigantic puzzle—I can figure it out." Arjun shut his eyes and pinched the bridge of his nose. His fingers fidgeted as he ran possibilities through his head. Breath slowed. His mouth tightened in concentration.

Seconds ticked by.

Then, minutes.

Ziven's stomach growled, breaking the silence. "Sorry. What I'd give for some tacos right now," he muttered, then stood to busy himself with organizing gear.

"Baby boy," Blaze said, rapping her fingers on the table. "We don't have all day."

Arjun's eyes flew open. "I've got it!"

"What is it?" Karaia unclenched her fists, noticing the deep half-moons her nails had left in her palms.

"Is it possible to kill the neural link and do the brain jump-start *after* Karaia is already inside Seromela?" Arjun asked Blaze and Ziven.

Blaze lifted her chin to the side. "Yeah, I guess we could. But why?"

"Because we're going in the front doors! Just like in *Goblin Warrior 3!*" Arjun puffed out his chest, grinning at the others as if expecting applause.

Karaia and Blaze stared at him blankly.

Ziven suddenly lit up. "That's brilliant! Why didn't I think of this? I knew I liked you, man." He strode over and clapped Arjun so hard on the back it nearly toppled him out of his chair.

Straightening his posture, Arjun said, "So in *Goblin Warrior 3*—one of the best VR games ever made, by the way—the only way to infiltrate the castle and defeat the evil warlord is to march straight in the front gates. No sneaking."

"Even if Karaia could walk in and out the front doors, she can't get the EMP inside to disable the safe," Blaze countered. "The entrance security would flag it instantly."

"That's because she's not going to bring the EMP." Arjun leaned forward, energized. "She's going to scan Griffin's brain waves and use his own scan to open the vault."

"I'm not exactly following ..." Karaia narrowed her eyes at him, suspicion prickling in her gut. She had a sinking feeling that she knew where he was going.

And she hated it.

"Get to your point," Blaze interrupted.

Arjun lifted his brows at Karaia, expectant.

Karaia's stomach clenched. "No."

"It's better than the first plan, and you know it," Arjun pleaded. "Griffin will willingly go into privacy mode with you. All you have to do is make sure he naps afterward, like he often does. It's really the perfect setup."

He spun in his chair smugly.

Karaia inhaled slowly, then exhaled through her nose, forcing herself to stay calm. Sneaking into Griffin's vault had already tied her stomach in knots—*but this?* This was worse. What Arjun was implying made her skin crawl.

"What am I missing here?" Ziven asked. "How is Karaia supposed to get Griffin Marshall into privacy mode *and* convince him to nap in the middle of the day?"

Arjun cleared his throat. "Let's just say Karaia has ... a special relationship with Griffin."

Blaze's jaw dropped. She shot Karaia a look that dripped with disgust. "Eww."

Ziven chuckled, pulling up a picture of Griffin Marshall on the main holo-screen. "I don't know ... he *is* an attractive man."

"Z, really?" Blaze slapped his arm, giving him an equal look of disgust.

"What? He is!" Ziven shrugged.

"We're getting off target." Blaze folded her arms.

"I'll do it," Karaia said.

Stay focused on the end goal.

"Good." Arjun pressed his palms onto the table, eyes focused. "Then when he's asleep, Karaia will scan his brain using my PET." He pulled it from his pocket, giving it a small caress as if it really were an animal. "Using the scan, she can open the vault, take the tech, and be out all before the neural jump-start."

"It's risky, but I love it," Ziven said, grabbing a small earpiece from a nearby drawer and holding it up. "We can program a timer to this—to fry your neural connection." He showed it to Karaia. "It'll also serve as a comm link to us. It runs on the same frequency as NIVA, so the entrance scanner won't flag it. That gives you just enough time to get in, get out, and reach the rendezvous before it goes off."

He plugged the earpiece into the main computer; his fingers flicked across the keyboard as he programmed it.

Blaze added, "We won't be able to come back here—this location is compromised." She glanced sharply at Arjun and Karaia. "Here are directions where I'll be waiting to exchange your necklace and the tech for directions to Avani." She scribbled on a small piece of paper. "You'll get your brain jump-start there, and then it's goodbye from us. You're on your own."

Ziven unplugged the comm and placed in Karaia's ear.

"You'll have exactly eight hours from now before the jump-start happens. That gives you time to get home, sleep a few hours, go to work, and meet Blaze at this address by noon tomorrow. Got it?"

"Got it," she said, nodding.

Out loud, Karaia sounded confident. Inside, the weight, the reality of her decision, was crushing her. Her chest tightened. Her mouth went dry. Her hands trembled. *What if I die tomorrow?* The thought clawed at her. She wanted to run, to take a hundred NeuroCredits, to hide under her bedcovers.

Instead, she sat still. Her fear held at bay because she knew this was what she had to do.

Blaze rose from the table. "Now we need to pack up and move out." She smiled—small, but the first Karaia had seen from her. "Good luck."

"Thank you." Karaia forced a return smile, mustering the courage for her task ahead. She breathed. *I'm not a little lamb anymore.* "Even if this all goes as planned," she said, "how am I supposed to get the tech out the front door? Won't it set off alarms?"

Ziven grinned mischievously. "Actually, it won't. It's made of wood."

"It's made of wood?" Karaia echoed.

"Yep. Griffin Marshall has the other half of the key to the Chest of Immortality, and you're going to steal it."

CHAPTER 40

MIRYAM

"Are you certain you are ready?" Ved asked as he clasped Miryam's hand, guiding her back to the abbey's small wooden door.

Questions swirled in her mind—about the order, about her strange new powers, about what it would mean to go home and face Dempsey again. Yet most of all, she thought of Ved, and of a life they might share. Her chest swelled at the thought of their being together.

Ved had said he *loved* her.

Such a small word to contain the most thrilling, most consuming of feelings. Miryam's heart fluttered with sheer joy. She hopped through the doorway, clinging to the warmth of Ved's rough hand, not wanting to let go. But once her feet touched the monastery's cool stone paths again, reality returned. She loosened her grasp, though every part of her resisted. For now, they were but two students, one preparing to take his vows, and the other about to face her initiation.

She let her hand fall to her side.

For once, Miryam was content. Content not to have answers to every question. Content to wait before feeling Ved's skin against hers, before tasting his lips, before holding him close.

Because she too was in love.

With Ved by her side, she felt as if she could endure anything. Right now, that meant her initiation. It was less about joining the order and more about discovering her own strength and her true ability to wield pleroma. She *had* to complete this for herself.

"Yes," Miryam said at last. She stopped walking and turned to face him. "But I want to speak with you about what you said back at the creek."

Ved's face flushed a soft pink. "I got caught up ... my words ... they tangle when I am in your midst, and—"

"I love you too," she burst out. Her cheeks ached from all the smiling she had done since they'd walked back from the forest.

Ved's own smile bloomed, slow and radiant.

Butterflies flitted about in Miryam's stomach.

"You do?"

"Of course, I do!" she gushed, bouncing once on the balls of her feet, trying to keep her excitement contained. In a whisper, she leaned forward and said, "I have never felt this way about anyone. Ved, I want to spend the rest of my life with you."

Ved sighed.

"What is it?" Miryam asked, a sudden pang clawing at her blissful heart.

"I do not know what to do about my vows." With his brow in a deep crease, he glanced around, making certain no other monks lingered nearby. Then he leaned in, pressing his forehead gently to hers and drawing her close.

She breathed him in—he smelled of the forest after rain, earthy and alive.

"But I know we will find a way," he murmured. "Let us speak more after your initiation."

Miryam longed to stay with him. Yet she knew this moment was hers alone—her trial, her power to claim. Plus, she reminded herself she had a lifetime with Ved ahead. "I know we will too. I will count the seconds until I see you again."

They slowly pulled back from each other, hands clinging desperately.

Ved opened his mouth as if to say more but then closed it. Instead, he gave her hand one last firm squeeze, let go, and walked toward his chamber.

Elated from the last few hours, Miryam skipped down the corridor, leaping over puddles as she went in search of Sophia for her initiation.

She felt lighter than air, stronger than stone. She could have tackled a dragon, had one crossed her path that was. As she strolled, she let her mind wander to daydreams of her and Ved's wedding. Not in a church, but in the meadow by the abbey's pond. Fields of lavender and chamomile swayed in the breeze, their sweet fragrance curling through the air. She would don a simple cream gown, barefoot in the grass. Ved would be clad in soft linen to match. They would lean forward to kiss and—

"Ahh!" Miryam yelped, pain jolting her shoulder. She had plowed straight into Sophia, who was coming out of the kitchen.

A bundle of bread loaves went tumbling through the air.

"Watch where you are going, dear girl," Sophia said.

"I'm sorry—I was ... never mind. Let me help you." Miryam scooped up the fallen loaves. Through gritted teeth, she asked, "Are they still good?"

"They should be." Sophia raised an eyebrow as she inspected the bread. "Now, help me to the kitchen."

Miryam scurried along next to her, loaves in hand, nodding.

Through tight, even lips, Sophia asked, "Where have you been?" Her eyes scanned Miryam's damp gown. "You are sopping wet."

"'Tis why I must speak with you," Miryam said, her face glowing with excitement. But she was careful not to trip or drop the bread again. "I finished my lesson. I truly understand how to surrender. It was messy—and wet—but I am ready for my initiation."

They entered the dining hall and placed bread on the two main tables, one for men, one for women.

"It will not be easy," Sophia said, "but we knew you would be ready tonight." She winked. "Father Thomas has had the cave prepared."

"Really?" Miryam's voice rose, and a nun nearby shot her a look.

"Yes. But this is no light matter. You are ready, my dear," Sophia whispered, placing a gentle hand on Miryam's shoulder. "After the evening meal, we will meet you in the cave. But you will not want to eat, for you shall need an empty stomach for this last step."

Between her nerves over Ved and the anticipation of initiation, Miryam doubted she could have eaten even if she had tried. Her whole body thrummed, alive and restless. Yet every second passed slowly after that moment. She sipped a chamomile tonic while the rest of the monks and nuns ate their evening meal. She tried hard not to steal too many glances toward Ved, who sat at the men's table. To distract herself, she helped wash the dishes as they finished. Eventually, one by one, everyone rose and drifted to their nightly tasks.

Except for the order. It was finally time.

Miryam stepped into the courtyard and lifted her eyes to the sky. The Sun had long since set, and the Moon had not yet risen. The heavens stretched clear and black above her. A cool wind brushed her skin, as if ushering her toward the cave. She drew a steady breath and began her descent down the stone stairs.

With each step down, the air became noticeably chillier, wetter, and heavy with stillness. As she entered the cave, candlelight wavered, sending restless shadows against the rocky walls. An earthy sweetness lingered in the air as Father Thomas and Matilda bent over a steaming pot in the corner, whispering as they stirred some concoction. Murmurs carried softly around the chamber.

Miryam walked forward until she reached Sophia, standing at the head of the gathering. Most of the order members already sat, waiting in their semicircle.

But not Ved.

A sudden panic rose in Miryam's chest. She wanted—needed—him beside her.

Father Thomas lifted his hand, motioning for the circle to begin a low, steady chant that reverberated against the surrounding cave.

Sophia stepped forward, holding a small wooden cup. "This is a sacred plant brew, meant to guide your journey. To one's body, it is harmless. Yet ... for the mind, the heart, and the spirit, it is powerful."

Miryam's heart pounded hard against her ribs, and her palms grew slick with sweat. *Where was Ved?*

"This initiation shall open the way into unseen realms," Sophia explained, "where you must discover your pleroma. You may behold visions not of this world. You may feel as though you have no control. And none here can aid you. The path to your gift will most likely lead you straight through your deepest fears."

Eyes darting around the shrinking room, Miryam didn't know if she could go through with this without knowing why Ved wasn't there.

Sophia caught Miryam's worried eyes. "You shall be fine, I *know* it. The journey will last until dawn. This is the moment for which you have been prepared." She held the cup upward.

"Where is Ved?" Miryam blurted above the chanting. "Should we not wait?"

"Ved will not be with us tonight," Sophia said gently.

"Why not?" Miryam asked, brows knit.

"Now is not the time for fear, my dear," Sophia said, resting a warm hand on her shoulder.

At once, a current of pleroma flowed into Miryam, filling her, calming the building storm inside her chest. She understood. *Surrender.*

"You carry one of the strongest auras I have yet seen," Sophia assured her. "Lean into your gifts. You need no one else to aid you." With that, the wave of Sophia's pleroma dissipated from her body, leaving her empty—alone.

Except, she wasn't alone. Not really. Feeling her own strength fill her body, pleroma weaving its tendrils through her, Miryam nodded.

She reached for the brew.

Sophia lifted the cup gently to her lips. "Once you drink, lie upon this mat. The chant will rise, and you will drift from this world into another."

The thick liquid touched Miryam's tongue, and at once she wanted to gag. The brew was vile and bitter. She held it in her mouth before forcing it to slide down her throat. Her stomach lurched, eager to send it back up.

"Hold it," Sophia urged.

Clapping a hand over her lips, Miryam willed it to stay down. A queasy warmth gurgled in her belly, threatening to spill over. *Surrender to it,* she whispered inwardly, until the brew began to settle.

"Now lie back, and let the medicine do its work," Sophia said.

Miryam stretched out upon the small woolen mat, closing her eyes. Doubt crept in almost at once. *What if the plant does not work for me? What if nothing happens?* She fought to hush the thoughts, to lean into trust.

The chanting grew louder around her, low and steady, until it seemed to reverberate through her bones. Her body swayed to its rhythm as though carried upon a tide. A dizzy swirl overtook her head, and her fingers tingled.

Am I truly moving—or only imagining it?

Her body felt distant, as though she were rising above it, lifted by unseen feathers brushing her upward, carrying her into another realm.

Floating.

Up.

Up into the air.

She opened her eyes, half-afraid, half-hopeful, to see if she truly rose—or if it was the plant's work upon her. The cave shimmered, awash in a flood of color. Vivid patterns wove themselves through the air—forming, shifting, geometric shapes.

She reached out.

At her touch, the shapes rippled and changed, bursting into brighter hues that leapt from her fingertips. Waves of color danced outward, circling through the chamber, twining about the other members of the order.

Miryam stared in wonder. *Is this what always surrounds us unseen? Is this pleroma or only my mind's trickery?* She laughed softly and played with the energy, letting the light swirl and twine through her fingers, until her eyes fluttered shut again.

Then, came the heaviness. Her body—or was it her soul?—began to sink. The lights ebbed, and the floating faded. *No, not yet. Let me stay here.*

Something tugged at her from the pit of her belly, strong and unyielding. She fought to cling to the brightness, to hold herself afloat in that glowing realm.

The pull won.

Down she went, deeper and deeper.

Into the darkness.

Miryam flashed her eyes open.

The shapes and colors were gone. The cave was gone. The order too.

Frantic, she cried out. But no one answered. She screamed for them, but only emptiness met her desperate moans. Her stomach churned, twisting and gurgling. The brew clawed its way back up. A sour wetness filled her mouth, and she heaved. Rolling to her side, she emptied chamomile-flavored bile onto the floor. But the floor was not there.

She forced her eyes wide, straining to see. Nothing. Just darkness. All-consuming darkness.

Vomit surged again from the pit of her stomach. Miryam retched again, but this time only a few sour drops of acid slipped past her lips. Her mouth felt parched and hot. She wiped the sweat from her brow—her skin was on fire.

Something was wrong.

She forced herself to remember her past lessons. *I must surrender.* Drawing in a deep breath, she closed her eyes once more. *Breathe.* Calling to mind that day in the forest with Ved, and all the hours of meditation since, she imagined her body filling with air, then emptying.

The pull in Miryam's stomach began again—like a rope cinched around her waist, dragging her down. This time, she did not resist. Her body fell deeper into the black until it swallowed her whole. The darkness wrapped around her like a spider's web, smothering every trace of who she was. *Who am I? Where am I?* Her thoughts tangled, slipping from her grasp. Faces, voices, and memories swirled together, dissolving like smoke. Did she even have a body anymore? She could not tell. Nothing made sense.

Then—*thud.*

Miryam hit the ground hard. Pain jolted through her, sharp and cold. She lay there for a moment before peeling herself off the damp Earth. Slowly, her eyes adjusted. Shapes emerged. Trees. Leaves. The familiar forest near her village, the floor littered with rain-soaked debris. She blinked, dazed, then looked down. One foot was bare, her toes curling into the dirt. *Where's my shoe?*

It was night, though the Moon lay hidden beneath a thick cover of clouds. An eerie stillness blanketed the woods. Miryam recognized the path that led to the lake. To her right stood an old stump.

Then, she remembered.

This was where Dempsey had attacked her.

Her heart pounded. Breath quickened. She scrambled to her feet, spun in place, scanning the dark. No Dempsey. Yet every part of her body whispered she was not safe.

The clouds parted above her head, and she glanced up to find a full bright Moon. Its moonlight cut through the tree canopy, spilling a silver glow across the forest floor.

Wait, the light never shines through here.

A rustle in the bushes snapped her head around. Nothing. Another sound behind her. She spun faster this time. Still nothing. With every turn, the sound followed. Again and again, always behind her, just out of reach.

Holding her breath, she slowly turned just her head.

There it was—her shadow.

And yet ... not her shadow at all.

It shifted on its own. A shape alive. Watching her. Mimicking her.

It moved, rustling the leaves beneath it, swaying this way and that. Rising, the shadow grew into a large swirling mass of clouds. It coiled and twisted, becoming heavier, more solid, until at last it took the form of a huge, snake-like creature.

Towering high above Miryam's head, it had shed its former shadowy self and stood as a giant, silvery serpent, spitting and hissing. Its cold black eyes, pits of infinite darkness, and in the center of its chest burned a single, glowing red ember where a heart should have been.

The serpent lunged.

Miryam cowered, screaming.

Helplessness crashed through her heart and mind as she hovered near the forest floor. Images flashed of her childhood, her father's face, the mother she had never known, her loving sister, and a future life with Ved. She reached for them, grasping at memory, past and future alike, real and imagined, but the harder she tried, the more they dissolved between her fingertips. She desperately wanted a fulfilling life, full of love, freedom, and happiness.

Yet a hiss of a voice resounded in her head, one she had carried since childhood. *You do not deserve one. You were born different. Born sinful.*

The serpent snarled louder at that last word. *Sinful.* It echoed throughout her mind, and the creature rose higher, looming over her.

Maybe this was it. *Maybe I must finally surrender to my fate—that I do not deserve the life I so desperately want.*

Then, a tiny voice stirred within her soul and whispered, *No, darling girl. That's not it.*

Despite the fear coursing through her veins, Miryam chose once more to defy—or perhaps, *to define*—her own fate. She scrambled to her feet, palms slipping against the damp leaves. In the struggle, she scraped her hand against a stick. She looked down. No blood. No pain. She tilted her head to the side. A heavy fog seemed to press against her thoughts, clouding all reason. Still, Miryam forced herself to remember.

And the still small voice spoke once more. *This is not real.*

The serpent lunged again.

Miryam darted aside. It came so close she felt its hot, fetid breath on her skin. Droplets hissed from its fangs, black eyes boring straight into her soul. Yet, she picked herself up off the ground. Looking for something to defend herself with, she seized a thick branch from the forest floor and swung it at the serpent.

The beast slipped aside with ease, its massive body gliding closer.

She swung again. And again. Each strike met only air.

Her rage grew. The coal in her chest flared, burning red hot, a mirror of the serpent's ember-heart. Suddenly, the tip of the branch she held lit aflame. She swung again with the flaming staff, but instead of touching the creature, it only seemed to rouse and embolden it.

Miryam imagined the serpent as Dempsey. As her old life. The life of a weaver's daughter and promised bride, shackled and powerless.

Life without Ved. Without magic. Without her strength.

With every furious swing, the serpent grew larger.

Its scales scraped the Earth as it lunged at her, each strike faster, heavier.

There was no fighting this.

"What do you want?!" Miryam shouted.

The beastly serpent halted its attack. Tilting its massive head, its eyes pierced into her mind. *I am you.*

Her chest heaved. "What does that mean?"

Yet even as the words left her lips, she knew.

Miryam lowered the stick. At once, the flame sputtered out. The serpent dove toward her, its fiery breath scorching her skin. But she did not flinch. She sat on the ground and drew a deep breath in. And out.

The serpent circled her, restless, hissing, slithering.

Miryam continued.

In.

Out.

The thrashing slowed. The hisses quieted. The terrible beast shrank before her eyes. Smaller. Weaker. Until it was no more than a grass snake, coiled and trembling.

Miryam reached down. Without fear, she lifted the tiny creature into her hands. She tilted her head back, bringing it close to her lips. The serpent slid down her throat, wriggling for a moment before settling in her belly. Warmth spread through her core. She could feel it coil inside.

Not an enemy now, but a part of her.

A gentle tingling stirred at the base of her spine, rising slowly and steadily. Gooseflesh prickled across her skin. Her breath came quicker, shallow and sharp. Her heart raced so fast, she thought it might leap from her chest. The feeling continued to rise. Climbing higher, through her belly. Surging through her heart. Her body swayed as if she were a reed in a storm-ridden creek. The power grew stronger, every fiber of her being alight with radiance. It pressed against her throat. She screamed as the force burst upward, forcing her spine erect. The power filled the space behind her eyes with brilliant light. Then, at last, the serpent's power shot through the crown of her head and erupted into the night air.

At once, stillness washed over her.

Miryam felt it—*a connection*. To the Earth beneath her feet. To the trees whispering above. To the Moon, the Sun, the stars. All of existence moved through her and with her. A boundless thread stretched from sky to soil, a living stream of energy flowing up and through her.

Tears streamed down her cheeks. Not of sorrow, but of pure, blissful joy.

Then, everything went white.

CHAPTER 41

LEAH

I t felt like someone had dragged Leah down to the depths of the deepest trench and scraped her along the rocky bottom. She couldn't find a way back up. Part of her wanted to lie down and die. Sleep forever. She could hear her mother's voice in her head. *You brought this upon yourself. You could have provided for Hana better by finishing your degree. Instead, you chose the simple route. And look where it's gotten you.*

Kat placed a hand on her shoulder, snapping her back into the present moment in the courthouse's hallway.

"Sweetie, you're not a bad mom," Kat said.

"Yeah, Mom, you're not. I would know," Hana agreed.

"He twisted your past to make it sound that way," Tate assured her.

Why are they all being so fucking nice to me? Leah's warped mind wanted validation for her own negative thoughts. Wanted to fall back into her usual pity party. She didn't deserve their kindness. The creeping migraine pressed on her skull.

Please, not now.

She thought of Miryam's journal in her bag. However, there was no magic pill—or magic journal—that would save her from the pain of this custody battle. She reached up and held her head, rubbing her temples, wishing for relief.

"Another migraine?" Kat asked.

"Yeah, they seem to have *perfect* timing." Leah rolled her eyes. This one seemed more intense than normal. And it was coming on quickly.

The fiery pain shot through her brain, making her wince. She reached into her bag to get the journal. But as she did, her head spun, and vision blurred. Arms out, she tried to steady herself. "I need to sit down."

Tate rushed forward—one hand steadying her elbow—and guided her to a nearby bench. "It's okay, we've got you."

Hana and Kat hovered around her.

Leah's head swirled.

"We'll get to tell your side of the story," Tate said. "The judge will see that Seth was twisting the truth."

"I hope you're right," Leah said, voice cracking as she clutched her head. The pain was overwhelming.

"Did you hear from the doctor yet?" Kat asked with a deep crease between her eyes.

"I need my bag ... the journal ..." Leah's tongue rolled in her mouth, trying to form words. Every ounce of her wanted to curl up into a tiny ball in bed and never come back out. She wished for a glass of wine—or four—to wash away her problems and this raging migraine. If only she could hold the journal, then maybe she could think clearly.

"You're not making sense, Mom." Hana rubbed her back.

Leah licked her lips. *Why is this happening to me?* Normally, she would never have the thought: *things happen for a reason.* But now, she was out of practical reasons, and she just wanted answers. She thought of Miryam, the journal, the silver piece, and her strange connection to them. Old Leah would have chalked it up to coincidence or would have given up and ignored it all.

But something shifted in her mind.

"My bag ... get me my purse," she managed.

Tate scanned the ground and found her purse lying where she had first come out of the courtroom. He rushed to grab it, handing it to Leah.

Reaching inside, she placed a hand on the journal and instantly—miraculously—the pain subsided.

"How much time do we have?" Leah asked, looking at Tate.

"About two minutes."

She nodded. "Okay, I'll meet you in there."

Clasping the journal, Leah sprinted down the hall toward the restrooms.

"Be careful. And ... don't be late," Tate shouted after her.

Leah stared at herself in the bathroom mirror. The gray in her hair was almost more than the light brown now. She had bags under her eyes. And those damn wrinkles were still there.

She glanced at the journal in her hand and thought about Miryam, going through her initiation into the order, facing her inner demon head on. She could do the same with Seth. *I will not make myself a victim anymore.*

Leaning forward, Leah gazed intently at her own eyes. Pale streaks of brown and green decorated the edges of her dark irises. *I see a loving mother. A survivor. A woman who has been tested and endured. Someone who will learn from her past.* She let out a deep exhale. No more running away.

"Now, go back out there and give it everything you've got," she said out loud.

Clutching the journal to her chest, Leah ran out of the bathroom, down the hall, and to the courtroom. She stopped running right before entering. Slowing down, she repeated her mantra in her head: *Breathe, just breathe.*

Softly, she opened the door. Everyone was already seated and glanced at her as she walked in.

Fuck, I'm late.

"Ms. Webb," Judge Scarborough said, "you're right on time. You and your lawyer have the floor."

Leah gave Tate a huge smile as she sat down at their table.

He stood up to speak.

"Thank you, Your Honor," Tate said. "I want to talk to you today, not about Seth Gray, but about Leah Webb and why she is a wonderful mother to her daughter, Hana." He turned to look at Leah with hope in his eyes. "All you heard from Mr. Gray and his lawyer is why they believe my client is unfit. However, he skewed the truth, and I'm here to show you the other side of Ms. Webb."

Tate continued to explain how deeply Leah loved her daughter. He read her personal statement, as well as Hana's, which clearly stated that she wanted to continue their joint custody. Plus, he gave a clear and hopefully compelling rebuttal to all the shit Seth and his lawyer had spewed earlier.

Still, Leah wasn't sure that would be enough to convince the judge.

"Yes, we all make mistakes," Tate continued. "My client, Ms. Webb, will be the first to tell you she isn't perfect. But is she a negligent mother?" He shook his head. "No, and her daughter doesn't think so either. We have plenty of witness statements, which also agree, as you can see from the additional documents we provided."

The judge looked down at her papers, nodding.

"Your Honor, may I speak?" Leah interjected.

Tate raised his eyes at her, confused. This wasn't part of their plan.

But Leah couldn't let Tate fight her battle.

"Mr. Vega, are you finished?" Judge Scarborough asked, tilting her head.

"Yes, Your Honor. Go ahead." Tate nodded to Leah and sat down.

Leah rose, drawing in one more deep breath before clearing her throat. "Thank you. Your Honor, have you ever felt like you were *meant* to do something important?"

Judge Scarborough's eyes narrowed. "Ms. Webb, I fail to see how this is relevant to this hearing."

"Please, bear with me. It is," Leah said, straightening her spine.

A pause, then the judge nodded at her to continue.

"What was it?"

Judge Scarborough looked mildly annoyed but—curious. "I felt I could make a difference for children in our community by becoming a family attorney, and now a judge in the family court system."

"That's wonderful. And thank you for the work you do." Leah reached for her water, letting the moment stretch as she took a sip. Then, she met the judge's eyes. "Psychology tells us that humans are biologically designed to seek purpose—meaning—in life. But you see ... I've never had a sense of purpose. I believed life was meaningless. We're born, we live, and we die—and in between, sometimes good things happen, but mostly bad things do." Her voice softened. "Then, I had Hana."

Tears welled in Leah's eyes. Normally, she would swallow them down, but this time she let them spill, warm tracks sliding down her cheeks. "Hana is my world. I would do anything for her. But I still didn't feel like my life had a purpose outside of her. But something has changed." She swallowed hard, steadying herself with a palm against the table. "I feel connected to a larger purpose now. It's terrifying. But it's also the most thrilling feeling I've ever had." She drew in a shaky breath, shoulders rising, then let it out. "So ... why is this important to this hearing?"

Scarborough leaned back, her expression unreadable. "Please, Ms. Webb. I'd like to hear that."

Leah nodded, wiping her cheeks with the back of her hand. "It's important because everything changes when we have a purpose. When we feel connected to something bigger than ourselves, we don't fill the void with alcohol, distractions, or poor decisions." Her voice cracked, and she pressed her palm to her heart. "I know I can't show you in a document, but ... Your Honor, I am here—with God, Spirit, whatever you want to call it—as my witness, to say that the *old Leah* is gone." She forced herself to hold the judge's gaze. "I can't change the past. But I can change the future. I will be better for Hana. But also—for myself." Nodding, her legs shook as she lowered herself back into her chair.

Tate reached for her hand, squeezing it gently.

She smiled and mouthed, *thank you.*

Judge Scarborough closed her file. "Well, Ms. Webb, Mr. Gray—you've both given me a lot to think about. I'll review the statements and documentation again. You'll receive my final decision early next week." The judge's eyes lingered on Leah.

Then she rose and swept out of the room.

Leah gaped at the now-empty chair. The echo of her heartbeat throbbed in her ears. "That's it?" she whispered to Tate, hoping for more of a resolution.

"You did great," Tate said, neatly shuffling the files and papers into his bag. "I'm proud of you."

From across the room, Seth's voice cut through. "What a fucking sob story, Leah. Oohhhh," he said, waving his hands in the air. "You finally found a purpose in life, and conveniently, just in time for the custody hearing."

Tate stiffened, standing to his full height, as he turned toward Seth.

"I can handle this." Leah rose, touched Tate's arm to pull him back a step, then leveled her gaze at Seth. "It wasn't a story. You don't have to believe me—but you'll see. I get you want your perfect little life, and I just put a big, ugly knot in it. But we can be reasonable adults and figure out a way to parent our daughter together, but separately. It's what Hana wants."

Seth's eyes burned into hers, his face flaming red. Leah could feel she was hitting a nerve, and that made her lips curve into a grin she couldn't suppress.

"What are you smiling about?" Seth snapped. He huffed out a bitter laugh. "It's not over yet. The judge still decides. Who knows? Maybe I'll stop by Betty's house later with a little ... gift."

Barclay cleared his throat sharply. "Mr. Gray, stop talking."

Normally, Leah would have been fuming too, but instead, a wave of sadness settled over her. Seth was nothing but petty remarks and vindictive moves. She had to believe in a world where people like him didn't always win.

It was her only way forward.

"Let's go," she said to Tate, her voice steady. "He isn't worth our time." She shoved the journal, her notes, and her water bottle into her bag.

Then, they walked out of the courtroom together.

The hallway felt brighter, louder, causing Leah to blink. She pressed her fingers to her temple—the migraine edging its way back in. She had hoped the journal would have eased it completely by now.

"Mom! How'd it go?" Hana's voice rang out as she barreled toward her. She wrapped her arms around Leah in a hug that nearly knocked the wind out of her.

Leah squeezed back. "When did you get so strong?"

Hana giggled and loosened her grip.

Leah brushed a strand of hair from her daughter's face. "I did my best, and that's all I can do. Until then ..." She managed a smile. "We should celebrate with some ice cream."

"Twice in one week?!" Hana bounced on her toes.

Leah stepped forward, but a jolt of pain shot through her head. She winced and faltered.

"You okay?" Tate caught her arm, steadying her.

"Yeah, I just ..." The world spun, and Leah grabbed her head. "... feel a little dizzy." Tiny black dots bloomed across her vision as the migraine surged back with full force, threading through every crevice of her brain.

"Tate, get her to the bench—hurry!" Kat's voice seemed far away.

"I think ... I'll be fine ..." Leah slurred out, knees buckling.

Falling in slow motion, her feet slipped out from underneath her.

As the hallway tilted, Kat and Tate's faces blurred above her, frantic and worried. Their words muffled as if she were underwater. Leah's eyes fluttered closed as she wished the pain away. It pulsed outward from the center of her skull like an expanding star. When she opened her eyes again, blackness crept in from the edges of her vision, narrowing to a thin tunnel of light.

And then—suddenly—the pain was gone.

Leah found herself staring down at her own body, lying on the courthouse hallway's hard tiles. Weightless. Floating. For the first time in forever, blissful.

I feel better. Why are they all so upset?

Kat was crying into her phone. Tate hunched over her body, gently tapping her cheek, his lips moving with urgent words she couldn't hear. Hana kneeled beside her, wailing.

Then, everything went white.

CHAPTER 42

KARAIA

Karaia's mouth fell open. "Griffin Marshall has the other half of the key to the Chest of Immortality?" She clutched her necklace, twirling the silver snake piece between her fingers. *How on Earth did he get the other half?*

"We don't have time to explain," Blaze snapped. "You need to go. Once you have both pieces, we'll do the trade-off, and you'll get the info to get to Avani. Got it?" The words were more like a command than a question as she stuffed the remaining tech into boxes and bags.

Across the room, Ziven worked quickly, wiping the memory of their computers and holo-screens. He paused, lingering at the wall of books and sliding open its fiberglass encasement, then took a deep inhale of their musty smell. With a heavy sigh, he whispered, "I wish I could take all of you." Guiltily, he slipped one slim volume into his pocket.

"What's going to happen to the rest of the books?" Karaia asked, fiddling with her newly placed earpiece.

"Like I said, no time," Blaze answered. "Z, wake the kids. We need to move—like yesterday."

Ziven nodded and headed down the hall. A crackle sounded in Karaia's ear. "Check, check. Karaia, can you hear me?"

She pressed the hidden comm. "Yeah, I can hear you."

"Great. We'll be on the move for a few hours. If you need us, just ring. But try to use it as sparingly as possible. There's always a chance that Seromela picks up on the wavelength." His voice faded as she caught the sound of shuffling feet and Ziven gently ushering the kids from their room.

"Got it, thank you," Karaia whispered.

Turning to Arjun, she nodded as they left the bunker, made their way up through the winding maze of stairs, and finally pushed out through the salon doors.

A faraway Sun was rising in the distance. A few early risers stirred on the tube's walkways, the city slowly waking to another day. Karaia drifted in a haze, still reeling from everything they'd learned overnight. Arjun looked no better, and she wondered how many credits he'd already popped since they were back in the tubes.

She paused by the window while they waited for the rail. Beyond the city's towers and tubes, the scorched Earth stretched to the outer walls. "What do you think it's like out there?" she asked.

"Huh?" Arjun blinked in a sleepy fog.

Karaia imagined a radiant sunrise surrounded by lush green trees and pointed mountains. "Past the walls. On the ground. With the soil beneath my feet."

"Oh." He rubbed the back of his neck. "Probably scary. Deserted. Bleak. Treacherous."

Karaia grimaced at him. Despite her own fear, she still refused to take a credit.

Arjun corrected himself as the rail slid into place. "I mean ... I'm sure it won't be that bad. You're tough."

They stepped onto the floating rail car.

"I hope you're right." She rolled her eyes, not feeling tough at all. The weight of leaving the only life she had ever known pressed upon her. She drew in a long breath, then pulled Arjun into a hug. "I'll miss you, you know."

"I know." He let out a small laugh, then added quickly, "I mean, I'll miss you too. But hey, this isn't goodbye. I need to program my PET for you at the office."

She nodded as they found seats. Arjun leaned his head on Karaia's shoulder. The rail silently pushed on. Almost instantly, she could feel him nodding off to sleep. Her eyes begged her to do the same.

Five stops later, she was shaking Arjun awake.

"See you at work," he said while yawning and stumbled off the rail.

Karaia followed suit the next stop after. Dragging her tired body to her front door and inside, she promptly set an alarm for two hours—not nearly enough time—and fell fast asleep.

~ഗ~

NIVA's voice cut through. *Good morning, Karaia. Would you like to get up or snooze?*

I'll get up, she answered silently.

Peeling herself from the comfort of her sheets, she knew snoozing wasn't an option. She moved on autopilot. Shower, get dressed, drink coffee, eat breakfast. Everything looked the same. Except it wasn't the same at all. Today would be her last day at Seromela. With NeuroCredits and NIVA.

The last day working for *Griffin.*

Her stomach lurched. She forced her breakfast back down, jaw tight, spine straight. She refused to let him derail her resolve. With one last sip of coffee, she headed out the door.

That morning, she was going to steal a magical key from her former lover and employer—the president of New Soteria—to potentially save the world and return magic back to humanity.

Karaia laughed aloud at the absurdity of it.

The first chuckle burst into a full, rolling laugh that shook through her chest as she walked down the tube toward the rail. People glanced and stepped aside, but she didn't care. Everything she was about to do sounded impossible. Still, something in her gut insisted it was the right thing.

That was her new normal.

Once she was on the rail, she pressed the small device in her ear. "Hello? Ziven?"

"It's about time." Blaze's voice was terse at the other end. "You have less than *three* hours. Are you at work?"

"Not yet." Karaia winced. "You're sure this earpiece won't be detected going through the entrance scanners?"

Ziven's reply came steadily. "You'll be fine. Tell us when you're through."

She clicked the comm off.

Karaia thought about calling her grandmother or her brother but had no idea what she would say. She couldn't tell them goodbye, not really—not about what she was about to do. Instead, she queued a future message through NIVA to be sent tomorrow, hoping it would still go out after she severed her connection to Seromela's servers. She told Gram and Cass she loved them, that she was safe.

Most importantly, not to look for her.

Tears cascaded down her face. She swiped them away quickly, hoping no one on the rail noticed. They'd wonder why she wasn't taking a credit. Fortunately, most passengers were lost on NeuroTryps or immersed in VR games.

Karaia tried to focus, forcing herself to run over the plan again in her mind like a mantra. Still, the thought of leaving without hearing her grandmother's voice one last time gnawed at her.

NIVA, call Grandma.

Calling Cecelia Pine.

"Karaia!" her grandma exclaimed. "I didn't expect to hear from you before work."

"I know ..." Karaia hesitated, unsure of what to say. "... it's just ... I have this thing later. I didn't think I would have time to call on my way home."

"How are you? I heard everyone at the gala received a free upgrade to NeuroTryp! I almost wish I could have been there just for that." Her grandma laughed.

I'm not fine. And no, you don't. If you only knew.

The flashes of dead bodies and explosions surged in Karaia's mind. But her grandma wouldn't understand. "I'm fine. I love you, Grams. Have a good day."

"Oh, you sound so serious," Cecelia gawked. "When was your last credit? Did you catch the latest episode of *On the Verge* when Brian was talking about—"

"I have to go." Tears blurred Karaia's vision as the rail slowed to her stop. "Tell Cass I love him too."

Her heart felt heavy knowing that might have been the last conversation she'd ever have with her grandma. Maybe someday she could tell her parents about Grandma and Cass—and tell Grandma about her parents—if she ever saw either of them again. Wiping her tears away, she knew she had to stay focused on the mission for now.

She marched through Seromela's front doors.

At the entrance scanners, Karaia noticed five armed guards. *Why have I never noticed them before? Probably because I never needed to.* She stepped forward. The brain scanner whirred around her head.

Beep! A green light blinked.

Relief flooded her chest. She exhaled.

"Good morning, Karaia Pine," the machine intoned as she passed through.

Once alone in the next hallway, she pressed the comm and whispered, "I'm in."

"Great," Ziven replied. "Remember, only use this if you need to. If we don't hear from you, we'll assume things are going as planned. Good luck—you've got this."

"Thanks," Karaia muttered.

She was on her own. Sliding quietly through the halls, her nerves danced within. Employees typed at keyboards, eyes glued to holo-screens, absorbed in Phase Two's latest project. No one noticed her.

She made her way to Arjun's office and knocked.

"Come in." He swiveled in his chair, dark circles under his eyes. Even credits hadn't helped, but he still managed a smile.

"Hey." Karaia slinked in, closing the door behind her.

"Hey."

Both knew every word was recorded. They chose them carefully.

"So ... that project you're working on," Arjun said at last. "I've got some tech to help."

"Thanks." Her voice was terse, holding back the tears from earlier.

He pulled out his PET. "I've reconfigured this for you. Hold this button near the *object* for thirty seconds to scan. Then, press this button to use it. Simple."

Karaia slipped the PET into her inner pocket of her jacket and zipped it shut. Through heavy breaths, she whispered, "I wish you could come with me. You'd be a lot of help."

Arjun pursed his lips. He wasn't an emotional person, but Karaia could see this was hard for him too. "It's not my type of work. I'm better here." He hesitated. "But I have a feeling this won't be the last time we work together."

"I hope not." She lingered for a few more seconds. Then, not caring what Seromela's cameras picked up, she rushed across the room and hugged Arjun hard, sinking into his arms, wishing he really could come with her. Choking on tears, she held him tight. This hug was the push she needed. She buried her last cries in his shirt, then pulled back, wiping her eyes.

Karaia strode out of the office and toward the elevator, checking the time. Two hours left. *Enough time to get in and out.* At least, that's what she told herself.

Griffin Marshall's office sat on Seromela's top floor. By now, close to lunch, he would be there—he never missed his midday meal or the latte he sipped at his desk.

Karaia braced herself as she walked. Could she face him, knowing what he was and what he'd done?

All those lies. Lies she'd helped tell. *Safe. Happy. Healthy.* That was New Soteria—at least for those who obeyed, didn't question, or fight back.

She nodded to Griffin's receptionist, Priscella, on her way down the hall. The woman didn't even glance up from scrolling her holo-feed. Turning the corner to Griffin's office, Karaia reached for the handle—then froze. *Voices.*

Leaning close, she pressed her ear to the door.

Griffin and ... Stellan. *Shit.*

"I need to know you're committed to the project," Griffin said sternly.

"I am," Stellan replied, his voice heavy. "I'm just not sure the way you're going about it is—"

"You're overthinking." Griffin huffed. "As always. Projecting your feelings. This is what people need. What *our world* needs. The gala attack had to happen. Don't you see?"

"Dad, people *died*," Stellan emphasized as he began pacing the room. "You—*or anyone*—shouldn't be able to decide things like that."

Griffin retorted, "You'll understand in time. Trust me, we had to do it. We can't return to chaos. We can't let the Defiers get what they want."

His voice was so firm, so unwavering, and so confident in his decision to ... *murder* people. Karaia's breakfast churned in her stomach.

He went on. "You, of all people, should know that. I would never wish what I went through with you and your brother on anyone else."

Silence followed.

Karaia leaned in, her pulse hammering. She couldn't believe it. Blaze had been right—Griffin had planned the gala attack, not the Defiers. She couldn't face him now. The thought of seeing his smug face made her sick. There was no way she could go through with what they had planned.

Stellan spoke up, his voice rising. "You know I want to be part of the business—like what you had planned for Kai. Let me prove I can do this."

"But you're not Kai," Griffin snapped. "He had been prepared for this role since childhood. He had my drive. My ambition."

"But he's not here. I am." Stellan's voice cracked. "Just give me another chance. That's all I'm asking."

Griffin sighed, then said, "We'll talk later. It's time for my lunch. Priscella!"

"Yeah, okay. See you, Dad," Stellan muttered.

Karaia's chest tightened. He was leaving the office—and coming straight toward her. At the sound of the knob turning, she quickly slipped back around the hallway corner.

But it was too late. Stellan rounded it and collided with her.

"I'm sorry—" he blurted, then froze, recognition dawning across his face. "You. From the gala?"

Why did he feel so familiar? Electricity crackled between them, drawing Karaia in. She couldn't look away from those eyes, searching hers—for something—what was it? Biting down on her lip, she forgot all about the mission.

"Hi," she breathed. "I finally know your name. Stellan Marshall."

The surname jolted her back into reality. *Marshall.* Just like Griffin. Stellan knew the truth about the gala—and that knowledge repulsed her. Whatever warmth she was feeling, she tried to force it back.

"Yeahhh." He rubbed the back of his neck. "I thought ... maybe I could have one night when I wasn't the heir to the world's largest tech corporation. Didn't really work out." His head dropped, heavy with resignation.

Karaia narrowed her eyes at him. Her mind drifted back to the gala. To the dying man, and his love for his wife. The memory left her aching. Not just for their loss, but for a love she'd never had. And for a flicker of a second, she imagined it—with Stellan.

"No, it didn't," she said, lips pressed tight.

"Though," Stellan said, lifting his gaze back to her, "we'll always have our little island getaway, won't we?"

He smiled, but torment shadowed his eyes, a battle raging inside him. Part dutiful son, part ... something else. Karaia didn't know what it was, but it tugged at her, pulled at her very core. She wanted to say yes. To join him in that dream. To be whisked away into something beautiful and blissfully their own.

But she couldn't let herself. She knew too much.

Averting her eyes, she hastened, "Excuse me, I have to go."

His face fell. "Oh, of course. I hope to bump into you again, Karaia." His voice lingered on her name before flashing a devilish half-smile.

Fuck. That would ruin her someday.

He stepped past her and continued down the hall.

Karaia hurried back around the corner toward Griffin's office and pressed herself against the wall. She drew in a long breath, preparing herself for the mission ahead. *Be brave.*

Then, she knocked.

"Come in," Griffin called.

Karaia slinked inside.

Griffin sat at his desk, leaning back in his chair.

When he saw her, he perked up, grinning. "What a pleasant surprise. I didn't know what to think after seeing you at the gala, not wearing the dress I bought you. You're always keeping me on my toes. Get over here and make it up to me."

Bile rose in her throat. She wasn't sure she could pull this off.

"Mr. Marshall." She nodded stiffly, inching forward.

He arched a brow. "Formalities now, Ms. Pine?"

"I mean ... Griffin."

At that moment, another knock rapped at the door, and Priscella stepped inside with Griffin's lunch and latte. Head down, she set it quietly on the desk and swiftly left the room again.

"Now where were we?" Griffin snarled, hungry for more than just lunch.

Karaia shuddered a breath and let her body take over. She strode across the room, letting her jacket—with Arjun's PET tucked inside—fall to the floor. Sweeping his papers aside, she slid in front of his desk and straddled him.

"This is what I'm talking about." He leaned in to kiss her.

Karaia's back stiffened, muscles taut.

"You seem tense," he murmured, drawing her close.

He knows. He's going to figure me out. I can't do this. Her mind raced, but her body stayed in place, trained by habit and determination. She'd done this before. What was one more time? She willed herself to believe it.

"NIVA, privacy mode," Griffin ordered.

The blinds snapped shut. The door lock clicked.

He lifted her shirt off, exposing her bare chest, trailing wet kisses along her neck, her collarbone ... then, lower. Her nipples hardened under his touch. Karaia fought to keep her face still, her body planted, and her mind—anywhere but here. It flashed to Stellan. Their island fantasy. She pictured the crash of the waves, the salty breeze, and the soft embrace of his arms. His lips against hers—

She shook her head. *Not that either.*

"You okay?" Griffin cocked his head.

"Let's move this to the couch," she answered quickly.

With her legs still wrapped around his waist, Griffin rose and carried her across the room. He dropped her onto the cushions, pressing hard against her.

A shiver ran up Karaia's spine—not from desire, but from disgust. She had to get through this somehow. So, she clung tighter to the fantasy of Stellan. And her body loosened, though shame nipped at her. *I can't believe I'm imagining him right now with ... his dad on top of me.* She closed her eyes.

Griffin peeled the rest of her clothes off, his mouth marking every inch of exposed skin. Each touch made her want to recoil, to shove him off—but she forced herself elsewhere. *Stellan. The beach. Far, far away.* She clung to that image. With every vile flick of Griffin's tongue, she drifted farther from the moment, letting numbness and bodily pleasure carry her away.

The rest was a blur.

When it was over, Griffin sprawled naked on the couch, smug. "What a great *fucking* lunch," he said, smirking.

Karaia's stomach rolled as she dressed hurriedly, ensuring Arjun's PET still lay in the inside pocket of her jacket and hadn't been exposed. Her breath was becoming rapid. Her pulse was on fire. She couldn't believe what she had just done. Just the thought of Griffin disgusted her so much—

Vomit rose into her mouth.

She cupped a hand to her face, holding it in. And—back down. *Just breathe*, she told herself.

Griffin hadn't seen any of that, luckily. Across the office, he sluggishly tugged on his clothes, stretching with a large yawn. "I should probably get back to work."

Not yet. If he did, everything she endured would be for nothing. Karaia smoothed her outfit, trying to keep her voice calm. "Why not relax? After the big launch—and the attack—you've had a hell of a week. You must be exhausted."

"I am, but life keeps going—and so does business," Griffin retorted.

Think, Karaia. She strode over, pressing her thumbs deep into his shoulders.

"That feels good," he murmured, sinking into the couch. He rolled onto his stomach, giving her full access to his back.

She rolled her eyes, letting out a small exasperated sigh.

Thirty minutes later, Karaia's hands ached, but Griffin was snoring. Loudly.

What time is it? she asked NIVA.

No response. *Oh, yeah.* Griffin's privacy mode was still enacted for the entire room, as his didn't have a time limit. She pulled up her holo-screen. *11:53 a.m.*

I have less than ten fucking minutes! Karaia's heartbeat quickened as she rubbed her arms, palms sweaty, thinking. It wasn't enough time—no way to reach Griffin's vault, steal the key, and get out before her brain rebooted.

She frantically tapped the earpiece. "Guys, you there?"

"Yeah, you out?" Blaze's voice crackled.

"Not exactly ..."

"What does that mean?" Ziven asked. "You do realize you have about ten minutes."

"Of course I do," she whispered, a deep crease forming between her eyes. "Things took longer. Griffin just fell asleep. I'm still in his office."

"What the fuck are you waiting for?" Blaze pushed.

Karaia pressed a palm to her head. "What happens if I don't get out in time?"

"We'll figure it out," Ziven replied steadily. "Just get the key piece. And call us when you have it, okay?"

"Okay," she huffed, cutting the line and moving close to Griffin's sleeping head.

Karaia's hands were trembling as she slipped the PET from her pocket. She did exactly as Arjun instructed. Holding the scanner over his temple, she pressed the side button. The device hummed. A thin beam pulsed across his skin. She counted the seconds in her head until the scan was complete.

Then, she tiptoed toward the vault door, heart pounding in her ears, the less-than-ten-minute clock ticking louder with every step. She pressed the PET against the scanner, praying it would work.

She held her breath.

A soft green light blinked on. "Welcome, Mr. Marshall."

Air whooshed out of her lungs. She glanced back—Griffin still snored on the couch—then pulled the heavy door open. A narrow flight of white marble stairs led down into the vault.

Karaia descended in swift, quiet steps.

The room below gleamed—sterile, immaculate, absolutely Griffin. Rows upon rows of artifacts stretched before her. Polished shelves held objects from across the world: a grotesque mask, a small stone idol, a carved wooden cup. Strange, ancient, out of place in this pristine tomb.

Her stomach flipped. *What the hell is he doing with all this?*

She checked the time. Three minutes remained. Her pulse spiked. She glanced at the hard marble floor. *That's going to hurt.*

She forced herself to keep looking, narrowing her gaze, scanning each shelf.

And then, she saw it.

The other half of the key to the Chest of Immortality.

It mirrored the one she wore around her neck—identical in shape and design—except this one was carved from wood, not silver. Small. Plain. Seemingly insignificant. Yet ... there it was again, the ache of familiarity.

She reached for it, then froze. *What if it's rigged? What if the second I touch it, alarms go off—and I'm lying here unconscious when they drag my body away?* The absurdity of her situation tugged a nervous laugh out of her.

Two more minutes.

No time for hesitation now. Karaia pressed her fingers around the wooden piece and lifted it. A small gasp escaped her lips as she held it. And her mind flashed to Stellan—no, to someone else—a young man in a long robe, standing in a cave. Wide-eyed and blinking, she shook her head. *Stay focused.*

Silence. No alarms. No shouts. She exhaled and slid the chain over her head, the wooden half of the key resting against its silver twin.

Ninety seconds.

Karaia lowered herself to the floor so she wouldn't crack her head on the marble when the reboot hit. As the seconds ticked by, the silence pressed in until she could hear every beat of her heart, every shaky breath. Trembling, tears dripped from her eyes as she slowly laid her cheek on the cool stone. She wished for someone to hug her tight, telling her it was all going to be okay.

Thirty seconds.

When she woke—*if* she woke—nothing about her life would be the same. The thought terrified her. She had never felt so alone. A credit would have dulled this pain, but that escape was long gone.

Ten seconds.

She desperately hoped she wouldn't open her eyes to Griffin standing over her, or a squad of New Soterian officers. Mind spinning with unanswered questions, Karaia counted down. *What if I'm arrested? Die outside the walls? Never find my parents? Never know love? What if…*

Three, two, one.

Then, everything went white.

CHAPTER 43

THE BEACH

W aves crashed against the beach shore, rushing water over Kara-ia's shoes. She wondered what the sand would feel like be-tween her toes. Then, in an instant, her shoes were gone, and she was digging her bare feet into the cool, wet sand. *This must be a dream.* But it seemed so real. Never had she felt this much awareness inside a dream. *Maybe it's VR?* She stretched out her hand, wiggling her fingers, straining to find the illusion she was sure had to be there. If it was, it was the most realistic simulation she had ever experienced.

The Sun sank low on the horizon, painting the sky in brilliant shades of orange and violet. Leah drew in a long breath of crisp, salty air. Peace at last. The throbbing pain that had plagued her head was gone, as if it had never existed. The hearing, the courthouse, all of it felt like a distant memory. She bent and picked up a seashell, marveling at the iridescent swirl of colors that seemed to mirror the beauty above her. She turned it over in her hand, smiling softly. *I could stay here forever.*

The warm sea wind whipped around Miryam, sending her dress and hair into a wild frenzy. A tingling energy spiraled into her core, warming her from the inside out, pulsing with each heartbeat. Laugh-ing out loud, she twirled, letting the joy of it all enwrap her. She had completed her initiation, faced her fears, and discovered her pleroma. She embraced all parts of herself—the dark and the light, the good and the bad. The power within her no longer terrified her. It fueled her.

But then, why am I here on a beach? She slowed her spin and looked around to find two women standing before her.

Crinkling her nose, Miryam asked, "Who are you? Is this part of my lesson?"

"Lesson?" Karaia reached down to touch the sand, rolling the grains between her fingers. "This *is* a strange dream."

Leah said nothing at first, simply watching the other two. One of them was young—probably still a teen, with long, red hair. Something about her felt familiar, though she couldn't place why yet. The other woman was older than the girl but younger than Leah, not yet thirty, with darker skin and short, curly hair. Leah's gaze drifted over their clothes—one wore a sleek, synthetic-looking jacket and pants, the other a long brown woolen dress. They looked as though they had stepped out of two completely different worlds.

"'Tis not your dream," Miryam snapped back. "'Tis my initiation."

"I have no idea what you're saying, but ..." The memory of the brain reboot sent a shock through Karaia. Pressing a palm to her stomach, her sixth sense flared like a signal of something important. "I'll wake up soon, and this will all be over."

Miryam tilted her head. "What is a ... brain reboot?" She spoke the words slowly, as if trying to wrap her tongue around something foreign and strange.

"How did you know what I was thinking?" Karaia crossed her arms, narrowing her eyes at the girl across from her.

"I heard it too," Leah finally spoke. Her usual urge to flee echoed in her mind—but something deeper told her to stay, to get curious instead. "Why can we hear each other's thoughts? Wait—can you hear this?"

Pink elephants, she thought deliberately.

"What are elephants?" Miryam asked, cocking her head.

"Elephants are extinct creatures," Karaia answered, letting her arms drop, her curiosity piqued. "I've only seen them in holo-movies."

"They aren't extinct," Leah shot back, shaking her head. *What the fuck is happening?* She strained to recall the moments before she had appeared here. *I was coming out of the courtroom ... then my migraine got worse. I got dizzy and ... passed out?*

340

"What is a *migraine*? A *courtroom*? What is all *this*?" Miryam exclaimed, throwing her hands wide. She was so confused—yet elated. The pleroma coursing through her body made everything shimmer with light and possibility. This was magical, beyond anything she had ever dared imagine.

"This is the wildest dream I've ever had." Karaia laughed. Surely, she'd wake up at any moment, slip back into her mission, and set off for Avani. But her gut told her otherwise. This wasn't just a dream. It was *more*. That's when she remembered—Griffin's vault and the genuine possibility that New Soterian officers would find her body soon. *How long have I been out?* Panic should have gripped her. Her heart should have been racing. Instead, she felt only peace.

"Why do you both speak in such peculiar ways?" Miryam's frustration grew. This couldn't be part of her initiation, could it? She longed to be back in the cave with the order.

Leah held up her palm, deep in thought. "Let's be logical and start at the beginning. What are your names, and where are you from?"

"I am Miryam, and I hail from Oakeshire, England."

"Karaia. I live in New Soteria."

"And I'm Leah, from Southern California."

"Wait." This time, Karaia shot up a hand. "California doesn't exist anymore. Do you mean the California Keys?"

"Noooo ..." Leah asserted. "I live in Los Angeles, California, in the United States of America." She iterated every word. "By the way, where's New Soteria? I've never heard of it."

Karaia raised a brow. "It's only the world's leading corporate government, ever since the United States fell."

"What's the United States?" Miryam blurted.

"It's official—I've gone insane," Leah said as she started pacing. "I hit my head when I fell, and now I'm in some crazy-ass nightmare where nothing makes sense and the United States doesn't exist. Awesome."

"What does a donkey have to do with this?" Miryam grunted, growing weary of this confusion. She longed to see Ved again soon.

Walking toward the ocean, Leah just shook her head.

Karaia dug her heels in the sand, determined to find answers. "So, you're saying the United States *does* still exist?"

"I mean, yeah," Leah said, turning to face her, "unless I time traveled."

Taking a deep breath in, Karaia closed her eyes. She leaned into the sensation that stirred within, stilling herself—listening—not to her own thoughts but to something *deeper* and more ancient. She flashed her eyes open. "Wait—what year is it?"

"The year of our Lord 1307," Miryam answered.

"2017," Leah said.

"And for me, it's 2307 C.E.," Karaia added, eyes wide, waiting for them to catch on to what she was thinking.

"You're saying we're all from different times?" Leah asked, eyes narrowing. "And this" — she pointed around them — "is a *real* beach? Enlighten us. Where are we?"

Karaia's shoulders fell. "Well, I don't know where—"

"Truly, this makes sense now!" Miryam exclaimed, eyes widening.

Both Leah and Karaia turned to her.

"Do you not see?" Miryam's voice rose in excitement as she marched across the beach, kicking up sand with the hem of her dress.

She ran toward the ocean, threw her hands in the air, and splashed up a crest of seawater with the fling of her arms, freezing the water in place mid-air.

Karaia gasped. Leah's mouth fell open.

Miryam moved her palms across the air, and the frozen water moved with her, conforming into beautiful fluid shapes, ebbing and flowing to the beat of the waves. With one flip of her wrist, she let go, and the water came crashing back down to shore.

She swirled to face the others again, smiling wide. "See! We are no longer of our world. Sophia said I may experience other realms. We must be in a world where time does not exist. 'Tis why we speak and think as one. Cannot you feel it as well?" Her chest heaved as she waited.

"I don't know what I'm feeling," Leah replied, still staring off where the twisting water once was. "But honestly, these last few weeks have been wild. So, sure." She shrugged. "I'm at the point of accepting there might be something bigger than myself going on here."

Karaia's sixth sense thrummed in agreement with Miryam's words; nevertheless, she hesitated. To admit this would mean she was connected to the Chest of Immortality, and ... magic was real.

"You know of the Chest of Immortality?" Miryam bounced on her heels, excitement radiating from her.

Then it hit Leah. That face. That fiery hair. She was the girl from her vision. From the journal. "It's you ... Miryam."

"Yes, I told you as much."

"No, I mean—I *know* you. I have your journal. Well, seven hundred years after you wrote it." Leah's voice wavered, the truth sounding absurd even as she spoke it. "You wrote about the chest. I have the silver half of the key."

Karaia gaped. "You do? I have the silver piece too. Do you think ..." Her hand went instinctively to the necklace resting on her chest. "... it's the same one?"

Miryam's brow furrowed. "How do you know of the chest and the key?"

Karaia launched into the prophecy and what Ziven had explained. The story of magic sealed inside the chest, waiting for the key to release it. She explained her mission—how she was stealing the other half for those who wanted to see humanity free.

Miryam shook her head firmly. "No, 'tis not right. Not in my time, at the very least. The chest does not contain *humanity's* magic. Every person holds their own pleroma within." She pressed a hand to her chest. "'Tis what we call the force that flows through all." To prove it again, she lifted her hand. A shimmer of golden light flamed from her fingertips, curling into the air like fiery sparks caught in the wind. "See?"

Leah and Karaia both stood frozen, their eyes wide, the glow reflecting—*resonating*—within them.

The gears in Leah's mind clicked together. "So, somewhere between your two times," she said, pointing from Miryam to Karaia, "humanity's magic gets locked up in that chest. What if we could stop it from happening?"

"What if we're *meant* to stop it?" Karaia added. It was all making sense—and yet, none of it did. Still, deep down, she knew this was why she had learned of the prophecy, why she was connected to the chest.

"But how?" Leah asked.

Karaia answered, "We need to touch. Hands—or something."

Miryam nodded, lifting her palms toward them.

Leah stepped forward and raised hers too.

The three women formed a triangle, palms facing one another. The moment they connected, a surge of energy sparked between them. Wisps of colorful pleroma unfurled from their fingers, weaving into luminous threads that whipped around them, stirring the air and sand in a spiral.

Karaia's chest swelled. She had never felt anything like this before—the warmth, the connection—it brought tears to her eyes.

Miryam breathed it in, surrendering to the current of pleroma as it wove its way through her, knitting itself into the very core of her being. It was like the time in the forest with Ved, only a hundred times more powerful.

Leah's eyes locked on the others. She knew what she—*they*—had to do. Their thoughts intertwined with hers, thin tendrils of consciousness braiding together until her own sense of self blurred, indistinguishable.

As one, their thoughts drifted together. From the attack in the woods, to Miryam's deep love for Ved and the power that still pulsed in her veins from overcoming her fiery inner demons. They witnessed the woman struck down in the alley, and the bombs that rained from the gala's glass ceiling. They felt Karaia's fierce resolve to protect the people she loved, her burning drive to do what was right. Then, came Leah's loneliness, her battles with depression, her exhaustion from years of silence. But they also felt her devotion to Hana, the fire that had carried her through the hearing when she finally stood up to Seth.

The surrounding air swirled faster, tugging at the edges of their beings until their separate lives blurred. They saw the passage of time, humanity's history and future, all blending and moving as one living consciousness. Sadness. Heartbreak. Apathy. Rage. But also love.

Joy. Beauty. Wonder. The breadth of human emotion and experience washed through them like a crashing wave.

Then, creeping in slowly, like smoke through a crack, came the darkness.

It was impossible to tell when it began—only that it spread, little by little, until it thickened into a choking fog. The depth of feeling, humanity's essence, its magic, smothered. Humanity was—or would become—dead inside.

The swirling pleroma settled, and a hush fell across the three of them.

"Not dead," Karaia whispered, her voice cutting through. "Just asleep."

Then, it all turned white again.

PART THREE

"Waking up to who you are requires letting go of who you imagine yourself to be."
— Alan Watts

CHAPTER 44

MIRYAM

Fluttering her eyes open, Miryam found herself back in the comfort of the surrounding order. Most of the candles had burned low, their light little more than faint glimmers against the stone. She lay on the mat, feeling the small rocks of the dusty cave floor press into her back, yet they brought no pain. The pleroma still hummed within her, soft and steady, masking any discomfort.

She glanced around the dim room. Some members still sat in their circle, chanting in low, steady tones. Others—mostly the students—had drifted asleep, their bodies slumped against the wall in quiet rest.

Sophia stepped forward and bent to help Miryam sit upright. "Welcome back, dear one. You have passed through your initiation." Her wrinkled eyes gleamed with warmth. "Tell me, did you find what you were seeking?"

"I did." Miryam rubbed her eyes, still hazy, her body unsteady. The medicine's grip lingered, pulling her between two worlds. But her voice was sure. "I know what I am meant to do."

Miryam explained that, in the future, humanity's magic would become trapped in the Chest of Immortality and that she was to play a vital role in stopping it and ensuring people stay connected to their pleroma. "We must protect the chest," she asserted. "And we must tell people about pleroma as well. The future ..." Her head hung low, shaking. "... it is so bleak. The Earth is dying. Humans are cut off from one another. They have forgotten who they are."

Sophia exhaled. "You have glimpsed a great deal in the spiritual realm," she said gently. "But let this knowledge rest within you for a time. Oft, 'tis not clear how we interpret the messages we are given."

Miryam frowned, though she knew Sophia was probably right. The chest was safe. There was no need to do anything rash.

Matilda, half-yawning, broke the silence. "So ... what is your gift?"

The other students rustled, waiting for her answer.

"I do not yet know." Miryam rose, stretching her sore limbs. "There was a serpent. I ... well ... it is *in* me now. I can feel it as we speak, scaling my spine." She rubbed her arms, a faint smile playing on her lips. "'Tis a bit ... tingly."

"Interesting," Father Thomas said as he cleaned up from the initiation. "The power of the serpent—one of the wisest creatures on this Earth. I have heard but one other person to have such a gift. For 'tis not one ability, but *seven*." His brows raised at Miryam. "It will be a rare delight to have someone in our order with so many gifts."

"That's not fair," Matilda muttered, folding her arms with a huff.

Sophia eyed Matilda and the other students. "We do not choose our abilities. They *choose* us. Miryam will have a most difficult time learning to be responsible with such power. It will not be easy."

"Sorry, I misspoke." Matilda bowed. "For I need rest." She left the cave.

One by one, the others followed until only Sophia and Miryam remained.

Miryam turned to go. She wasn't tired in the least, but she knew she'd want to write everything down in her journal before sleep claimed her.

"Wait." Sophia's voice stopped her in her tracks. "There are two things I must say. First, like the other students, you are not to use your gifts if you stray outside these walls. Do you understand?"

"Yes." Miryam nodded as she helped Sophia snuff the last of the candles. "And the second?"

"Also," Sophia said, her voice low, "Ved has spoken to me of your bond."

Miryam gasped. "He told you?"

"Aye. I am the closest he has to a parent, and he sought my counsel. He confessed he shall not take his vows—in order to be with you."

Heat rose in Miryam's chest. "'Tis his choice—his life, *our* life. We would be together. You cannot forbid it."

"I said naught of forbidding." Sophia laid a steady hand on her arm. "I only asked him to stay away tonight. You needed to do your initiation on your own. You are still young. I warn, do not bind all your strength to another. You must first learn it within yourself."

"And what if we are to be wed?" Miryam pressed her lips tight, her heart quickening, praying Sophia would say they might remain in the order.

"I must speak with Father Thomas and the elders," Sophia replied. "Yet if it were mine to decide, I would allow it."

Miryam's eyes widened.

"Once wed ..." Sophia added. "... you would need your own quarters, but I see no reason you should not continue to train and practice your gifts."

A smile broke across Miryam's face, and she couldn't contain herself. "Oh, thank you, thank you, thank you!" She flung her arms about Sophia, her joy echoing through the dim cavern. "This gladdens me more than I can say."

Sophia returned the embrace. "Naught is certain yet. Now, off with you. Rest well, dear."

Miryam was abuzz with energy and hope for what lay ahead. She hurried to her room and poured every detail of her initiation onto the page—every vision, every feeling, and all she could recall of her time with Leah and Karaia on the beach. Knowing that Leah would one day receive her journal, she flipped to the first page and wrote, *For Leah*, in her best handwriting possible. Then, she imagined her future and wrote down every dream she had for a life with Ved.

At last, her hand grew weary, her quill slipping from her grasp. A yawn overtook her as she glanced out the small window to see dawn's pale light breaking in the east. Sleep tugged at her, insistent. There would be more time tomorrow.

She crept beneath her blankets, her head heavy upon the pillow, and let her thoughts wander to Ved—what it would be to kiss him, to stand at his side on their wedding day. She played out the whole ceremony—and wedding night—as a gentle fog pulled at her eyelids, making her mind fuzzy with dreams.

When she woke again, Miryam found she had slept an entire day. The next morning's Sun shone brightly, and it was a crisp autumn day. She stretched, feeling more alive and more hopeful about her future than ever before. That very afternoon would be Bella's wedding—the first time she would set foot in the village since the night of her attack.

But she was no longer afraid. Because she would marry Ved. And Dempsey would trouble her no more.

She dressed quickly, tucked her journal into the small satchel Sophia had given her, and scurried out the door. Rather than follow the usual stone path, Miryam ran down through tall grass and wildflowers, brushing her fingers across their petals while the morning Sun kissed her cheeks.

At the pond's edge, Ved sat in his quiet meditation, the surface of the water shimmering like glass.

"I have much to tell you!" she exclaimed.

He turned, cheeks flushing, and smiled. "I cannot wait to hear it."

She dropped beside him and poured out everything—her initiation, her strange visions of Leah and Karaia, the serpent's gift, and even Sophia's words about their future together in the order. When she finally paused for breath, she asked, "So ... have you heard from the elders?"

Ved replied, "Not yet. They have been in council since dawn."

Miryam let out a sigh and rested her head upon his shoulder as they gazed at the pond. "They do talk for a long time."

"Well, it would be the first time they allowed anyone in the order who did not follow the monastery's ways," he said.

"True, I am simply impatient." She laughed.

"I had not noticed," Ved teased, nudging her with his shoulder.

Miryam gasped in mock outrage and gave him a playful shove. "Hey!"

"I only speak the truth." He winked, grinning wide.

Miryam's heart leapt, and it took all her strength not to fling herself into his arms. She bit her lower lip, pulse quickening. Slowing, she asked, "Would you come with me to the village today? You could meet my family—at Bella's wedding."

"I would love nothing more, but—"

"But what?"

His gaze fell to the ground as he twisted a cloverleaf between his fingers. "I must remain here. I received a message from the Akashic realm, and I am still discerning its meaning. And ... I believe this is a path you must complete on your own." He lifted his eyes back to hers. "But I shall miss you."

Miryam seized the front of his robes and drew him close until their foreheads touched. Energy sparked across her skin, humming between them. She longed to pull him close and press her lips to his. Taste him. Feel him.

She squeezed her eyes shut.

They could not. At least, not yet.

"I'll miss you too," she whispered. Then, reluctantly, let go.

She sighed heavily before rising to head out of the abbey gates and make her way toward the village.

Bird chatter and the rustle of fallen leaves filled her walk. Miryam tried to carry the lessons of the order into the outside world, breathing with intention on every inhale and exhale. Yet the joy within her burst too high to keep still. She broke into a run, skirt flying, and made a cartwheel down the path, shouting with such delight that a flock of sparrows burst from the trees in alarm. She laughed aloud, certain no one could ever be happier than she was at that moment.

At the edge of the forest, she stopped just before heading into town, taking one long breath. *In. Out.* Nodding, she assured herself that she was brave enough to face whatever lay ahead.

Villagers bustled about like any other day—women hauling water, children darting between carts, men herding sheep. Except, it was not any day.

It was her sister's wedding.

Miryam opened the door to her family's cottage to find Isabella and her father getting ready for the ceremony.

"Father, the flowers do not feel right," Isabella fussed, adjusting the garland in her hair.

"Bella, I can see them plain enough, and they look fine," Simon retorted.

"Can I help?" Miryam asked softly.

"Miryam!" Her father dropped what he was doing and ran to her, pulling her into a crushing embrace.

She clung to him, tears rising fast. It felt so good to be in his arms again. And from the way his shoulders shook with quiet sobs, he had missed her just as much.

"My girl, my darling girl," Simon choked out. "I would not have believed it until I saw your face. I thought we had lost you forever—" His words broke into a coughing fit.

Isabella's worried eyes met Miryam's over his shoulder. Miryam mouthed, *I am sorry,* for leaving her sister to bear this alone.

Simon cleared his throat into a small rag. When he pulled it away, Miryam could see a spot of blood.

"Oh, Father, I am so sorry I did not come sooner." She rubbed his back.

"No need for apologies, my dear. You are back now, and 'tis all that matters," he said, moving to find his seat next to the hearth.

"Are you feeling improved at all?" Miryam asked, though she could already see the truth in his weary frame.

He straightened as best he could, mustering dignity. "We will not speak of me today. This is your sister's day, and we shall celebrate." He clapped his hands lightly. "Now, you may take over helping her prepare."

Miryam nodded and turned to her sister. "Bella, you are radiant and look absolutely fit for a bride."

"Thank you," Bella said as she fussed with her hair again. "But can you help me? Father seems to think my hair flowers appear fine, but they feel out of place."

Miryam walked over to Isabella and straightened the flowers in her hair. "There. How do they feel now?"

"Perfect. Now that you are here, what do you think of my dress?" Isabella asked, smiling as she gave a twirl in her wedding gown. "Gawain's father had it made for me by Demp—"

Her eyes flashed at Miryam.

"All is well," Miryam said quickly, steadying her sister with a reassuring grin. "You need not worry about me. Because—" She paused, swallowing her own secret joy. This was Bella's day, not hers. "Because you are the most beautiful bride I have ever seen!"

She caught her sister's hands, and the two of them spun around the cottage, laughing and dancing until their cheeks ached and their breath came short.

"We mustn't spoil my hair," Isabella said at last, still laughing as she pressed a hand to her head. Then she stopped and eyed Miryam up and down. "But what in God's name are you going to wear? You cannot go dressed in *that*." She gawked at the plain brown dress.

Miryam laughed. "I had but little choice of garments. Let me change, and I will be ready."

Miryam sauntered to her corner of the cottage. Everything was just as she remembered it—her narrow cot, the worn blanket, a small stack of books, and a few simple gowns hanging neatly at the side. She chose a blue wool dress and changed hastily. While her heart swelled for Bella, and she did not want to steal the momentous occasion from her, Miryam knew she must tell her father she would not wed Dempsey.

Returning, she started, "Father, I must speak to you about—"

"No time to talk now, Miryam." He scurried his girls toward the door. "'Tis time to get our dear Bella to the church."

"But, Father—"

His sharp, fatherly look silenced her. Miryam pressed her lips together and nodded, falling in step with them.

"Wait," Isabella said as she ran back, plucked a sprig of lavender from the bundle hanging over the hearth and placed it gently into Miryam's hair. "There. Now we can go."

They stepped out of the cottage, and the three of them linked arms—one daughter on each side of their father. For a moment, it felt like old times. Only then did Miryam realize how deeply she had missed them. Yet her mind strayed to the abbey—the order, her new powers, Ved. She walked between two worlds now, so different from one another. Could she truly belong to both?

The wedding was held in the town square before the church, as was custom. Isabella and Gawain looked the part—the devoted bride and the steadfast knight—hands bound with ribbon as they pledged themselves as one under God. The ceremony was brief, but sentimental.

When it ended, the bells tolled, and the crowd flowed inside for mass. That part stretched on much longer, the priest's voice echoing through the stone walls, but Miryam let her thoughts wander. She imagined her own wedding day—her hands fastened to Ved's, their vows spoken beneath an open sky, and a wedding night that would satisfy the deep longing she felt in her groin every time Ved drew near.

Miryam wiggled in her seat, and the priest shot her a glance as if he could read her impious thoughts. She huffed gently, knowing he couldn't.

At last, mass concluded, and the people poured outside once more. Cheers rang out as Isabella and Gawain stepped through the doors, faces bright. The square filled with well-wishers, laughter, and clapping hands.

Miryam let her gaze roam the crowd. Neither the earl nor his family were in attendance, which was hardly surprising. Gawain was not quite noble enough for such attention. Still, many of the earl's knights were present, for Gawain was now a knight in the castle of the Earl of Norfolk. He stood tall in polished armor beside Isabella—the perfect couple. A pang of envy flickered through Miryam, but it was quickly tempered by genuine happiness for her sister. Her heart swelled, knowing her own time would come soon enough.

She hadn't seen Dempsey yet either. Perhaps he wasn't here. Perhaps he had gone back to London. Perhaps he had died of a painful, incurable disease.

She prayed it was so.

"You look rapturous," a sniveling voice hissed from behind.

An icy chill ran down Miryam's spine.

"Dempsey," she said, turning slowly. At the sight of him, her breath faltered, all the color draining from her face. The fiery coal she had extinguished in her heart begged to be relit. It took everything in her to resist the temptation. Everything about him, from his oily smile and fish-stained odor, made her skin crawl.

"And here I thought you were gone forever, my elusive bride," he said, bowing with mock ceremony.

"I am not your bride," she bit back.

"Are you not?" He spread his hands as if at a bargain. "Your father has promised you to me. So, I take it we have unfinished business."

Miryam's jaw hardened. She stepped forward until she was close enough for only him to hear. "I will never wed you. However, I forgive you — *not* for your sake, but for mine. I refuse to let *you* define me." Then her voice dropped to a calculated whisper, and she hissed, "But mark me, should you ever touch me again, I will rip you apart."

He recoiled, eyes wide, one hand pressed against his chest. For a fleeting moment, he looked honestly afraid.

Then he smoothed his coat, forcing his sneer back into place. "You cannot threaten me, girl. I have the earl's favor behind me. Now come—take my arm. We shall enter the feast together, as the betrothed we are."

He held out his elbow to her.

"I will never," Miryam snapped, folding her arms tight.

Before she could say more, her father appeared, smiling faintly.

"Ah, I am most glad you found each other." Simon patted Dempsey on the back. "I told him you had escaped those wretched men in the woods. Now at last, I will see both my daughters wed. 'Tis the greatest gift a father could ask."

Her father's voice was hoarse, and the rasp lingering in his lungs made Miryam's heart twist with worry. She sighed heavily, forcing her mouth not to spout off. She would not crush his joy here, not today. Later—tonight, or tomorrow—she would tell him about Ved. About her choice. About the truth.

For now, she forced herself to nod. "Yes, Father."

"Then, my dear girl, there is no need for that sullen face. Let us celebrate!" Simon threw his arms into the air. "And Dempsey—come. You are family now."

Miryam shivered.

Her father started toward the church hall, glancing back to be sure they followed.

Dempsey stuck out his elbow again to her and said, "Shall we?"

Miryam's eyes flicked from his smirk to her father's beaming face. Slowly, she uncurled her arms from across her chest and placed one, stiff as wood, through his. Her father's smile deepened, satisfied, and he turned back toward the feast.

Leaning close, Dempsey breathed, "I knew you could not deny an ailing father."

The once-extinguished coal flickered in her chest, and it took all her strength not to strike him or cry out. No, not today. Today was Isabella's day. Today, her father was happy. She would not ruin either.

For now. She repeated the words to herself like a chant, clinging to them as they walked.

Guests made their way into the church, which had been transformed since the earlier mass service. Benches had been moved aside to prepare the hall for the wedding feast, and smells of roasted meat and fresh bread drifted through the air. Soon, people were piling on pieces of turkey legs and turnips, filling their glasses with ale. Lively music struck up, and Isabella and Gawain led the floor, spinning in the first dance as others joined with laughter.

Dempsey turned to Miryam, bowing slightly. "My lady?"

She turned her nose up. "Never." Then, louder, for any listening ear, she said, "Ah, my dear, I am weary from the day's excitement. My frail frame begs a moment's rest." With that, she glided toward a pew along the wall.

"Then I shall keep you company, future wife," Dempsey declared as he followed.

Miryam blew a sharp breath through her nose. *Is there no escaping him?*

Her thoughts darted to her newfound powers. She closed her eyes briefly, stilling herself, and pictured her throat center spinning with pleroma. Faster, stronger—it would take but a thought to send him into a coughing fit.

But then Sophia's warning returned. *No powers beyond the abbey walls.* She conceded and let the pleroma dissipate within her. Instead, she resolved to treat the evening as a meditation—utter silence for the rest of the night. *Maybe he will eventually grow bored with me? I can only hope.* With that, she slumped down at the end of the pew.

Dempsey sat next to her, scooting close. "Have you heard the latest from the earl's hunt for heretics?" he asked.

Miryam pursed her lips.

He droned on. "Word is, there is a secret group practicing witchcraft under the guise of the Catholic Church."

She sat stone-faced. No response.

"They say the witches hide in a nearby abbey, dressed as Benedictine monks."

Her heartbeat quickened.

Dempsey gave a pious nod and crossed himself. "Can you imagine? What blasphemy against God. The earl plans to see them arrested and quartered in the square within the week."

Miryam's eyes widened with panic. She forced her hands to stay folded neatly in her lap, though her fingernails dug into her palms. Pressing her mouth shut, she tried not to speak. But the words tumbled out without regard. "When is this going to happen?"

"My dear, I do not know such details." He rolled his eyes as if they were speaking of the cabbage harvest or next year's wool supply—trivial matters.

Except this was far from trivial to Miryam.

Dempsey continued, waving a hand flippantly, "I only know that 'tis happening soon. Lord Amalric speaks too freely when I am measuring for his outfits." Narrowing his eyes at her. "Why the sudden interest?"

Miryam willed her body to remain still, though her heart hammered in her chest. Her mouth turned dry as ash. She licked her lips, searching for moisture, then seized the nearest chalice of mead. Tilting it back, she drained it in a single swallow.

"No reason," she managed through tight lips. "I only find it ... terrifying."

"'Tis what I am always saying. How terribly dreadful it is!" He clutched his chest. "Have no fear, my future wife. Lord Amalric will see the heretics rooted out and slaughtered."

Dempsey reached for Miryam's hand.

She snatched it away.

The music, the laughter, the crowd—all dimmed to a dull hum. Heat flushed her face. And only one thought pulsed through her like a drumbeat. She had to warn the order.

She had to save them—save Ved.

CHAPTER 45

LEAH

The smell of hand sanitizer and stale hospital food hit Leah as she drifted out of her deep sleep, forcing her to wrinkle her nose even before opening her eyes and blinking to adjust to the fluorescent lighting.

"She's awake, guys," Hana said, rushing to her side.

Kat, Tate, Felix and even her mother, Karen, crowded around her bed.

"Now, now, I'm going to need some space," the nurse said, weaving his way through her friends and family.

Leah strained her eyes to focus, but the room, her friends, the nurse—everything—was blurry. She squinted at the name tag that leaned over her. It said *Blod*.

Or Brah. Or Brad, she wasn't sure.

"Ms. Webb," 'Probably Brad' asked as he checked her blood pressure, "how are you feeling?"

"Call me Leah, and ... I feel ... okay." She rubbed the back of her head, feeling a giant bruised knot. "What happened?"

"Mom, you fell. It was so scary," Hana explained, tears streaming down her cheeks. "I never want to experience that again. I thought you had died. Please, *please* never do that again." She collapsed in a heap on Leah, squeezing her legs through the hospital sheets—not letting go.

On the other side of Leah, Kat rubbed her back, smiling through soft tears. "She's right, though. We were so scared. Glad to have you back, sweetie."

"Your mom and friend is in good care," the nurse said, heading for the door, "but it's good she's here now. I'll get Dr. Paulson, and she'll explain more."

'Probably Brad' left, and immediately Felix popped his head out the door, gawking as he walked away.

"Mmm hmm ... I knew he'd have a nice ass." He swung back around. "Leah, honey, before you leave this hospital, can you seriously find out if your nurse is single—*and* get his number for me, pretty please?" He batted puppy-dog eyes at her.

Leah just rolled her eyes, shaking her head. "How long have I been out?"

Tate, eyes puffy and red, stepped up near her bed. "About six hours." Gripping her hand tightly, he said, "We were really worried about you."

Looking from him to Hana, to her friends, and even to her mom, everyone looked worn and exhausted.

Her mother, Karen, cleared her throat loudly. "I knew when Kat called, and then Hana called twice, something was serious." She began straightening and smoothing the hospital sheets, then moved to Leah's face and hair. "Look at you. Are you taking care of yourself? Eating enough? Is it depression again? Have you been drinking?"

"Mom, stop," Leah said, nudging her away. "Give me some space." She rubbed her head, still trying to process what had just happened. What she had seen, experienced, felt—with Miryam and Karaia. *Was any of it even real?* She really didn't need her overprotective mom hounding her now.

"Of course, be difficult. I just wanted to help." Karen threw her hands up. "Nothing is easy with you. I'm going to get a soda." She exited the room with a huff.

Leah exhaled with relief just as the doctor walked in.

"Hi, Ms. Webb," the doctor said, flipping through her chart. "I'm Dr. Paulson."

"She goes by Leah." Brad—whose name tag Leah could clearly read now—chimed in from behind.

"Leah," Dr. Paulson repeated, inclining her head, "I've been in touch with your physician. It looks like you were waiting for some MRI results, correct?"

Leah nodded.

"Unfortunately, there was a mix-up. They thought they had called you, but ... hadn't. Their office is very sorry about the mistake."

Gripping her blanket, Leah asked, "What are the results? Please—get to it."

The doctor glanced at the others in the room and then at Leah again. "Would you like to go over this in private?"

Leah shook her head. "Go ahead."

"There's no easy way to say this." Dr. Paulson pressed her lips together for a moment, flipped a page of the chart, then continued, "The scans show a tumor near the pineal region of your brain. That's a small gland deep in the brain's midline. These kinds of tumors can block normal fluid flow, which causes pressure to build up. That pressure explains your headaches, dizziness, and memory problems. Your fainting episode most likely resulted from that."

Leah's mouth went dry. "Is it cancerous?"

Tate squeezed her hand.

"We don't know yet," Dr. Paulson explained. "The only way to know for certain is to do a biopsy. The more urgent problem is the pressure. If it continues to build, it can become life-threatening."

Tate clasped Leah's hand harder.

"One option is to do a biopsy and place a shunt to relieve the pressure. If the tumor is benign and not growing quickly, we may not need to do anything else beyond monitoring it over time." Dr. Paulson glanced up from her charts.

Swallowing hard, Leah asked, "And what's the other option?"

"We go straight to surgery—remove the tumor—whether it's cancerous or not. Depending on its exact location, we may need to remove part or all of your pineal gland. Fortunately, there are medications you can take to replace the gland's functions."

Dr. Paulson paused, letting her words settle across the hushed room.

Nervous glances darted between Leah's loved ones. She hated this. Hated seeing them fret over her. Hated feeling this helpless.

"Personally, I would recommend the surgery," the doctor added. "Any time we operate on the brain, there's risk. Why take that risk *twice* if it turns out to be cancer after a biopsy? This is your decision, though. Press the red button if you need anything or once you've decided. We'll need your choice by the end of the day." Nodding, she turned promptly and left the room.

Leah sat frozen, her chest tight, like she couldn't breathe. She thought she'd learned her lesson—to truly *live* life. Not back away. Own her power. Learn to love. Yet here she was again, feeling like the world had just piled more on top of her, crushing her from all sides.

"Sweetie, how are you feeling?" Kat asked gently. She unscrewed a bottle of water and handed it to her.

Leah gulped it down, her hands trembling. "I don't know ... I thought it all made sense. I was getting better. And then, I was on a beach. And the key piece and ..." Her mind felt foggy as she searched for the right word. She closed her eyes, trying to grasp the fragments of her vision—or was it a dream?

"Are you talking about the journal?" Tate asked.

"Yes." Leah opened her eyes, the memory flooding back to her. "I saw Miryam—from the journal. When I was unconscious, I was with her. And another woman, Karaia, from the future. It turns out we're the same person—*the same soul*—but from different lifetimes. It's confusing. Like, was I talking to myself? Or to them?"

Her friends all stood there with blank expressions on their faces. She wished they could have experienced it too. See what she saw. Felt what she felt. Then, maybe they would believe her.

"I know this sounds crazy, but it has something to do with this tumor and my migraines. Whenever I have that journal with me, my mind is clear. The migraines go away. You'll see. Just hand me my purse." Leah reached out toward the chair with her things on it, but no one moved to help her.

"Tumors don't just go away on their own," Felix said, crossing his arms.

"Yeah ..." Kat stared down at the floor, then finally raised her gaze to meet Leah's. "Maybe you should rest for a few hours before deciding. Personally, I think you should do the surgery."

"But I can't decide until I figure this out. It's all connected, don't you see?" Leah's eyes pleaded with Kat—surely *she* of all people would understand.

Kat's eyes flickered back to the ground.

Felix shifted his weight, sighing. "Kat's right, honey. I believe you think you experienced something magical, but sometimes things just ... happen. Not everything has a grand purpose. But this tumor *is* real, and you can't ignore it."

"What I experienced was *real*," Leah shot back, her lips tightening. "And there is a larger purpose. I *know* it." She looked from Kat to Felix, to Hana, then to Tate, searching their faces.

A sudden wave of pressure surged through her skull. She squeezed her eyes shut, pressing a hand to her temple.

"You're having another migraine," Kat said, placing a gentle hand on Leah's shoulder. "Doesn't that tell you this needs to be addressed?"

"I'm not ignoring it, I just—" Leah winced, her voice catching as the pain pressed again. "I just need the journal."

"We just want you healthy," Felix said. "Then afterwards, we can figure out your mysterious medieval connection. Totally jealous, by the way. Do you think I was a dashing knight in my last life?" He struck a dramatic pose, hands on his hips like a regal knight.

Despite herself, the corner of Leah's mouth twitched.

"Mom ... they might be right," Hana said quietly. "But what do I know? I'm just a kid." She buried her face against her mother's chest and squeezed her tight.

Leah knew this was too much to ask a child to weigh in on.

"This might be the first time you didn't give me your opinion," Leah murmured, kissing the top of Hana's head. She lifted her eyes to Tate. "You've been quiet. What do you think I should do?"

Tate exhaled slowly, his shoulders rising and falling. "I support you in whatever decision you make. You're a responsible adult. No one else can make this choice for you."

Leah rubbed the heel of her hand between her brows, trying to knead away the pain and think clearly. "Kat, isn't the pineal gland supposed to be the body's spiritual center? The third eye in a lot of cultures? What if I do the surgery and lose my connection to the spiritual realm?"

Kat's expression softened. "Oh, sweetie. I love that you're into all of this spiritual stuff now. But what's more important at this moment?"

Leah massaged the spot between her eyes harder, her thoughts spinning. She couldn't run away from this. She had to choose. Yet something deep in her whispered that the tumor, the journal, the otherworldly visions—they were all connected. She just had to figure out how.

Only then could she decide.

She exhaled, and for the first time, Leah really *took in* the hospital room around her, like she was prepping for a psychic reading, paying attention to every minor detail. Directly to her right, a monitor beeped a slow, steady rhythm. An IV bag hung above her, its clear fluid dripping into a thin tube that snaked into her clammy hand. The oversized hospital gown itched against her skin, and she wished for normal clothes. But they were draped over a chair in the room's far corner, along with her purse—and the journal. A tray of untouched food sat on the table to her left—congealed meatloaf, lukewarm mashed potatoes, and a wobbling square of red Jell-O beside a half-empty water bottle—beside where Felix and Kat stood, both with puffy eyes. Felix shifted his weight from foot to foot, while Kat fidgeted with the crystal hanging from her neck, rolling it between her fingers. Further down on Leah's right, Hana still clung to her through sterile bed sheets. And next to her, Tate hovered, standing firm, emotion tightening his jaw. His body language said he wanted to lean in closer, but he held himself back, along with the tears in his eyes. Out in the hall, nurses and doctors passed by with hurried steps, their eyes glued to charts.

"Fine," Leah said at last, letting out a long breath. "I concede on the journal stuff. But first, I need to rest. I'm going to nap for a while. Then, when I wake up with a clear head, I'll decide—biopsy or surgery."

She knew what she must do, and no one was going to stop her.

"Sounds like a plan." Kat nodded. "We can take Hana with us, if you'd like. Or get your mom ... or call Seth?"

"Not Seth." The words came too quickly. Leah tried to soften them. "I mean—it's up to you, Hana. Who do you want to go with?"

Hana smirked. "As much as I'd love to sit here and watch you sleep in this stinky hospital room, I might take Kat up on her offer. I can probably talk her into ice cream for the *third* time this week." She laughed, breaking the tension in the room.

And for the first time that day, everyone smiled.

Leah's mom came back to give her a quick goodbye hug before leaving with Kat, Felix, and Hana. Leah promised she'd call everyone as soon as she made her decision.

Tate lingered by the bed. "I can stay with you, if you want," he whispered, brows deepening. "Just in case anything happens."

"I'd love that," Leah said, reaching for his hand. "And thank you."

"For what?"

"For not pressuring me. No pun intended." She laughed and forced a smile, knowing what she was about to do.

Even Tate let out a little chuckle, but she could tell it pained him to see her like this. He gripped her hand harder.

"Hey," she said, eyeing the untouched tray, "would you mind grabbing us some fresh food from the cafeteria? I'd like to eat something before I rest—and that meatloaf looks like it's been embalmed."

"Of course," he said, picking up the tray. "What do you want?"

"Surprise me."

"Okay, I'll be right back." He hesitated a beat, then leaned down and pressed a gentle kiss to her forehead.

The moment he was out of sight, Leah moved.

She yanked out the IV line with a wince—the adhesive tugged at her skin, and a trickle of blood welled from the site. The heart monitor immediately shrieked a flat, continuous tone. *Shit!* She scrambled across the room to pull on her clothes, pausing as a wave of dizziness made her sway. She grabbed the chair for balance, whispering under her breath, "Come on, brain—just stay with me."

Grabbing her purse with trembling hands, she darted to the door. Peeking into the hallway, she spotted two nurses chatting at a faraway counter—one scrolling on her phone, the other flipping through a chart. No Tate. No Dr. Paulson. No Nurse Brad.

She slipped into the hall, trying to look like she belonged there. *Just act normal.* Then she saw the bright hospital band around her wrist. *Damn it!* She tried ripping it off to no avail. Instead, she crossed her arms and kept walking toward the elevator, willing her legs to cooperate. *Almost there.* A wave of dizziness crashed through her. Her vision blurred. The hallway tilted.

Leah stumbled, reaching for the wall to catch herself.

Quickly she straightened, scanning the hall, certain she'd been caught. But no one noticed her. A few more careful steps got her to the elevator doors. She jabbed the call button repeatedly, her pulse hammering in her ears.

Glancing over her shoulder, she saw him—*Tate.* He was rounding the corner at the far end of the hallway, a tray of food in his hands.

Leah's panic kicked into overdrive. She turned back to the elevator, watching the numbered lights tick toward her floor. *Four ... five ... six.* "Come on, come on ..." she whispered.

She really didn't want Tate to see her like this. Running away. *Again.*

The doors slid open, and Leah darted inside, slamming her finger against the button for the first floor, still watching, waiting, and praying Tate didn't see her.

He stepped into her hospital room.

The elevator began to close.

Then, rushing back into the hallway, confusion spread across Tate's face as he frantically looked around. About to run to the nearby nurses—he stopped. His mouth fell open, and the tray clattered from his hands, food and utensils scattering across the floor.

His eyes met Leah's through the narrowing gap of the elevator doors.

"Leah!" Tate shouted, sprinting toward her.

"I'm sorry," she squeaked out.

It was too late. Whatever the doctors said, whatever anyone thought—nothing was going to stop her now.

The doors sealed shut, and Leah was gone.

CHAPTER 46

KARAIA

The marble floor felt cool against Karaia's cheekbone. Her mind, her heart, and her gut thrummed as one steady pulse throughout her body. She pushed herself upright, blinking through the fog in her mind, like she was waking from a dream that had seemed so real. *Was it real?* She consciously breathed, grounding herself in the reality that she was still in Griffin's private vault.

No alarms. No guards. No Griffin. She was alive.

What time is it? she asked automatically.

Silence.

NIVA was gone, along with her connection to the Seromela server.

For the first time since she was born, Karaia was truly alone inside her own head. The quiet felt foreign, unnerving, but also ... freeing.

Except she wasn't entirely alone. If what she'd just experienced was real, she was connected to something far greater than herself—a lineage of women that stretched backward and forward through time. Lives interwoven. Souls echoing across centuries.

Maybe the prophecy was true after all.

Narrowing her eyes, her gaze fell on the wooden piece she'd stolen, looped around her neck. It was identical to her silver one, a serpent coiled into half a key. *What secrets do you hold?* Together, she gave them a squeeze—their pull toward each other undeniable—and exhaled deeply.

She still had to get out of this building in one piece.

None of what she'd experienced or what she had done would matter if she didn't get out alive.

My earpiece. She'd forgotten—she still had a direct link to Ziven and Blaze.

"Ziven? Blaze? Can you hear me?" she whispered, pressing the comm.

"You made it?!" Ziven's voice rang out on the other end.

Karaia rose to shaky legs. Her right foot had fallen asleep, and it tingled as she put pressure on it. "You sound surprised."

"Well, you never know when jump-starting brains ..." Ziven said, his words trailing. "Anyway ... you out?"

"Not exactly." She grimaced. "I'm still in Griffin's vault."

"Fuck," Blaze muttered.

"Thanks for the confidence," Karaia shot back. "Can you get me out? I can't exactly stroll through the front doors anymore."

"Yeah, yeah. Hold on," Ziven said, the sound of rapid typing filling her ear. "I'll pull up the building schematics and guide you out through a maintenance hatch."

As Karaia crept back through the vault, she felt untethered to her body—part of her still on the beach with Miryam and Leah. But she forced herself to focus, one step at a time. The room was silent. No alarms. No flashing lights. Everything was untouched—well, everything except for the missing key piece. She climbed the marble steps and pressed her ear against the heavy vault door.

She couldn't hear a sound. Maybe Griffin was still asleep.

"Karaia, you there?" Ziven's voice crackled in her ear.

Pulling back from the door, she whispered, "Yeah, do you have my exit plan?"

"You'll need to get to the building's southwest corner on the fortieth floor," he said. "There's a conference room with a maintenance hatch. That hatch leads outside to a ladder—take it down to the top of the main-level tube. From there, you'll find another hatch that leads into an alley off Fifth Tube. Once you're back in the tubes, head straight to the rendezvous point. Blaze is already there waiting for you."

"The fortieth floor in the southwest corner?" Karaia whispered, pulse quickening. "I'm in the northeast quadrant. And that's the *gov-*

ernment side. I'm not even cleared to go over there. There's no closer way out?"

"Wellll," Ziven said through gritted teeth, "technically, yes—there's a maintenance hatch on your side too. But there's also a conference of international tech trillionaires in there, soooo ... no."

A heavy silence followed. The weight of what Karaia would have to do sunk in. *What is one more impossible thing?*

"After everything else I've already done," she muttered, rolling her eyes, "this should be a breeze."

Ziven gave a strained laugh. "That's the spirit."

He tried to sound upbeat, but Karaia could hear the worry in his voice.

She pressed a hand to her forehead, running through the building's layout in her mind. Four tower quadrants—two Seromela, two government—linked by tubes on the tenth floor, where central security sat. She'd have to get past all of it to reach freedom. *I've made it this far. This will be easy, right?* She tried to convince herself as well.

Taking one more steadying breath, she hushed, "Okay, I'll let you guys know when I'm out. See you soon, Blaze."

Then she clicked off the comm.

Pressing her ear against the vault door again, Karaia strained to hear through it to no avail. She'd have to crack it open to ensure it was safe to exit. If Griffin saw her, she'd be arrested on the spot. Slowly, she pushed the massive door an inch open, hoping that there was no one in the office, or if they were, they wouldn't notice.

"Sir, there are more reports in Sector Five of an uprising among the factory workers," Raven's voice came through. "We have armed officers at the ready. How would you like us to proceed?"

Raven. Of course, she knew of the protests in Sector Five. She was head of security. Still, it saddened Karaia to hear her talking with such a casual tone about suppressing the workers there.

Chewing muffled Griffin's reply. He was still finishing his lunch. Which meant he did not suspect a thing.

Karaia let out a breath she hadn't realized she had been holding in. *He probably thinks I just left after we ...* She shuddered, forcing the thought away, and leaned her ear closer to the door opening, straining to hear.

"Don't send in officers yet," Griffin said between bites. "Last year, when those protesters in Sector Three organized, we barely contained it. What we need now are complimentary NeuroTryps for every worker there. Immediately."

"But sir," Raven said carefully, "we've already offered that, and some are refusing to upload."

"I don't fucking care, Ms. Ryder," Griffin asserted, his voice firm. "Upload the program *for* them. Send them all on NeuroTryps. This can't get out—to the public or the news."

"Understood, Mr. Marshall. News won't be an issue. Sector Five has officially been quarantined," Raven said. "We infused rumors of a new virus spreading. No one will go there, and no one will get out."

"Perfect," Griffin said, taking a loud slurp of cold coffee. "Now leave me. I have a board meeting, and I want to finish eating first."

"Of course." Raven nodded. "I'll update you if there are any developments. One last thing though ... how is your *other* project going? Still in development?"

Other project—what was that?

"Yes, it is," was all he said back.

Without time to think on this other project more, Karaia heard the office door open, then shut. Raven was out of the room, but that still left Griffin. She just had to wait for him to leave for his meeting with the board.

Those five minutes felt like forever.

Finally, she heard the click of the doorknob a second time. And she counted another sixty seconds before pushing the vault open all the way and exiting, tiptoeing her way through the office. She was sure to keep her head down—out of the cameras' prying eyes—now that Griffin's privacy mode had ended. *Just get to the other side of the building.* Escaping alive was what was important now.

She was so close to finding out about her parents, the prophecy, and finally getting answers to all her questions. But the *knowing* in her gut twisted and gnawed as she thought more about what Griffin was doing in Sector Five.

But that isn't my fight.

A quieter voice inside whispered, *Then, whose is it?*

Slinking out of the office, Karaia spotted Priscella, the secretary, sitting at her desk. She froze, prepared to be caught, turned in, arrested—or worse. Then, she saw a small light on Priscella's temple and let her shoulders relax.

Karaia strolled on unnoticed, making her way to the elevator and pressed the button for the tenth floor. As she waited, she glanced at a nearby holo-screen projecting the news. There it was—reports of a virus in Sector Five, quarantined for the safety of all. She gaped at the words on screen, then stepped onto the elevator. For as long as she'd known, there had always been a reason people didn't travel outside the walls or between sectors—viruses, air quality, terrorists, the list went on. That's what she'd been taught. What they'd all been told. The walls were there to keep them safe. The tubes, there to keep them healthy.

Furrowing her brow, Karaia wondered how much—*if any*—had been the truth.

The doors opened again onto the tenth floor, and the bustle of noisy people shocked her back into the present moment. She slowly inched off the elevator and gazed around. Being the busiest floor of the entire building—the hub that connected all four quadrants—Seromela employees and New Soterian government workers alike hurried in all directions, living their lives blissfully unaware of what was really happening in their country. No one knew she'd severed her NIVA link. No one suspected what she had taken.

Or what she was about to do.

Instead of heading southwest like the plan, Karaia marched toward the northwest corner. *One more thing*, she told herself. She couldn't let it go.

She slipped inside Arjun's office.

He lounged with his feet on the desk, holo-screen glowing—clearly in the middle of a game. "Whoa, you surprised me," he said, snapping the screen off and sitting up. "Aren't you supposed to be gone by now?" He leaned forward, lowering his voice. "Did you get the *thing* you wanted?"

"Yeah. It's here." She tapped her necklace, hidden beneath her jacket.

"Then why are you still here?"

"I have to do something before I leave." Karaia shifted in place. "And ... I need your help."

Arjun arched an eyebrow. "What is it?"

Karaia mouthed, *privacy mode,* knowing how dangerous it would be if Arjun's NIVA connection heard what she was about to say next.

He paused, then nodded.

Then, she pulled out Arjun's PET, swiped up the small holo-screen, leaned over it so only Arjun's eyes could see, and quickly typed a note to him.

It read, *We need to infect the NeuroTryp program with a virus.*

"What?" His mouth dropped open.

"I can't leave knowing what is happening here," Karaia whispered, staring at him. She wanted to say more. But she couldn't. Not with Seromela potentially listening to their every word.

Arjun's eyes lit up as he snatched his PET from her hands. Flicking through different holo-screens, he typed into the device. A long beep rang out, and he released a whoosh of air from his lungs. "Now, we can talk. I set up a dampening field around us. It should hold as long as we stay within ten feet of the PET."

Karaia smiled, determined. Then, the words spilled from her mouth as she started pacing the small office. "NeuroTryp is turning us into living robots. Griffin has complete power to do whatever he wants. He's forcing Sector Five factory workers to upload NeuroTryp so they stop protesting. I can't get Kiron's face or the people at the gala out of my mind. Griffin staged the attack. For what, more sales?" She stopped, swung and faced Arjun, her eyes wet. "When does it end?"

Arjun pressed his lips together, then said, "What you're talking about is nearly impossible. We'd have to plant it in the central core where the program's hard-wired."

"I know," she said, calming her voice. "But I just can't do nothing. Please—help me."

He frowned, sinking into thought. "You'd need my brain scan to access the core." He was already pulling up a 3-D map of the center of Seromela. "And a pre-programmed virus."

"Exactly," Karaia said, pacing again. "If I get traced, you can claim I stole everything from you. You'll have plausible deniability."

Arjun's face went pale. "If anything happens to you, I'd never forgive myself..." He shook his head. "It's too risky. You already have the key pieces, so why not just go?"

Karaia's voice cracked. "But those children—"

"That's why I'll do it," he interrupted.

She halted, cocking her head to the side. "What?"

"*I* will get the virus into the core. You get out with the key pieces," he insisted.

"We'll both do it," Karaia said firmly, her eyes meeting his. "I'm not letting you do this alone. From there, I'll get out, I promise."

Arjun hesitated, then gave a small, resigned nod. He pulled up the holo-screen from the PET again and began moving like a man possessed, tapping and swiping flashing images and hidden code.

After a few intense minutes, he grinned.

"What?" she asked.

He spun in his chair. "You know, this reminds me of the epic last level of *Red Robo-Hounds of Planet X*."

She laughed, shaking her head. She was so glad Arjun was by her side during all of this, knowing that if it weren't for him, she wouldn't have been brave enough. It pained her to think of leaving the walls without him. "You're such a dork. Does everything remind you of a holo-game?"

"Pretty much, yeah," he said, shrugging.

"And do they all make it out in one piece?" Karaia asked between tight lips.

Arjun's sideways smile gave her the answer she needed.

CHAPTER 47

MIRYAM

T he wedding feast lasted longer than Miryam had hoped. Every second she waited, the tightness in her chest increased. She tried to go back to breathing, her meditation, but it all seemed so shallow when all she wanted to do was run and warn the order about the impending attack.

Listening to hours of Dempsey's nasally voice drone on about Lord Amalric and his family while everyone else danced and drank, she tapped her foot incessantly on the wood floor, impatiently waiting, begging, for the festivities to end. She tried to think of scenarios in which she could get out of this sooner. Fake a headache or stomachache? That would confine her to bed. Feign tiredness? Also bed. Sprint out the front doors when no one was looking? Highly unlikely with so many people around. Say she needed some air and then sneak away into the night? Maybe her best chance. But Miryam didn't want to worry her sister or father again.

So instead, she sat. And waited. And groaned silently.

When the feast at last came to an end, Miryam's only thought was of the abbey. She had to reach the order before it was too late. But young women could not wander alone after dark, so she returned home with her father, counting every heartbeat as she lay awake, waiting for the sound of her father's deep, rumbling snores to fill the cottage air.

At last, they came.

Miryam slipped from beneath her covers, donned a wool cloak and leather boots, and crept to the door. Outside, a thick cloud layer blanketed the sky, and the air was cold and stiff, biting at her exposed skin. But she did not care. Her mind was singularly focused on reaching the monastery.

Her feet hit the path that wound through the sleeping village and into the forest, and she ran as hard as she ever had. Her lungs burned, and a sharp stitch jabbed her side, but she did not slow. The world was hushed but for her own gasps for air and the pounding of her heart. All she could think of was protecting Ved and the order.

At last, Miryam reached the great wooden gate, breathless and trembling. The night was still—eerily so—just as it had been the first evening she arrived seemingly a lifetime ago. She rested her hands on her knees for a moment, catching her breath, before rapping gently on the door.

A bleary-eyed apprentice answered, squinting into the dark. When he recognized her, he gave a sleepy nod.

Inside, the courtyard glimmered with a few dying candles, their flames flickering against the stone walls. Every window was dark. Every door was shut tight. It seemed so peaceful, and Miryam wished she could preserve this stillness, especially knowing what was to come.

She also knew she should wake Sophia or Thomas first. But her feet carried her elsewhere—toward Ved's room instead.

Down the familiar corridor she went, her pulse drumming faster with every step. She had never entered Ved's chamber before—men and women kept strictly to their quarters—but she had watched him disappear behind that door often enough to know it by heart.

She knocked once, then stepped back, biting down on her lip.

After some rustling inside, the door opened a crack. Ved stood before her, tousled hair and clad only in a linen night tunic.

Miryam froze, the warning bells in her mind drowned out by the sight of him. She had never seen a man so undressed before. Well, her father, but this was very, *very* different from that.

"Miryam?" Ved whispered, rubbing his eyes and opening the door further. "What are you doing? Someone might see you. Hurry—come inside."

She slipped through the door.

Ved lit a couple of candles, their glow spilling across the small chamber. The room was even sparser than Miryam's—little more than a horse stable. In one corner, a narrow bed made of hay with layers of wool covering it lay beside a rough piece of sanded wood that posed as a desk, stacked high with books, parchment, and ink. The rest was bare save for a prayer mat and crucifix against the opposite wall.

"Miryam," Ved said again, his voice confused. "What are you doing here?"

The flickering light revealed the lines of his chest beneath his thin tunic. His toned chest muscles distracted Miryam from her purpose, heat flushing across her face as her gaze drifted down his torso, past his waist, down to ...

Ved hurriedly grabbed the nearby wool blanket, wrapping himself in it.

She blinked hard, forcing her thoughts back to the danger that had driven her here. "I came to warn you. To warn everyone," she said, her words tumbling out. "Lord Amalric's knights—they are planning to attack the monastery. They know about the order. They say ... we are heretics."

Ved stared steadily, unfazed.

Her desperate voice sped up. "We must go tell the others. Now. Dempsey says they mean to have everyone quartered in the square."

He did not move.

"We must leave." Miryam seized his wrist, trying to usher him to the door, but his feet stayed planted. "Why are you simply standing there? Get dressed—we must warn Sophia and the others before 'tis too late!"

Ved's brow creased, deep in thought.

"What is it?" Miryam asked, her voice trembling with urgency. "Why are you not as alarmed as I?"

He didn't answer.

"Ved," she pressed, "what thoughts lie in your mind?"

At last, he stepped closer, pulling her into his arms. The blanket slipped from his shoulders as his eyes met hers. "Do you trust me?"

"Of course, I do." Her gaze sank deep into his eyes.

"I received a message last week during meditation," he began. "I did not understand it then—'tis never clear at first—but my visions often foretell what is to come. They guide the order when we lose our way."

"And?" she urged.

"Now ... it makes sense." His eyes darted between hers. "The message was about the attack. It is *supposed* to happen."

"No, it must be a warning," she retorted quickly. "And we are meant to keep everyone out of harm."

He shook his head. "I do not think so. My visions—no matter what we do, they shall come to pass."

"I refuse to accept that," Miryam said, gripping his hand tight. "We cannot simply let them capture us. We must try to flee. Come, Sophia will know what to do."

"No," Ved said firmly. "'Tis meant to happen. They shall attack—but we shall *escape.* There is nothing to fear."

A wave of relief washed through Miryam. "You could have led with such revelations." She rolled her eyes and gave him a playful nudge. "Still, why wait for the attack when we can flee now?"

He pulled her closer, and the air between them thickened.

"I know this is how it ought to happen," he explained, "because I have faith."

"I do too ..." She frowned, burying her face into his chest. "At least, I think I do. How can you be so calm amidst such danger?"

Ved's hand found her chin and lifted it gently. "Miryam, do not mistake my faith for fearlessness. I *am* frightened. This message has weighed on me for days. But we cannot pick when to trust God and when to turn away."

His words sank into her like water soaking into parched Earth. She wanted to trust God—and Ved. But her own heart protested in naive rebellion. However, her own desires had betrayed her once before, and she was ready to trust something greater than herself now. Closing her eyes, she resigned. "Very well. What do we do now?"

Ved pulled her closer, his muscled arms wrapping around Miryam's shoulders, folding her into him. She melted into the embrace, letting herself surrender to the moment. He smelled of sweat, fresh bread, and wildflowers—a scent both earthly and heavenly—and purely intoxicating. She could have stayed there forever.

"Marry me," he whispered.

The words jolted her. She had dreamt of this moment a hundred times, but hearing it aloud was different—stronger, sharper, more real. And so much better.

"What?" Miryam breathed, wondering if she had imagined them, needing to hear it once again, to know it was real.

"Marry me," he choked out again.

"'Tis what I thought," she said softly. "I only wanted to be sure I was not dreaming." She gazed into his deep blue eyes and knew, with all her heart, she wished to spend the rest of her life looking into them.

"Well ..." his voice cracked, "... what is your answer?"

She realized she'd kept him waiting. "Yes," she said, breathless.

Ved's shoulders relaxed.

"A hundred times, yes! Is there any other answer? Ved, I love you." Miryam wanted to leap and shout for joy, but instead, she pressed her face into Ved's shoulder and let out a muffled scream into his tunic. Her heart swelled until she thought it would leap from her chest.

"I love you too," Ved said with a smile.

Though it looked as if something lingered behind his eyes—something held back, unspoken. Miryam noticed it but knew Ved well enough that he'd tell her in time. For now, they had an order to protect—and a future wedding to plan.

"Did the elders approve of our being wed and remaining as students in the order?" she asked.

He nodded. "Yes, we have their blessing."

The last few hours had been an emotional whirlwind—fear, hope, love—all spinning through her like a storm.

"Then we may tell Father, and I shall not have to marry Dempsey." She straightened, the questions flooding her brain. "But what of the attack? Will we flee the abbey? The village? Will I see my family again?" Her eyes widened. "When shall we be wed?"

Ved laughed, his eyes warm. "I love all your questions and cannot wait for a lifetime of them. But I've only one answer for you." He paused, a grin spreading. "Now."

Miryam tilted her head to the side. "*Now?* For what?"

"The wedding," Ved said with quiet certainty.

"In the middle of the night? Here—in your chamber?"

He gave a small, nervous smile. "Aye, well ... what I mean is, we may handfast now. Only if you wish it. Later, we shall have our ceremony before others."

The candlelight flickered over his brow, catching a glimmer of sweat. He was warm too—proof she was not the only one burning despite the cold.

Miryam's thoughts spun like autumn leaves in the wind, and pleroma fluttered within her as she strained to think clearly. She was not yet betrothed by law—only promised by her father—so there was nothing keeping her from binding herself to Ved.

Nothing except nerves. But she pushed through those easily.

Taking a deep breath, she whispered, "That sounds perfect. What must we do?"

Ved walked over to his 'desk' and pulled a ribbon from a small satchel, along with something else Miryam could not quite see. Then, he led her to the low woolen bed, where they sat facing one another.

"We hold our hands together like so," he said, lifting her hand to his, their sweat mixing. "And we take this ribbon, wrap it around here." His free hand shakily intertwined their hands in the soft blue ribbon.

"'Tis almost as if you had this planned," she teased, raising a brow.

His face flushed in the candlelight. "I had hoped to know your answer. Sophia also helped me prepare." He cleared his throat, refocusing on the ceremony. "This ribbon marks our unity. Now we each speak our vows and offer a gift. I shall begin." Taking a deep inhale, he said, "I, Ved, son of Joseph, hereby take thou, Miryam, daughter of Simon, to be my wife and thereto plight thee my troth."

Releasing his breath, he nodded to Miryam to say her vows.

She tried to speak, but her voice caught. Tears welled up, spilling before she could stop them. She laughed through the sobs. "Forgive me—I do not oft struggle for words."

"I have not once noticed," he said with a faint smile.

She tried again, gathering herself. "I, Miryam, daughter of Simon, hereby take thou, Ved, son of Joseph, to be my husband and thereto plight thee my troth."

"Now for the gifts." Ved reached aside to pick up a small item.

Her eyes went wide. "But I've naught to give you." She glanced around the chamber as if a worthy gift might appear, but to no avail.

"'Tis fine, you do not—"

"Wait, I do."

Miryam reached up and plucked the flower sprig from her hair, still there from Isabella's wedding. Holding it out before them, she closed her eyes and focused on the center of her heart, feeling the energy begin to swirl and quicken. Lifting the flower to her lips, she blew softly upon it, breathing her pleroma into its petals. Tiny sparks of rose-colored light shimmered from her mouth and cascaded into the bloom, glowing with life-force energy.

"There," she whispered. "Now a part of me dwells within it ... for you."

Ved accepted the flower and tucked it into the ribbon binding their hands.

"Thank you," he said. "Now, for my gift. I promised I would read you one of my poems." He lifted a piece of parchment toward a candle, hands trembling as he read,

"Across a tempest sea,
my thoughts drift oer the waves.
A lone star shines in the night sky,
calling me homeward.
Like braids in an ancestral rope,
a boundless thread.
As the Earth needs the Sun,
yearning for one another.
Seeking always, never satisfied,
until our union is One.
Spirit, hear me, oh, mysterious world,
fill me with God's love.

For the only thing that has ever existed,
exists in me now.
The vow I promise transcends
death, time, and thy Earthly plane.
The light in my heart will always shine
and find my way to you."

Ved closed his eyes, drawing a slow breath as he set the paper aside.

Miryam reached across and lifted his chin, his gaze meeting hers. "'Twas the most beautiful poem my ears have ever heard."

His cheeks reddened. "I wrote it for you."

Miryam's face flushed hot too. Swallowing hard, she said, "Thank you. Now ... what doest we do?"

A quiet hush fell across them.

Ved hesitated. "We ... uhh ... we are to consummate the handfasting. 'Tis only if you wish it. I would never press you. We may wait. 'Tis the wise choice—"

Miryam silenced him with a kiss.

The ribbon slipped from their joined hands as her fingers explored his chest, feeling the smoothness of his skin beneath the thin linen.

"Wait," Ved murmured, pulling back just enough to search her eyes. "Are you certain? I would not have you do aught against your will."

Miryam smirked, her breath mingling with his. "And I love you all the more for saying so," she whispered, placing a finger on his lips, "but hush now."

She drew him back to her as the world outside the small chamber disappeared. Together they sank onto the small woolen blanket that served as his bed, the candlelight flickering over their bodies.

He did not question her again.

Ved's lips found hers in a slow, intentional kiss. As he did, his hands undid the buttons of her outer cloak, revealing Miryam in nothing but her nightgown. He took a quick breath at the sight of her shadowed body beneath it.

Then, he leaned in, gently brushing a strand of hair from her neck, and left a trail of soft kisses along her nape, leaving Miryam breathless.

Every place he touched her, her skin came alive with goosebumps, magic dancing in their wake.

Only two thin pieces of linen separated their bodies now.

Miryam's fingers clawed at Ved's back as he pressed into her, wanting him closer—to feel every inch of him. She pulled him into a deep kiss, their tongues swirling with one another, hungry for more. The place between her legs awakened with warmth, tingling with every caress of Ved's hands upon her.

Pleroma surged through her just like it had during her acceptance of her power during the initiation, but this was more visceral, raw with bodily emotions, pulsing with their heavy breaths. It lit up her spine's energy centers, all the way from her root through her heart and out through the top of her head, filling the room with a swirl of passionate energy.

Ved gazed at her. "Do you feel that?" he breathed. "'Tis pleroma, but never like I have felt before. 'Tis running up my spine. Is that from you?"

"I think so," Miryam whispered. "Doest that mean—"

He nodded. "We are connected."

She could sense the energy flowing between them, and she felt as though she could stay in this moment forever. She didn't know how it could get better than this.

Then, Ved sat up, lifting his night tunic off, revealing his whole body to her.

She gulped.

It could get better.

The candlelight flickered off his toned chest and stomach. He wore only the wooden key piece around his neck. Bending down to kiss her again, he dotted a line of kisses from her cheek, then to her neck, and pulled down her nightdress to expose her breast. He gently kissed her there, swirling his tongue around her nipple, making her arch her back in bliss.

A soft moan escaped her lips.

He gently pulled her undergarments off over her head.

Miryam felt both vulnerable and safe at the same time as she bared her naked body before Ved. He paused for a moment, drinking her in.

"What is it?" she asked, her voice quivering.

He smiled. "'Tis you. I may die in the wake of your beauty. My heart feels as if it might burst."

"I do not think 'tis your heart that will burst." Her eyes cast down, giggling.

"Maybe 'tis both," Ved said as he joined her in laughter.

As their eyes met once again, a hush fell over them with nothing but their hurried breaths and rapid pulses echoing throughout the small chamber.

Miryam nodded as she parted her legs around Ved's waist, and he gently lowered his body down onto her. As he pressed himself inside her, she quickened a brief gasp.

He paused, muscles taut, breath heavy.

Miryam let the feeling of him filling her rest for a second, relaxing into the unfamiliar sensation within, her lips blooming around his hardness. Then, she wrapped her legs around him and pulled him all the way in, moaning in ecstasy.

Ved rocked against her in slow, deliberate waves, picking up pace with each crest. He pressed into her harder, sending jolts of pleasure through her body, pulsing from the base of her spine to the tips of her fingers and toes. Every fiber of Miryam's being exuded pure, tantalizing bliss.

Their hands found each other again, gripping and grasping wherever. Kissing every bare inch of skin, tasting each other, moving in sync. Their bodies knitted together as one. Pleroma flowed through and around them, mixing and mingling in the air, expanding to fill the room with a soft glow of light. Ebbing and flowing like the ocean knocking hard against the shore. Their bodies disappeared, leaving only their souls, swirling, dancing together on an infinite plane of ever-building waves of pleasure. Like a crescendo of music, peaking, begging to come forth.

Miryam didn't think it could get better.

But then again, she had thought that before.

Ved thrust deep into her, sending a final explosion through her body, and Miryam cried out in ecstatic pleasure. She forced her mouth down onto his shoulder, digging her nails hard into his skin, trying to muffle her screams, as a throb pulsed from between her legs, holding onto him still inside her. Floating in a tingling, blissful haze, her mind went blank.

Ved slowly pulled away and flopped down next to her in exhaustion, his body sticking to hers with sweat.

She laid her head on his chest. Listening to the quick thrum of his heart and heavy breaths, she lulled herself to sleep, where she dreamt of Ved, of the ocean, of waves crashing over her, and of dancing on the stars.

Miryam didn't even notice when the smoke entered the tiny window and filled her nostrils … until she was coughing it up.

CHAPTER 48

LEAH

Smoke wafted into Leah's nose as she rushed out of the hospital. A young boy, probably sixteen or seventeen, sat on the curb, a cigarette hanging from his lips. His head hung low, shoulders slumping. He probably hadn't slept for days. Leah guessed he had a family member here in the hospital dealing with some illness.

It made her think of her own family and friends. How they must feel seeing her lying in a hospital bed. They just wanted what was best for her. And how they would feel when they heard she had run away.

But I'm not running away. I'm running toward *something.*

Then why did it feel like she was running away?

The Sun came out from behind a cloud, hitting Leah's eyes and the spot between them where the migraine pressed. She got dizzy for a moment, grabbing a railing to brace herself. She thought of the journal. Snatching it out of her purse, she held it close to her chest, and the pressure lifted immediately. *Fucking magic.*

Something was happening here, and she couldn't decide about the surgery until she understood what it was.

Her phone buzzed. It was a text from Tate.

Where are you going? Please come back and we can talk.

A taxi pulled up and let someone out at the hospital doors. It began to pull away.

"Wait!" Leah yelled, waving her arms above her head.

The taxi stopped, and she got in.

"Where to?" the driver asked without turning around.

Leah still stared at her phone screen. "Uhhh ..."

"C'mon, lady, I don't have all day."

Leah shoved her phone into her purse. "Um, sorry. Can you take me to the corner of Elm and Granger? I don't know the exact address."

"Sure thing."

And the cab took off just as Tate ran out of the hospital, throwing his head in all directions looking for her, only to finally let his gaze fall.

Leah was gone. For now.

Her phone buzzed again. She peeked into her purse. Still Tate.

Please respond. I'm worried about you.

She got another text. This time, it was Kat.

WTF. Tate just told me you left the hospital. Where r u?

Leah started texting back before she deleted her response. Instead, she clicked her phone off.

The driver pulled up at the corner. Tate's office was just a block away, but he wouldn't be there, of course. Leah paid the cab driver and then stepped outside.

Disappointing her friends distressed her, but she felt compelled. She walked cautiously up to front of the bookstore—*Baba Yaga's Books and More.* The little shop had started it all weeks ago, setting Leah off on this strange, inner journey. She narrowed her eyes, peering through one of the small front windows. It appeared dark inside.

Taking a large inhale, she knocked on the door and waited.

And waited.

No answer.

Her shoulders sagged. *Damn.* She turned to leave, disappointment pressing on her mind. She'd been so sure Gertrude would have the answers she sought—something to make sense of this connection to the journal.

The door creaked open. "Can I help you?"

Leah spun back toward the voice. A young woman stood in the bookstore doorway, eyes rimmed red and puffy.

"Is Gertrude here?" Leah asked, her pulse quickening.

The woman hesitated, gaze dropping. "Oh ... you haven't heard." Her voice cracked. "My mom—Gertrude—passed away yesterday. How did you know her?"

Leah took a step back, stunned.

She'd just seen Gertrude a few days ago, bright, animated, and *alive*. Her heart ached even though she hadn't known her long. "I got an old book from her. A journal." Leah lifted it, her hands trembling slightly. "She gave it to me."

The woman gaped. "You're *Leah*?"

Leah blinked. "Yes ..."

"I'm Annabelle," the woman said, wiping her nose. "Gertrude's daughter. My mother talked about you all the time. Honestly, I started to think you didn't exist." Her eyes widened as she studied Leah. "You became this sort of fairy tale when I was young. But then, a few weeks ago, she told me you'd finally come to the store. I still wasn't sure I believed her. And now—here you are again."

Leah just stared at her, speechless. *Talked about me ... when she was little?*

"I'm confused," she managed, wrinkling her brows. "Your mom and I met only a few weeks ago. You said she'd talked about me when you were little?"

Annabelle nodded toward the doorway. "Come in. She left you something else."

Leah drew a steadying breath, tucked the journal inside her purse, and stepped inside.

The store looked exactly as she remembered. Messy, disheveled, only quieter and emptier now. The air itself felt heavy, dull, and even the many colors were less bright. Annabelle led her toward a narrow doorway in the back. The room beyond looked like a cramped apartment—Gertrude's living space.

It was total chaos. Bright scarves and vintage dresses piled high on the couch. Stacks of books and old magazines littered the floor. The sink overflowed with dishes, and a faint sour smell hung in the air. In one corner, a huge spiderweb stretched like fine lace, untouched.

"I apologize for the mess," Annabelle said, creasing her brows. "My mother wasn't the tidiest of people." They both let out a small laugh despite the moment. "Toward the end, she wasn't doing well. Some days, it was like she wasn't even in the same world as us. The doctors said it was dementia, but she refused to take her medicine."

Leah shifted awkwardly, unsure what to say to someone freshly grieving. "Are you selling this place?" she asked, regretting her choice of question instantly.

"Probably ... in time," Annabelle answered, her voice lingering. "This was my mother's passion. I run a nonprofit that keeps me busy enough." She cleared a spot at the table for them. "Oh, and don't mind Ralph there."

"Ralph?"

Annabelle nodded toward a large spider dangling from the web in the corner. "He eats only flies. As you can see, he's thriving here."

Leah chuckled, glancing at Ralph before taking a seat at the table. She let her gaze drift to the rest of the small apartment. A row of tiny plastic army men marched across the top of the refrigerator. A battered firefighter's helmet hung on a wall. Bright plastic tubes, like a hamster playground, wound their way from the floor to the ceiling. Against another wall stood a full-sized suit of armor, sword and shield in hand, as if keeping watch.

She looked around the cluttered apartment and thought about her own life—the strange, winding path that had somehow led her here.

It was ridiculous.

A laugh slipped out before she could stop it. Then another. *Look at me.* She shook her head. *What the hell am I doing? Sitting in a dead woman's apartment with a spider named Ralph, trying to decode some ancient prophecy about my past lives.*

The laughter burst out of her, uncontrollable now. Her stomach cramped, gasping between giggles. "I'm sorry—I can't—stop. Sorry," she said, finally pressing a hand to her mouth.

Annabelle just stared at her, wide-eyed. Leah was sure she was about to be asked to leave. Slowly, Annabelle started to chuckle too. Within seconds, the sound filled the tiny apartment, both women doubled over, tears of laughter streaming down their faces. When it finally subsided, Leah leaned back in her chair, breathless, a smile escaping her lips. She let out a long sigh. For the first time in days, she felt lighter.

Annabelle blew her nose with a handkerchief. "It's okay. This is exactly what my mom lived for. She was special. Many people said she was just sick. But that didn't explain everything."

"I think you're right." Leah nodded. "She changed my life. I wish I had told her that. The last time I saw her, I was so rude and asked her to leave my shop." She let her head drop.

"She was very forgiving," Annabelle said, pulling out a large envelope. "My mother wrote this right before she died. She asked me to get it to you, but I didn't have a phone number or address. And then you just showed up. Of course!" Throwing her hands up in the air, she shook her head in disbelief. "My mom always knew things. Things she had no way of knowing." She slid the sealed letter across the table.

The front just said *LEAH* in scratchy handwriting.

She opened it and read silently to herself.

Dearest Leah,

When you read this letter, I will be DEAD. But don't worry!!! That old meat sack wasn't me! I will be back. Or will I be forward? The illusion of linear time messes things up. That, and world religions. We are told we are sinful, when in fact we are just separated! Separated at birth—from ourselves and from each other. This leads to so much pain, hate, and confusion in our world.

So why do we choose to come into these bodies? I asked this question in so many of my lives. But I think that for each of us, the answer is different. Yet we all have a purpose, down to the tiniest bugs (Please see that Ralph gets fed).

Can you feel your purpose? It is BIG!!! I know you can feel it. And would you tell Annabelle two things? First, tell her I love her so much. Second, tell her to scoot two feet to the right. Like, RIGHT NOW, tell her that.

Leah paused. She glanced at Annabelle with raised brows, and said, "Your mom says to scoot two feet to the right—now."

Annabelle tilted her head but still scooted her chair to the right.

Crash! A massive chandelier smashed on the ground, shattering into thousands of tiny glass shards—exactly where she had been sitting only moments ago.

"Thanks, Mom," Annabelle said, looking to the sky.

Leah kept reading.

> *Meant to fix that chandelier a year ago, but you know ... more important things to do!! Inside this letter, I left you a brochure and money for a treatment center in Oakeshire, England, that works on the mind, body, and spirit at the same time. Go there! I know you have so many questions, but I cannot say more.*
>
> *See you again,*
> *Gertrude*

Leah set the letter down and pulled out the brochure.

Oakeshire ... It rang a bell in her mind.

Within the brochure, a stack of crisp one-hundred-dollar bills lay. She shuffled through them. It had to be around $10,000. Her jaw plunged.

"So, did my mother give you what you were looking for?" Annabelle asked, leaning forward.

"I think so," Leah said, her brow knit tightly. "But I can't take this money. You should keep it ..." She glanced around. "... for the cleanup here, or the funeral."

Annabelle waved her hand away. "Oh no, my mother was quite clear she left this letter and its contents for you alone." She nodded. "Plus, my mother always had a way of investing in just the right stocks. I'm not hurting for money."

Still stunned, Leah stashed the money and brochure in her purse, tucking it snugly against the journal. "Thank you." She nodded slowly. "But the question that keeps nagging is '*Why me?*' I'm nobody special."

Annabelle reached over and flipped the letter to its backside.

P.S. Why not you?

Leah pressed her palms to her cheeks and smiled wide. There was no denying it. Not anymore.

Rising from the table, she let out a huge exhale. "Thank you, Annabelle. So much. Your mom was truly an amazing person, and I really hope we get to see her again in another life."

Annabelle pulled her into a hug. "I have a feeling we will. Good luck."

Leah stepped onto the sidewalk, back into the Sun and fresh air, feeling like a completely new person—hopeful and ready to be guided by the Universe, or whatever spiritual force she felt within. Cringing and laughing at herself, she turned her phone back on.

Six new voicemails. Twenty-nine missed calls. Fifty-three new texts.

Biting her thumbnail, she scrolled through the texts. Most were from Hana, Kat, Tate, and Felix. One was from her mom. Everyone had been looking for her. Everyone was worried.

But then she saw one—a long one—from Seth.

Our daughter is here crying because she can't find you, her mom, who should be in the hospital. You're scaring us all. I reported this to the custody judge, and she is taking it into consideration in her final decision. I sent out patrols looking for you as well. Meet us at the hospital.

Or else.

Leah breathed deeply. *Or else what?*

It hurt her to go against logical thought, everyone she knew, and risk losing Hana, but she had to trust that things would work out this time.

At least, that's what she assured herself as she called for another cab.

CHAPTER 49

KARAIA

"**D**on't look suspicious," Arjun whispered as he and Karaia slipped out of his office and headed toward the center of the building where the central processing core was located.

"Don't say things like that in a suspicious whisper, and I think we'll be good," Karaia hissed under her breath. She gently nodded to a person who passed them in the hallway. "No one knows what we're doing. Let's keep it that way."

As they walked, Karaia counted their pace, anything to keep her brain from going into overdrive thinking about all the hundreds of ways this could go wrong. She was already too far in, and there wasn't any going back. It still didn't stop part of her from wanting to turn around, take a now-impossible credit, and sink into the comfort of her old life with every step forward. But despite her sweaty armpits and trembling hands, she knew—in her gut—this was what she was supposed to do. She had never felt more certain in her life.

They reached the entrance. Typically, only senior engineers were cleared to enter the core. Luckily, Arjun was on that short list.

He leaned forward, letting the door scan his brain for entry. "You're not authorized to go in here."

"Arjun, my brain isn't connected to the server anymore, remember?" Karaia smirked, letting the weight of her decision settle. She liked the idea of not being trackable. "They can't trace me." She slinked in after him.

Lowering his voice, he said, "If someone is here, I'll say I'm training a new hire." Then, bent toward her, raising his brows. "You're the new hire."

"I got that." She stifled a laugh as they weaved through the banks of machinery.

Seromela's central core consisted of seemingly endless rows of identical ceiling-high computers. Few people worked there unless they were physically inspecting equipment. Most engineers and programmers, Arjun included, operated remotely from offices or home. That worked to their advantage now that the place was empty.

To Karaia, it just looked like a giant room of big, boxy boxes. But Arjun saw something completely different.

He wandered between the racks with a silly grin. "I've always wanted to show someone the core. Isn't it amazing? These computers run every program Seromela uses for the entire country. Every brain in New Soteria is linked to this server, essentially making up one giant *super-brain*."

They walked up to a large terminal. Arjun tapped a few things on the keyboard, let it scan his brain again, plugged in his PET, and a holo-screen pulled up in front of them. He started explaining what he was doing as he typed.

Karaia nodded along, trying to follow, when a familiar twinge stirred in her gut. "The computer virus can't hurt people, right?"

"No, of course not," he said, eyes glued to the computer. "I am programming the virus so that when someone is on a NeuroTryp, the virus will give them an error message. It's not permanent—Seromela will patch it in a few hours—but maybe that window will be enough to let the Sector Five protests gain traction."

Karaia frowned, her stomach twisting. She'd hoped for something bigger—something lasting. Leaving New Soteria while people remained at Griffin's mercy didn't sit right. What even *was* his plan? World domination? More money? Total control? It still hadn't fully sunk in that the man she had worked for—and slept with—was a murderer. Responsible for the gala deaths. For Sector Five. For who knew what else?

"I guess ... that's fine," she said, exhaling sharply. "What did I expect? To take down the entire system? Free people from their shackles to NeuroCredits? Wake them up to what is really happening in our world?" She threw her hands up in frustration.

Arjun faced her, lips pursed. "I know you want to help people. But you've already done a lot—for me, for your family, for those you saved at the gala." His shoulders slumped, knowing anything he said wouldn't be quite enough. Turning back to the terminal, he said, "I'm in the backend of NeuroTryp. What do you want the error message to say?"

Karaia held up her hand. "Give me a second." She clutched the pieces around her neck, closing her eyes to ask her sixth sense what to say. This alone seemed wild to her, being that less than a day ago, she was certain God didn't exist and spirituality was a relic of the past. But after what she experienced with Miryam and Leah, and knowing Griffin had the other half of the key, she was sure now there was more going on than she could perceive. As she stilled herself, the knots in her stomach loosened too.

Within less than a minute, she knew her answer.

Flashing her eyes open, she asked, "Can you program the virus to show a video instead of the error message?"

Arjun tilted his head to the side. "I could ... but it would have to be short. The longer the video, the larger my virus, and the more detectable." He narrowed his eyes. "What are you thinking?"

"Record me," Karaia said, back straightening, becoming more confident as she spoke. "Well, not *me*. Can you show an avatar in my place?"

The feeling in her stomach—the one that had been gnawing—ceased completely.

Arjun perked up at the talk of video game characters. "Which avatar do you want to be? I have hundreds of games on my PET. You could be Mistress Mayhem. Oooo, or The Flyer Crusader. Or Grysella from—"

"I already know." She leaned forward with a grin. "The Silver Serpent."

"Perfect choice!" He shouted and then lowered his voice. "I always loved her in the *Battle for the Elixir* when she slams down on the great stone right in the middle of the castle's courtyard before she takes her blade—"

Karaia rested a hand on his shoulder, shaking her head. "Not the time."

"Right." Arjun nodded curtly. "Okay, give me a minute to reprogram." He swung back to the terminal and furiously typed new code. "So what was it like?"

"What was *what* like?"

"Dying."

"Oh, yeah. That," she said, realizing she had thought little of it.

She had wanted to dwell more on her otherworldly experience, but with stealing half of a prophetic key from her boss, and then trying to escape the world's most secure country, she hadn't had the time to take it all in.

"So, this is going to sound weird ..." Karaia began. Then, she told Arjun about her experience on the beach with Miryam and Leah, the feelings she felt inside, and that she might be the one to give humanity back their magic—as briefly as she could.

"Whoa." His mouth dropped as his fingers continued to fly over the keyboard. "You're starting to sound like Ziven."

Karaia elbowed him lightly, rolling her eyes. "I know it sounds crazy—humans having magic and all—but I've never felt more certain."

Arjun turned toward her with a soft smile. "Hey, no judgment here. I'm just jealous. You're going on this epic adventure outside the walls, and I have to keep living ... here. Maybe someday we'll make your story into a video game!"

"Of course," she said with a grin just as the terminal blinked green.

"We're ready for your message." Arjun held up his PET's holo-screen and aimed it at her. "You have ten seconds. Tell me when to start."

She rolled her shoulders, stretching her neck a few times. "Just to confirm—they won't see or hear me, only the Silver Serpent?"

"Right," he said.

"Okay. Go." She nodded.

He hit record.

Karaia shoved her shaky palms into her jacket pockets. Calming herself with one more steadying breath, she spoke. "People of New Soteria, you have been deceived. Our government has been lying to us. The Defiers did not cause the gala attack; it was Seromela—and Griffin Marshall himself. The reported infection in Sector Five is also a lie, created to hide the ugly truth—that children are being forced to work in factories there. NeuroTryp is an intentional distraction to keep you from what's really happening in our country."

Arjun gave her a quick nod—time was up.

The PET clicked off.

Karaia exhaled, her shoulders sinking. "Do you think anyone will believe it?"

"No idea." He typed into the computer as fast as possible. "Okay ... I'm programming the virus to be released in fifteen minutes. That way, if someone were to go on a Tryp now, they wouldn't get the error message yet. We should be far away by the time it begins."

"Sounds good. But what about your brain scan?" she asked, frowning. "Won't they be able to see that you were in here?"

"Yeah, they could. Except I already erased it." Arjun smirked. "I memorized Raven's authorization code from the other day."

She smiled. "Of course, you did."

"Almost finished ..."

Karaia took the moment of silence to go over what lay ahead—get to the maintenance hatch, exit the tubes, reach the rendezvous point, and leave New Soteria. It was a lot, and she slowly breathed through it, clenching and unclenching her hands. She was getting better at regulating her own emotions without credits. *How did people live like this all the time?* Closing her eyes, she imagined the beach again. Peace. Bliss. She tried to feel the all-encompassing feeling again. *Love.* That's what it was. She settled into it, letting the feeling wash over her—

Weeeee-ooooooo! Weeeee-ooooooo! A loud alarm blared, and red lights flashed above their heads.

"Arjun, what happened?" she asked, panic flashing in her eyes.

"It wasn't me. The virus isn't even active yet," he said, finishing up and yanking his PET from the terminal.

Raven's face flickered onto the holo-screen as the alarms quieted. "We have had a security breach. A personal item has been stolen from Mr. Marshall's private vault. All employees and guests are to remain inside the building. Security officers will perform routine searches on all floors. I repeat, do not leave the building. To assist in our search, report any suspicious activity. We will notify you when it is safe to leave. Thank you for your cooperation."

"Shit, shit, shit," Arjun muttered, closing his eyes for who-knew how many credits.

Karaia's heart pounded so loudly it filled her ears. She had been so focused—so determined—to reach Avani, she hadn't really entertained the idea that she might not escape. Until now.

She shook Arjun out of his blissful state and shouted at him. "Arjun, it's not the time for credits. We need to get out of here!"

Coming back to, he blinked. "I guess ... this is goodbye?"

Tears already littering her cheeks, Karaia pulled him into one last hug, fueling her for the mission ahead. "Thank you for everything."

"Good luck, Silver Serpent," he whispered in her ear.

They rushed outside to find that the hallway was much louder and more hectic now than when they had entered the central core. Red lights flashed. Alarms blared. People hurried about in a gentle panic despite taking credits.

Arjun headed off toward his office.

Karaia paused, pressing her hand to the key pieces against her chest. Then, she marched toward the government side of the building. *Stay calm and look like you know what you're doing.* She walked, back taut, face straight-ahead. *Not too serious-looking!* She relaxed her shoulders. If she were seen on the security feeds, she shouldn't flag concern. She was an employee here, and as far as she knew, they didn't know it was she who had stolen the key piece yet. She hoped. *Fuck, this is harder than it should be. Just get to the elevator.*

A few officers passed by, checking offices.

Finally, Karaia reached the elevator doors and pressed the up button with sweaty fingers. As she waited, Griffin Marshall himself popped up on the holo-screens in the hall as the alarms died down momentarily.

"Greetings, everyone. Thank you for your cooperation. We are asking all employees and anyone in the building to go on a complimentary NeuroTryp. Please find a place to sit and enjoy a trip to your favorite vacation spot. All NeuroCredits are complimentary as well. This will assist in our search for the intruder as we believe they are a Defier terrorist without a Seromela neural connection."

People gasped, freaking out and scrambling toward their offices.

Karaia would normally have joined them. The idea of a terrorist being in their building would have been terrifying if it weren't her who was the *terrorist*. Yet she still had to play the part, so she began fidgeting, glancing around nervously while waiting for the elevator.

More officers marched past her.

For all they knew, she was just trying to get back to her office and go on a NeuroTryp. It would take a few minutes for everyone else to reach their offices, which meant that was exactly how long she had before she would be the only one walking around, except for security officers.

It really was the perfect way to root her out.

The elevator opened, and she rushed inside, pressing the button for the fortieth floor.

"Karaia, you still there?" Blaze crackled in her ear.

"Yeah, there was something I needed to do," she replied with a shaky voice, watching the elevator tick up floor by floor. "I'm on my way out now ... well, hopefully. Seromela knows someone stole something from the vault. Officers are looking for ... me."

"What the fuck could have been more important than getting yourself and the key pieces out?" Blaze shot back.

Karaia winced, then said, "Arjun and I leaked a virus into the NeuroTryp program to release a message about what's really happening in New Soteria."

The line was silent.

"Blaze?"

"Fuck yeah! Little lamb, you're turning out to be—"

"A Silver Serpent." Karaia smiled. While she was nervous about her escape, she couldn't help being proud of herself for doing *something*—trying to make a difference—before she left.

"Well, I wasn't going to say that, but I like it." Blaze chuckled. "Do you think you can still get out?"

"I'm in the elevator now. Then, to the conference room. And I'll let you know when I'm outside," Karaia said, drawing in a deep breath as the elevator crept closer to her stop.

"Okay, keep us posted," Blaze said, cutting her comm.

The elevator dinged and opened onto the fortieth floor.

Directly ahead, three security officers strolled down a hallway, leaning into office doorways one by one, swinging their laser guns from side to side. They were facing away from Karaia, but in the direction she needed to go. Luckily, each quadrant looped around on itself, so she could still reach the corner room—it would just take longer. Forcing her feet to cooperate, she slipped out and hastened down the hallway to her right, praying she wasn't met with more officers.

This hall was empty ... and eerily quiet.

Good on the officer front. Bad because that meant that most employees were on NeuroTryps.

Karaia scurried down the hall as quietly as she could, sweat dripping down her brow, pulse pounding in her ears. She pressed herself against the wall just before the next turn, catching her breath and steadying herself. Wiping her forehead, she slowly peered around the next corner.

Two more security guards were shuffling up the corridor, checking offices. They were headed toward her.

Karaia yanked her head back and pictured the building's layout in her mind. Each quadrant mirrored the others. She squeezed her eyes shut. *Think, Karaia, think.* If this floor mirrored hers exactly, then across from her should be a long row of connected offices parallel to the hallway. At the end of the last office, there's a door that leads back into the main corridor, which should take her to the conference room—and around the officers. It was a roundabout path, but it might work.

She edged around the corner one more time.

The guards were close now. There were only two more offices before they reached her position.

She had to go.

Taking a long breath in, she waited until they checked the next set of offices, then darted across the aisle toward the connected office spaces, praying they hadn't seen her.

One by one, she slinked past occupied desks, unnoticed. Everyone was miles—and minds—away. *Wait, the virus. How long has it been?* Her message would interrupt their virtual vacations. Would that chaos give her a distraction—or would everyone suddenly see her, the only conscious person in their midst?

Karaia reached the end of the office row and peered cautiously into the hallway.

No guards.

Forcing her shoulders to ease, she stepped out—then jerked back against the wall, her breath quick and uneven. Closing her eyes, she tried to slow down, to quiet the pounding in her chest. She inched forward. With each painstaking stride, her destination felt heavier, her feet refusing to cooperate. Staying safe—staying here in New Soteria—even if that meant being arrested, seemed easier at this point.

The quiet whisper in her gut echoed, *the time for easy and safe is over.*

Determined to push on, she glanced around one more time as she peeled her body down the last hallway. One foot in front of the other. For her parents. For unanswered questions. For the knowing she couldn't explain.

Her thundered pace picked up speed. The door she needed was in sight.

Twenty more feet. That was it.

"Well, this is interesting." A voice rang out.

Karaia halted in her tracks. She knew that voice. Slowly, she turned to see Stellan Marshall standing behind her.

CHAPTER 50

MIRYAM

Smoke burned her lungs, and Miryam awoke in a coughing fit. Panicking in the darkness, she had forgotten where she was, groping the air with blind hands. Then, she felt Ved's warm sleeping body next to hers and she calmed. But only momentarily, as she choked on another inhale of heavy smoke, sending her into another fit of swollen, raspy breaths. She glanced outside. The Sun had not yet crested the horizon, and only a faint flickering light danced through the tiny window—*fire*.

"Ved, wake up." Miryam shook him, her voice cracking with worry. "There's a fire. We must get out!"

His eyes flew open, groggy at first, then wide with alarm. "What? No—'tis too early."

"What do you mean, *too early*?"

He shook his head sharply. "Never you mind. Let us go."

They dressed in haste, crouching low to the floor to avoid the thickening haze around them.

"Here," Ved said, tearing a strip of cloth from his night tunic and handing it to her. "Cover your mouth."

She wrapped it around her neck and face while he did the same, fear filling her mind with thoughts of the impending attack and how she could have warned the order when she first arrived, but then ... she had come here first. Furrowing her brows, she asked, "Ved, do you think 'tis Lord Amalric—"

He pulled her close to him, kissing her quickly on her forehead as if he could read her mind, easing her guilt. "It does not matter now. We must protect the chest above all else." Then, grabbing her hand, he led her toward the door. "Whatever happens, know that I love you, Miryam."

Before she could respond, he pulled her out of the room into the chill of the early morning. Instantly, the acrid scent of burning timber filled Miryam's nose, sharp and suffocating. Though darkness still shrouded the abbey, shouts echoed from every direction.

Ved wove them down the corridor toward the main courtyard, never losing grip on her hand. As they moved closer, the chaos swelled. He slowed, pressing them against the stone archway hidden in shadow, and held a finger to his lips.

Miryam stilled, forcing her breath quiet.

They peered around the corner into the ravaged area. Charred beams crashed in sparks. Smoke rose in heavy plumes from smoldering heaps. A cluster of monks huddled by the front entrance, terrified. One lay dead, his blood painting the stones. The great wooden gate that usually barred the abbey lay in a blackened ruin. A knight stood sentinel before it, sword drawn, posture ready for slaughter.

At the far end, flames had already taken hold of the kitchens and the cathedral. Two knights rode through the yard, torches in hand, setting alight any timber they found. The narrow cave entrance still looked untouched. For now.

Amidst the screams and sobs, one mounted knight shouted to his companion, "Get to their private quarters—start at the back and force them into the open."

The other barked back, "Lord Amalric bids us to show mercy as God would. With heretics, 'tis none. Burn them all!" With a cruel kick, he spurred his steed and swept off.

Blinking a few times in shock, Miryam pressed her hand to her chest, her heart thundering in its place. She couldn't believe what she was hearing and seeing. She glanced at Ved, standing next to her, his gaze fixed on the cave entrance. "Ved, we must help," she whispered. "Where are the order members? We can use our powers to fight the knights."

"We are not meant to use pleroma for combat," Ved replied shakily, squeezing her palm tighter.

Frantic, she pulled him to face her, searching his eyes for answers. "*You* said we would get out safely. How else shall we do that?"

Ved's voice steadied, though his face remained pale. Lifting their interlocked hands, he said, "The chest must come first. If the chest is lost, all is lost. Our mission is to secure it and flee to the safe house a mile hence. That is where the others will gather."

"And what of the others?" she retorted, feeling the heat in her chest rising. "What good are these gifts if we do not use them when needed?!" Huffing, she threw her hands out in protest. "We can protect them *and* get the chest."

Ved found her hand again and pressed it against his tender lips, softening her determined stare.

"Please," she whispered, releasing his grip, "this time, trust *me*. Wait for my signal, then make haste to the cave."

He stiffened, but before he could stop her, Miryam stumbled out into the courtyard toward the knight guarding the front entrance.

"Help! Help!" she cried, limping on one leg and clutching her side in feigned pain.

"M'lady, what are you doing here? 'Tis not safe for you!" the knight shouted, lowering his blade as he rushed forward.

"I am hurt. Please, sir, help me," Miryam gasped before collapsing in the middle of the courtyard.

She gave a quick nod to Ved, still hidden in the shadows. He sprinted toward the cave entrance, swiftly dodging charred wood and crumbled stone, staying close to the outer wall in hopes of not being seen.

The knight knelt beside Miryam. "Where are you hurt? I do not see—"

"Oh, I must be mistaken," she interrupted. Her tone turned cold. "'Tis you who are hurt."

She summoned the fire burning in her chest, focused its energy into her palm, and released it toward the knight in one sharp burst. The blast hurled him back toward a wall, stones cracking and tumbling down upon him.

With her palm still held out, Miryam stared at the crumpled knight, unmoving. Was he dead—or merely stunned? Had she killed someone? Shuddering, her breath caught in her throat. She hadn't meant for anyone to die. Glancing at her trembling hand, she felt the pulse of pleroma still coursing through it. It frightened her. But then, she remembered Ved, the order, and the innocent monks who called this place home. She was doing this for them.

She clenched her palm into a fist. Turning toward the frightened monks still huddled by the gate, she shouted, "You are free. Go! Get to safety or help fight, if you can."

They scattered at once, stumbling over one another in their hurry out the gate and into the woods. None were fighters.

But Miryam ... was she?

Now was not the time to dwell on it. She turned toward the cave to follow where Ved had gone, but before she could reach it, three knights emerged from a side corridor—two on horseback, one on foot. Between them were Fern, Matilda, and Father Thomas, shaken and terrified.

Fern wept, his face streaked with soot. Matilda thrashed and shouted for release, while Father Thomas stood silent, his head bowed low.

Before she knew it, Miryam's instincts took hold. She lifted her hands high above her head, feeling the pleroma stirring to life from within.

"You! Stop where you are!" one knight bellowed.

"I am," she said evenly.

She focused her breath, syncing it with the surge of power building deep inside of her. A spark ignited at the base of her spine and soared up to her outstretched arms. Miryam drew upon the very pulse of the Earth beneath her feet—more than her own strength. More than just her own pleroma.

The Earth's power flooded through her. Upward it climbed, through her limbs, into the sky itself. High above them, clouds began to gather and churn. The air crackled. Wind tore through the courtyard, whipping cloaks and banners. The horses whinnied, and one reared violently, casting its rider to the stones. Leaves and cinders spun into the air, veiling everything in a whirlwind of smoke and dust.

"Witch!" one knight shouted. "By order of the king, cease at once!"

The one still astride his horse drew his sword to strike Miryam—but the blade froze mid-air. His arm quivered, unable to move. Tiny blue lights, near invisible to the eye, danced around the sword, lifting it from his grasp.

He gawked. "What sorcery is this?"

"Nay, not witchcraft," Father Thomas said, standing tall now. "'Tis but some old friends come to lend their aid."

The blue fairies carried the weapon as though it were weightless, gliding it into the whirling sky and away. The dismounted knight, seeing this, pulled a dagger with a trembling hand and lunged toward Father Thomas.

Miryam threw all her focus into the storm.

The heavens roared in swift reply. Icy rain lashed the Earth, soaking them through. Lightning flashed—then struck the dagger a moment before it could reach its mark, its thunder splitting the air.

The knight convulsed at once, his weapon dropping from his palm. Then, his body clattered to the ground in a heap.

Father Thomas turned to face the two remaining knights. The one still on horseback sat frozen in disbelief, his swordless hand still shaking. The other stood firm, blade drawn, with Fern and Matilda held behind him.

"Release my friends," Father Thomas commanded calmly.

"Never," the young knight spat. "We are sworn by the earl's order to seize the heretics and bring them to the castle. And you, old man, are chief among them."

The knight raised his sword high.

Father Thomas stepped back as the blue lights reappeared, swirling up and seizing the weapon. But this knight was stronger than the last. He gritted his teeth and pressed forward, fighting against the fairies' invisible pull. The blade hovered merely inches above Father Thomas's head.

"Do not harm him!" Matilda cried out. She wriggled forward and threw out her hands toward the nearest wall.

A thick vine tore loose from the stone, slithering across the ground like a serpent. It wrapped itself around the knight's ankle and yanked.

He slipped hard onto the cool flagstones, armor and sword clanging as they struck the solid Earth.

Then, from the cracks and crevices of the walls, dozens of rats poured forth like a living tide. They swarmed over the fallen knight, his screams echoing through the smoke-filled courtyard as the creatures enveloped him in a writhing mound of slick, wet fur. The sound turned from agony to silence as the rats dragged his body away into the shadows, leaving only the clink of his sword upon the ground.

Matilda turned to Fern, wide-eyed. "Did you summon those rats?" Fern gave a small, sheepish grin.

"We are not done yet, though," Matilda said, gently pushing Fern behind her and stretching out her hand once again.

Another vine snaked its way upward, growing to the height of the final knight still atop his horse.

The man's eyes went wide with terror. He spurred his horse hard, shouting, "Witches! Witches! Flee for your lives!" He galloped through the smoke and out the monastery's ruined gate.

Matilda and Fern exchanged astonished looks, laughter spilling out.

"Did you see that?" Matilda yelled, hopping up and down. "We fought off three knights. 'Twas incredible! Father Thomas, did you see?"

He gave a weary nod, releasing a long breath.

Then, their eyes turned to Miryam. She still stood, eyes closed, arms lifted toward the sky. The storm above showed no sign of calming. It raged on, fierce and untamed—like something greater had taken hold of her.

Father Thomas called out, straining over the wind. "Miryam, you may stop!"

But she did not hear him. She had become a vessel for the power coursing through her veins, the pleroma-fueled storm pulsing with every beat of her heart.

Matilda and Fern joined in, shouting above the thunder.

"Miryam!"

"Come back to us."

The voices echoed distantly in the back of her mind. Miryam strained to identify them. Still foggy, she tried to slow the surge of energy flowing through her. *Slow*. She breathed. Starting with just a wiggle of her fingertips and toes, she started to come back into her body. Then, she could shake her head, stretching her neck, loosening her shoulders. And finally, she broke free from the storm's grip.

The fury of the storm waned. The clouds thinned, and the rain softened to a gentle drizzle, dripping from the broken eaves and pooling across the stones.

Her eyes fluttered open. "What happened?" she asked in a daze.

The courtyard had grown dim. All the fires were out, replaced by a heavy stillness in the air.

Fern inched forward, excitement spilling forth. "We defeated them! With our powers. Did you see what I did with the rats?"

"And me with the vines!" Matilda shot in.

He nodded fervently, then continued, "And you, Miryam—you summoned a storm that doused the flames! I've never seen aught like it." He launched into a breathless retelling of the battle, hands flying in all directions.

"Come, come," Father Thomas said, laying a steadying arm around Matilda's shoulders, ushering them all forth as Fern still jabbered on. "Let us be gone from this place. 'Tis not safe to linger."

Miryam let out a deep sigh, letting her body relax. No one had been hurt. They would get out safely, just as Ved predicted they would. Now she only needed to find him and the chest before she would leave with the others.

She took a step toward the cave—when Fern staggered to his knees beside her.

Miryam swung around and froze, staring down in disbelief as blood darkened Fern's tunic, dripping to the stones.

"I do not feel well ..." His words broke as a blade protruded clean through his middle, slicing his flesh like softened butter.

From the shadows, a knight pulled the blade back through Fern's torso, just as Matilda screamed, her cries echoing off the smoldering ruins of the abbey.

This wasn't supposed to happen. Miryam lunged forward, reaching for Fern—when the knight leveled his bloody sword at her.

"If you wish not to end like your friend here," he growled, "you'll follow me—by order of the Earl of Norfolk, Lord Amalric."

Miryam slowly rose to her feet, her gaze intent on the knight. "No," she said, her voice low and trembling with fury.

The knight sneered, pressing the end of the blade to her sternum. "What did you say to me, girl?"

"No. I will not follow you," she said, each word sharp as the steel tip that pierced her cloak. "You killed my friend, and now you will pay."

"And what shall *you* do about it?" He rolled his head back in laughter for a second. "You are but a woman and an unarmed one at that." Then, leaning in close enough that Miryam could smell ale and smoke on him, he whispered, "Oh, and what I will do to you once you are in the castle dungeons, where no one can hear you scream."

The burning coal in Miryam's chest flared into an inferno as the knight's sword pushed harder into her, biting through her skin.

She never once broke her stare.

"'Tis not what I am going to do. 'Tis what you will do to thyself," she said.

The knight cocked his head to the side.

Miryam pulled her focus inward to the center of her skull and felt the pleroma there swirl faster and truer. With it, she reached out, threading her will into the knight's mind.

She raised her arm slowly out to one side.

The knight's own hand began to twitch, battling his grip on the sword. Confusion creased his brow as he fought an unseen force. "Pray, what are you doing, witch?" he spat.

Miryam held him in that silent current, her arm taut to the side, strengthening the link that hummed between them.

Slowly, his fingers could not maintain their position, and they dragged the blade away from her breast. His arm floated out to his side, mirroring hers.

"Stop this!" the knight roared. "You shall burn for such heresy."

"Miryam ..." Father Thomas warned. "'Tis not the answer."

She ignored both.

The coal in her chest burned brightly, feeding a fierce, hot resolve for justice, as pleroma flowed between her and the knight, knitting her will upon him. She imagined the blade in her hand, moving her palm toward her throat. His weaponed hand obeyed, copying her motion as if pulled by strings. A thin line of blood trickled down his neck, between his armor, as the real blade gently pressed against his flesh.

"Please—do not do this," the knight begged, pleading through hurried breaths under his helmet. "I have a family, a daughter born but a fortnight ago, and a—"

Miryam held her gaze, yanking her hand hard across her neck in one swift slicing motion. "Fern had a family too."

Blood spurted from the knight's neck as his sword followed suit.

For a moment, he stood like a statue, hot liquid gurgling out of his mouth and neck, spewing down his armor and covering the front of Miryam's cloak. Then, in one fallen heap, his body crumpled, and the sword clanged to the ground, a growing red puddle surrounding him.

A shuddered cry escaped Matilda's mouth as she clung to Father Thomas.

Miryam drew in a sharp breath, standing frozen before the bloody scene. The fiery coal in her heart dampened, and she felt nothing—no triumph, no grief, only emptiness.

"Hurry," Father Thomas urged, his voice low and firm. "We must reach the safe house. The others shall be there before more knights come."

"But Fern ..." Matilda sobbed, rocking back and forth in Thomas' arms. "We must bury him."

"We've no time," he said, ushering them to move. "Come now."

Miryam blinked hard, snapping herself out of her trance. "Ved," she breathed. "He has not come out of the cave yet."

Without waiting, she turned, running toward the cave.

Father Thomas and Matilda did not follow. The old man's tone resigned as he called after her, "I do not suspect there is any use in arguing with you on this."

Miryam spun back around to face them before descending the stone steps.

"You have proved you can hold your own," Father Thomas said, face weary, nodding slowly. "I must get Matilda and the others to safety.

Meet us at the safe house. 'Tis one mile straight east of here, out the back gate."

Miryam gave him a curt nod back.

And down into the cave she flew, her voice and footsteps echoing against the damp stone. "Ved, Ved!"

No answer.

Most of the torches had gone out, and the air was thick with smoke. She groped her way forward, the rock walls slick and cold beneath her fingertips. Something round caught her foot—a turnip that had spilled from the shelves of the root cellar. She stumbled, nearly falling into the heavy curtain that hid the inner chamber.

Pulling it back, she froze.

Ved sat slumped against the wall, the chest clutched tightly in his arms.

Miryam rushed to him, grabbing the lone torch that still lit the cave. "Ved!" Dropping to her knees beside him, she glanced down at his tunic—dark and soaked with blood. Her eyes went wide. "'Tis blood! Are you hurt?"

He shook his head faintly, lifting his chin toward the shadowed corner. A knight's body lay sprawled in a crimson pool.

"I had to fight," Ved murmured, trembling. "I ... I did not mean to hurt ... anyone." His eyes glistened with tears.

"I know ... me too," Miryam said, casting her eyes down. "They killed Fern, and I had to—" Her voice wavered as anger clawed to rise from her chest, but she swallowed it down. Another feeling rose to meet it—*love*—fierce and all-consuming. It burned brighter than her rage, and she let that love for Ved envelop her instead.

She leaned the torch against the wall. Then, she pressed her lips to his, kissing him tenderly, breathing in his familiar scent. "You are here. And you are alive," she whispered, resting her forehead against his. "I do not know what I would do if I lost you."

Ved drew a shuddering breath. "We must get the chest out of here."

She nodded, helping him rise. His weight leaned heavily against her for a moment before he found his footing.

Miryam's brow furrowed. "Are you certain you are well?"

"Aye," he said, rolling his shoulders with a wince and securing the chest in his arms. "Only sore from the fight. Naught more than that."

She exhaled, the tension in her chest easing just a little.

Miryam snatched up the torch once more and led them up the narrow stairs. The flickering light cast long shadows along the damp walls as they climbed toward the open air.

Ved gasped when he saw the sight.

For the first time, Miryam truly saw the destruction. Fern's body lay beside the fallen knight, still and pale. The abbey was little more than ruins—charred beams, smoldering rubble, and skeletal walls reaching toward a sky veiled in smoke. The once-living heart of their order now looked like ancient rubble, centuries old.

Ved's voice cracked. "All our books, our texts ... our home. 'Tis all gone?"

"But we have each other." Miryam gripped his hand in hers as she led him through the burned courtyard. "And we have the chest."

He nodded faintly, his eyes still scanning the remains. "You are right. Let us go."

They turned down the corridor toward the back gate—only to freeze at the sound of a voice behind them.

"I cannot let you leave."

Miryam stiffened. She knew that voice. Turning slowly, she met Gawain's eyes.

"Please," she said, her voice pleading but steady, prepared to do what she needed to protect Ved and the chest. "Let us go. We are friends—*family* now."

Gawain stepped forward, removing his helmet. "What are you doing here, Miryam?" His face looked torn, and his voice lowered. "With these people? These ... heretics?" His hand hovered above his sword hilt, trembling.

"They are not heretics." She crept forward to meet his gaze, gathering the swirling pleroma within her, just in case. "They simply want to live peacefully—like anyone else. Please ... you can trust me. Let us go."

The last thing Miryam wanted was to harm her sister's husband, but if he drew his blade against Ved, she would defend them both without hesitation.

The pleroma bubbled inside of her—ready to strike.

"Do I know you?" Gawain asked quietly. His eyes searched hers, flickering with doubt. "Tell me the truth. Are you part of this order we have been sent to apprehend—the ones accused of heresy?"

Miryam hesitated, her heart quickening. Then, she straightened and lied with all the confidence she could muster. "No."

His eyes narrowed, studying her for a long moment.

Finally, his hand dropped from the hilt of his sword. "Very well," he breathed. "I am sorry you had to witness this, truly. You must know it was necessary—to root out those who threaten God and the Church."

Her shoulders relaxed, and she let the pleroma soften. "You are only doing what you think is right," she replied with a weary nod.

Gawain lifted his chin to them and placed his helmet back on. "Be safe, dear sister, Master Ved. There are still knights scouring these woods, and they will not know you as I do." With that, he bowed and turned away.

Miryam exhaled the breath she hadn't realized she was holding as she and Ved made their way quietly to the back gate, slipping through the opening.

Once they reached the forest edge, they broke into a run. Only slowing to cross the creek's icy waters, its cold teeth biting into their ankles as they waded.

On the other side, Miryam paused and glanced back at the burnt abbey. Smoke curled into the pale morning sky, rising from what was once their home, as the first rays of sunlight crested the horizon.

CHAPTER 51

LEAH

Or else what? The vague ending of Seth's text gave Leah pause. Was she willing to risk everything and journey across the ocean to find a cure, but also answers about how she was connected to Miryam, Karaia, and this prophecy? Or she could stay, go through with a surgery she wasn't sure about? Or a biopsy to see what she was dealing with first? They didn't even know whether this tumor was cancerous.

Everything was moving so fast. As she rode in the cab, gazing out at the passing Los Angeles landscape, Leah realized she didn't want to make this choice alone. That's what she had been doing for years. Keeping people out. And she didn't want to do that anymore.

She picked up her phone and dialed Tate.

He answered immediately. "Leah. Are you all right? We've been so worried."

"I'm fine, really," she assured him, strain in her voice. "I'm sorry for worrying you and leaving the hospital. There was just something I had to do."

He exhaled, telling the surrounding others she was safe. "And did you?"

"Yes, but now ..." She glanced down at the brochure and journal in her purse. "... I need to make a choice, but I don't want to do it alone."

"That's great." Tate's voice rose with excitement. "We're at the hospital café—even Seth is here, and he seems worried too. Do you want me to pick you up? Then, you can let the doctor know which route you want to go with for surgery."

No answer.

"Leah ...?"

"Tate, that's not the choice that I need to make."

"I'm not following," he said, voice cracking. "What are you talking about?"

Leah drew in a deep breath. "Please *don't* tell anyone—especially Seth. He sent me this weird, threatening text, and now, he's got patrols looking for me. I promise I'm fine. But can you meet me at the beach where we first met?" She scrunched her face, waiting for the reply.

This time, he didn't answer.

"Tate?"

"Yeah, I can do that," he murmured. "See you soon."

Thirty minutes later, Leah slipped off her sandals and sank into the warm sand. She dug her toes in deep until the grains hugged her feet. The warmth against her skin felt grounding—real. The Sun was sinking low in the sky, bleeding orange and pink across the horizon. She took a long inhale of salty air, letting it fill her lungs.

Pulling the journal out of her bag, she held it tight to her chest, and the tension in her body eased. She lowered herself, sitting on the cushion of sand. With the journal in her embrace, she felt lighter—clearer. *Maybe that's the answer? I just have to carry this with me everywhere.* A small laugh escaped her. *If only it were that easy.*

"Leah?"

She turned to see Tate striding toward her, his figure framed by the setting Sun. He looked as handsome as ever; the wind tugging at the edges of his linen shirt, curving around the muscles of his chest.

Leah bit down on her lower lip. "Thanks for coming."

"Of course." He dropped beside her, the sand shifting under his weight. After a pause, he slipped off his shoes too, pushing his feet into the sand until they disappeared. "So," he said, glancing at her, "what did you want to talk about?"

"I don't even know where to start," Leah said, reaching down to grab a handful of sand, watching it fall between her fingers. "Well ... you know about the journal—and the vision I had while I was unconscious—but you don't know how it *felt*." She turned to face him, letting out a shaky laugh. "I know I always made fun of the woo-woo hippie yoga stuff—"

"Hey, I'm a yogi." Tate feigned offense, laughing with her.

"I know," she said with a grin, nudging his shoulder. "I made fun of you too."

He smirked, shaking his head.

"But now look at me." Leah tossed her hands in the air. "I sound crazier than a crystal-toting, foil-hat-wearing New Ager at a psychic fair."

"I've already told you," Tate said, steadying her hand, "you're not crazy."

"I know," she said, smiling, squeezing his palm. "That is just my brain's default programming—always trying to pull me back to 'no rmal.'" She reached into her bag, pulling out the brochure. "Anyway, this is what I wanted to show you." She handed it to him.

He flipped through the brochure, scanning the images and text as the ocean breeze whipped at its corners.

"So, the choice I have to make is between going *here* for treatment—or staying and doing the surgery." Leah paused, watching a wave roll in and crash softly against the shore. "But you know what's even crazier? *This* is the same town where Miryam—my past life—grew up. I feel like everything's leading me there, like that's where I'm supposed to go."

She lifted the journal from her lap. "See, look here."

"Wait—what's that?" Eyes wide, Tate pointed to the shiny piece tucked into the back pocket.

"This?" She drew out the small silver snake, the last of the sunlight glinting off its curves. "It's one half of this ancient key, supposedly meant to unlock a chest that contains humanity's magic." Rolling her eyes at her own words, she continued, "If I can find the other half, maybe I can start understanding some of this mystery."

Tate's gaze stayed fixed on it. "Can I see it?"

Leah handed him the silver piece and watched as he turned it over in his hands, studying the delicate engraving in the fading light.

"Tate," she said quietly, her voice catching, "I finally feel like I'm connected to something greater than myself. Do you know what that feels like? It's exhilarating. It's like I can see a glimpse of this infinite *web* that connects us all." She held her palm out to the sky, her fingers floating between the emerging stars as if she could weave them with an invisible thread. "Life, the Universe, God—whatever it is. Right now, I just have one strand, but if I keep following it ..." She traced the lines between stars, then let her hand fall. "... ugh, I'm not explaining it well."

He laughed softly. "I think I get the gist."

Turning to look deep into his eyes, she asked, "What do *you* think I should do?"

Tate met her gaze, smiling. "I think you called *me* instead of Kat or Felix because you knew I wouldn't tell you what to do. You already know what you want."

He handed the silver piece back to her.

Leah took it, nodding slowly. "Yeah," she said, the corners of her mouth curving into a grin. "I guess that means I have a trip to England in my near future."

She tucked the journal and key piece back into her purse and leaned into Tate, resting her head against his shoulder. He slipped an arm around and pulled her close, warming her from the inside instantly.

Together, they watched the Sun sink behind the horizon—quiet and fleeting.

It was a beautiful moment.

That didn't last long.

Sirens blazed behind them, and red and blue lights flashed across the sand. Leah turned around, her stomach dropping, as two police cars pulled up to the beach. Officers climbed out and started toward them.

She twisted toward Tate, heat rising to her cheeks. "You told them where I was? You told Seth?"

"Leah—"

She threw his arm off her. "I thought you wanted to support me, but you were just *stalling*—waiting to get me back to the hospital?" Her voice cracked as she stood, brushing the sand from her dress with trembling hands. "I trusted you."

"Wait," Tate said, reaching out to her. "I swear I don't know how they found you. I didn't tell anyone."

Leah froze for a moment, tears welling at the edges of her eyes, torn between believing him and the familiar pull of betrayal that had lived in her for years. *This is what always happens.*

She turned away from Tate, her vision blurring, head spinning. Then she ran—barefoot across the heavy, uneven sand, hot tears streaming down her face as the sirens wailed behind her.

"Ms. Webb!" one officer shouted. "Stop right there. We have orders to take you back to the hospital."

Leah's feet pounded against the sand—raw and slipping with every step—willing her body to keep going despite the ache in her side and the fire in her lungs. She clutched her bag tight against her side. The journal. The money. That's all that mattered now. But her calves screamed at her. *Why is running on sand so damn hard?*

"Leah!" Tate's voice echoed behind her.

She glanced around—ocean to her right, flashing lights to her left. Where was she going? The length of the endless beach stretched ahead of her, taunting her every step forward. She slowed to a jog, panting, heart pounding in her chest.

"Ma'am, don't resist," the officer called, his tone calm but firm as they moved in. "We don't want to hurt you. Chief Gray asked us to bring you in, for your safety."

Bullshit. Seth didn't care about her. He never had.

The ocean breeze stung her face, mixing salt with tears until she couldn't tell one from the other. Leah's breath came in ragged gasps. She wanted to disappear into the sea—sink below the waves like the Sun had just done, vanish before anyone could pull her back. Her jog slowed to a stumble as pain knifed at her side, forcing her to a stop. She bent slightly, one hand gripping her ribs, the other clutching her bag like a lifeline.

But there was no escape.

Tate reached her first, huffing lightly. "Leah, I swear ... I didn't tell them." He caught her hand, trying to catch her eyes too. "Please. Look at me."

Leah kept her gaze fixed on the ground, her lips pressed tight.

Then the officers arrived, their flashlights cutting sharp circles of light around her. "Ms. Webb," one said as he crept carefully toward her, his tone low and authoritative. "We need you to come with us. We'd prefer not to use restraints—but we will if necessary."

Finally, she glanced up—and froze. Felix, donning his police uniform, leaned against one of the cop cars, swirling lights flashing across his sullen face. Their eyes met. And in that instant, she *knew*.

It was he, not Tate, who had ratted her out.

She didn't know how Felix had known where to find her. Maybe he remembered this was her favorite beach. Maybe because he had been here when she met Tate. It didn't matter. The guilt on his face told her everything.

Leah spun toward Tate, desperate to make it right. "Tate, I believe you."

But he was already walking back toward his car, shoulders rigid, not turning back at the sound of her voice.

Fuck. With shoulders sinking, Leah followed the officers to a waiting car.

The drive back blurred past her in silence.

When they brought her back into her hospital room, everyone was there—Seth, Kat, Felix, Hana, her mother, even a security guard.

Everyone but Tate.

Dr. Paulson entered a moment later, flipping through Leah's chart. "Ms. Webb, there are a few things we need to discuss before surgery in the morning."

"Surgery?" Leah blurted. "I haven't consented. I want the biopsy and the shunt first. Then, if it's cancer—"

"I'm sorry, Ms. Webb," the doctor interrupted gently.

"It's Leah."

"Leah ... sorry, I thought someone had spoken with you already."

There was a hush across the room.

"And told me what?" She frantically searched the doctor's eyes, then turned to her friends and family. "What is it?!"

Dr. Paulson glanced at the paperwork. "Your medical power of attorney has been transferred to..." Her eyes scanned the page. "... Mr. Seth Gray."

Leah's migraine pressed on her skull. She shook her head and said, "You can't do that. He's my *ex*. He has no right."

"I signed off on the transfer after you left the hospital." The doctor eyed Leah, raising her eyebrows. "Given the circumstances—and your recent statements about a magical journal and prophecy—it was determined you cannot make sound medical decisions at this time. If you need a moment to process, I'll be just outside."

She left, the door clicking shut behind her.

Leah's mouth hung open, her heart thundering in her ears, as she looked from Felix to Kat to Hana to her mother. Then her gaze met Seth's.

He stood smugly by the window, arms crossed, a faint smirk on his lips.

He had won—and they both knew it.

CHAPTER 52

KARAIA

S tellan stood just a few feet from Karaia in the hallway. A New Soterian security vest fit snugly over his pressed, buttoned-up shirt, and a laser gun holstered at his hip. She remembered the last time they had spoken—the pull she'd felt toward him, the emotions she'd tried to fight, knowing what he knew, and how impossible it was for them ever to be together.

Her mind flashed to Griffin's weight against her body, then Stellan's face in his place, imagining they were far, far away on their Californian isle. His lips on hers, tongues dancing, hands grasping at one another—

She shuddered a heavy breath, blinking hard to bring herself back to the present.

She was a fugitive, and he was the president's son.

"Hi," she managed.

"Karaia?" His mouth hung open for a second before words tumbled out, eyes frantic. "What are you doing here? Everyone is supposed to be in their office on a NeuroTryp. We're looking for a terrorist. It's really dangerous for you to be walking around here."

Stellan sounded genuinely concerned, and Karaia ached to tell him the truth. Her gut told her she could trust him—but her mind wasn't convinced. She searched his eyes for something, *anything*, that would prove her instincts right.

He gazed back at her, biting the inside of his lip.

It was obvious he wasn't a fighter by nature. He shifted his weight from one foot to the other, sweat glistening along his forehead. His hand was nowhere near his gun. And his eyes—*those eyes*—belonged to someone trapped in the wrong life, the wrong family, trying to make sense of his place in it all. Her gut told her he was everything his dad wasn't. And that only made her want him more. She watched as he closed his eyes for a moment, then—the familiar ease of tension and fall of his shoulders as he took a credit.

Coming back to, Stellan rolled his neck and asked Karaia again, more calmly this time, "What are you doing here?"

Taking a deep breath, she began, "I need to tell you something—"

Without fear coursing through him anymore, his quick gaze swept over her disheveled hair, the jacket zipped tight to her chin to hide the necklace, and the rapid rise and fall of her chest. "Wait," he said, wrinkling his brow. "Don't you work in the Seromela sector ... not here on the government side?"

He stepped toward her, his eyes sharpening as he pieced it together.

Karaia shifted to the side, holding his gaze. "Stellan—"

He inched closer.

She stepped aside again.

They moved in sync, circling each other in the narrow hallway like two equal forces pulled by the same magnetic field. With every step, the tension thickened—until Karaia's back met the wall, and Stellan stood between her and her escape route.

Stellan rubbed the spot between his eyes. "You were by my father's office earlier. Someone broke into his vault and stole—"

"I can explain," Karaia blurted, raising her hands.

His hand shot to the gun at his side, hovering over the holster—but he didn't draw it. Not yet.

"I hope so," he said, sweat soaking his shirt under the arms.

She edged toward him, palms still raised. "You're right, I was in your father's office, but it's not what you think."

"Then what is it?" he snapped, shaking his head. "Give me one reason I shouldn't call security right now. Tell me you're not the one we're looking for—that you're not the terrorist."

"I'm not a terrorist," she said firmly. "But I ... can't tell you I'm not the one you're looking for."

Karaia searched his face, desperate for the empathy she'd glimpsed before—the version of him she'd heard in Griffin's office, the one who questioned the violence. And the one she had danced with at the gala.

"Your father is doing awful things in our country," she said. "I know you know this. He planned the gala attack."

One more step forward.

"I know." Stellan's head dropped, his hand slipping from his gun. "I don't know what to think. He says he has a larger plan—that he *had* to do these things to stop the Defiers." Rubbing his temples, his voice broke. "Karaia, they *killed* my brother."

She could see the torment behind his eyes—the years of conflict, of trying to reconcile the father he loved with the man he feared. She wanted to comfort him, hold him, take him with her. Maybe there was a world where he would run away with her.

"I know you want to be a good son." Karaia nodded, taking one more step in, feeling the pull between them, letting her hands find his, giving them a squeeze. "But there's more that you don't know about him. About the Defiers. Are you even sure it was them who kidnapped you and your brother?"

Stellan pushed her away, throwing his hands up. "What are you saying? That my dad had something to do with Kai's murder? He *loved* him." His brow furrowed deeply, and his hand drifted back toward his gun.

It was too far, too fast.

Letting her fantasy go, Karaia realized then she would have to get out of here alone.

"Sorry, I didn't mean to imply that. There's just more happening than we've been told ..." She reached for him again, searching his eyes. But he wouldn't meet her gaze. "I just need to get out of here. *Look* at me. I'm not a terrorist."

Stellan squeezed his eyes shut for a moment, his breath coming in rapid succession, trembling hand still hovering over his laser gun. He took another credit—or ten. Finally, he glanced up at her. "I'm not as

strong as you, Karaia. I want to believe you, but ... my dad. He's just ...
he's too ..."

She wondered how many times he'd had this same argument with
himself. How many times he's tried to numb himself with credits.
How many times it hasn't worked ... enough.

"You see, my dad always gets what he wants." Stellan exhaled.
"There's no point in fighting him. I'm going to call security, and I'll
try to help you out of this mess, I promise." A familiar stare blanketed
his face as he alerted NIVA.

"I hope you can forgive me." Karaia swung her fist into the side
of Stellan's face as hard as she could. The instant she hit him, a sting
radiated back through her hand.

Stellan stumbled back, clutching his ear.

A few drops of blood hit the floor.

Karaia shuddered a gasp. *What did I just do?* She'd just struck the
son of the president of New Soteria—and possibly the only man she'd
ever thought she could love. She hoped that what she was doing was
worth throwing all that away.

But security would be there any second.

She snatched Stellan's laser gun as he hunched over, switched the
setting to *stun*, and pressed it hard against his side.

He stiffened as the electric charge surged through him.

"I'm so sorry," Karaia whispered as Stellan's unconscious body
slumped to the floor.

She leapt over him and sprinted toward the conference room, glancing back just long enough to see security charging down the hall after
her.

"Hey! Stop!" they shouted.

Karaia flung the door open and locked it behind her. It might hold
them off—for a moment. She glanced around, trying to think clearly
past the roar of her own heartbeat and the ache in her stomach after
hitting Stellan. The room was larger than she expected, more like an
auditorium. Rows of desks stretched between her and the far wall of
windows. She bolted down the center aisle.

Behind her, the officers reached the door. A rattle of the handle. Then silence. Then—*pew!*—laser fire blasted the knob clean off. The door crashed open.

Finally—the distraction she needed.

An eruption of chatter echoed as people poured from their offices into the hall beyond the conference room. No one was linked to their NeuroTryps anymore.

The virus was live.

Karaia could hear the chaos behind her—the officers shouting orders, trying to calm the panicked crowd. Voices overlapped, questions rising about the gala attack and Sector Five.

The distraction lasted less than a minute.

But it was enough.

The officers stormed back into the room. One drew his gun and fired. The blast struck a desk beside her, leaving a black scorch mark inches from her arm. She winced instinctively but kept running. Almost there.

Another shot sizzled past, grazing her leg. Pain seared through her thigh, causing her to stumble. But she didn't stop.

Finally, she reached the enormous wall of windows at the far end.

Straining her eyes, she desperately scanned for the maintenance exit, checking each window for a hidden latch. An opening. Something, but—

She found nothing.

For a heartbeat, dread flooded her being. It had all been for nothing. She was sure she was going to die here with the next laser shot.

Then—in the corner, she spotted what she had missed upon first look—a single window with a small latch.

Exhaling, she rushed to it.

With all her strength, she pried it open. A rush of cold air hit her face—sharp, sweet, and startlingly fresh.

A laser blast shattered the glass above her head. Karaia ducked, shielding her face from the shards scattering around her. *Were they intentionally missing?*

Maybe the orders were to bring her in alive, not kill her.

She scrambled onto the narrow platform outside, blinking as sunlight flooded her eyes. The metal led to a long, slim ladder descending the entire side of the building. Karaia looked down at the massive landscape of buildings and tubes below her—instantly dizzy. Cupping her stomach and drawing in a long breath, she pressed herself against the wall, trying to calm herself.

There was no time.

Any second, the officers would be outside too.

She had to go.

But her feet refused to cooperate ... again.

Spotting a small stepladder leaning against the structure beside her, she slammed the window shut and wedged the ladder in front of it. It wouldn't hold long, but maybe it would be long enough.

And every moment counted.

Karaia gripped the metal railing and inched herself toward the edge again. This time, she didn't dare look down. Lowering her foot down onto the first step, her whole body trembled, but she maintained her footing. Focusing on her breath, she clung to the metal ladder. Just one step at a time.

She took another step down.

And another.

The graze on her leg burned with every movement. Sweat slicked her wet palms as she squeezed each rung. *Focus. Just focus.* She moved faster.

And whatever I do—don't *look down.*

Internally, her nerves were on fire, and she wasn't sure how her heart hadn't yet pounded out of her chest. But then she realized something—just a few weeks ago she would never have been able to do this without a shitload of credits in her system.

Probably not even then.

Now, here she was, scaling the side of a skyscraper while the feisty wind whipped through her hair and the intense Sun beat down on her skin, reddening her cheeks. Terror coursed through every fiber of her body, but beneath it—there was something else. A spark. Bravery. Courage. Finding out just what she was capable of.

And it felt fucking amazing.

Karaia smiled.

A laser blast cracked the air from above. She flinched, nearly losing her grip. The beam sizzled past, missing her by inches. She gripped the ladder and climbed faster.

Another shot zipped past her.

Karaia's blood thudded in her veins.

Another miss.

With each step down, each breath she took got more punctuated.

Keep going. Don't look down. Or up.

Just keep going.

Finally, her foot landed on something solid. Had she just descended forty floors? It seemed like forever and an instant all at once. Wiping her brow, she glanced around. There were no more shots coming from above. Instead, all she saw were tubes and rails stretching for miles in all directions, connecting one building to the next. She squinted into the tube below her—*Fifth Tube*—its glass and metal glinting in the sunlight.

Karaia turned in a steady circle and scanned the top of the tubes for the next maintenance hatch that would lead her to the rendezvous point to meet Blaze.

There it was—about a hundred feet away.

Karaia pressed her heels to the metal and sprinted toward it. Crouching, she tried to wrench it open. It wouldn't budge. She slammed her shoulder against it. Nothing. Panic rose in her throat. She had not gotten this far to be locked out of the tubes.

Pressing her earpiece, she breathed, "Blaze? Are you there?"

"Yes—where the fuck are *you*?" Blaze yelled, causing Karaia to recoil.

"I'm just above Fifth Tube. The hatch won't open." She furrowed her brows as she stared at the hatch, willing it to open for her, pulling, pushing, using everything she had in her to open it.

"Just hit it hard. It should open from the outside," Blaze instructed.

"I tried that!" Karaia yelled, slamming her fist down again. Blood trickled from her knuckles as pain flared through her hand.

"It might be ... sealed shut," Ziven's voice cut in.

"What do you mean—sealed?" she shouted, shaking her swollen hand. "What do I do?"

Then—Karaia saw them.

Dozens of armed New Soterian officers poured out of Seromela's front doors and into the tube below her. One of them pointed upward toward her hatch.

Frantic, her eyes darted back and forth between the hatch and the oncoming threat. "Um, guys," she said, voice trembling, "security officers are coming this way. Tell me what to do!"

"We have to change plans," Ziven said sharply. "Follow my instructions exactly. If you don't ... well, just follow them, okay? Start running down the tube to your west. Now!"

He didn't need to tell her twice.

With every ounce of strength she had left, Karaia ran.

CHAPTER 53

MIRYAM

The leaves crunched beneath their hurried steps as they fled through the dense forest—away from the monastery, away from danger. The air still reeked of smoke and ash, stinging Miryam's lungs, yet adrenaline fueled her onward. She would not stop. Not now.

"Wait," Ved gasped, holding a hand up. "I must rest. Only a moment."

"We cannot stop." Miryam turned, tugging his arm forward.

But he stumbled, panting heavily as he doubled over with one hand pressed against his tunic. The fabric was dark and wet with blood.

Brows deepening, she asked, "Are you hurt?"

"'Tis simply a slight wound ... I reckon," he said between ragged breaths.

"You *are* hurt. Let me see." Panic surged as Miryam reached to pull up his tunic, but he caught her wrist, shaking his head.

"We've no time for that," he insisted. "You said it thyself—we must keep going. The safe house lies just beyond this wood." He winced as he straightened, then held the chest out to her. "Here. You'd best carry it."

Miryam hesitated, her heart twisting, but she took the chest from his trembling hands. It pained her to see him like this. He was clearly suffering more than he was letting on, but how much she didn't know.

They turned to carry on when the ground trembled beneath their feet. Leaves rustled in the trees overhead, and a flock of birds burst into the early morning air. A crash of crumbling stone followed. Both turned toward the sound, breath shallow. Behind them, faint shouts and the clatter of armor carried through the trees. The knights were still hunting.

"What was that?" Miryam shuddered, gripping Ved's hand tight.

"The monastery," he said hollowly. "They are destroying it. Everything. My home. 'Tis all I have ever known ..." His words faded, but the grief in his eyes said what he did not.

She pulled him close, resting her finger gently on the center of his chest. "Life is more than stone walls and old books," she whispered. "Aught we need is right here." Then, she pressed her lips to his.

Ved kissed her back, though the passion was missing from it.

"You are right." He nodded solemnly. "Let us go."

They continued until they reached a small, half-buried cottage deep in the woods. Miryam could see how easy this place would be to miss if you weren't looking for it. With a moss-covered roof blending into the hill and vines climbing across its front, there was but a single wooden door visible.

"Here," Ved said, knocking three times, pausing, then twice more.

A latch clicked from within. The door creaked open, and Sophia stood there.

"Come in," she said, motioning them inside. "Hurry."

They stepped into the dimly lit cottage. Cobwebs hung in the corners, and the air smelled of damp Earth. The space was larger than Miryam expected, stretching deep into the hill. A few cots lined the walls, and several hay mats lay scattered about. On a small wooden table sat a few loaves of bread and some root vegetables. A few monks and a nun—not part of the order—were there among them. The nun cried softly to herself as she nibbled on a piece of bread. The two monks knelt in prayer on the ground. Father Thomas sat on a mat while Matilda snored next to him.

"Where are Will and Catherine?" Miryam asked, gazing around.

Sophia met her gaze with puffy eyes. "I fear they have been captured."

Miryam thought of her friends, feeling the coal burn hot in her chest. "That means they will—"

"Aye," Sophia said, bowing her head. "Be executed."

Helping Ved to a cot, the spot between Miryam's eyes narrowed. She couldn't stand the thought of anyone else being murdered simply for being who they were. She turned back to Sophia and blew out a small huff, stomping her foot. "We must try to save them. Can we free them from the castle dungeon?"

"And reveal our gifts to the world?" Sophia's voice was soft but firm. "If our power fell into the wrong hands ..." She shook her head. "... we cannot. 'Tis far too dangerous. We shall rest here, then travel southwest tonight. If need be, we will cross to France by boat." She paused, searching Miryam's face. "You are welcome to come, but we cannot remain."

Conflicting feelings tightened in Miryam's chest as she clenched and unclenched her hand. Part of her wanted to fight. Part of her only wished to live quietly with Ved.

But Sophia spoke the truth. The order could not stay here.

She and Ved had only escaped because Gawain had known her—and trusted her, even when she lied. *Am I truly willing to give up my whole life, never see Father or Bella again, to flee with Ved and the order?* The question echoed in her mind, though she already knew the answer.

"I will join you," Miryam said, nodding.

Sophia inclined her head, then addressed the others. "We all must regain our strength. One of us shall keep watch while the rest sleep. I shall take first watch."

Miryam turned to Ved, who had barely spoken since they left the abbey. His skin was pale, his breath shallow. "Before we rest, let me see your wound. It needs cleaning." She reached for his tunic again.

He caught her hands, his grip weak and his hands icy cold. "I am fine, Miryam," he murmured. "Let us lie down."

But when he lowered himself onto the cot, he winced.

"You are clearly not fine. Sophia—tell him," Miryam urged, glancing toward her mentor.

"Ved?" Sophia raised a brow.

"I am well, truly. I only need rest," he repeated.

Ved held Sophia's gaze for what felt like an eternity. Something unspoken passed between them.

Frustration welled within Miryam. "What are you not telling me?" Her eyes darted between the two of them.

"Ved is correct," Sophia said, her voice catching. "Miryam, get some rest."

"No, but—" Miryam began, her protest faltering as Ved reached for her hand and drew her gently toward the cot.

"I know you do not understand," he mumbled, pulling her close. "You will soon enough. For now, rest beside me."

She hesitated, then sighed and nestled into the crook of his arm, her head tucking beneath his chin. Feeling the soft hum of Ved's breath on her, she hadn't realized how weary she was until that moment. Her heavy eyelids pulled closed, and sleep claimed her swiftly.

"Wake up." Sophia's whisper stirred her from a shallow slumber, a hand nudging her shoulder. "I shall fetch water from the creek for our journey. Would you keep watch while I am away?"

"Yes," Miryam said groggily, rubbing her eyes. She eased herself out of Ved's embrace and sat upright.

"I shan't be long," Sophia murmured before slipping quietly through the small wooden door.

The room was still and dim, the air thick with the scent of the surrounding Earth—*rainstorms and mushrooms*, Miryam thought. She fought to keep her eyes open, her body swaying slightly as exhaustion threatened to pull her under once more. The last few adrenaline-filled hours—or was it just an hour? She didn't know—flashed in her mind. Fern's death. The knight she had killed. The terror when Ved hadn't come out of the cave. For a moment, she had thought he might never.

Her gaze fell on him now, sleeping soundly beside her. She brushed her fingers through his dark hair. He felt clammy and cool—*too cool*.

Miryam's chest tightened. She touched his cheek, then his neck, then his hands.

All cold.

Her eyes darted to the crimson stain on his tunic. Slowly, she lifted the fabric and gasped, cupping a hand to her mouth. A deep gash split his stomach, blood still seeping from it.

"No, no, no..." she whispered, her pulse hammering in her chest. *Why didn't he tell me? Why would he keep this a secret?* Unless ...

She shook her head hard.

No, I won't think it. I won't say it. But the thought was there, along with the fresh tears streaming down her face.

... unless he knew he would die.

Hot tears blurred Miryam's vision as she scrambled to her feet, searching the room for anything to stop the bleeding. She knew little of healing, but she knew one thing—blood belonged inside the body, not out.

She couldn't lose Ved. Not now. Not when they had so much ahead of them. They were supposed to have a whole life together.

Desperate, Miryam scanned the cottage for something to tie around his wound. She glanced down at her own nightdress. It would work. She lifted the bottom hem and pulled as hard as she could at the linen, ripping a long piece off, pressing it hard around his waist.

Ved flinched, gasping in pain, and his eyes fluttered open.

He looked at her and then down at his wound. "You know?"

"Know what?" Miryam snapped through trembling lips. "That you were wounded and kept it from me. That we could have aided you sooner. That you are too cold now and losing blood." She gently tied the linen around his torso, letting out a shuddered cry. "That I love you—and I cannot imagine this life without you." Her voice broke, the ache in her chest spilling out in ragged sobs.

"Miryam—"

"What?" she screamed, then lowered her voice. "What could you possibly say that would make this right? That would justify doing naught to save yourself?"

"I can hear your anger," Ved said, his voice low.

"I am not angry. I am sad, and I ..." she said, wiping her cheeks only for new tears to replace the old. "I do not understand why ..." Pressing herself onto his chest, she muffled her cries with his tunic, trying to take in his scent, trying to feel every ounce of him, trying to hold him closer than was possible.

Silence stretched between them, too heavy to bear.

Miryam peeled herself off, busying her hands by checking the linen strip was tight around Ved's waist. "There," she said, forcing steadiness into her voice. "You shall not lose any more blood. You only need water, food—then you shall gain your strength for the journey ahead."

"Miryam," Ved began, his voice ragged, "I will not be—"

"Do not speak," she interrupted, shaking her head. "I cannot hear it." She buried her face against his chest again, her sobs rising and falling like waves.

Ved's hand trembled as he lifted her chin, his eyes glistening. "Please," he whispered, "let me explain."

Miryam hushed, eventually nodding her head.

"When I told you I had received a message about the attack—that we would escape the abbey—I did not lie," Ved began, his breath shallow, "not entirely." He winced, squeezing Miryam's hand. "The message said we would escape, yes, but ... most would not make it farther than that." He looked into her eyes, voice cracking. "Only you, Miryam, will survive this."

For a moment, her mind went blank. The words hung in the air, heavy and hollow. Her gaze darted between his eyes, searching for some hint that he was mistaken. "What are you saying? What about Sophia? Father Thomas? Matilda?"

Ved's eyes cast down.

"Do they know?" she asked, dread in her throat.

He nodded slowly. "The elders do."

Miryam shook her head, tears spilling freely again. "No."

"No, what?"

"I refuse to accept it," she asserted, her voice rising. The coal burned brightly in her chest, fueled by her desire to save Ved and the others. "We can change it—we can change *everything*. I will not sit here and watch you die. I can heal you—I *know* I can."

Closing her eyes, Miryam placed her palm gently over his wound. She focused on the pleroma rising within her, the energy centers of her body whirling faster and faster with golden warmth. She imagined it flowing through her hands, knitting his torn flesh whole again. She felt the energy surge from her to him, bright and alive.

Then, she waited.

And waited.

Flashing her eyes open, she raised her voice in a panic. "'Tis not working—why is it not working? I can conjure storms and control minds, but not this?"

Ved took her trembling hands and pressed his lips to them. "Miryam," he whispered, "I love you with all my heart. But we do not choose when we live or die."

"We still must *try*," she pleaded. "There's a difference between lying here bleeding out and trying to escape—trying to live. Do not you want to live?"

He was silent for a long while.

Miryam studied his face, trying to memorize it. The slight wrinkle between his deep blue eyes. The perfect curl that always fell onto his forehead. The dimple that only donned the left side of his smile. She loved it all. And she couldn't imagine a world in which he didn't exist. She didn't want to be a part of that world.

Finally, Ved nodded. "Of course, I do. When Sophia returns, we shall wake the others and try. For you, I will do anything." He pulled her into a deep kiss, and this time, it was filled with every ounce of passion left in him.

"Thank you," she breathed against his lips.

"But first, do one thing for me," he said, his voice barely above a whisper.

"Aught," she replied at once.

Ved reached beneath his tunic and pulled out his necklace. The two halves of the key hung from it—one wood, one silver. He must have taken them when he retrieved the chest from the cave. "Help me take this off, would you?" he asked, leaning forward slightly. Even that slight movement made him grimace.

Miryam's hands trembled as she reached around his neck, untying the leather cord. The necklace slipped free, and she held the two halves in her palms. "What are we to do with these?"

"Has anyone ever told you the story behind these?" he asked, reaching for the wooden piece.

She shook her head.

"Well," he said, each word a struggle, "the chest did not always have a key."

"It did not?" Miryam tilted her head, gazing at the silver piece in her hand, feeling its smooth edges between her fingertips.

"No. After the chest came into the possession of Jesus Christ, it—"

"How did he get it?"

Ved raised a brow at Miryam and let out a hoarse chuckle. "Are you really going to ask questions now?"

She smiled through her tears. "Go on."

"Jesus trained with the Essenes, who believed him to be the Messiah and thought it fitting that he safeguard the chest. But word spread of the mystical object's power, and both the Romans and the Jewish authorities sought to claim it. They feared anything—or anyone—who might challenge their rule." He continued, his voice steadier now, the story itself lending him strength. "They could not stand thinking a poor carpenter's son could usurp their power, so they attempted to steal the chest. To keep it safe, Jesus and his disciples forged a key in two parts—one of wood, for our bond with the Earth, and one of silver, for our bond with the Heavens. Together, they represent the union of the divine and the mortal within us all."

Ved lifted his gaze to Miryam's as they each held one half of the key. "And they call out to each other. Can you feel it?"

"Yes, 'tis amazing," Miryam breathed. She could feel their soft pull—magnetic, yearning, reaching for each other. The energy between them shimmered like invisible light, tugging gently, begging to be made whole.

"Well, I have a theory," he said between short, uneven breaths. "I think these pieces can link two souls together. And I do not know how much longer I have in this body."

"Do not speak like that. You shall be fine," Miryam insisted, checking the wrap around his torso.

Ved winced but smiled faintly. "You do not know that. So, before I go, I want to bind our souls to these pieces. That way, no matter what happens, we will always find each other again. The two halves want to become one—and if they do, so shall we. Even if death, or distance, or time itself divides us, we will always be drawn back together. If not in this life, then the next ... or the next."

Miryam looked into his eyes—the blue that once shimmered like bluebells now dulled, framed by the gray pallor of his skin. Yet his spirit still burned within them, and she wanted to remember that light forever.

"Alright," she whispered.

"Close your eyes with me," Ved said.

She obeyed, and the moment her eyelids shut, she felt the hum of the keys intensify. Their energy throbbed softly from her palm to Ved's, like one heartbeat.

"Now," he instructed, "take a deep breath in ... and out. Feel the pleroma rise within your heart."

The world around Miryam faded.

The damp smell of Earth, the flickering candles, even the fiery coal that burned for revenge, for justice, within her—dissolved into pure white light. She saw the swirl of energy at her heart center spinning fast.

Ved continued, "Imagine that divine spark—the part of you that is eternal and pure—stretch outward. Let it flow into the silver piece."

Focusing on the warmth of her love, Miryam poured the pleroma from her heart into the key piece. In her mind's eye, she saw threads of light wrapping around the silver, infusing it with her essence. She could feel that Ved was doing the same, but with the wooden piece. His pleroma bound itself around the grains of the wood, weaving in and out of it.

The two halves began to tremble, pulling toward each other even more as their souls knitted together, connected, bound across time and space.

Miryam gently opened her eyes. A faint glow—soft pink and gold—illuminated their faces, the air thick with swirling pleroma.

Each half lifted from their palms, hovering in the air between them.

Chapter 54

LEAH

"This can't be." Leah's voice broke as the hospital room seemed to shrink around her, walls closing in until she could hardly breathe. Everything was crumbling down. This was not how it was supposed to happen. She pressed her palms to her temples, the migraine throbbing like a hammer behind her eyes. "How the hell did Seth of all people get power of attorney over me?"

Hana rushed to her side. "Mom, we're worried about you, and Dad is just trying to do the right thing."

Leah barked out a bitter laugh. "Your father is not in the business of doing the right thing. He's only in the business of serving himself."

"Is an entire career built upon protecting and serving our community not enough?" Seth stepped forward, his jaw tight, his voice rising with each word. "Haven't I paid your bills when you couldn't? Made sure Hana had everything she needed—the best schools, every opportunity in life? Fuck, Leah, I've been doing the right thing this whole time. It's you who is selfish, and now this—" He waved his hands in the air. "This fantasy you're spinning about being some *chosen one* chasing magical keys and an ancient chest. You need help, and we're trying to help *you*."

He exhaled sharply, shaking his head as he stormed out of the room.

The air in the room grew heavy. Leah sat trembling in bed, one hand gripping the rail, the other still rubbing her temple.

She looked to her best friend. "Kat, how ..." She sniffled, choking on her words. "... how does Seth know about the journal?"

"It wasn't her," Felix admitted, his eyes downcast. "I told Seth. I'm worried about you. We all want you well." He glanced around the room, and one by one, the others nodded slowly.

Kat squeezed Leah's hand. "I rarely agree with Seth—well, never—but—"

"But what?" Leah snapped, yanking her hand away. "Now you think he's suddenly doing something good for once?"

"I don't know." Kat's face softened, sighing. "But I *do* know you're sick, sweetie. You have a tumor, and it needs to be taken care of. This isn't something you can run from."

I'm not running. Leah wanted to say, but the words weren't forming properly in her mouth as the migraine surged harder in her skull, clouding her thoughts, halting her speech. Squeezing her eyes shut, she focused. Why was this happening? She had been doing everything right—surrendering, following the signs, learning her lessons.

Then she remembered. *Gertrude's letter.*

"Where's my bag?" she said suddenly, scanning the room. Her voice rose with urgency. "I need my purse. You'll see—it's all there! The journal, the letter from Gertrude. There's a clinic in England. I promise I'm not running away—I'm going to get treatment. Where is it?"

"It's here, Mom." Hana dragged the bag from a nearby chair, slowly handing it to her.

Leah yanked the brochure out, flipped it open, holding it up with shaky hands. "See! I'm *not* running. I can go here for treatment." She turned to Kat, her eyes pleading. "You, of all people, can understand this. It's spiritual, not just physical."

Kat pressed her lips together, leaning over to read the brochure silently, then said, "Leah, I *love* that you believe now—that you finally see there's more to life. And I'll explore that with you, promise. But ... *after* the surgery. Get the tumor taken care of first. The spiritual meaning behind it isn't going anywhere."

Leah massaged her forehead, a dull ache pulsing from within. "I can't believe this is happening," she muttered. "You're all against me." She lay back on her bed, shoulders slumping. "Can I just ... be alone for a while? I need some sleep before the surgery tomorrow."

Kat and Hana exchanged a wary glance, raising their brows.

Leah caught it. "There's a security guard at my door," she said, forcing a small smile. "No sneaking out this time. I just want to rest."

"Mom, I love you so much." Hana let out a big exhale, wiped her wet eyes, and wrapped her arms around Leah one more time. "That's why we're doing this."

"I love you too." Leah squeezed her daughter back.

"I'll be at Dad's tonight," Hana said quietly. "Call me if you want to talk before the surgery, okay?"

Leah nodded and watched as they filed out of the room—one by one—until she was finally, achingly, alone, with nothing but the persistent beep of the heart rate monitor for company.

Adjusting her head on the scratchy hospital pillow, she tried to think despite the searing tentacles that wove their way through her brain. She stared up at the ceiling tiles. Images from the last few weeks flashed in her mind. The beach with Tate. The custody hearing. Standing up to Seth. Her renewed fervor to really *live* her life fully. She thought she was learning and following her path. She'd believed this was all happening for a reason. *Then why am I here—trapped in a hospital room against my will?*

A soft knock interrupted her thoughts, and the door creaked open. Leah's heart jumped. "Tate?"

Nope, just me again," came Dr. Paulson's voice.

But it wasn't just her. Seth stood behind the doctor, arms crossed.

"Does he have to be here?" Leah wrinkled her nose.

Dr. Paulson gave a professional but apologetic nod. "Actually, yes. Since Mr. Gray holds your medical power of attorney, he's required to be present for decisions about tomorrow's procedure."

"How did he even get that?"

The doctor glanced down at the clipboard. "Get what?"

"Power of attorney. I would *never* allow that." Leah could feel the heat rising in her throat as she spoke—feel Seth's grip clamping down on her life.

Dr. Paulson flipped a page. "According to your advance directive, you filed it thirteen years ago." She turned the document so Leah could see. "Here—it lists Seth Gray as your medical proxy."

Leah gaped at the paper in disbelief. She didn't even remember making one. Then—she saw the date. Hana's birth.

Slowing shaking her head, she growled, "You fucking bastard."

"Ms. Webb," Dr. Paulson said sharply, "I need you to refrain from that kind of language, please."

Leah looked up, eyes blazing, but said nothing.

"It's okay," Seth said smoothly, stepping closer. "She's under a lot of stress right now. Anyone would be. It must be frustrating to think you are part of some elaborate past-life hallucination, only to have your hopes dashed by reality." He smirked at Leah. "But as you can see, your signature is right there. And honestly, you're lucky. If it weren't, we couldn't get you the help you need so quickly."

Leah let out a low grunt. She couldn't stand the sound of his voice. "That's *old,*" she snapped. "I signed that when I was in labor with Hana. It wasn't meant to last this long."

Dr. Paulson adjusted her glasses, maintaining her calm. "Ms. Webb, an advance directive remains active until it's revoked or replaced. Do you have documentation showing you appointed someone else?"

Leah cast her eyes down. "No."

"Very well. Then, there's no point arguing. Let's go over your procedure, and then we can all get a good night's rest." The doctor turned to her chart. "We'll perform a craniotomy and remove the mass. Depending on how much of the pineal region the tumor involves, we may need to remove part—or all—of the gland. If that's the case, you'll likely need long-term hormone replacement to regulate sleep and mood. I won't know the full extent until we're in the operating room."

Leah barely heard her. The doctor's words blurred into a hum, drowned out by the thud of steady pressure in her brain.

"The procedure's scheduled for eight a.m.," Dr. Paulson finished. "You'll be prepped at seven. Goodnight."

She gave a last nod, then she and Seth left the room, the door clicking softly behind them.

Leah was alone—again. She could see the outline of the security guard who stood watch at her door as she flicked the light off. Closing her eyes, she tried to sleep. But the insistent beep of the monitor coupled with the throbbing in her skull, she tossed and turned in the stiff hospital bed—for minutes, maybe hours? The paper gown clung to her damp skin as she writhed in place, trying to find peace, comfort, anything to remove the pain—the pain of the migraine, the pain of dealing with Seth, the pain of living. But sleep wouldn't appease her.

She sighed and reached for her purse, pulling out Miryam's journal. The leather cover felt warm against her fingertips, and the migraine finally eased. She flipped to the last page she'd been on. Miryam had just completed her initiation into the order—something about being given the "power of the serpent." It read like pure fantasy. Did she really have magic? Or was it symbolic? A metaphor for transformation, spirit guides, and all that mystical stuff Kat was always talking about?

Leah rolled her eyes at herself. *Yeah, now I sound exactly like Miryam.*

She was a skeptic at heart, and she still couldn't quite believe some of the stuff Miryam wrote about. Her thumb hovered over the page. No wonder her friends and family thought she couldn't make her own decisions. If she were them, she probably wouldn't believe her either.

But then, there was Tate. He *had* believed her—and she'd doubted him when it mattered most. A pang of guilt tightened in her chest. She wished she could tell him she was sorry, but she feared that moment on the beach might have been their last. Maybe that was for the best. She didn't deserve him anyway.

Leah flipped to the next page in the journal. It was blank.

She turned again. Blank.

"What happened to you, Miryam?" she whispered, running her fingers over the pages. "Did you get your fairy-tale ending with Ved?" She hoped so.

But that was never what happened in real life.

Leah tucked the journal under her arms, rolled onto her side, and finally—mercifully—drifted into uneasy sleep.

She woke with a jolt, gasping for air, heart hammering in her chest. She had dreamt of a fire—an attack. Then, someone chasing her. Her lungs burned. Blood covered her hands. She looked down, flipping over her palms repeatedly, stretching her fingers out. It was just a dream. No blood. No threat.

I'm still here at the hospital.

And it was still dark outside. She let out a shaky breath, glancing at the clock. 5:06 a.m.

Three hours until the surgery.

With a stomach in knots, Leah thought about how all she had been through might have been for nothing. *What if I do this surgery and lose my connection to Miryam and Karaia? Or worse, what if that means it wasn't real? Or even worse—what if I lose Hana?* Shuddering heavily, she flipped on the bedside light and reached for her purse, searching for her own journal to write in.

While rummaging through it, she felt something *new*. Something that hadn't been there the night before. A small pouch. With a folded note pinned to it.

It read,

> *I still believe in you.*
> *Tate.*

She smiled, warmth spreading through her cheeks as she unfolded the lip of the pouch. Tipping it into her hand, a small, twisted piece of wood rolled into her palm—smooth, carved with delicate grooves. Her breath caught. It perfectly mirrored the silver piece from Miryam's journal.

That meant ... *Tate had the other half of the key?*

Her brow deepened. It seemed impossible. But impossible was becoming her new normal.

Leah reached for Miryam's journal under her pillow, slipping the silver fragment from its pocket. Placing the two halves side by side in her lap—one wood, one metal—she could *feel* the pull between them. There was a gentle hum in the air, magnetic and alive, like static before a storm. It was as if the pieces wanted to weave themselves into one key, invisible threads calling to the other.

Her breath calmed. She didn't know what would happen if they merged, but she had to find out. Hesitating for a moment ... then, unable to resist, she held the pieces up—one in each hand—and slowly brought the two halves together.

CHAPTER 55

KARAIA

With her heels pounding hard against the tube's outer metal, Karaia sprinted in the direction away from Seromela. Below, officers started after her, their boots echoing in the tunnel.

She huffed, "Ziven, where are you sending me?"

His voice crackled in her ear. "I'm rerouting you to the rendezvous location—just on *top* of the tube—instead of *in* it."

"I'm here *waiting* ..." Blaze chimed in, annoyance in her voice.

"Don't worry about B," Ziven said. "She's just mad that our new location doesn't have a beats pod. It's where she went to chill out."

Karaia couldn't imagine Blaze chilled out—*ever.*

"When you hit the upcoming intersection, head north," Ziven instructed.

She pivoted sharply. The officers turned with her.

"Now head west again at the following intersection," he said. "You'll be right next to the city square."

She pressed on, coming up to the gigantic dome, glancing down to her right. There it was—the perfect emerald lawn, scattered trees, people strolling about, and her grandma's favorite fountain glinting in the Sun. Her stomach tightened. *Gram. Cass.* Would they be okay without her? She hoped.

For a brief stretch, the square's large trees offered her cover from the barrage of marching soldiers below her. Maybe it would buy her a few extra minutes. Maybe ... it would be enough.

"Take the next tube north. You'll follow it for about two miles."

"Two miles?!" Karaia exclaimed, her lungs already feeling the difference between this and her normal VR workout program.

"Just be thankful you don't have a belly like Z." Blaze chuckled over the comm.

"Heeeyy!" Ziven retorted.

Karaia managed a small laugh. Wiping her brow, she didn't slow, following every direction exactly, zig-zagging farther from Seromela and the city's heart. She felt lucky she was in shape, or running this much would have been much more difficult. Despite that, she had to take a break now and then to catch her breath, gulping the fresh air, praying the officers below her needed the same.

Once, she made the mistake of glancing over the tube's edge. Thirty feet down, the ground spun beneath her. Dizzy, she flailed—screamed—barely catching herself before she slipped. She thudded to a halt, resting her hands on her aching thighs.

"Karaia, are you okay?!" Ziven shouted through the other end.

Between rapid, shallow breaths, she managed, "Yeah ... just almost fell to my death. Where to next?"

"You're almost there," he said. "Any sight of officers?"

"Not at the moment," she said, scanning the tube beneath her, "but they can't be far behind."

"Okay, you should reach a T soon. Tell me when you're there." He clicked the comm off.

Karaia pushed off the metal ground again, forcing herself to keep a steady pace. Despite the towers and upper tubes surrounding her, the Sun and the wind still beat down on her raw skin, sweat dripping into her eyes and stinging her burned cheeks. She wiped her forehead with the back of her hand. Every ounce of her body begged her to stop—lungs pinching, thighs burning, her jaw tight. She wasn't used to the outside elements—no one in New Soteria was.

That's when reality really sunk in about where she was headed—outside the walls, on the bare Earth. How many times had she wished to feel the ground beneath her feet? And now—she would. But would she survive it? Would she reach Avani or die on the journey, never finding her parents, never knowing more of the prophecy? Fear crept like a spider up her spine. So much of her thoughts had been consumed by *how* to escape, not what her world would be like once she did. Rolling her neck, she felt the tightness in her upper back.

She needed a distraction. *Oh, how nice a credit would be right now.*

"Ziven," Karaia asked between ragged breaths, "I haven't asked you guys, did you all make it out all right? The kids—are they okay?"

"Yeah, thanks for asking," he answered. "We're prepared for that sort of thing."

Blaze added, "We have locations all over—for situations exactly like this."

Karaia frowned as she ran. "How often do things like *this* happen?"

"More often than you think," Blaze said flatly.

Karaia's stomach sank. Years of media flashes replayed in her mind—nothing about child labor, uprisings, no crime *at all* within New Soteria.

Glancing down, she crinkled her brow. No officers. There had been none for some time now. Did she lose them? It seemed unlikely.

She looked back up and nearly ran into the side of a building. Skidding to a stop, she breathed, "Okay, I'm at the T."

"Great," Ziven said. "There should be an air duct on your left. B, can you meet her there?"

"On it," Blaze replied.

Karaia scanned the area, holding her stomach, trying to slow her rapid breathing. She wondered how far she had run. She was in a part of the sector she wasn't familiar with.

A moment later, Blaze appeared in the tube below wearing a full metal helmet, gloves, and a chest plate. She was holding some kind of device—part laser gun, part remote control. She looked like a knight out of one of Arjun's VR games.

She aimed the device at the air duct and—

Boom! An explosion rattled through the metal. Karaia flinched as the waves reverberated around her, shaking the tube beneath her feet. She crouched, steadying herself with her hands, ears ringing.

Ziven cracked on the comm. "I forgot to say. You'll want to back up. Now."

She shouted, "You could have warned me sooner."

"Sorry ..." Ziven squeaked out. "Blaze is opening the air duct. I'd stand back. There will be sizzling metal—like five-thousand degrees hot metal."

She stepped away and peered down through the glass as Blaze methodically cut along the grate's edge, sparks flaring as she worked. It was slow—*too slow*. Karaia tapped her foot on the metal impatiently, scanning both directions down the tube. She felt exposed and powerless—alone on top of the world.

The waiting left her mind with too much room to wander.

Pursing her lips, she clutched the two key pieces beneath her jacket. *Why did Griffin have the other half of my necklace?* He must have noticed hers over the years—of course he had. Her thoughts shifted to Stellan. The guilt clawed at her. Beneath all his inner turmoil, she knew he was good. She hated that she'd hurt him. But what choice did she have? He wasn't like his father—but he was still working for him.

"Blaze, are you almost done?" she asked, impatient.

"I'm working on it," Blaze shot back. "You try melting Tungstenium X, the world's strongest metal."

That's when Karaia saw them—Seromela security and New Soterian officers storming down the tube.

"Uh, Blaze ..." she licked her lips, the crease in her brow becoming heavy.

"I said I'm almost done!" Blaze hissed over the crackle of molten metal.

"It's not that." The words spilled out of Karaia's mouth as fast as she could muster. "It's Seromela. They've found us—they're coming down the tube from you, less than a block away."

Blaze froze, glancing over her shoulder. "Shit, shit, shit. I'm almost done ... just one more side left."

"Get out of there, B!" Ziven yelled, frantic through the comm. "It's not worth your life. We'll figure another way."

"Almost done ..."

A final slice of metal clanged against the floor, and suddenly, Karaia was staring through a gaping hole at Blaze in the tube below.

"There!" Blaze clapped her gloved hands together.

But the officers were close now. Karaia could hear them shouting commands, boots pounding against the floor. Half a block at most.

"Take it," Blaze said, shoving a backpack up through the opening.

Karaia narrowed her eyes. "Take what?"

"The key. Both pieces. Get them to Avani—find a man named Xander. He'll know what to do." Blaze thrust the pack toward her again as she glanced at the oncoming soldiers. "Supplies and directions are inside. Now go!"

"But what if—"

"There's no fucking time to argue!" Blaze cut her off, voice sharp. "I'll hold them off. Ziven will get you out. Go—now!" She lifted her helmet, staring deep into Karaia's eyes, nodding. "Be the Silver Serpent we need."

Karaia obeyed, grabbing the bag.

Below, Blaze dropped the cutting tool, and drew two laser pistols from inside her jacket, spinning toward the oncoming officers.

Zap! She fired. And fired again. *Zap! Zap!*

Karaia felt utterly helpless, shaking her head, as she watched the scene unfold before her. The officers fired back tenfold. Blaze dodged the first few shots. One hit her armored chest plate, bouncing off, but one slammed into her hip, jerking her backward. Another grazed her uncovered cheek—blood splattered against the tube wall. She slammed her helmet back down and turned on her heels to run, pivoting to fire her gun every so often.

But it was too little, too late.

One shot to her back was all it took.

Karaia gasped, clapping a trembling hand over her mouth. Blaze's body stiffened mid-stride, then crumpled onto the tube floor.

"Blaze?!" Ziven's voice cracked in her ear.

Karaia's lips quivered. Her eyes burned. "Ziven ... she's ... gone."

A strangled cry erupted from the other end of the line. Karaia's pulse thundered in her ears. She forced herself to look down—darting her eyes away from Blaze's bloodied body—the officers were shouting, pointing up at her. They couldn't shoot through the tube, but they could follow.

And now—there was a massive hole leading them straight to her.

Karaia slung the backpack over her shoulder and ran again. She didn't know where she was going, only *away*.

"Ziven? You still there?" She panted as slow tears welled in her eyes. No answer.

"Ziven," she cried, feet pounding on the cooling metal as the Sun sank behind buildings in the faraway sky.

"I'm here," he finally said, sniffling, his words breaking with each breath. "Blaze was like an older sister to me." A heavy silence followed. "We met when I was a kid. She had just been rescued from a factory ... and I've been with her ever since. I can't believe she's gone."

"I'm sorry," Karaia said, now with tears streaming down her cheeks. "I can't imagine what that must be like."

Ziven quelled his sobs. After a beat, his shaking voice said, "Blaze would want you to get out. Follow my instructions again. Getting you out of New Soteria from the top of the tubes is going to be... a little more difficult."

"Of course it is." Karaia rolled her eyes and kept moving.

She followed his directions for what felt like hours, stopping only to allow her desperate, hungry lungs to grasp more air than was possible. Her muscles burned, sweat soaked through her clothes, and her throat itched—raw and screaming for water—but she couldn't slow down. Even though she'd outrun the officers who killed Blaze, Seromela still had eyes everywhere.

They wouldn't stop—*Griffin* wouldn't stop.

"Ziven, how much farther?" she gasped.

"You're almost to the rail station. From there, you ride."

"What?"

"Just tell me when you reach it, okay?"

Karaia's pace faltered, then slowed to a stop. She bent forward, hands braced on her knees, panting. "Ziven, I don't think ... I can go ... much ... more."

"Just a little more. You've got this," he urged.

She hobbled to the edge of the tube and looked down. The world spun for a second. Then she saw it—the rail station.

Here, the rail wasn't enclosed in a tube. It was open to the air, gleaming in the faint light of the afternoon Sun, stretching for miles into the horizon. And she realized, for the first time in her life, she could see so far. Her heart fluttered at the expanse.

Until that moment, she hadn't believed the world was truly this big.

"Wow," she said, half-crying, half-laughing, all delirious. "I made it."

"You did? For a sec there, I thought maybe you had gone the wrong way ..." Ziven echoed in her ear, stifling a small sob. "Anyway ... welcome to Sector Two. The rail in front of you is for cargo only, so it won't have any passengers. You need to get on top and ride it to the edge of Sector Six. From there, you'll reach the wall—and after that, well ... you know."

"How do I get onto the rail?" Karaia asked, still catching her breath.

"In exactly two minutes, the next scheduled rail will arrive," he explained. "Climb down and get on top while it's stopped. There'll be employees loading and unloading cargo ... don't let them see you, okay?"

"Got it." Karaia nodded, thinking that was the least of her worries now. "How long is this ride exactly?"

"Ummm ..."

"Ziven?"

"Six hours."

"Six hours?!" Karaia's mouth fell open. "I can't make it. I haven't eaten or drunk anything all day." Her stomach growled right on cue.

Ziven sighed. "Blaze didn't tell you what's in the bag, did she?"

"No ..."

"Check it," he said. "There are supplement pills that'll last you months—water, vitamins, food replacements, meds—everything you'll need for your trip to Avani."

Karaia unzipped the bag. Everything was meticulously organized. She pulled out a small pouch labeled *H2O* and popped two pills into her mouth. Instantly, her thirst vanished. She licked her lips, savoring the relief, even if it was synthetic.

"Oh, thank you." She exhaled. "I needed that. Now, to get on this rail ..."

She scanned the surrounding area. Straight ahead of her, the magnetic strip of New Soteria's rail system stretched out for miles. Below her, just to the right of that, was a long platform that connected to inside the tubes, marked by secured doors on either side. To her left, there was a narrow ledge a few feet down—just enough for her to climb onto and make a small jump onto the next train car.

But now ... she really needed to pee.

Fully hydrated, she wouldn't be able to hold it much longer.

"Ziven," she said, squeezing her legs together, "you can't, like ... see me or anything, right?"

"No, why?"

"No reason. Be right back." Karaia clicked off her comm, glanced around, then yanked down her pants and underwear, squatting on top of the tube—praying no one appeared at this exact moment.

Another sigh of relief left her body.

Pulling her pants back up, she hopped down to the small platform above the station just as the next rail arrived—exactly when Ziven said it would. A sudden flurry of activity unfolded below as both humans and machines moved in rhythm, loading and unloading cargo.

They were all too busy to notice her.

Karaia took a deep breath, sat on the edge, and dangled one foot down. Then the other. The rail was still a good six feet below her.

Just jump, she told herself—but her body froze, suspended between fear and resolve. Her mind screamed it, but her muscles refused.

"Karaia, are you on yet?" Ziven asked. "It will leave in exactly one minute."

Go! With no further thought, she launched herself off the ledge. Her feet hit the train squarely—but with a heavy *thud*.

A worker glanced up in her direction.

She stiffened, bracing for it—a scream, a shout, a cry of *There she is. The terrorist!* But nothing came. The worker simply turned back to loading the rail, a small white light glowing on his temple. They had already fixed the program and rid NeuroTryp of her virus.

"Thanks for one thing, Griffin," she muttered into the breeze.

"What was that?" Ziven asked.

"Nothing," she said, crouching low. "I'm on the rail."

"Oh, good." Ziven loosed a sigh.

Narrowing her gaze, she looked for something to hold on to. Just ahead, some vertical bars lined the top of the rail. She inched toward them and settled into a secure position, gripping them tight. That's when she heard the shouting—boots ringing against the metal tube below. The Seromela officers had found her.

"There! She's on top of the rail!" one yelled.

"C'mon, c'mon, go," she whispered through clenched teeth.

Zap! A laser shot whizzed past her head, so close she felt the wind whip through her hair. She flattened herself against the train car.

And another. *Zap! Zap!*

"Stop the rail!" an officer barked.

Then, silence.

Karaia slowly peeked her head up.

The workers froze. Their temple lights flickered off. One replied, shrugging his shoulders, "We don't control it. It's automatic."

The officer pressed his gun against the worker's chest. "What do you mean? We're apprehending the Defier terrorist. Where's the emergency brake?"

The rail began to move—slowly at first, then faster.

"Stop that fucking rail!" The officer slammed the butt of his gun into the worker's cheek, sending him flying to the ground, clutching his face.

More shouting below.

Then, more laser fire toward Karaia.

She ducked, pressing her body onto the rail again, clinging to it, praying it wouldn't stop. After a few seconds and increasing speed, she dared to peel her cheek from the smooth metal just enough to see the officers shrinking in the distance, still chasing, but falling behind.

Once she was sure she was safely away, she let her body relax, shifting and stretching in place, feeling the tension melt from her muscles—at least as much as she could riding atop a rail at high speeds. She adjusted her arms around the bars, lay down, and rested her head, ready for the long ride.

She tapped her comm. "Ziven, I'm on and moving."

"Ohhhh, good," he exclaimed, letting out a whoosh of air from his lungs. "I was so worried. Now, just hold tight. I'm going to get some ..." He shuddered a cry. "... rest. Talk in six hours."

The rail thrummed beneath her—steady, rhythmic—exhaustion washing over her like a tidal wave, unable to stop it. Before she could even say goodbye to Ziven, the vibration lulled her to sleep.

Every now and then, Karaia would stir in a haze, drifting in the space between waking and sleeping.

Still moving.

Still alive.

Time blurred. Images of Miryam, Leah, and the beach swirled in her foggy mind. Sometimes, she thought she was there again—feeling the wind in her hair, the grains of sand between her toes, the magic whirling in the surrounding air. At other times, she thought she *was* Miryam or Leah. She lived their lives, felt their feelings—their love, their pain. Then, Stellan appeared beside her, a beach house and garden plot blurred in the distance, a smile spreading across his face as he held a hand out to her. She tugged him close, kissing him deeply, their bodies weaving together, warm and safe.

But then, Karaia's hand slipped through his skin. Shaking her head, she watched as he slowly dematerialized. She tried to cling to him, to hold on to him—but she failed.

His body faded into sand.

And Griffin's face flashed across her dream.

He lunged for her, grip tightening, forcing her to obey—as he yanked the key pieces from her neck.

"No!" she screamed.

"Karaia?!" Ziven crackled in her ear, startling her awake. "You okay?"

She blinked, disoriented, then remembered where she was. But just in case, she felt for the necklace. *Still there.* "Yeah, yeah—I was just having a bad dream." She shook it off, forcing her breathing to steady, heart still pounding in her chest.

"You're coming up on the end," he said.

Karaia rubbed her eyes and peered into the night sky. The Moon hung full and luminous, brighter than she had ever seen through the tube windows. Something stirred inside her, mouth agape and eyes wide, as she gazed upward. The stars shimmered like tiny living things, expanding out forever. *Our world is so big*. And she had seen only a fraction. A surge of anticipation rose from the pit of her stomach, momentarily overtaking her near-constant fear. It was beautiful—achingly beautiful—and she had barely scratched its surface. She wondered what existed beyond New Soteria's walls. Beyond the oceans. Beyond Earth itself.

There was so much she didn't know, and it thrilled her.

The rail slowed and then stopped. Karaia pulled her sore body from the cool metal and glanced below. The workers and machines were busy again, oblivious to her.

Still, she moved quietly off the rail and onto long grated platform that ran the distance of the outer wall.

"Ziven," she whispered, "where to next?"

"Well ..." he hesitated. "You might not like it."

She rolled her eyes, half chuckling. "That's becoming a pattern."

"You're going to need to get up on top of the wall."

Karaia gaped at the mountain of a wall towering above her. "What about New Soteria's security system? Aren't there torpedo launchers and defense missiles?"

"Most of that isn't true ..." Ziven said through gritted teeth.

She raised an eyebrow. "Most?"

"You'll be fine. It's all for show—to keep people inside. There hasn't been an actual attack on New Soteria in, well, *ever*," Ziven stated.

Karaia shook her head. "Are you serious? Add it to the list of things Seromela has lied about. So, how do I get up there?"

"It's not that far, actually," he said. "Look around. There should be a ladder."

"Another ladder?" she groaned, spotting it.

"Can you climb up it?"

Karaia hesitated. Every muscle in her body screamed for more rest, but she trudged toward it. Gazing up, she drew in a long breath and compelled herself upward, fingers gripping metal, feet searching for holds. Somehow, she found the strength. Every pull burned, but she didn't stop until she had hauled herself to the top.

"Is it time for the swimming portion yet?" She panted, trying to joke through the pain in her side.

Ziven let out a laugh. "Thanks for that."

"For what?"

"Making me smile. Giving me some hope. With everything today ... with Blaze ..." He shuddered, his voice trailing off.

Karaia stood on the outer edge of the wall—at last. Her breath calmed, shoulders loosened, and a hush carried over her body. *This is it.* Her sixth sense whispered to her. Everything beyond was unknown. But maybe—somewhere out there—were the answers she had been searching for.

She peered over the edge. Thousands of trees blanketed the Earth below, for as far out as she could see, and so densely she couldn't peer the forest floor. *But they told us Earth was scorched.* Turning, she looked back at New Soteria. The ground inside the walls was barren and brown, lifeless compared to the wild green beyond.

Another lie.

"Ziven," she asked, gazing at the expanse ahead of her, "how do I get down?"

"This is the part you're not going to like," he said.

"I thought we already did that," she said, moaning. "So, what is it?"

"You have to jump."

"Jump?" Karaia's eyes widened. "As in *off this wall?* Into trees? The tops of them are at least ten—no, fifteen—feet down, and that's if I'm lucky enough to hit the canopy. If not, it's more like..." she stared down again, "... *dead.* That far."

"At least there are trees," Ziven said, trying—and failing—to sound cheerful.

Karaia blew out a breath. "Give me a minute."

She stretched her arms and legs, shaking them out. She made sure her backpack and the necklace were secure, and took one last steadying inhale ... and exhale.

That's when she heard the low hum of something mechanical, growing louder by the second. A sharp buzzing cut through the air. Lights flashed behind her.

Karaia turned, and her stomach dropped.

A hoverjet was speeding toward her, lightning fast.

"Ziven, I've got company—a jet coming straight at me," she said, her pulse spiking.

"Then *jump*!" he urged. "They won't be able to see you through the tree cover."

"I can't."

"What do you mean, you *can't*?"

Her legs refused to move—again. "Soooo, this thing has been happening to me ... where my body doesn't want to cooperate with my crazy plans."

Karaia could hear Ziven at the end of the line shaking his head, a gentle laugh emitting into her ear. She knew it was silly. But here she was frozen, her legs unwilling to budge from the wall.

He finally said, "What other option do you have?"

"I don't know." She huffed a laugh herself. He made a good point. Squeezing her eyes shut, she tried to think as the jet's roar grew louder, vibrating through her skull.

A voice boomed through a loudspeaker. "Put your hands up. You are being taken into custody. Do not move. We repeat—do not move, or we will shoot."

Karaia tilted her head, recognizing the voice instantly. "Raven?"

"Put your hands up," Raven repeated.

Karaia hesitated. She had to jump now—but she couldn't make her body obey. The jet hovered closer, its spotlight locking onto her. She tensed, bracing for capture, or worse—death.

But no shots came.

With her eyes still closed, she felt a faint tingling against her chest. At first, she thought it was a bug, gently brushing it away—but it wasn't. The sensation was subtler than that. It came from the key around her neck. She glanced down, pulling the key halves from beneath her jacket. The silver, serpent-shaped piece quivered softly in her palm, while the wooden one pulsed with a steady, grounded energy.

Karaia slowly reached behind her neck, unclasping the chains and slipping the pieces free.

In her open hands, the two halves seemed to vibrate—*calling* to each other, yearning to be whole once again. A faint, shimmering light danced between them.

It shone brighter as she drew them closer to one another.

Chapter 56

THE KEY

A cross the threads of time, the two halves of the key drifted toward one another, suspended in a current of pleroma, weaving ribbons of gold and silver through the air. Each half pulsed with its own magical rhythm—one humming with electricity, the other deep and ancient—until their swirling energies intertwined, harmonizing into a single breath. Brighter, they glowed, drawn together by an invisible memory.

Then, they touched.

Two became one.

Connected—eternally bound—the singular key flamed a brilliant white.

CHAPTER 57

MIRYAM

Closing her eyes, Miryam let her body sway, her pleroma twining with Ved's like threads in a loom. A rush of pure bliss surged through her, enwrapping her in a blanket of swirling, warm energy. She forgot where—or even *who*—she was, the edges of herself dissolving. Time blurred, and she wasn't sure if she was Miryam, Leah, or Karaia.

But none of that mattered. In that infinite, all-encompassing space, only she and Ved—*or was it Stellan or Tate?*—remained.

Had ever remained.

Would always remain.

Everything else faded away. All she knew was—*love*.

The feeling rose within her, a soft whisper from beyond. She realized then that it had always been here. This *love* was not something found—but remembered. It flowed through her, around her, through every fiber of her being. She wanted to hold it forever. Reaching for it, her fingers cupped the air, as though she could grasp the feeling itself.

But she couldn't.

The tighter she tried to grip, the more it slipped through her fingertips.

Miryam wanted to freeze time—to keep this moment, this eternity. She held her breath, hoping that if she did not move, time would stop with her.

But her breath demanded release.

When she finally exhaled, the warm swirling blanket ebbed, the veil lifted, and the world around her returned.

Miryam opened her eyes. "Look," she whispered.

Ved's eyes fluttered open, blinking.

Before them, the two halves of the key floated in the air, now fused together—whole and radiant—glowing like a small Sun suspended between their palms. The golden light filled the cottage.

"It worked." His frail lips curved at the corners.

Miryam wanted to return Ved's smile—but the light, now dimming, revealed how pale and hollow he had become. "We must get you aid soon," she said, stroking his cheek.

With that, the key slipped from the air and fell onto the cot between them. Its glow faded entirely, leaving only the dim candlelight flickering on the walls.

The door creaked open, and Sophia entered, a few leather pouches of water in hand. Her voice was urgent and low as she woke the others one by one. "We must leave. The knights are close—I scant returned without being seen."

The group stirred from their slumber and started packing, the air thick with quiet panic. Father Thomas gathered the food. Matilda hurried to roll up the blankets. Miryam turned to Ved, tightening the bandage around his waist, then looped her arm behind him to help him to his feet.

He tried to stand, but his legs gave way beneath him. "I cannot."

"Yes, you can," Miryam insisted. "Together, we can do aught." She tried to lift him again, but as she did, Ved let out a brief howl of pain, and the weight of his body collapsed on her, his head rolling forward.

"Ved! Ved, come back to me!" she uttered a sharp cry, lowering him back to the cot as Sophia rushed to help.

For a long, terrible moment, he was still. And Miryam was breathless—frozen, waiting, scanning his body for movement, for breath, for any sign of *life*.

Then—he gasped and gulped air through his ragged lungs. "Miryam," he breathed, barely audible.

"What are we to do?" she pleaded, her voice breaking and her wet eyes darting around the room. "Sophia, help—there must be aught we can do!"

"Miryam ..."

"I know. We will make a cot to carry you," she said frantically, tears streaming down her face. "If we break apart the table, it could serve as a—"

"Miryam ..." Ved's voice cracked a little louder.

She didn't stop. Instead, she began to rise. "If we pull the table legs off—"

Ved grasped her arm in a weak embrace. "Miryam!" he shouted, followed by wretched wheezing coughs emitting from his mouth.

She froze—turning to face him.

"'Tis too late," he whispered.

"No, no, no ..." Miryam said firmly, shaking her head vigorously. "We shall keep trying. I must. I cannot live without ..." Her words blurred into heaving sobs that bellowed up from her chest, up her throat, and out of her mouth, echoing against the walls of the small cottage.

Those around her hushed in quiet reverence.

"Please ... stop trying," Ved managed, reaching for her hand, his fingers like ice.

Miryam halted a breath, stilling herself, but not the cascade of hot tears that stung her lips; those flowed freely down her face. Then, she gently sat beside him again, placing a trembling hand against his chest. His heartbeat was faint—so slow she feared each one might be his last.

Their eyes met, and the rest of the world melted away.

"Miryam, you must *live*," Ved rasped, drawing shallow breaths between each word. "Live for me. Live a long, and happy, and," — he gave a slow smirk — "ridiculous and fun and adventure-filled life. I am utterly grateful for the time I have had with you. And now ... I can die in peace knowing I have loved and been loved so deeply." His gaze drifted briefly toward Sophia and the others before returning to her. "I love you, Miryam ... more than you know."

Miryam's chest caved under the weight of his words. She could not breathe. Gulping for air, her eyes blurred, and her heart ached for the life that she would never live—refusing to accept the fate she had been doomed to endure.

"But we were to be wed." Her voice broke between sobs. "And write poems to one another. And gaze at the stars. And chase our children through lavender fields. And die old and wrinkly ... together." She shuddered a cry, squeezing his hand tightly as if her grip could force her will upon the world. "'Tis what I want. So, you see, I cannot let you go." Burying her head in Ved's chest, she wailed, her whole body shaking with each breath.

Ved lifted her gaze, cupped a hand to her cheek, and wiped tears from it. "I know," he whispered. "I wanted all of that as well. But I love you too much to let you die here with me ... which is why you must go."

His body quivered as he reached for the key lying beside them. With great effort, he pressed it into her hands. "The silver half," he said, "shall always be bound to your soul. And the wooden half to mine."

Sophia knelt beside them, her own eyes shining with tears. She laid a gentle hand on Miryam's back and murmured, "'Tis time to go, my dear."

"No!" Miryam cried, spinning toward Sophia and the others. "I cannot believe you would all leave him here to die."

Their response was a heavy silence, with eyes cast down.

Only Sophia met her gaze. "Miryam," she said softly, "we grieve as you do, but we must keep moving. The earl's knights are not far."

"She is right," Ved murmured, voice weak. "Go—all of you. Protect the chest."

Sophia breathed a ladened sigh, resting a hand on Miryam's shoulder. "You must choose. Come with us ... or stay."

Father Thomas cracked open the cottage door, and they started to slip out into the early morning light, the distant thud of horse hooves shaking the forest floor.

"They are close," he hastened a warn.

Miryam turned back to Ved, her heart breaking into a thousand pieces, knowing it would never be whole again. She pressed her lips to his, lingering there, tasting a mix of tears and smoke and a life cut short. Pulling back a little, she studied the curve of his mouth, inhaled his sweet earthly scent, felt the hum of his breath against her skin, and melted into *his eyes*—the eyes that caught her from the first moment they met, like bluebells in the springtime. Blinking slowly, she knitted them all into memory.

"Miryam," he breathed, "I promise—I shall find you again."

She nodded through her tears and forced herself to stand. Her legs trembled as she hurried toward the door after the others.

Outside, the forest was alive with danger—knights' torches flickered, voices shouted, armor clanked like thunder.

"This way," Father Thomas ushered, leading them further into the woods.

Miryam moved to follow—but Sophia caught her arm, drawing her close.

"You must take the chest," Sophia whispered, thrusting the wooden box into Miryam's hands. "Hide it beneath your cloak. Everything Ved saw has come to pass. The rest depends on you. Go."

She shoved her in the opposite direction.

Miryam's brow furrowed. "But where do I go?"

"'Tis up to you, my dear. But you must go—now," Sophia insisted, then turned and sprinted after the others.

Miryam gaped at the chest in her arms, her heart thundering against it. On one side, she could see the knights closing in, their torches bobbing in the distance. On the other, were the silhouettes of the order—her friends—vanishing into the trees.

She fled north. Away from both.

Branches tore at her cloak as she ran. Her thighs burned, and her lungs screamed for air, but she didn't stop until the shouts behind her faded into silence. Everyone must have also escaped by now, she told herself. Tears stung her eyes, but she forced them shut. *No more crying. Not now.* Keeping to the trees, Miryam circled wide around the abbey's smoldering remains and followed the path toward the village. She pulled her cloak tighter, concealing the chest beneath its folds, and tried to look and act as normal.

She had to—for Ved, for the order.

When she reached her father's cottage, she found Isabella by the chicken coop, scattering grain to the hens. Of course, she'd be helping with their father's farm chores. Even as a married woman now, she would always be the dutiful daughter.

"Bella," Miryam managed.

Her sister turned. "You are well!" she cried, running to embrace her.

Beneath her cloak, Miryam shifted the chest to her side, praying Isabella wouldn't feel it between them.

"Gawain only returned from the abbey but an hour ago," Isabella said breathlessly. "Lord Amalric had sent them to capture the heretics in the night. If we had known you were there—oh, my!" She hugged her again. "But you are safe now."

Miryam only nodded.

"Come, let us get you inside and cleaned." Isabella shook her head at the sooty cloak, leading her toward the cottage. "Can you believe there were heretics among you? I cannot imagine what you must have seen."

"Aye." Miryam swallowed hard, following. "'Twas dreadful indeed."

Their father greeted Miryam warmly, pressing a kiss to the top of her head and pulling her into a deep hug. His belly laughed up and down with joy, despite his ragged weakening breath. Isabella, ever the caretaker, fetched a damp cloth and began gently wiping the ash and dried blood from Miryam's face. They were so happy to have her back. And she wanted to be happy to see them as well.

Yet—she felt nothing.

Miryam was simply *there*, going through the motions, with no feeling behind anything she did. Then she remembered ... the chest. Still gripping it beneath her cloak, she had to protect it. That was her sole focus.

"May I have a moment?" she asked quietly.

Isabella cocked her head, gaze narrowing momentarily, then she said, "Of course, sister. You have endured much."

"I only need to rest," Miryam said, spinning toward her small cot.

Their father and sister exchanged a look and took the hint.

"Father, I shall help you clean the chicken coop before getting back to the castle. Gawain will expect me tonight for dinner. A married woman can only spend so much time at her father's now," Isabella added, heading for the door. Simon gave a small nod and followed.

The moment the door shut, Miryam moved swiftly. She dragged her cot aside and knelt on the ground. Pulling the chest and key out from cover, she quickly hid them in the hole under her bed. The two halves of the key still glimmered faintly in the dim light. *I will protect you,* she nodded. *With my life, if I must.*

For now, this was safe enough. But she knew she'd need to find a safer place soon—especially with what she feared was to come. Her *marriage* to Dempsey.

The thought sent a chill down her spine.

Too tired to think further, too hollow to cry, Miryam slumped onto her cot and curled into a ball under a thick blanket. Still, the cold clung to her. Her heavy eyes closed, but unable to sleep, her mind drifted straight to Ved. He swirled through her thoughts—his voice, his touch, his lips on hers—and their brief time together. It wasn't meant to end this way. Pressing her mouth against the covers, she let out a quiet scream against a cruel world. The pull in her heart was so great it felt as though it had been ripped from her chest.

Nothing remained within her.

Well—*almost* nothing.

That hard red coal where her heart used to be burned hot, swelling inside her. And a plan started to emerge of what she would do. But that was for another day. Today, she begged sleep to carry her away. And eventually, it acquiesced, the next sunrise and sunset going by in a blur of fiery nightmares and faraway dreams of Ved.

"Miryam," her father whispered, shaking her gently, "you have slept all day."

No response.

"There is to be an announcement in the square by Lord Amalric. Will you join me?"

Still no answer.

"Miryam."

"Yes," she huffed, peeling her body from the cot. "I shall come. But first, I must change."

"I shall be outside." Simon frowned but made his way out of the cottage.

Once alone, Miryam pushed her bed aside, checking her secret hole. The chest and key were still there. She lifted the key, and it fell into two separate pieces in her hand. Shuddering a breath, a flicker of feeling wanted to surface at the ache of losing Ved. She shoved it back down. The time for emotions was over. Then, she took both halves, threaded them through a bit of twine, tied them around her neck beneath her dress, and headed out the door.

With her father in tow, Miryam's feet carried her to the village square, where the cathedral loomed high, its shadow stretching over a newly built wooden stage. Already the crowd of villagers chattered, wondering what the announcement might be. Gawain stood nearby in full armor with the rest of the knights, his polished breastplate catching the sunlight. He gave them a small nod. The knights formed a line, making way for the Earl of Norfolk, who marched down the path toward the stage, with his wife and son. Behind the noble family trailed servants, guards and the rest of the castle dwellers, among them Isabella—and Dempsey.

As Lord Amalric and the procession drew nearer, Miryam noticed a gated cart at the end of the line. Her eyes darted to the center of the square—four horses stood at the ready, ropes tied to their harnesses.

Her breath caught. *No.* Realization set in as she thought of the order members who had been captured in yesterday's attack, and a frenzy of painful feelings begged to come forth. *I cannot watch.*

She turned to leave.

"My future wife," Dempsey sniveled, looping his arm in hers, dragging her back. "Master Simon." He nodded to her father.

The red coal within Miryam's chest blazed as she felt its heat rise in her.

The cart rolled to a stop beside the stage, and when she saw who it carried, her blood ran cold—Catherine, Will, Sophia, Father Thomas,

Matilda, and several monks who had nothing to do with the order, all huddled together in chains.

No one would survive, save her—just as Ved predicted.

Miryam's nostrils flared. Her fingers curled into a fist as the heat from her chest surged down her arm. When she opened her palm, a small flame flickered to life between her fingers.

Lord Amalric raised his arms and called out, "Greetings, good people of Norfolk. 'Tis with great satisfaction I can announce we have rooted out the heretics. As promised, I have rid our land of these vile creatures. Now, we shall release their damned souls from their bodies so they may be punished for their sins."

The crowd roared with cheers, egging him on.

As Miryam listened, she felt nothing but fire. She rolled her fingertips gently at her side, flames licking upon them, and she found that the surge of anger flowing through her veins transformed her. The young, naive girl she had once been withered away, shed like a snake's skin, no longer needed. How had she been so foolish to believe love would last forever? Now she understood. *Life is harsh, and people take what they want.* And what she wanted was to destroy those who had hurt her and those whom she loved.

And she could—with the flick of her wrist.

They had no inkling of the power that dwelled within—what fury fueled her. She could kill Lord Amalric with one stroke of her hand. Tear those knights limb from limb. Rip Dempsey's whiny little head clean off.

She could do it all.

But—she was no longer the brash young woman who acted on impulse. No longer the hopeless romantic led by her feelings. No, now she could see life more clearly, because she was stepping into her true power. As she scanned her surroundings, she calculated the impact of striking at this time. It would only reveal herself to be a heretic as well. Lord Amalric would simply be replaced by another of his sort, and they would keep coming after her—after others who practice magic, wield pleroma, and hold secrets that threaten their reign.

It would only mean more lives lost in the end.

So now, she would bide her time.

Today I shall not kill you, she thought, staring daggers at Lord Amalric. *I shall plan. Plan to make you suffer far more than you have caused me. Make you feel more pain than you thought possible. And when you least expect it, I will take everyone you have ever loved. And you shall feel what I feel now.*

Miryam let the flame gutter out in her palm, quelling the fire within her, and watched the rest of the speech. But she would not watch her friends be torn apart.

"Excuse me, my future husband," she whispered to Dempsey.

"Yes?" he said, mouth bending into a sneer at her last word.

"May I take leave? I grow faint." She held the back of her hand to her forehead in a dramatic fashion. "I do not think my frail composition can endure such horror."

"Of course, my bride." Dempsey reached out for her, but she was already stepping away. He called after, "I shall meet you at your cottage afterward. We've much to discuss of our betrothal."

"Yes, we do." Miryam bowed to him and bade her father goodbye.

She left the village square and marched straight for the old orchard. The very place where she had once climbed the gnarled apple tree and wished for a life she would never live. They said magic always comes with a price. She scoffed. She would show them—and have her revenge. The tree looked nearly dead in its preparation for winter as only a few leaves still clung to its mangled branches. From the distance, the townsfolk—drunk on bloodlust—cheered and shouted.

Then, the first of the bloody screams split the air, startling a murder of crows nearby, sending them flying into the sky.

A flame ignited in her palm again with ease. Drawing her arm back, she hurled a burning orb of pleroma toward the old behemoth. It struck true, erupting the tree in a fiery blaze.

Crumbling to her knees, Miryam cried out in righteous anger at the heavens.

Chapter 58

LEAH

A burst of white light exploded between Leah's hands, the hospital room disappearing. She flinched, blinded, squeezing her eyes tight, as the two halves fused into one. For a moment, everything was pure white—weightless and silent.

Then, darkness swallowed the space whole. The heart monitor beside her gave one final *beep* before flatlining into silence. Leah reached over and tapped the machine. Nothing. The digital clock beside her bed was dead too. She stretched her eyes wide to see in the pitch-black room when she heard the commotion.

Outside in the hallway, chaos erupted in a frenzy of noise.

Shouts. Alarms. Footsteps pounded down the hall. Leah slowly crept out of the bed, arms out, feeling her way to the door. Pressing her ear against it, she caught fragments of hurried shouts.

"Code Triage!"

"Outage on every floor."

"Backup power's down!"

Leah cracked the door open. The hallway, once a quiet, sterile space for nurse gossip, was now a blur of movement—hospital staff rushing about, flashlight beams cutting through the dark.

And the security guard who'd been stationed outside her room was gone.

Her pulse quickened. *This is it.*

But then—*Hana.*

Leah froze, chest aching just thinking about life without her daughter in it. She could never leave her behind. Not even for a few weeks for treatment in England. No, she would bring Hana with her. Her mind raced ahead, calculating the fallout, what Seth would do, every possible consequence of her actions—

She pressed her eyes closed. *Don't think. Just move.*

Rushing back inside her room, she scrambled to grab her things. The journal, the key, her purse—double-checking for the brochure and cash from Gertrude. She hurriedly changed into her regular clothes and darted for the door.

Then—she thought of Tate and Kat, and her stomach sank.

They will forgive me later. She hoped.

Peering left and then right, Leah slinked into the dark hallway, joining the chaos, and made her way to the emergency stairs exit. No one even noticed her leave.

She managed to get home in a cab, pack a bag of clean clothes, and grab their passports. Just as she was about to head out, she remembered Hermes, their tomato plant. She rushed to Hana's room, scooped up the mangled, yet still-living plant. She knew they couldn't take it with them, but she hoped this was the next best thing. Snatching a small shovel from the closet, she took the plant outside, dug a shallow hole, and placed it there, tamping soil around it. She gave it a good drink of water before standing to go.

"Good luck, little guy," she told the plant. "Grow strong while we're gone, okay?"

Grabbing their things, she rushed out the front door.

It was early morning, and the Sun was just beginning to peek over the horizon as she turned onto Seth's street. To be safe, Leah parked a few houses down and crept toward the side of the house where Hana's room was.

Pulling out her phone, Leah texted, *Hana, are you awake?*

Then, waited.

What if Hana didn't answer? What if her phone was off—or dead? The seconds dragged by. Leah tapped her foot, staring up at Hana's window, willing her to wake up.

Finally—the phone buzzed.

yea

A sigh of relief escaped Leah's lips.

Do you trust me? she typed.

mom what are u talking about? ofc i do, Hana texted back.

Leah quickly explained that she was outside, what her plan was, and that she hoped Hana would come with her to England. She really didn't want to do this alone.

Three blinking dots appeared on her phone. Leah's palms grew damp as she held her breath.

Then Hana replied, *ok let me get a few things and then I'll meet u outside.*

The tension in Leah's shoulders eased, and she exhaled deeply.

Just be quiet. And don't let your dad hear you, she texted.

duh mom

Leah rolled her eyes, smiling, and waited.

A few minutes later, Hana slipped through the back gate, backpack slung over one shoulder. She grinned widely when she saw Leah, and they fell into a quick, tight hug. Hana glanced back at her dad's house with a deep furrow in her brow.

"What is it?" Leah asked.

"It's strange. Normally, Dad has the house alarm set at night." Hana tilted her head, then looked at her mom. "But tonight, he didn't."

That was odd. It wasn't like Seth not to be surveilling and protecting everything he owned. Maybe he had forgotten in the chaos of the past twenty-four hours. He was still human, right? Leah wanted to think more about it, but there wasn't time.

"He probably just forgot, sweetie," she whispered, nodding, trying to convince herself. "Now, we really need to get out of here—fast."

They moved quietly down the street to the car.

"I hope you know what you're doing," Hana said with a nervous laugh.

"For the first time in my life," Leah replied, "I think I do."

At the airport, Leah approached the ticket counter. "Two seats on the next flight to London, please."

The clerk at the front desk typed into his computer. "That would be our 8:25 a.m. departure."

"Perfect," she said. After gaping at the price of the last-minute flights, she handed over a wad of cash to the man, who gave her a side eye, but accepted the payment.

With tickets in hand, they shuffled toward the security line.

"Ooooo," Hana exclaimed, tugging on Leah's arm. "Can I pleeeasse get a coffee drink? What if they don't have them in England?" She motioned to her favorite coffee shop just outside the security gates, then turned, giving Leah her toothiest smile.

Leah huffed and checked the time. Two hours until boarding. Still no calls or texts or police infiltrating the airport looking for them. "Okay," she agreed, "but we need to be quick."

Hana bounced up and down, running to stand in line for her large single-shot salted caramel mocha, with extra whipped cream.

"And we order breakfast too," Leah added, shuffling behind her.

Leah ordered the largest black coffee she could get and a bagel egg sandwich, Hana, her drink and breakfast burrito, then they made their way to a small table.

That's when she realized she hadn't had a single twinge of her migraine pain since she had left the hospital. She laughed to herself, shaking her head, still not really knowing how any of this magical shit worked. But sitting there in an airport café felt strangely *normal*—the most ordinary thing she had done in weeks, and she liked it. Taking a long sip of coffee, she let her eyes close as the warmth slid down her throat. For the first time in what felt like forever, everything was falling into place.

"Mom?" Hana said.

Leah opened her eyes. "Yeah, honey?"

"We're coming back, right?"

"Of course we are," Leah said, gently squeezing Hana's hand across the table. "I just couldn't let your dad ... I couldn't let them operate on me yet. I can't explain it, but I *know* this is what I'm supposed to do."

Hana nodded and continued scrolling on her phone.

Leah checked the time. Ten minutes until they really needed to be in line for security. Her phone notifications were still blank. That was good. It meant that no one knew she had escaped yet. She only wished it didn't have to be this way. Sneaking out again. Running away. *But this isn't running away, not this time. I'm running toward something.* She just didn't know what yet.

Taking a bite of her sandwich, her chest tightened at the thought of Kat and Tate. Kat would forgive her—she always did. But would Tate? He'd once said he wanted a woman who was mature, grounded, and sure of herself. *That's not me. At least, not yet. Better to let him go.*

Leah exhaled deeply as she stretched her tense shoulder muscles, trying to let go of Tate. But the feel of his hands pressing on the small of her back, the tingle of his lips on her skin, and his fresh linen scent mixed with the salty beach air clung to her mind. For now, that would be enough.

Standing, she drained the last of her coffee, wincing a little as it burned her tongue. Still, the jolt of caffeine was worth it. "We better get going," she said, shoveling their trash into a nearby can.

Then, they joined the security line, which luckily was moving at a fast pace. Still nervous, Leah's eyes darted around, sure the police would be here any moment. Tapping her foot as they waited, she checked her phone again—no calls or messages.

"Passports and tickets, please?" the security agent asked.

"Oh, sorry," Leah said, scrounging through her purse. "Hold on—I know I have them in here somewhere." The woman behind them gave a little grunt. "Uh ... go ahead of us," she motioned the woman ahead, forcing a polite smile.

The agent handed back their passports, and Leah and Hana stepped aside.

"Mom," Hana whispered, "where *are* our tickets?"

Digging through every corner of her bag, Leah's pulse quickened. *Fuck.* Of course, this would happen. Just when things were feeling right. *Why did I think this would be easy?*

Life was *never* easy.

She mentally retraced their steps—the line, the café, the ticket counter.

"I'll be right back! Keep our spot in line!" she called to Hana, already sprinting toward the table where they'd been sitting. She scanned the area—the floor, the walkway, under the chair legs. Nothing. With shoulders slumped, she started back toward Hana when she saw—the trashcan.

She hesitated, then lifted the lid and peered inside. Wrinkling her nose at the stench, she slowly sifted through the top layers of garbage. Between half-eaten food and coffee-drenched paper, there they were—their tickets. She held her breath, then reached down into the mess.

"This isn't how I thought I'd find you," said a familiar voice behind her.

Leah froze. She pulled the crumpled tickets free and turned. Tate stood a few feet away. He looked exhausted—eyes red, shoulders tense—but still painfully handsome.

"How did you find me?" she asked, stunned.

Tate loosed a heavy sigh. "When I brought you that piece last night, you were already asleep," he explained. "So, I left it in your purse. I came back early this morning to talk to you, but you were already gone. I didn't know for sure if you'd be here—I just had a feeling." Wiping his eyes, he shook his head in disappointment, staring at the ground.

Leah began. "I can explain—"

"No, I don't want an explanation. Don't you get it?" Tate's voice cracked, raising his eyes to meet her gaze. "I want *you*. That's all I've wanted this whole time. But I can't keep doing this—this back-and-forth stuff you keep putting me through."

"I know," Leah said with a sigh. "But *I* am a mess right now. How can I possibly be in a relationship when I can barely take care of my daughter? I can't pay my bills. I'm chasing after a magical connection to a prophecy. Hell, I can't even get on a plane without losing my ticket in the trash." She threw her arms into the air.

"When you put it that way ..."

Her heart sank. *He's finally realizing I'm not worth it.*

Then he smiled, reaching for her hand. "I was kidding."

"Oh." She couldn't help but smile back.

"I mean, you *are* kind of a mess—and a little crazy ..." Tate chuckled, squeezing her palms. "But you're also witty, funny, and smart. I know it sounds strange since we've only known each other for a month," — he shook his head knowingly — "but it feels like I've known you *forever*."

"But I can't stay here," Leah said, glancing down at her phone, the time glaring back at her. "They're going to force me to do the surgery. I have to leave."

Tate drew a deep breath. "That's why I ..." He hesitated, then said, "I packed a bag too. I was hoping you'd let me come with you. I can be there while you go through treatment—to support you, help you ... and love you."

Upon hearing the word *love*, Leah's mind went abuzz.

No one had said that to her in years—except Hana. Her thoughts spiraled, her mouth went dry, and her first instinct was to push him away as the familiar feeling that something bad would always happen came over her, so it was better to stay safe. *Ughh ... just say something.* But words wouldn't flow from her mouth. And the questions kept building inside. Why did he have to come into her life now? Why did he have the other half of the key? Why was it so hard to make a different choice than she had in the past? Everything felt like too much. She froze. Too much time had passed.

Don't fucking ruin this.

"Tate, I can't ..." Leah uttered.

Fuck. Wrong thing to say.

"What?" He dropped her hand, eyes narrowing in disbelief.

"I have so much going on inside of me I still need to work on." Her voice trembled, tears rising within her. "This—right now—is a perfect example. I can't even say a simple *yes* to a man I'm falling for because I still don't think I deserve to be happy. You said you wanted someone mature, someone who knows herself. That's not me."

"I don't care if it's messy," Tate said softly. "I just want to be with you."

But Leah could see his eyes losing their fervor.

She tried to picture it—Tate beside her in England. "Okay, say you come with me. Where would you stay? What would I tell Hana?

Would we be dating, or friends, or something else? And we haven't even talked about the key or the chest or this insane prophecy."

"We don't need to figure that out right now."

"What if this *is* cancer? What if I ..." She couldn't finish the sentence.

What if I ... die?

Tate took a step closer. "That's life." He huffed, clearly exasperated. "It's ugly and complicated and sad sometimes, but people still fall in love. Sometimes they break up—but sometimes they don't. Sometimes they find the love of their life, and they don't want to let them go." His voice broke on the last word.

Leah nudged him. "Are you talking about other people—or yourself?"

"I'm serious," Tate shot back, frustrated. "The only thing I need to know is—do you want me too?"

He gazed at her, the crease in his brow deepening, his eyes red from crying, waiting for her answer.

Yes. That's what she wanted to say. *Yes, yes, yes. Just let him in. Yes!* But nothing came out.

Tate stood motionless, lips pressed tight. He closed his eyes, trying to steady himself. The silence between them grew unbearable.

"I guess I know your answer," he whispered, turning to leave.

Leah lifted her hands, desperate. "Wait—what I mean is—"

"No," Tate said, shaking his head. "It's clear what you want. Have a good time in England. I hope you find what you're looking for."

This time, he spun and started walking away.

Chasing after him, Leah caught his arm and turned him to face her. His eyes brimmed with tears. "I *do* want you," she said, squeezing his arms tight, pulling him close. "I'm just afraid. I don't want to fall in love and then lose you ... if I die." She lifted his chin to meet his gaze, but his eyes looked past her. "What about when I get back? When I'm better, when all this tumor stuff is behind us? We can be together."

Tate wouldn't look her in the eye.

"Say something. Please?"

He drew in a heavy breath. "Everyone is afraid. There's no magic button that makes life easy. But we all want love. And we all die. You don't get to choose how either of those happens."

"So?" she murmured.

Tate lifted his eyes to hers at last. "I can't promise I'll wait. Maybe we leave it up to the Universe when you get back."

Leah swallowed hard and muttered, "I'm just not ready."

"Then, I guess this is goodbye," he said, shuddering as tears began to spill from his eyes.

She tilted her head to him, already regretting her decision, but knowing she'd fuck it up if she tried to be in a relationship now. "One last hug?"

Tate hesitated, then wrapped his arms around her. Leah pressed herself against him, taking him in—warm skin, the smell of linen and sandalwood, taut muscles, and the feeling of being *home* in his embrace. She held on as long as she could, knitting it in her mind.

"Find me in another life," she breathed in his ear.

When Leah finally let go, she watched Tate walk away—out of the airport and out of her life. She rested a hand on her chest, where her heart ached, hollow and heavy. Wiping her eyes, she squared her shoulders and headed back to the security line with her coffee-stained tickets.

A few minutes later, she and Hana made it to their gate.

Leah hoped she'd made the right choice. She kept telling herself she had. If she and Tate were really meant to be together, they'd find each other again—right? For now, she needed to get healthy, to work on her own shit before letting anyone else in. Because she'd only ruin it anyway. That made sense. That was the rational choice. But then if it was, why did it feel like her heart had been ripped out?

"Mom, are you okay?" Hana asked, glancing up from her phone.

"I will be," Leah said, forcing a small smile. To distract herself, she inclined her head toward Hana's screen. "Want to play one of your phone games until it's time to board?"

That's when her own phone buzzed.

And buzzed again.

And again.

She knew the steady onslaught of texts and calls from friends, from Seth, from the hospital wouldn't end. So, she turned off her phone.

A few seconds later, Hana's phone chimed.

"It's Dad," Hana said with a grimace on her face.

Leah's stomach twisted. "What does it say?"

"He says we have to come back to the hospital right *now*." Hana furrowed her brow. "Mom, are you going to get in trouble for this? I don't want anything bad to happen to you."

Leah took a long, steadying breath and patted Hana's knee. "We'll be okay. Just turn off your phone for now. We'll figure it out when we get there."

Hana paused, then smirked faintly. "Okay. But this means you owe me a year's worth of ice cream—any flavor, any time I want."

"Deal," Leah agreed, laughing softly.

Five minutes later, the loudspeaker crackled to life. "Boarding Group D to London."

They gathered their things and boarded the plane.

As Leah settled into her seat for the long journey, engines rumbling beneath, she reached into her purse and pulled out the key. The moment her fingers touched it, the two halves fell apart in her lap. She hastened a breath. *Tate.* He was connected to this too, so why had she turned him down? Clinging to the key pieces, she hoped he'd find her again. And maybe that time, she wouldn't say no.

Letting out a slow exhale, Leah leaned her head against the window and watched as the plane lifted from the ground, the city shrinking until it vanished into clouds. Despite herself, she knew she was headed toward something great—something she couldn't quite explain. She smiled softly, tracing the edges of the key halves with her thumb, as a single tear slid down her cheek.

CHAPTER 59

KARAIA

A surge of energy shot up Karaia's spine as the two halves locked together, fusing into one singular key. Stunning white light illuminated the night sky for an instant. And just as quickly, the burst of light dissipated, the afterimage burning in the center of her vision. She blinked hard, straining to see—nothing, but darkness and echoes of shapes danced before her.

Dropping onto her hands and knees, she steadied herself against the outer wall, waiting for her vision to return, hoping that meant Raven in the hover jet couldn't see either. From the sound of the now-distant hum, the jet had pulled back when the light exploded. *This is my chance. I have to make the leap.* She reached out into the empty air, feeling for the wall's edge.

Slowly, Karaia's vision was becoming clearer. But now—it was darker out. The previous lights that had cascaded their beams onto the wall stood as tall statues of darkness, nothing more. Cool metal met her fingers. Pulling herself back up, she peered over the ledge into a black abyss. Only the Moon and stars cast their reflections onto the forest, leaving only a whisper of shadows below. Crinkling her brow, she tried to remember what the trees had looked like—how far down they were, how far she'd have to jump.

"Ziven," she whispered into her comm, "are you still there?"

There was no response.

"Ziven?" Her pulse sped up. "I need your help."

Still silence.

A cold realization sank in. The key's uniting must have disrupted the electrical systems nearby. That's why everything was darker. Why Raven had pulled back. Why Ziven was gone. She was on her own from here.

Karaia yanked the small communication device out of her ear, threw it to the ground, smashing it. Then, she drew a deep breath and placed one foot on the wall's outer edge. Her hands trembled as she gripped the metal on either side of her foot, trying to steady herself.

Ready to launch.

She imagined the motion—pushing off, leaping into the unknown—but her body refused to move. She rolled her eyes. Not again. *Why can't I just do this?*

But in her gut, she knew why. Jumping meant beginning again—a life beyond the walls. A life she knew nothing about. One filled with uncertainty and danger. Was she really brave enough to face it all?

Then, a memory surfaced, one she hadn't recalled until that very moment.

She was little again and had been hiding a tiny blue bug in her room. She had never seen such a creature with its fuzzy body and many legs. Not knowing what it was, she still cherished the small animal and named him Neptune after her favorite planet. For days, she had kept him tucked inside a small container, sneaking him carrot tops and spinach leaves.

When her mom had discovered Neptune, she had scolded Karaia.

"You need to dispose of it right now," she said. "You know we're not allowed to have any unapproved living beings. It could carry a disease. Get rid of it, then wash your hands, and take a credit. I've already transferred one for you."

"But Mommy, this is Neptune. He's my friend. I can't throw him away," little Karaia pleaded.

"Then I'll do it," her mother said, snatching the tiny creature and marching toward the kitchen. The sound of the incinerator filled the air.

Karaia burst into tears.

Her father came running in, sweeping her up in his arms. "Honey, it's okay. Your mother's just following the rules." He rubbed her back gently. "Just take the credit, and you'll feel better."

"But, Daddy, I don't wanna."

"Why not?"

"What if I forget my love for Neptune?"

"Oh, sweetie." He wiped a tear from her cheek. "I hope you never forget that. You have so much compassion."

"What's com ... pass ... sun?" Karaia asked, tilting her head.

"It's when you care deeply for another person or animal or thing," her dad said, placing a finger on the tip of her nose, which made her smile. "You know what?"

"What?"

"I want you to remember something for me."

"Otay."

"I want you to always be *yourself*," he said, squeezing her tight. "Sometimes this world will try to keep you down—try to change you. Don't let them. Even if you have to hide it. You are Karaia, and you're amazing, compassionate, and so, so very brave. You're the only *you* that will ever exist."

It was Karaia's turn to wipe the tears streaming down his face. "Daddy, why are you crying? Do you miss Neptune too?"

Her father managed a smile and looked deep into her eyes. "I read this old book once while I was working in the California Keys. It said, '*Our greatest fear is not that we are inadequate. Our deepest fear is that we are powerful beyond measure.*' And it's true." He nodded, then lowered his voice to a whisper. "But the people in power don't want us to know that. There might come a time when I'm not here anymore, but you have to stay brave for me—and always lead with your heart." He kissed her on her forehead.

Karaia never did take her credit that day. Just listening to her father's words had made her feel better, even though she had not understood half of what he was saying.

Dad, I'm coming for you. I'll be brave and strong and always remember.

With that, she launched off the wall's edge, arms spread out wide. For a split second—she was weightless, free.

Everything felt right. Karaia's gut told her this was what she was meant to do. In her mind, she still didn't know if she believed in the prophecy or if what she experienced with Miryam and Leah was real. But it didn't matter—not really. All that mattered at that moment was that she was ready to *live*. To *feel*.

Truly experience life. No holding back.

Crash! The impact with the trees knocked the breath from her lungs. Pain ripped through her body as branches scraped and tore at her skin. She tumbled through a storm of leaves and twigs, unable to control her speed or direction. Her hands clawed desperately for something—anything—to stop her fall.

Finally, her fingers caught a branch. It held and didn't let go. She gripped tighter, her arms trembling, and reached up with her other hand.

There she was. Really living. Really *feeling* it.

Every bruise. Every cut. Every sore muscle, as she dangled in the air, heart pounding in her chest.

Karaia gazed up, and a small drop of blood dripped into her eye. Trying to blink it away, she could see the top of the wall far above her now, maybe forty feet, she didn't know exactly. Her eyes cast downward. The forest floor was about ten feet away. Swinging her aching body toward the trunk, she caught her foot on a thick branch. From there, she climbed down, branch by branch, until her boots hit the ground.

The damp Earth felt squishy beneath her feet. She shifted her weight back and forth, feeling the give, the warmth, the aliveness. Nothing like the cold metal floors she was used to. Before she knew it, she was removing her shoes and sinking her toes through the lush green moss and into the dirt below. She hushed a breath—a steady calm radiating from the tips of her toes, through her core, and out the top of her head. It was everything she had hoped for. So, despite the stinging cuts and the pain spreading through her limbs, Karaia smiled.

Then, she set off into the unknown.

EPILOGUE

With his feet propped on his desk, Griffin Marshall leaned back in his chair as he swiped through footage of Karaia's theft and her escape from the building on a large holo-screen. Across from him, Stellan sat, rubbing his side, still sore from being stunned.

A knock came at the door.

"Come in," Griffin said, still scrolling.

Raven entered the office and approached the desk, her back taut. She hesitated for a moment before speaking, then said, "Sir, she got away."

Stellan's head snapped up. "How did she get away? We have the world's best security."

Griffin's gaze never left the screen as he flicked through the holo-images, analyzing each frame before moving to the next. He flipped to an image of Karaia on the rail, then another as she climbed the ladder of the outer wall.

"We can still get her." Raven cleared her throat. "She won't get far on foot. Mr. Marshall, how would you like us to proceed?"

No answer.

Stellan began, "Dad, I want to—"

Griffin raised a hand, cutting him off. He stopped at one scene, zooming in, swirling the three-dimensional frame to see it from all sides. Raven and Stellan leaned closer, narrowing their eyes as well. The holo-screen showed footage from the hover jet, moments before the flash of light had knocked out its camera. In it, Karaia held the two halves of the key together.

"There you go," Griffin whispered to himself. "Now, where will you take it?"

"I want to help," Stellan blurted, straightening in his chair.

Griffin lowered his feet and turned to face his son, a mocking sneer spreading across his face. "You think after she *tased* you with your own laser gun you can catch her?"

Stellan's jaw tightened as he stared back at his father, resolute. His eyes were unsure, but his voice was not. "Yes."

"I'd much rather send Raven here with her security team."

"Please," Stellan said, his voice cracking. "Let me prove I can be useful to Seromela—to our country ... to you. I *will* find her."

His last words lingered in the air.

Griffin went back to flipping through the images.

Stellan's brows knit together. This time, he stood. "I know I can find her. And if I don't within a couple of weeks, send someone else. Just give me this chance." His hand closed into a fist as he held his breath, waiting for his father's approval.

Griffin swiped the holo-screen off.

"Very well," he said. "You may take a hoverjet, a pilot, whatever weapons you want. But—" He held up a finger. "She comes back alive. You hear me?"

"Of course." Stellan nodded slowly, stunned his father had agreed so easily. "I won't disappoint you."

"Good. Now, Raven and I need to discuss some security matters." Griffin waved his hand in the air.

"But—"

Griffin shot Stellan a familiar glare. "No buts. You have a mission. Get on it."

"Yes, sir." Stellan turned and hurried out of the room.

Once the door shut, Raven cocked her head at Griffin. "Everything went exactly as you said it would—from Karaia stealing the artifact to Stellan insisting on finding her. How did you know, sir?"

"Because ..." Griffin said with a half-smile, "... this is what always happens."

ACKNOWLEDGMENTS

I'm not even sure where to begin. I still can't quite believe I've written a novel. Maybe that's because this story doesn't feel entirely mine—it is and it isn't. The idea came to me on a long drive in 2020, playing out like flashes of a movie in my mind. Daydreams like that aren't unusual for me, but this one wouldn't leave me alone. After a few weeks, I finally thought: *I should probably write this down.* What started as scattered scenes on sticky notes became a full poster board of color-coded ideas—characters, plots, timelines—and a realization that this was only the beginning of something much bigger.

Six months later, I had written the first draft of book one.

Five years later, I quit my full-time job to publish this book and figure out how to support myself creatively.

Which brings me back to that feeling that this story isn't fully mine. As humans, we are intricately connected—to one another, to our ancestors, to the families and communities that shape us. I am who I am because of so many incredible people who have supported me, believed in me, and reminded me that dreams are worth chasing.

To all of you, I am endlessly grateful.

To my loving partner, Will, thank you for standing beside me through every up and down, for holding me in the hard moments, and for cheering me on through every twist of the publishing process. I'm so grateful to be walking this life with you.

To my son, Elijah, you never doubted me for a second. When I told you I was quitting my job to publish a fantasy novel, you had complete faith that I'd figure it out. You've always believed in me, and that means more than you'll ever know.

To my ex-husband, Tracy, thank you for giving me the space and time to write this story, and for recognizing the importance it would have in the world.

To my sister, Sarah, my first supporter in life and the first person I call with every wild notion, and to my brother-in-law, Bryce, for cheering me on from afar.

To my mom, who's no longer here but whose spirit is woven through everything I do—I know you'd be so proud of me.

To my friends and family—near and far—thank you for believing in me, for loving me through all my crazy ideas, and for reminding me that community is what keeps us going—Jeff, Jack, Jenn, Melissa, Kara, Amanda, Becca, my St Louis family: Gwen, Jenny, Sue, the Tarletons, the Reschkes, the James', my Washington family: Dad and Brenda, Grandma Louise, the Austin clan, my California family: Aunt Cathy and Uncle Bruce, Aja, Wes, Eric, Kyle, Nana Goat, Grandma Lorraine—I have been lucky to be surrounded by so many loving people in my life.

To my Substack community—the dreamers, the idealists, the artists, the writers of the world—you guys rock! I can't believe that complete strangers (now dear friends) have championed my work and encouraged me through this last year. David, Anna, Kate, Jared, Ceylan, Charles, Lis, Gabriel, Jason, Andrea, Norman and many more—thank you for believing in me. To Hal Gill, my first founding member of *Wildest Dreams*, and to all my paid and free subscribers—thank you for your support.

To my St. Louis writing group—Kell, John, and Cole—you reignited my spark for writing this year.

To my Kirksville Book Club ladies—Amy, Maria, Stephanie, Mandi, and Naomi—thank you for your excitement to read this book.

To my beta readers—Cole, Christen, Eric, and Emily—thank you for your insights, your time, and your feedback to make this story even better.

To my incredible team—Maria Lewytzkyj-Milligan (editor), Mandi Wiser (proofreader), and Juan Padrón (cover designer)—I truly couldn't have done this without you. You brought my words to life and helped shape this dream into reality.

And to my cat, Moon, and dog, Jake—thank you for keeping me company during long writing hours and for reminding me to move once in a while to take you on walks.

And lastly, I'm just grateful.

Grateful to be alive.

To be here.

To be writing.

To be connected—to Spirit, to our Earth, and to Love.

Because in the end, that's where we'll all return.

About the Author

Jessica Ann is an author, intuitive, and creative entrepreneur who believes in living a life guided by passion and purpose. Her storytelling blends fantasy and spirituality into genre-bending explorations of life, fate and free will, and the invisible threads that connect us all. Drawing inspiration from myth, nature, and her own personal journey, she writes stories that blur the line between the mystical and the everyday—reminding readers that magic is not something to be found, but something to be remembered.

Before stepping fully into her creative calling, Jessica built a diverse career as a nonprofit founder, city council member, and educator. Her work has always centered on community, connection, and the belief that small acts can ripple outward to create a more compassionate world. Now, she continues that mission—helping other authors and entrepreneurs bring their dreams to life.

When Jessica's not lost in a story or mentoring other dreamers, you can find her baking sourdough, foraging for wild edibles, dancing barefoot in her kitchen, or spending time with her partner, children, cat, and dog in Missouri. She's endlessly inspired by the cycles of nature, the resilience of the human spirit, and the mystery of the unseen forces that guide us home to ourselves.

Follow Jessica Ann's journey and creative work at jessanncreates.com and @jessanncreates on Instagram, Facebook, and Substack, where she writes her newsletter, *Wildest Dreams*—a call to courage, creativity, and living a life you love.